EARTH 2.0: PRISON PLANET

EARTH 2.: PRISON PLANET

WILLIAM CROW JOHNSON

iUniverse, Inc.
Bloomington

EARTH 2.0: PRISON PLANET

iUniverse books may be ordered through booksellers or by contacting:

iUniverse
1663 Liberty Drive
Bloomington, IN 47403
www.iuniverse.com
1-800-Authors (1-800-288-4677)

ISBN: 978-1-4759-4018-3 (sc)
ISBN: 978-1-4759-4019-0 (hc)
ISBN: 978-1-4759-4081-7 (e)

Library of Congress Control Number: 2012913356

Printed in the United States of America

iUniverse rev. date: 08/01/2012

For Will,

who as a boy asked, "Why can't life be more like the movies?"

CHAPTER ONE

September, 2442
Transported

Alexander Khan came aware in a howling blizzard. Driving snow billowed before him like the veils of a dream. Bitter wind lashed his skin, and he realized he was standing naked in thigh-deep snow. He did not know how he had suddenly come to be here. He shook his head to remember, but it wouldn't come.

Commando training kicked in. He turned his back to the wind and cupped his hands between his legs for warmth while he surveyed his environment. Blinding snow stretched away in front to a far suggestion of mountains. A kilometer or two to the right loomed a tree line. To the left and behind, the horizon fell away. No trace remained in the snow of how he had arrived. The overcast sky had a pinkish tinge, suggesting a red-giant sun. Or a large, Martian-like iron-oxide desert somewhere on the planet.

The planet. Yes. It was coming back. The trial. The sentence.

Too numb to be sure, he pulled a foot out of the snow and checked. No boots. No clothes, and no knife strapped to his waist. Urban myth was wrong. Nothing. He permitted himself one sardonic smile. Transported. Earth Central Government had replaced execution three hundred years ago with the more humane banishment to Prison Planet. In practice, lower-level bureaucrats had dumped him naked in a blizzard to die.

In the cold gale, he had thirty to forty minutes before he froze. And it seemed to be getting darker by the second. He shook his head again to clear the cobwebs and took an experimental step. The snow was uniformly deep. It wasn't going to get easier the farther he went. But at least there was grass under the snow instead of rocks. And the snow was dry powder. Could have been worse.

He made for the tree line. There was a chance there of finding or building shelter. He strode quickly, rhythmically, almost a run, counting on his body generating heat from fighting the deep snow to counterbalance the cold. He did not run for fear of damaging his numb feet on sharp rocks under the snow. Even with the strenuous activity, the wind sucked the warmth out of him fast.

The tree line turned out to be 1232 strides away. Roughly a kilometer. It guarded a declivity sixty or seventy meters deep and was mainly leafless deciduous trees. But usefully, there were some firs similar to white pine, with long, soft needles.

He was sweating slightly under the arms from the exercise, but the rest of his body was growing numb. He could not decrease his activity level or he would freeze. He immediately began stripping off small pine boughs, shaking off the snow, and piling them up under a large pine with a bed of pine straw beneath it. The tree itself was heavy with snow but bare beneath.

When he had a pile roughly waist high, he took a couple of deadfall branches and plunged back into the snow. He used the branches to uncover the heavy grass beneath, a patch roughly four meters square. Then he began pulling large tufts, shaking them free of snow, and piling them beside his pile of pine boughs. After a couple more such squares, he had a pile of dry grass roughly half a meter deep and a meter and a half wide.

He was starting to shake uncontrollably. Without further delay, and with only an occasional wary glance down into the cut to look for predators, he made a bed against the trunk of the pine tree. First he heaped up pine needles fifteen or twenty centimeters deep. Then he laid pine boughs over them to keep them in place, followed by dried grass to lie on. Finally, he lay down on this bed and covered himself first with dried grass. Then as a last step, he pulled the rest of the pine boughs over him to hold the grass in place and to insulate himself from the cold air.

It wasn't comfortable, but within ten or fifteen minutes he was much warmer. He wouldn't freeze to death for at least the next few hours, and he would have time to think. And now that he was warmer, his brain was on fire.

No longer was he Major Alexander Khan of the galactic-arm-ranging Internal Movement Control, but Alexander Khan, criminal. No longer Alexander Khan, scion and board member of Khan International, mission-driven developer of freedom technology, but Alexander Khan, pauper. And no longer son of a vital, living Lucian Khan, but son of a man brutally murdered by an ECG operative.

The memory wipe started immediately after the sentence – Prison Planet – so he couldn't remember how he had been brought here. But he did remember the courtroom reading of his crimes: Distribution of Contraband Technology, Conspiracy to Destroy Harmony, Failure to Condemn Wrong Views, Failure to Initiate Positive Statements, etc., etc. And of course, there was that other charge that would have put him here by itself alone.

ECG controlled and tracked all interstellar missions, and had kept Prison Planet's location secret for 300 years. Even he as an officer in Internal Movement Control hadn't known where it was, or whether it truly existed. But people had always whispered of it, and urban myth provided details: 10,000 transported per year, tech development prevented by laser satellites, ECG operatives *never went to the surface of the planet,* just dumped prisoners, and no one knew if transportees survived or not. And here he was.

So the goals of his life – fully avenge his father's death, and set the people of Earth free from its bonds – no longer looked reachable. Even survival looked uncertain. But in his mind he heard the voice of Pierre, his childhood tutor in all things from Latin to martial arts: "Every environment has in it the tools for survival. You just have to recognize them." He would have to recognize them on his own, though, because there was no UAI on this planet. The dead link to his implant was like a black hole in his brain.

Warmer now and tired from his efforts, he grew drowsy. His mind began to run down. He resisted awhile, then gave in to sleep. He hoped it wasn't the deceptive warmth and inviting sleep of those who are freezing to death.

He awoke to a terrifying roar. Surrounded by darkness, he took a moment to realize where he was. – In survival mode, he remembered quickly. And his feet were freezing because in his sleep he had thrust them out of his carefully arranged cover. But the rest of him was warm and almost certainly generating scent. Whatever had roared sounded big enough to consider him food.

A twig snapped maybe twenty meters below in the cut. Then silence. The wind had subsided, but there was no starlight. His eyes had not yet adjusted. He could barely see.

He didn't even have a sharp stick. Suddenly he could hear quiet breathing no more than five meters away, slightly downslope. He strained to see. A massive dark shape crouched up toward him along the slope. It was two meters long and massed at least three hundred kilos. No physical details were visible, but he didn't need any. It clearly intended him as dinner. Soon. There was no reason for stealth and no more time.

Reaching down through the pine needles, he grabbed the hard object that had been sticking him in the back. It was a limestone shard twice the length of his fist. He pulled it from the soil and found one end sharper than the other. Better than nothing.

He slipped into the genetically enhanced intuitive zone he always entered when his life was in danger. His heart sped up. Time slowed to a standstill. He rose from his warm bed and faced the beast. The tree trunk was on his right, his bed to his left, and the beast in front.

The beast did not charge. It raised the front of its body from a crouch into a challenge posture, but kept its forelegs on the ground. It roared again, showing white fangs the size of commando-knife blades. Khan caught a glimpse of eyes. With no sudden moves, he crossed ever so slowly in front of the tree trunk while the beast watched, ready to spring, perhaps waiting for him to roar back. Then he abruptly moved on around the tree, out of the predator's sight. Behind the tree, he heard the animal give a low rumble, moving to intercept him when he came clear around the tree.

He counted, thousand one, thousand two, thousand three. Then, gripping the rock like death in his right hand, he leapt back out the way he had come, and charged the beast's left side, bellowing like a bull. As hoped, the beast was surprised, and hesitated for a split second. He jammed the point of the rock down into what he hoped was the creature's left eye, then quickly again where he thought the right eye should be, then the nose. Blood spurted onto his hand.

The beast screamed a loud falsetto shriek that belied its size and grabbed him with two small but strong arms and hands that unfolded from under its massive head. *Feeding arms*, he thought with a shudder, as they pulled him to within inches of the terrifying teeth.

His arm windmilled, striking over and over, hammering once each what he thought were ears, then actually breaking one of the fangs. Then the other fang sank through his left triceps and it was his turn to scream. He felt his bladder void.

The animal sensed now that it had him and began backing up, dragging him downhill. It was going to drag him back to its den and eat him there, he realized. The pain in his arm filled the whole left side of his body like molten lava, and because he was being dragged face down, the pain in his groin from being dragged over rocks and bushes was like a fury of knives. He was weakening, and for a brief moment was tempted by despair. But he still had the rock, and he could still use his right arm. Straining up, he jammed the rock into what he believed to be the beast's left ear hole. Then again. Again. Again. The beast gave him the predator's killing shake, but it didn't kill him because it had only his arm. It did, however, rip the fang through the muscle on the back of his arm and set him free. He sprang to his feet. At this point, they were on a steep part of the slope facing a drop-off if they continued downhill.

Traversing the edge of the drop-off was a dimly visible game trail, apparently the beast's objective. To Khan's right was a pin-oak-like tree, with many dead branches three to six centimeters in diameter. Familiar with such trees from the family's forest operations, he grabbed a branch and broke it off. It was dense, hard wood, and the break was sharp. He jammed the break into the same ear hole he had been working on. Then again, and again, and again. Finally the branch sank ten centimeters into the animal's brain, and the beast settled onto the ground like a balloon losing air. Then because it had backed too far during the final fight, it slipped over the edge of the cliff and fell. There was a two-second silence, then a crash from far below. Thirty meters, he calculated. Good enough to finish the beast off, since gravity felt close to normal, perhaps a bit light.

He now had two priorities: bind his arm so as to lose as little blood and function as possible, and find and butcher the beast. It was food and clothing. But first he had to quiet the uncontrollable shaking, from cold or adrenaline, it didn't matter.

He returned to the top of the slope and crouched in his bed for a few minutes to warm up. He took some grass fibers from the bed and used these to bind his wound. The pain had subsided slightly, but the wound hurt unbelievably when he cinched it up and tied it. He worried that he might go into shock, so he needed to keep moving.

There was no possibility of waiting until morning to skin the beast. The corpse would quickly attract carrion eaters and perhaps more dangerous predators. He had to find it first and somehow get the hide off and get a few pounds of meat, all in the dark. He had field-dressed and butchered his share of deer and wild boar on youthful hunts, but he had always had good knives, cleavers, and saws. He had to find some sharp stones. There was no time to search for chert and flint-knap himself a knife blade or two. He would have to make do with what he could find.

The height and peaked nature of the mountains in the distance had suggested a granitic/basaltic geology, but he sensed that the plateau-like area he was on had a limestone substrate. He couldn't see well enough, but was pretty sure some of the pain of being dragged downhill had been edges of limestone outcroppings. –Which suggested that the stream that was likely at the bottom of the cut had limestone outcroppings and shards.

He found the stream before the carcass. It still flowed, which suggested that the bitter cold was recent, maybe temporary. The stream bed was indeed limestone, and more luckily, had shale shelved between the layers. He selected as many sharp shale and limestone wafers as he could carry and went looking for the carcass.

The beast lay in a twisted heap about five meters upslope from the creek. A coyote-like creature was easily shooed away to a distance of twenty meters, where it sat on its haunches to watch. Khan went to work with his right hand, using his left hand only to hold. Soon the arm was numb and aching, and he wondered about deadly infection. Had he done enough to clean and dress the wound? He could wash it in the stream, but he wasn't sure about the water. On second thought, the teeth of any carnivore probably carried more harmful bacteria than a snow-melt mountain stream, so he decided to gamble. He took a few minutes to untie his grass-fiber bandage, kneel streamside, and wash the wound in the clear, cold water. The washing and the rebinding hurt astonishingly, but he gritted his teeth and refused to let it slow him. He went to back to work with the shale wafers. The sky was beginning to lighten, and he could see his work better. The water looked clean.

Had the animal been a deer back on one of the family estates, he would have field-dressed it, cutting it open from breast bone to pelvis and removing all entrails. Then he would have hauled it to a place more convenient for butchering and freezing. In this case, all he wanted was the skin and a few pounds of meat. So, tempting as it was to cut open the gut and thrust his icy hands and feet into the animal's warm blood, he didn't want to contaminate any cuts with whatever was living in the animal's system. He simply started at the neck to skin it. It was slow work because the shale wafers weren't very sharp and crumbled easily. However, they held their edge reasonably well, so if he found a good one, he stuck with it.

In an hour he had the skin off and a couple of kilos of strong-smelling meat tied in a piece of skin. It was cold, nasty work, but at least the wind didn't reach into the cut. Thin vines hanging from bare tree tops worked well as twine for tying bundles, though they were impossible to break and tough to cut.

Shelter was the next priority. The bed under the pine tree was too exposed. He needed a place where he could at least get his back to a wall. If a whole pack of the coyote-like creatures were to surround him in the dark under the pine tree, he wouldn't stand a chance. And of course, warmth was a pressing priority. His hands were in good shape because they had been busy, but his ears, knees, feet and privates were numb. He wasn't sure he'd ever have the chance to use the latter again, but he would certainly need the former. He couldn't afford frostbite. He needed a place where he could hunker down and not lose body heat.

The stair-stepped limestone shelves in the creek bottom suggested the possibility of a cave or a hollow in the side of the cut if he went downstream. Indeed, he found a two-meter deep hollow on a nice shelf a hundred meters downslope. The coyote had padded softly behind him, keeping its distance. Now it sat down at the edge of the shelf, looking more curious than dangerous. He tossed it a piece of meat, which it rose and snapped out of the air with skill. Then it sat back down on its haunches, licked its chops and looked to him for more.

"Forget it," he said. The sound of his voice surprised him. He realized he might never need it again. He assumed if there were survivors from other transportings, they would be few and far between. Even if three million prisoners really had been transported over three centuries, they could be spread over the entire planet. He might search for the rest of his life and not find anyone. And of course, there was the very valid question: did he want to find them? Not all would have been political prisoners. Some would have been murderers, kidnappers, anarchists, terrorists, rapists and thieves. Those probably hadn't changed their ways on this new planet, if they had survived. No, the best course was to survive on his own awhile, get good at it, and then begin carefully to explore.

He threw an end of twine-like vine over a scraggly tree that thrust out at an angle from the stone wall above his hollow. Then he pulled up his bundle of meat so an animal would have to jump nearly three meters to get it. The coyote-like creature gave him a reproachful look. "Sorry, I'm not your meal ticket," he said. "I'm not your meal, either, in case you're a lot tougher than you look." Then he took the skin and went in search of more pine needles and boughs.

He found another pine not far away. He made several trips back to the hollow, each time with the skin full of needles, which he dumped on the stone floor, and with as many feathery pine boughs as he could carry. When he had enough, he made himself another bed on the flat stone in the back of the hollow, with twenty centimeters' worth of needles between him and the stone, and with pine boughs on top for cover, and for insulation from the stone back wall. Then he pounded the rest of the pine needles into the raw side of the furry skin for thirty minutes or so, bundled it up, and hung it also from the protruding pole.

Nearly exhausted, and with his left arm completely numb, he took care of one last item before he permitted himself to get into his new bed.

He found a stout piece of oak-like deadfall about five centimeters thick. Finding a forked tree, he stuck the branch between the forks, leaving a long end as a lever, and pulled. It split longitudinally, as intended, leaving a long, sharp point. That would be his weapon.

Then he went to bed, such as it was, with his weapon beside him, and hoped that tomorrow, which was in fact already here, would be a better day. The coyote-like creature huddled three meters away. "Stay the hell away from me, Dog," he said. "Or I'll eat you, too."

He slept fitfully, waking several times with a start. In his dreams, he could still smell the beast's breath and feel its teeth. Once when he woke, Dog was gone. Another time he was only a meter away, watching, and Khan shooed him away. Finally he slept soundly and woke to light. Dog was again nowhere to be seen. Dog of course was no dog, or coyote, or wolf. His snout was too long, his canines too small, and his tail too parallel to the ground behind him, like a fox's. But he was not a fox, weighing at least thirty kilos, plenty large enough to give a good account of himself. He looked meant for preying on small game like rabbits or turkeys if such lived here.

The snowy ravine looked much less threatening in the light. The trees looked much as they would have on Earth, though without the snow storm going on, the sky was a pronounced reddish color in the direction of the sun. "Evening red and morning gray sets the traveler on his way. Evening gray and morning red brings down rain upon his head," he remembered. He wondered if it was a harbinger of more snow.

But the immediate concern was that his left arm was swollen to twice its normal size. The grass binding was cutting into his flesh. He found more grass for a better binding, then gently retied the binding with a new wad of soft grass for a pad over the wound. It hurt amazingly. He tried to force himself not to worry. It either would or would not become gangrenous and kill him. There was little he could do except try to maintain his strength. Certainly he couldn't cut it off if it came to that, because he had no tools to do so. Even if he had a knife, there was the bone to deal with. He had no saw. And of course, there was the brachial artery, which would bleed him out quickly if not tied off. And there was the doubt that he could manage the pain and horror of cutting his own arm off. So the only thing he could do was try to prevent the growth of the anaerobic bacteria that caused gangrene. Which meant keeping the wound open to the air and washed. On this thought, he laboriously removed the binding and painfully laved the wound one more time in the clear, cold water of the stream. The cold actually made the wound feel slightly better. Then he rebound it, but much more loosely this time. The key issue was the loose triceps, which by experimentally extending his arm he discovered had partially survived. Only part of it was bitten through.

He forced himself to eat a small amount of the meat from the bundle. He gagged repeatedly, not only from disgust at eating raw meat, though this meat was frozen, but because the meat smelled strong. The animal had been a predator, and its meat smelled like it. Carefully suppressing thoughts that might make him gag and vomit, he knelt by the stream and drank his fill. This helped, because it washed the taste from his mouth. He resolved to find another source of protein soon – nuts, fish, eggs, something – and to make fire to cook his meat.

First priority was to scout the area, but he needed protection for his feet. They were bruised and swollen. He would have appreciated a coat, but his naked body seemed to have adjusted to the cold. He wasn't shivering. But feet used to shoes would not last long in this rocky environment.

The skin of the lion, as he thought of it, might serve to make boots as well as a coat, but it would take several days to cure. And he wasn't sure there was enough tannin in the pine needles to do the job. He might have to go back to the animal's corpse and get its brains for their tanning agent. But tanning would take days. He needed foot protection now. He had once seen five-thousand-year-old dried-grass sandals in the Egyptian Museum. He would use those as a model.

Two hundred meters downstream, where the cut began to broaden into a valley, he found dried sedge grass growing beside a gravel bar. He knelt to pull it. As he worked, he noticed looking downward through the trees that the cut extended for hundreds of meters, then took a steeper turn out of sight. But he also caught a glimpse through the trees of what looked to be a broad plain at least a kilometer below his current level. And it was not covered with snow!

Excited, he began to make plans. He would descend onto the plain where it was obviously warmer, and look for people. Surely there were some survivors from the tens of thousands of other transportees. – Survivors who might help him.

He pulled an armload of sedge grass and took it back to his lair. Then, gingerly tiptoeing to protect his feet, he returned to the corpse. Though badly gnawed upon, its skull was intact. He smashed it open with a large rock and scooped out the brains. Disgusted but determined, he took the brains back and smeared them thoroughly into the hide. Then he replaced the coating of pine needles and hung the rolled-up hide once again from his flag pole. If the tanning efforts worked, he would have a hide to keep him warm for some time to come. He washed his hands perhaps longer than necessary in the creek.

The museum shoes had been made of grass braided into rope-like cords. He immediately understood the importance of this idea. The tightness of the cords would impart toughness and durability. As he braided dried grass into cords and set them aside, he developed respect for the skill of that ancient cobbler. By the time he had completed weaving and tying one sandal, that ancient workman had become a veritable master artisan. By the end of the day, he had a pair of sandals with soles two centimeters thick, and a band over the toes that would afford some protection and warmth.

Carrying his sharp stick for protection, he tried out the sandals by exploring downstream half a kilometer or so, looking for fish, edible roots, and chert beds. From Ancient History class at the Academy, he knew chert was a silicon-based rock used by stone-age people for arrow heads, spear heads, and knife blades, and that it occurred in limestone geology. The creek bed was a stair-stepped series of limestone shelves, so chances seemed reasonable. He marveled at the similarities between this planet and Earth, and thought again what a shame ECG's policy was, of limiting space travel to only government entities like the Space Navy and Internal Movement Control. This planet had possibilities.

The policy drummed into his head in Academy classes and in countless indoctrination sessions was that humanity was to achieve a self-sustaining Great Equilibrium on Earth before going to other planets and plundering them as humans had done on their home world. Perfect the species and the process on Earth before marauding into the galaxy. Only ECG could manage humanity to the Great Equilibrium.

A second reason for the policy, whispered among his less doctrinaire fellow officers, was the Encounter. This supposedly occurred shortly after the first star travel in 2062. The Eridani – from Epsilon Eridani, the star system where they had been encountered – had warned Earth explorers not to venture beyond certain nearby confines in the home galaxy. Frighteningly superior, they were from a distant star system they would not identify. They had only small outposts in Epsilon Eridani's asteroid belt, but they were clear: violate the ban and Sol would be destroyed. Fifteen star systems were permitted, all those closest to the Sol system, starting with Alpha Centauri and Proxima Centauri. The problem was, according to Navy surveys, no easily habitable planet existed in any of these systems, and the government didn't want self-appointed explorers venturing outside the permitted area and causing Earth's destruction. Thus, no space travel for the masses, and no colonization.

This all begged the question: where was he now? On Prison Planet, for sure, but this planet was clearly habitable. It certainly appeared, as he and many others believed, that ECG had made up the Eridani story. They used it to justify controlling the population, preventing people from developing colonies outside Earth's immediate control. Supporting this theory was the fact that the government had never broadcast pictures of the Eridani, or proof of their existence. It was hard to tell what was true. Under ECG's cloak of repressive secrecy, conspiracy theories sprouted like weeds.

But that was all behind him now. Indeed, if he didn't stay with it and learn to command his new environment, everything would be behind him.

He found a pool with two treasures: a chert bed on one side, where gravel had washed down, and in a tidal pool on the other side, something like cattails. Military survival training had taught him that cattail roots were edible, so he pulled several plants to see if the roots were still alive. They were. He washed one off and took an experimental bite, chewed, and swallowed. That would be enough for a test. The taste was earthy with a suggestion of onion, but it settled on his stomach with no pangs or twinges.

The chert wasn't as satisfactory, but better than nothing. With one exception, the pieces were small, suitable only for arrow heads. The one piece with promise was about twelve centimeters long and nearly as thick as his wrist. Big enough for a knife blade or a spear point if he didn't screw it up.

He took his treasures back to his lair and settled in for a flint-knapping session, starting with a small piece. Learn first, then try the big piece. The process turned out to be quicker than imagined, but every bit as demanding of skill. He ruined three promising arrow heads before completing a good one. He decided to make several. He had found no suitable bow wood, and he didn't yet have a knife to carve a bow with, but he could at least use the arrowheads to skin with. Compared with the razor-sharp arrow heads, the shale flakes he had used on the lion had been entirely unsuitable. And when he did find good wood for a bow, he would already have arrow heads.

After an hour he had several crude but usable arrow heads. His stomach had not yet rebelled, so he ate more cattail root. He considered eating some more lion meat but the thought palled.

Suddenly he sensed a presence. Reaching slowly for his sharp stick, he looked up to see Dog sitting on his haunches at the perimeter of his little camp area, with a furry creature in his mouth. The two regarded one another for some time. Finally, Dog cocked his head, much like a real dog, and took an experimental step closer. Khan reciprocated by scooting half a meter or so toward Dog without rising up. Experimentally, he extended a hand. But Dog was unwilling to come closer. He gave a slight growling whine, sounding very much like an earthly dog, though there was that unearthly long snout. He dropped the furry creature on the stone slab and retreated three meters to the edge of the stone slab.

He was offering to share.

Deeply moved, Khan got up slowly and approached the furry creature, white on the bottom, gray on top, much like a rabbit/hamster mix. Gingerly he reached down for the animal while Dog watched. Dog did nothing when he picked up the creature, which did in fact appear to be a hare,

oryctolagus cuniculus, but with rabbit markings, *sylvilagus floridanus,* details
flooding back from Khan's youthful wildlife biology studies. Before the
military. Either he was on Earth in a different time, the planet he was on
had fostered parallel evolution, or Earthly creatures other than humans
had been introduced here and had interbred with local creatures and
evolved. The latter seemed more likely.

Watching Dog out of the corner of his eye, he skinned the rabbit,
carefully saving the skin, then dressed it using one of the new arrowheads
as a scalpel. It worked amazingly well. When the rabbit was thoroughly
field-dressed, he took the carcass down to the stream and washed it. Dog
watched with interest, moving toward him with some apparent concern
when he put the carcass into the water, but still stopping at a distance.

Satisfied that the meat was clean, he cut off a hind and a fore leg for
himself and approached Dog with the remainder. Dog retreated a step for
each step he took, so he put the carcass down and backed away. Then he
sat down and took a bite of the raw meat himself, stifling again the disgust
of eating raw meat. Dog approached the carcass and made such short work
of the remaining meat that Khan quickly rethought his impression of the
animal. The speed of movement was extraordinary. This animal could kill
and eat any dog before the dog knew what was happening. And Dog had
made a clear gesture of friendship, which was not only welcome, it made
him wonder if the beast was much smarter than the average dog.

The sun glowed red in evening clouds, so he settled down in his nest
to rest. His meal would make him sleepy, but he did what he could to be
less vulnerable. He sat with his back to the wall, his sharp stick beside him,
and a wary eye on Dog and the perimeter.

He relaxed, thinking tomorrow he would search for more food sources:
roots, nuts, fish, game runs where he could snare rabbits, and maybe some
overwintering berries like multiflora hips. Then he would concentrate on
hunting tools – fishing gigs, knife blades, spear points, maybe a bow and
some arrows – and a fire-making bow and spindle. His swollen left arm hurt
any time he flexed it, but he could at least hold the firebow spindle with it
while he bowed with his right. He marveled as he dozed at what a full-time
effort survival was. He got an inkling of how the first farmers must have
regarded a full year's supply of grain laid back: leisure to think.

"Good night, Dog," he said, and Dog tossed his head, gave an answering whine, and licked his chops.

Khan went to sleep thinking of his plans. When he had weapons, fire-making tools, a portable supply of meat, and some description of clothes, he would set off down onto the plain to search for others like himself.

He awoke with a start to see Dog silhouetted directly in front of him in the darkness, dark against the snow downslope. Alarmingly, the animal's front feet were planted between his ankles. He was instantly wide awake. Was Dog preparing to attack, or trying to warn him? He had his right hand on his sharp stick, and was pretty sure he could bring it up before Dog could be on him. But he sensed no aggression. Looking upward, Dog made a strange double exhaling sound, similar to the warning sound deer use, but quieter. Khan wasn't sure of the message but sensed it meant danger. His eye was drawn upward to his meat pole. A dark, short-legged shape was creeping out along the pole toward his hanging meat bundle.

A thief. Carefully, slowly, he rose from his warm nest of grass and pine boughs with sharp stick in hand. He reached up quietly, preparing himself, then drew back and stabbed the creature with all his might. He felt the sharp stick penetrate the animal's hide. The reaction was instantaneous. The animal leapt from the pole growling and spitting like a mad dog, going straight for his throat. He sidestepped quickly, but was barely able to avoid it landing on him. As it went down, he saw white stripes starting at its nose and running down its back. My God, he thought as he prepared himself for the onslaught he knew was coming when it hit the ground and turned. A wolverine. One of the meanest, most vicious, hardest-to-kill animals for its size on Earth. And here it was on this planet.

He drew back his sharp stick to stab it straight down the wolverine's throat as soon as it landed. An old boar-hunting trick learned from Pierre, this would at least help keep the animal's teeth away, even if it didn't kill it.

But he need not have concerned himself. Displaying the same speed he had shown earlier, Dog streaked in from the side and took out the wolverine's throat before it hit the ground. It gurgled and thrashed, and died within a minute.

He and Dog regarded one another. "Remind me never to piss you off," he said. "I'm still not sure I trust you, but I owe you one." Dog grinned in the manner of dogs and hung out his tongue in a friendly way as if nothing had happened.

Khan shook his head and skinned the wolverine with one of his arrowheads, then shoved the carcass to Dog with his foot. After the taste of the lion, no way was he going to eat wolverine. Dog dragged the carcass downhill out of sight.

In a couple of minutes, there was a lot of coyote-like yipping and howling, and then more from the near distance, and ultimately, it sounded as though a pack of a dozen or more were enjoying a feast below his ledge. After he hung the skin to dry, he resolved to stay awake for the rest of the night. One animal like Dog was probably not enough to take him. Two or three could easily do the job, with one keeping his arms busy while the others attacked from behind. He was going to have to find more defensible shelter.

On the morning of Day Three, Khan awoke to see Dog sitting guard at his place at the edge of the limestone ledge. He chastised himself for going to sleep against his resolve and making himself vulnerable. His life had made him avoid trust. It was always dangerous. It was a prelude to suckerhood. But Dog had shown nothing but friendship so far. Khan decided to trust the animal. There was too much to do to be constantly on guard.

Hardly aware now of the cold except on his feet in snow, he felt eager to start the day's activities. He felt rested, and the pain and swelling in his left arm had subsided slightly – a good sign. He began to feel cautiously hopeful. Taking his sharp stick in one hand and two arrowheads in the other, he headed downstream. Dog watched him go and did not follow.

He found a pool where he could see fish, though they were not as big as he might have liked. He laboriously shaved a barbed gig from a sapling, then waded quietly into the icy water to try his hand. The fish were warier than they first appeared, but he was finally able to spear three slightly bigger than his hand. Using one of his arrowheads, he cut the filets off and ate them raw on the spot, nibbling them off of the scaly skin rather than attempting to use one of the arrowheads to remove the skin. The raw fish was much better than raw meat.

Farther downstream than he had ventured yesterday, he found another chert bed, this one also with mainly small stones, but with one chert lump partially buried in the stream bed. Dug out, it turned out to be a nodule the size and shape of a large, long potato – a valuable find. If he worked it and his other wrist-sized piece right, he could get a few knife blades and several spear points out of them.

He then ranged off into the woods and brush on the far side of the stream to collect a cousin to trumpet vine. Thin and tough, it looked and felt like the trumpet vine he had as a boy been required to clear from fruit and nut trees in the family's orchards. He selected young vines six or seven millimeters thick and cut them in lengths of up to two meters. When he had a bundle as thick as his arm, he returned to his lair. Dog was nowhere to be seen.

Using an apple-sized piece of granite, a lucky find in the mainly limestone geology, he was able to fracture the chert lump into five flakes a centimeter or so thick by eleven or twelve centimeters long. He congratulated himself on his newfound skill until he promptly broke one of the priceless flakes in half with his first effort to knap the edge. He then grimly set to work with extreme care to fashion points instead of knife blades. First things first: he needed a defensive weapon that could kill as well as fend attackers away from his body. That was a spear. Once he had two or three spear points, he could then make a knife.

It took half the day, and another foray into the creek bed to find a rock substitute for an antler point to make the fine edge flakes, but out of his chert potato, he finally ended up with three spear points roughly ten centimeters long, and plenty sharp enough to penetrate. The fourth flake also broke in the middle, but he was able to make a couple single-edged short knife blades out of the pieces. He set aside the other wrist-sized chert lump as if it were solid gold. It might be even more valuable.

Then he set to work with the vines. Using an arrowhead, he shaved off long fibers and laid them aside in rows. When he had enough, he made four-strand braids a couple of millimeters thick. Then in turn he braided those into thicker cords. He tried to break one and found it to be quite strong.

Altogether, he made three braided bow strings the length of his arm span, and a dozen half-meter-long three-strand braids suitable for tying on arrowheads and spearheads. He coiled up the bow strings to wait until he found suitable bow stock, and wrapped the binding strings around a couple of thick deadfall sticks. With the rest of the trumpet vine, he made himself a flat basket suitable for hanging from a rope belt and riding against his hip. He put his treasures into the basket for safekeeping, tied it around his waist with a length of trumpet vine, and went looking for spear shafts.

At the end of the day, he was armed with three sturdy spears at least two meters long, two knives, and three arrowheads, and he had sufficient chert to make at least three more spear points. He realized that if he was going to travel, he needed to make spear and arrow points ahead of time, because chert might not be available. He thus resolved to spend a few days doing so to fill his hip basket with points. And he reflected on the amazing fact that in three days, the measure of material value in his life had gone from Credits to lumps of chert.

That night no predators or thieves came to his hollow, or none he was aware of. In the morning, Dog reappeared, this time with a pheasant in his mouth. He came warily to within a meter of Khan and gently deposited the bird – a Korean Ringneck, if Khan was not mistaken – on the stone slab.

"You're a good dog," he said. "I'm not sure why you're being so helpful, but I'm grateful."

He dressed the bird, then decided it was time to use his fire bow. He quickly made one with a sixty-centimeter-long curved stick as the bow, keeping the string loose. For the friction drill, he carefully rounded the ends of a thirty-centimeter-long, two centimeter-thick hardwood stick. Then he split another piece of deadfall lengthwise by prying it between two trees, creating in one of the split pieces a groove where the heartwood went with the other piece. This he used as the bottom of his friction set-up, and a flint nodule as the top, and got the bow going, turning the drill stick back and forth at speed.

Soon the drill stick started squeaking and smoking in the wood groove, and he knew it was going to work. So he collected grass and thin twigs for tinder and some thin deadfall for fuel, and started again. In a few minutes he had a small flame going in the grass, which he carefully fed with the thinnest of twigs, then with bigger pieces of deadfall until he had a substantial fire. He built it up so it would burn down and create a bed of coals suitable for cooking. Then he sat back on his haunches and looked at Dog.

"I'll bet you've never seen anything like that before," he said, and Dog returned his look with an inscrutable one of his own. He did not seem surprised or frightened by the fire. "Then again, maybe you have."

The familiarity of some of the animals – the rabbit, the pheasant, the dog-*like* nature of Dog, the lion-*like* nature of the animal that had tried to eat him, even the bluegill-like nature of the fish he had eaten – all suggested an intermingling of Earth animals with the animals of this planet. Apparently ECG had not only been dropping humans onto the planet, but had also dumped animals, perhaps thinking they were providing transportees a source of food. But he didn't think they were that considerate. Maybe ECG really hadn't ever come down to the surface, but more was going on here than an initial orbital survey to determine environment, followed by three hundred years of prisoner dumping. It began to look like an uncontrolled three-hundred-year ecological and social experiment. – Assuming anybody else was around to add reality to the social aspect of it.

He roasted the bird on a spit and divided it with Dog, who licked the meat several times this time instead of snapping it down, and nibbled on it as if he were savoring the cooked meat. Which was delicious. Khan found himself wishing for salt. Then he gave a sardonic smile – the kind that used to get him into trouble. Here he was, enjoying roast pheasant four days into a survival experience, and he was churlishly wishing for more.

The day was reasonably warm – nearly up to freezing – and the sun was shining, so he took down the bundle of skin and meat and set the meat aside. Dog eyed it covetously, so Khan threw him a fist-sized chunk. Dog snapped it out of the air with the incredible speed he had demonstrated before. The meat stank so badly that Khan resolved not to eat another bite of it, but to save it for Dog, piece by piece, to keep the animal coming back to him. He put it into his hip basket and hung the basket from the pole.

He then lashed together a rectangular frame, tied the skin to the frame and leaned it up against the stone wall, raw-skin side toward the sun. He wasn't sure his tanning efforts had worked, though they had effected a change of color from pink to buff. In any case, stink or not, it was time to dry the skin and turn it into clothing. If it was stiff, he would pound it with stones until it limbered up.

Satisfied with that effort, he turned his attention to turning the rest of the chert into arrowheads and spear points, which took until afternoon. He wanted an axe head to more easily cut spear shafts, arrow shafts, and bows, but first he needed weapons for all eventualities, even if crude. He therefore made more crude but effective spears out of deadfall branches, tipped with his precious spear heads. The heads wouldn't take much lateral pressure before breaking, but they had all the strength they needed to be thrust into a body. With one of these, he headed downstream in the late afternoon in search of a piece of chert big enough to make an axe head.

This time he went farther downstream than ever before. He found no big chunk of chert, but he did discover his next big challenge. At the end of the cut, the stream plunged down a thirty-meter sloped cliff onto tumbled boulders that gave way to a forested slope. Half a kilometer farther down, the slope eased out onto the open plain he had seen earlier. And far across the plain, in a copse of trees, he saw smoke. His heart skipped. He looked and looked for a long time to convince himself he was not seeing things.

He was not seeing things. At least one other being on this planet – he cautioned himself that it might not be a human – was capable of making fire. And it didn't escape his attention that he was seeing evidence of this other fire shortly after he had made his own first fire. Had the other person seen his smoke? Was this a signal? Or a coincidence? What if the people dropped onto the planet had devolved into cannibalistic savages? Did he need to move his camp?

His mind ran at top speed while he looked up and down the stream bed for a chert knob big enough to make an axe. He didn't find one, but he did find several lumps of granite that might serve if he got them to fracture right and take an edge. He took them back to his hollow, thinking furiously. Had he made a mistake by making a fire and giving away his location?

He thought about all these things while he worked on the axe head, which he quickly realized was a two-day job. It was bigger than arrow heads, and the granite was much harder.

By the time he bedded down for the night, he had resolved to move the next day. He would finish the axe, catch some fish, and find another camp down the slope. There he would stay a day or two until he could cut and sew the skin into clothes of some sort. Then with the meager tools and weapons he had made, he would set off to find somehow, somewhere on this planet a way to get back to Earth and gain his revenge on ECG, and on Nathan Fox, the man who ordered his father's murder.

CHAPTER TWO

PEOPLE

Getting down the cliff face next morning was easier than expected. He tied his worldly goods – the hip basket, arrowheads, spear heads, axe heads, fire bow, a couple of freshly cooked fish left over from breakfast, and most importantly, the spears – together in a bundle tightly wrapped with lion skin. Then he lowered the bundle down with a long vine chain – five sections of vine ripped loose from trees and tied end to end. Finally, he climbed down the sixty-degree face gripping the vine chain with his fully extended left hand for steadiness and finding handholds with his right. This permitted him to use his left hand's grip without forcing the use of the torn left triceps.

The vine chain alone wasn't enough to hold him, but it steadied him and bore most of his weight on his way down while he found handholds and footholds. Out of breath at the bottom, but satisfied with his accomplishment, he left the vine in place in case he wanted to go back up later. Going up would prove much harder, but he would cross that bridge when he came to it.

Spear at the ready, he followed the stream downslope through the trees in the general direction of the smoke he had seen yesterday. He was looking for a place well short of the smoke where he could stash his things and make cold camp. The smoke – which was not visible today – had been roughly five kilometers from the base of the cliff. He wanted to approach no closer than three kilometers before finding a place to camp. It should be a defensible place to which he could retreat and at least get his back to a rock wall if necessary. – A new base of operations. He would scout the situation from there.

The stream tumbled over long limestone shelves like giant stair steps as it fell down the slope, and he quickly found another dry hollow where he could make camp. It was a meter or so above stream level on the outside of a bend, where it looked as if flood waters hitting the cliff face had hollowed it out. It was just high enough for him to stand in, about two meters deep, and beneath at least five meters of vertical wall – perfect for defense. And in front, between the hollow and the water, was a flat ledge where he could have a small fire and do flint knapping. And there would be no problem finding the place again. If he could find the stream, he would be able to find his hideout.

He hid his things in the hollow behind a pile of rocks, then covered himself with the lion skin. He had not wanted its interference while climbing down the slope, but now he made a slit for each arm, then tied it at the neck with a piece of his homemade string. Then, with his hip basket slung over one shoulder in case he saw promising pieces of chert, and a lightness of heart he had not felt for years, he set out with a spear at the ready. Something about the sunshine, the fresh air, the adventure, and the freedom from the ECG darkness of which he had been an unwilling part – made his heart dance. The lion skin was still smelly, but nonetheless soft – the tanning efforts had not been in vain – and instantly reminded him of how cold he had been. Warmer here at the lower elevation, the air was still only a few degrees Celsius above freezing. And yes, this quest for people might be about to get him killed, but the cloak was heavy and warm, his belly was full of excellent cooked fish, and he sensed opportunity like he had never felt on Earth, or on his brief missions to other worlds.

Away from the stream, the forest gave way quickly to grassland, as he had noted yesterday from above. He had the location of the smoke imprinted on his mind, and he would have to cut across open country soon, but he stayed in the stream's cover as long as possible. When he did cut out into the chest-high grasses, he stayed low and vigilant. The grasses were sharp, and he found himself making a path by swinging his spear back and forth. Occasional sharp noises and scurryings in the grass to his left and right heightened his alertness further. And he was pretty sure something was following him at forty meters or so, but every time he stopped to listen, whatever it was also stopped. The hairs on his neck remained on full alert.

After two kilometers, the grass gave way to thicket and trees. Suddenly he could smell smoke. He crept softly, toe first so he could feel twigs before breaking them. A boy's voice called out, "You're It!" and a girl laughed and answered, "No I'm not; you didn't catch me."

A knot Khan had not realized was in his chest gently loosened itself, and an unaccustomed smile came to his lips. There was civilization here. They spoke a standard language. And it was peaceful enough to permit children.

He crept forward cautiously, aware of his appearance, of his nakedness except for the lion skin, and aware that he might look threatening. He waited until he could see them – a couple of sunny-haired early adolescents dressed in baggy homespun linen, both wearing what appeared to be toy bows slung across their backs – before he made himself visible or audible.

"Hello," he said.

Faster than he could believe, both children unslung their bows, nocked arrows from quivers slung across their backs, and drew down on him. Suddenly the bows didn't look like toys any more. He judged them to be fifteen-kilo bows. Enough to put an arrow through him at this range of fifteen meters. And the arrowheads appeared to be steel.

"Can we talk before you shoot me?" he asked reasonably. He carefully laid his spear down and raised his hands.

"Maneater," challenged the boy, "the only thing I want to hear you say is, 'I'm leaving, and I won't be back.' Otherwise, you die now." The boy had deepened his voice to sound as intimidating as possible. Khan approved.

"Hold on just a second," he said, raising his hands. But both drew their bows tighter and he instantly entered the slowed-down world of the battle space in which he had been so many times before – the warrior state afforded by illegal genetic enhancements Pierre had arranged before he was born.

Both children shot. In his altered state he could see the expressions on their faces – both fear and disgust – could see that the arrows were rotating, indicating skilled fletching, could see that if he did nothing, both arrows would pierce his heart, indicating skilled shooting, and could suddenly see a comely blonde woman in the background, seventy or eighty meters away, dressed the same as the children.

He sidestepped and neatly snatched both arrows from the air, one in each hand, though moving so fast hurt his left arm enough to bring tears to his eyes. Ignoring the pain, he laid the arrows cross-wise on his palms and approached the children.

"You'll want these back," he said, offering the arrows. "They are well made."

The boy swallowed hard and took a quick look over his shoulder as if to scope out his path of retreat. Khan tossed the boy's arrow at his feet and the girl's at hers to show that he wasn't going to use them as weapons.

"I will not harm you. I need information, and medical care for my arm, if possible. I am, uh, newly arrived. Six days ago."

"You're not a Newby," said the boy. "You've got a spear and a cloak. You couldn't have made them that fast. You look like a Maneater. Except no headband."

"I assure you, I've only been on this planet – Prison Planet – for a few days, and you're the first, er, man I've seen. You don't look good to eat." He smiled. He wasn't used to making jokes, but he sensed that one might lighten the mood here. "Too stringy. For the last few days I've mainly eaten fish. Not bad. And a pheasant that a dog-like creature brought me."

As he spoke, the woman approached closer and closer, obviously listening. A hint of a smile lurked at the corners of her mouth. And accompanying her, several meters behind, was Dog, or one of his breed. "That is the dog-like creature I'm talking about, if I'm not mistaken," he said, pointing. Apparently happy to see him, Dog smiled and came closer, but not close enough to touch – wary, as before.

"We wondered where he had gone," said the woman. "He comes and goes as he pleases, but usually comes home at night. He was gone for most of three days. So you are saying that you are newly sentenced from Earth?"

"Yes. Arrived six days ago."

"Up in the high country? We saw smoke."

"Yes."

"The skin around your shoulders? May I see it? It looks to be a gryphon skin. How did you get it if you've only been here a few days? Who killed it and dried it?"

"It tried to eat me. I objected. It tore up my left arm pretty badly before I was able to kill it. It wasn't even good for eating."

All three sets of eye widened. "You killed a gryphon?" said the boy, a note of awe creeping into his voice. "With a spear?"

"Looked like a lion, had a set of feeding arms, and teeth like swords. No choice. Him or me. And I used a sharp rock and a stick. I hadn't made the spear yet."

"May I see the skin?" the woman said again. "There is an identifying mark I want to look for."

"I'm, uh, afraid I don't have any clothes other than the skin."

She smiled. "You don't like people to see you naked?"

He shifted uncomfortably. "Where I come from it's not done."

"We've heard that from other Newbies. Fine, turn and let me see your back."

"They put down their bows first, and you do too."

"We are not murderers, Mr., uh … –"

"Khan. Alexander Khan. At your service." He made a slight bow, as was the Earth custom.

Her eyes widened. "*The* Alexander Khan?"

He laughed. "I don't know how many there are. Major Alexander Khan, uh …, *former* Major Alexander Khan, Internal Movement Control, former board member of … former Khan Enterprises. But I can't see how you would know anything about me, given the blackout enforced on this planet. So I don't know if those things make me *the* Alexander Khan."

She motioned with her hand in a turn-around motion. He did. "You have a lot to answer for, Major Khan. It will be interesting to learn how you ended up here. And it's just as I thought. There's the white blaze on the back between the shoulder blades."

He sighed darkly and turned to face her again. "It's complicated. Some believe I have much to answer for. And I may. But they don't know the whole story. And I would have thought I could leave all that behind once I was on Prison Planet –"

"We call it Arcadia –"

"– and what is the significance of the white blaze?"

She flipped one side of the robe for emphasis, briefly exposing his bare body and taking a frank look down before it fell back. "This gryphon has killed fourteen people and countless sheep, hogs, and cows over the last twenty years. Not to mention deer. Old Merciless, we called him. You've done us a great favor. Come to the house and let me look at your arm. It's amazing you're alive."

"Mom," warned the boy. "He could be just a quick talker. He talks like a Lord or a Tech, but he looks like a Maneater."

"That's why you're going to stay behind him at all times, and your sister is going to stay in front of him. If he makes a false move, one of you will kill him. But of course, he's also a guest, so we're going to be polite. Bring his spear."

She looked Khan in the eye with a steady regard that demanded respect.

"Fair enough," he said.

True to their mother's instructions, the boy and girl kept him under bows at the ready the whole two hundred meters through the woods to the house. He watched everything for clues about their technical level. The house stood in a well-kept two-hectare clearing. Beets and turnips grew in a garden that was mostly fallow, which could mean it was either spring or fall. The house was a modest but well-made log structure with a cedar-shake style roof. There were shutters, but no glass in the windows. To one side was a woodshed with a saw-grass thatch roof, and in the back was a two-story barn with an open mow apparently full of hay. Significantly, the barn was sided with planks. Planks meant either a two-man rip saw and a saw pit, or a sawmill with a rotating blade. Either way, steel was involved, or at minimum, bronze.

The boy and girl still kept him under guard up onto the porch, where the boy carefully laid the spear flat on the porch next to the house wall, taking care not to bump the point. Khan approved. The boy understood the strength of flint points was end-to-end, not side-to-side. They could stab an animal to death, but be easily broken with no more than a thumb.

The girl led him into the house while the boy remained behind. Coals glowed in a massive flagstone fireplace in the front room, which was the room to the right of the entry door, and in the equally large fireplace in the kitchen, which was to the left of the entry door. Heavy, skinned-sapling furniture covered with thick colorful Afghans faced the fireplace in the living room. A ladder beside the fireplace led up through a hatch-like opening to a loft whose floor formed the front room's ceiling – logs covered by sawn planks. Khan was surprised that there would be a single entrance to the loft. These people were very cautious. He brought his gaze back down. Unlighted candles stood in whittled wooden holders on sawn-lumber end tables. Then he spied something that lightened his heart even further. A book lay on one of the end tables. No one on Earth used them anymore, but the Khan family library had had thousands of them. He was very familiar with them.

In the kitchen a trestle table and four chairs occupied the center of the room, and a smaller table with knives, pots, and spoons stood in front of the fireplace. Another ladder rose up between the fireplace and the corner. He smiled and looked up. He shouldn't have underestimated these people. He was willing to bet there was also an escape hatch through the gable at the other end of the house. The loft ended two meters short of the end of the house, with a railing to keep people from falling off. The ladder connected to a walkway along the side of the house that connected with the loft. In the open floor-to-roof space between the end of the loft and the end wall of the house hung bunches of dried fish, clusters of smoked hams, clusters of onions, clusters of garlics, bundles of dried chili-pepper plants with the peppers still on, and clusters of cheeses.

"Don't get any ideas," said the woman, watching his eyes. "We will feed you once, then you leave."

"I won't deny that that sounds good after my diet of the last several days, but I didn't come for food. I came to see who was making the smoke, get my arm looked after, and learn something about this planet. My responsibilities took me to many planets, but I've never been here to … Arcadia. To my knowledge, no one from Earth Central Government ever has. I know nothing about what has developed here in the three centuries since we started transporting prisoners here."

She lit a candle with a twist of grass ignited by coals in the fireplace and smiled wryly. "'We?'" she said, and indicated a chair for him to sit in. "Don't you now mean 'they'?" The boy and the girl still had beads drawn on him but he noticed that the boy had perked up considerably at the mention of other planets.

"Slip of the tongue," he said. "There was never a 'we' with me in it. There was only following the orders of the real 'we.'"

"Yes, we know about those orders," she said, taking his left wrist in her hand, "And we know what you did with them. Here. Let's take a look at that arm."

"'We?'" he said.

"The people of Arcadia," she said. "At least the Techs in the Deepeven and the Elves in the Leas. I don't know about the Beyond."

He said nothing. She carefully untied the dried-grass binding he had put around his wound the last time he dressed it. It was stuck in the wound, and partially scabbed over. She took a razor-sharp steel paring knife from the cooking table and cut the binding loose, exposing the rest of the wound. The movement and bumping hurt. He stiffened. She sniffed the wound, then looked up at him.

"You're lucky. It's already healing, and it smells clean, no infection. It's dried out pretty well, and scabbed over, so I'm going to leave those pieces of grass stuck in the scab, and cover it loosely with a stiff dressing that will keep it from breaking open if it gets bumped. A tighter bandage or a poultice would moisten it, and at this point, that would be a mistake. Could encourage infection."

"Agreed. You understand, I can't see it very well. All I have to go on is how it feels."

"It'll never work quite the same. He tore about half of your back-arm muscle in two, and it is actually starting to heal together – which is amazing for so short a time. About twice as fast as normal." She gave him a long look expecting some comment or explanation. He met her gaze but said nothing. Finally she gave a little nod and said, "It's healing, but it will never be as strong." She thumped him on the shoulder to let him know she was done with him. "Go out and wash your hands for lunch. Gareth and Branwyn will show you where."

"Yes, Ma'am."

When they returned from the dug well, where he was ordered by Branwyn to drop the wooden bucket on the rope into the well, then pour the water into a wooden washing trough, he asked the boy where the threats came from. "You're very cautious. You've been attacked. Who attacked you?"

"You don't know anything yet. You just got here. You'll learn."

"Who?"

"The Maneaters any time they're in the Leas. They roam around looking for anything to steal or eat. They'll eat people, too. And the Lords took Dad –"

"Gareth!" the girl said sharply. Then she looked at Khan, still holding her bow at the ready. "What he meant to say is, Dad will be back at any moment. And he's very large and strong and quick. At least a head taller than you."

They paused on the porch. "That's pretty big," Khan said. "Your Dad must be a pretty tough guy."

"Very tough," she assured him. "Tougher than you for sure."

"I see. Well, I don't intend to do anything that would make your father have to get tough with me … when he returns. I'll be on my way soon. Just not sure where to. Is there a village nearby?"

"Depends upon what you mean by 'village' and 'nearby,'" said the boy. "There are settlements all over the Leas and even bigger ones and towns in the Deepeven out to the east." He looked Khan in the eye. "But for their sakes, I'm not sure we should tell you anything. I've never seen anyone do that with arrows before. Come inside and eat, then leave, just like Mom said."

It was hard not to wolf his food and ask for seconds. He had not realized how hungry he was. He reflected that when you're eating nothing but things you can pull up from the ground or catch, much of which tastes revolting, your appetite is suppressed. The warm bread and butter alone tasted like a feast, but the smoked pork, boiled dried beans, and fresh beets, with beet greens as a salad, bested any high-society feast he had ever tasted, and he had partaken since boyhood of the best that high society and riches could provide – at least, until ECG Officer Academy. He forced himself to be moderate, especially since the boy, the girl, and their mother all silently watched his every move while he ate. They all ate too, but sparingly. – And by turns so at least one could have bow at the ready.

"You are very generous," he said, pushing back the stoneware plate. "What work can I do to repay you?"

The mother spoke. "We always need work done, but you make us nervous, and we prefer that you move on. Besides the fact that you – or your gryphon hide – really smell bad." She smiled. "Nothing personal. You asked for information. What do you want to know? Some things I'll tell you, and some I won't."

"What are the Leas, and what is the Deepeven?"

"The Leas are where we live. They are all around you: the fens, the meads, the glades, the groves, the dales, even the plateaus and foothills."

"How far do they extend?"

"From the mountains on the west, where you came from, seven days' foot journey to the northeast, twenty days to the south, and five days to the east. To the northeast and east then comes the Deepeven grassland, which goes on forever."

"And when you say, 'we,' you mean –"

"We Elves."

The hairs on the back of Khan's neck stood up for reasons he could not explain. He was not quite sure how to react. He knew of elves in Earthly lore, but he also knew they were supposed to be mythological creatures. He didn't believe in mythological creatures, and he didn't know anyone who did. This woman seemed perfectly rational, but …

She smiled. "Light Elves, not Dark Elves," she said, almost mischievously.

He gave her his best poker face.

"You are struggling, Mr. Khan, and attempting to hide it. It is probably good for you that you have spent your life as a military man rather than a business man. Your face gives you away."

He didn't like this at all, but at least it gave him information. They knew about military men, they knew about business men, and they didn't mind if he knew it. "I, uh …."

"We are called Elves by the Techs, primarily, but also by the Lords. We claim no special powers. They began using the name as an insult nearly three hundred years ago when the groups began to form by affinity. The nature spirits and Mother Earthers, as our ancestors thought of themselves, were considered impractical and addle-brained by the Techs, who were busy recreating as much technology and environmental destruction as they could, and by the Lords, who were and are nothing but predatory thugs, but who style themselves as knights and feudal lords. So you need not fear that we'll put a spell on you. We embrace the name because it causes a similar reaction among both the Lords and the Techs. – A reaction we encourage by hinting mysteriously of spells and omens, and by exceptional skill with the bow. Our children in fact shoot better than their warriors."

"Yes, I've seen that." He cast a nervous glance at the children, who still held their bows at the ready.

"Nobody is more superstitious deep down than a warrior or an empiricist. – Especially one who has seen an Elf shoot a running warrior dead at one hundred paces. It is skill, learned and practiced from early childhood, not magic. But we don't discourage their thinking it's partly magic."

Khan was taken aback by this speech. "You speak like an educated woman. I saw only one book in your other room. How do you come to know about empiricism, or mythology? Why has such knowledge not died back in the absence of libraries and the Net? And why would you trust me with this explanation about Elven magic with the bow when it would be logical to assume that I would become a Lord?"

"That's a lot of assumptions for an educated man. We do have books. Nothing is more precious to us. We also have a library maintained by us all. The list is available to all, and though they don't move, all books are shared. People travel far to study a book. Books are held in high regard by all three groups and protected even more than food. Only Maneaters and barbarians don't care about them. Even Lords revere them and commission their creation – usually about weapons and military matters. As soon as the First People had paper – which is an accomplishment the Techs love to talk about – they began writing down everything that everyone knew. It still goes on today. It's considered a duty to humankind. Learned groups review the writings and decide what to put into books. And I'm trusting you not to be a Lord because … ," and here she looked him directly in the eye for a long, evaluative silence, making the hairs on the back of his neck stand up again, "though you have done many bad things under orders, and you are dangerous and therefore not to be fully trusted, I sense you are … a decent man."

Goose bumps rose on his skin, and he cleared his throat. Her steady, clear, grey-eyed gaze was unsettling. He could understand how the Lords and Techs gave credence to the Elf thing. There was something indefinable about this woman. He shook it off.

"What about education?"

"Those who know, teach. We send children around to various worthies to learn what each knows."

"It suddenly occurs to me that you have me at a disadvantage: you know my name, but I don't know yours."

"Yes, I know," she smiled. "That's because I haven't told you. It leaves you slightly in my power, but it's also inhospitable. I am Maruil."

He got the goosebumps again. She pronounced it 'Mar-oo-il.' An Elvish name if ever he had heard one. And so, come to think of it, were Gareth and Branwyn.

Suddenly there were hoofbeats and shouts outside, and looks of real fear came onto the faces of all three elves.

"Maruil!" boomed a man's voice. "Out here now! Both brats too! No bows or we shoot!"

"It's the Lords!" said Gareth to Khan, wide-eyed. "That's Sillion, from Mander's Keep. Mander's oldest son. The one who took Dad!"

"What do you think they want?" said Branwyn.

The fear on the others' faces instantly brought Khan into battle mode. "Doesn't matter," he said, assuming command. "What weapons do you have besides those two bows?"

Maruil hesitated only a moment, pressing her lips together. "Baelmar's bow," she said, looking back at Khan, not with fear, but with a fell resolve. She looked at Gareth and hooked a thumb toward the loft ladder. "The machete, too." The boy disappeared up the ladder with speed.

"Maruil!" bellowed the voice. "We're coming in!"

"They wear chain mail," she said. "You'll have to aim for the neck."

"Try to keep them talking until the first one dies. Once that happens, they'll come after me. Get your bows and disable their horses. I'll try to get the armor from the first one, and then kill the others one by one."

Gareth came back down the ladder with a heavy bow, a full quiver, and a sheathed machete with a shoulder strap. He hesitated a second before handing them to Khan. Khan said, "In battle, you have to trust someone,

Boy." The boy handed the weapons over, and Khan was out the back door, first checking to left and right to see if the door was observed.

There were bushes close to the house, which he used for cover. He crept around the side until six mounted men came into view, facing the front of the house. They indeed wore chain mail and tabards and helmets and carried swords, bows, and shields, as if they had stepped out of *Chanson de Roland*. Khan waited until he saw the smile on the head man's face, heard him say, "Well, Maruil, you are as beautiful as ever," and heard Maruil reply, "What can a barbarian like you know of true beauty, Junior?"

Khan nocked his arrow and drew down, going to the battle space in his mind, thinking fleetingly of his boyhood years of relentless drilling by Pierre in the use of weapons. All weapons, ancient and modern. The Khans had powerful enemies, and he was to be a warrior as well as the well-schooled chief of the family empire when the time came. "We start with the sword," Pierre had said. "The most personal weapon there is. Its discipline and logic are well established, and its strategies transfer. Once you can fight a man with a sword, you understand fighting. Then we move to more cowardly weapons, like the bow, and finally the gun and the laser. You must master them all."

When Sillion threw back his head and roared laughter, Khan loosed his arrow and willed it to its target, as taught. But he had not shot a bow in years, and holding his left arm straight against the bow's tension was agony. The arrow went not into Junior's throat but through one cheek and out the lower jaw on the other side. Incredibly, the man was not even unhorsed. A big man in his late twenties, he roared in anger, broke off the arrowhead, and pulled the arrow back out the way it had come in. "Who did that?" he roared.

"Damn," said Khan to himself, and nocked another arrow. He knew this would be his last. Calculating that Sillion was at least weakened by his wound, he fired at the man to his right. This time the arrow went through the throat, and bright arterial blood spurted. The man made ineffectual grasping motions at the arrow, then fell from his horse.

"Grab the boy!" bellowed Sillion to the man to his left. "The girl, too, if you can get her! She's plain, but she'll warm a bed!" Then he looked directly at Khan, though Khan knew he couldn't see him. "Come out, Coward! Fight like a man!"

Khan was ready for this. He stepped out into the open, unsheathed the machete, took a wide stance, and threw the bow aside. "A man needs a man to fight with!" he roared. "Where is there a man?"

Sillion looked him over in surprise, then threw back his head and laughed, spraying blood from his cheek wounds. "You challenge a Lord, Maneater?"

"I don't see a Lord. I see a bandit who is used to running in packs and probably can't put up much fight by himself."

Sillion acknowledged this insult with a brief nod. "And I see a ragged, stinking Maneater who sneaks in the night to catch people to eat them because they are easier than fairer prey."

Khan nodded in return. "When I kill you, I will give your liver to my favorite animal, but I won't eat you myself. You look as though you won't taste too good. But as a matter of honor, if you have any, the girl, her brother, and her mother go free when I kill you – or your champion."

Sillion spat blood and thought this over for a moment. "Agreed, though I could kill you in the next minute and wouldn't have to worry about honor. But since you offer to fight my champion, and since I don't want to dirty myself with you, you can fight Bolodan." He gestured behind him, and a huge, blonde young man stepped his horse out from behind the others. He looked to mass about 130 kilos – about 30 kilos more than Khan. His arms were the size of Khan's thighs. "Bolodan needs the experience. I do not."

Bolodan swung a gigantic leg over his horse and dropped to the ground with a thump and a clank from his sword. He cracked his fingers as though he were going to play piano, cut the distance between them to two meters, and smiled shyly at Khan. He looked to be a good natured boy of about twenty, and not terribly bright, so it was going to be harder to kill him than if he had been more ill-tempered or evil-looking. Nevertheless, he looked deadly, and Khan prepared himself. *They look slow, but they are not,* he heard Pierre say in his mind. *Big doesn't necessarily mean slow.* And there were other dicta: *Whenever your opponent makes a move, use his momentum against him. If he doesn't get you, he's vulnerable until he reassumes his defensive posture. He's extended.* And the one he always ended up with: *Whoever is meanest quickest wins. Most humans are made not to want to hurt others. Those who hold back die.* Khan brought himself again to that quiet battle space in which time slowed, and his genetically modified body sped up to superhuman levels.

"Let us kill them, Khan," said Maruil reasonably. We can get at least four of them before the other one comes at us. You can slow the last one down until we can shoot him."

"You are a fine woman," boomed Sillion good-naturedly. "You are a fit queen for a Lord like me, and wasted as an Elf."

"I would kill you in your sleep and feed your manhood to the hogs for their breakfast."

As Sillion threw back his head and roared with laughter, Khan struck. Momentarily distracted by the exchange, Bolodan looked mildly surprised as the none-too-sharp machete plunged through his neck and bright arterial blood spurted out. His reflexes were fast enough to bring his sword up as a shield between himself and Khan, cutting Khan across the chest with its razor-sharp edge. The boy was fast, but not fast enough. He looked at Khan with confusion and disillusionment, as if to say, "How could you be that mean? You looked like a nice person." Then he slumped to the ground and slowly flattened out on his back.

Khan looked at the centimeter-deep cut across his chest and decided it was not serious. He leaned over and picked up Bolodan's sword. It was a finely made, doubled-edged weapon over a meter long with a generous forged-steel quillons and a leather-wound brass hilt. Then he removed the scabbard and buckler. It would come in handy.

Sillion's laughter died in his throat. He was thunderstruck. "Bolo!" he bellowed. "Brother, get up!" He slid from his horse and ran to the boy, kneeling at his side. He grabbed the boy's massive shoulders in his hands and tried to get him to sit up. "Bolo! Wake up, boy!"

But Bolo was never going to wake up again. Khan prepared for what he knew was coming next. Sillion rose to his full height and bellowed in rage. "You killed my baby brother! I am going to kill you!" He drew his own sword and came after Khan.

Now there was little chance for surprise, and Khan knew he was in a more dangerous fight. He could maybe use the brother's rage against him, but Sillion was almost certainly a highly skilled swordsman, and Khan was not. He was competent.

"You named him as your champion. Leave now, as you promised, and we will not kill the rest of you."

"Kill them all!" roared Sillion, and came for Khan with sword at eye level, clearly an experienced fencer.

The other three horsemen spurred their mounts and tried to ride Maruil and her children down, but they retreated onto the porch and started shooting. One of the men went down immediately, with an arrow through his larynx. The other two dismounted on the safe side of their horses and untied shields from their horses' flanks. Then they rushed the porch with shields and drawn swords.

Gareth leapt forward with his boy's imitation of a battle roar and started rapid firing one arrow after another at the three attackers, including Sillion, all ineffectual because of their helmets, their shields, their mail tunics, the greaves on their shins, the rerebraces on their upper arms, and the vambraces on their forearms. Only their feet, elbows, and shoulders were exposed. The boy had lost his temper.

"Think, Gareth!" shouted Khan. "Think! Still your mind!"

The boy nearly got killed while staring at Khan in response to this, but immediately thereafter put an arrow through one man's sword elbow. Then all three Elves turned and ran off the porch, pursued by the two swordsmen, though one of them lagged while picking at the arrow through his arm.

This left Khan alone with Sillion, who while Khan was distracted with Gareth nearly cleft Khan in twain from top to bottom. Only Sillion's uncontrolled rage saved him. The man was so enraged that he opened his guard, grasped his huge sword with both hands, and raised it over his head like a wood splitter's axe. Khan side-stepped in a split second's time, and the sword went into the dirt. Khan than slapped Sillion on the side of the head with the flat of his brother's sword.

"Stop fighting and go home," he said. "You've lost enough." He had not the heart to kill this man whose baby brother he had just killed. He knew of course that if he let Sillion live that he would have a lifelong enemy, but he couldn't do it. In his previous life, he wouldn't have hesitated a second. Since boyhood he had clamped down and stuffed back anything personal to play the roles required by Khan International and ECG. Now something had stirred. It was just him now.

Sillion stepped back in confusion and looked at him. "What kind of man are you?" he said, shaking his head. "I have never seen any man move that fast. You kill one brother and spare the other. I don't know your kind."

"I'm a man who has killed many and is tired of killing," said Khan. "Go home and leave these people in peace. Return their husband and father."

"You reach too far, Stranger. My father and my brothers and I rule the West Riding, no matter what these Elves may say or think. They are my serfs. I take them when I want them. "

"But not today," said Khan.

"No, not today," said Sillion, his spirit rallying. "But tomorrow or the next day. I will kill you and take them as I need them. You have not long to live. "

Khan said nothing as the man knelt beside the body of his brother in a brief moment of silence. Then, with more ease than Khan could have managed, Sillion pulled Bolodan's body up by the arm, slung it over his shoulder, and transferred it belly-down to the boy's horse. Then he bellowed, "Richard! Georg! To me!"

After a few moments the others appeared from behind the house with Dog nipping at their heels, protesting that they would have had the cursed Elf boy in another moment.

"Another day," said Sillion, speaking to them, but looking at Khan.

"Any time," said Khan, saluting with Bolodan's sword.

The three horsemen mounted and rode out without looking back. Khan knew he had made a mortal enemy that day, and that sooner or later he would have to kill Sillion. So be it. He had experienced the same before. He stood for a moment in silence looking at the sword, reflecting on life. Then he shook his head as if to clear it and buckled on the sword. It felt quite natural.

Maruil and the children reappeared from around the house. They paused for a moment as they looked at Bolodan's sword buckled at his side, and then at him. Their expressions said, "I knew it," but they said nothing. Finally, Maruil spoke.

"Thank you, Major. Without you we would have lost Gareth or Branwyn, one."

"I would have killed them all," protested the boy.

"You would certainly have caused them damage," said Khan, wanting to reinforce the boy's fighting spirit. "But you were not focused enough. When you are in a fight, you must go to a place inside yourself where there is no pain, no fear, and no hurry. You must imagine a calm place with no sound, where nothing has happened for a thousand years. This will permit you to focus completely on the fight."

The boy scowled slightly but took this in with a nod. He clearly now knew what Khan was talking about.

Maruil looked at him with a deeply sad look. "You have saved us, Mr. Khan." She made go-away motions to Gareth and Branwyn. They hesitated a moment, then made themselves scarce. "But you must go. Immediately."

He looked at her without speaking. He knew he scared her. He nodded. "The boy?" he said.

She nodded. "I don't want him admiring a man like you."

He nodded again. "I don't like violence, but I understand it. It comes from simple laziness: you can get what you want through violence, with no other effort. Most people are unprepared to resist. Violence is foreign to their nature. But there is always a violent minority, lazy and violent, or simply cruel and violent. So decent people have to master violence to protect themselves. It is an old, old story. You have to get good at the thing you hate. It has been my profession. "

She smiled grimly. "We have chosen the bow as a compromise. But we live as we do because we are a peaceable people."

"—who are victimized by people willing to use violence to get what they want."

"We make it hard for them. We make them pay. We send them away with arrows in them. "

"Yet they've taken your husband."

"We hope to get him back when he has trained their horses."

"The Lords have no incentive to give him back. Why do they want Gareth?"

"He is able to call animals. They come to him. I imagine the Lords want to use him as a hunting dog of sorts. They also like to steal boys and make them warriors. They do fight among themselves, one fief against another."

"I see. How far away do these Lords live?"

"Many days' ride before you come to the first fief, which is the Guido Hundred. Not bad, that one. Salvatore. Mander's the worst. We live at the far western edge of what they call the West Riding and we call the Leas. They don't normally come here."

"But they can any time they want." Khan would not let her off the hook.

"Yes, Mr. Khan," she said with some irritation. "There are always forces that can destroy us."

"Indeed. Fine, I will go, though I'm not sure where. I don't want to continue living in the Stone Age, but I don't want to fall into the clutches of these Lords, either. Do you have paper? Pencils? Will you draw me a map? I think I will journey to the Techs. Surely there it is more like what I'm used to."

She smiled wryly. "We are not barbarians, Mr. Khan. We do have paper and pencils, and we even have maps, of a sort. We have only two, but we will give you one as a token of our gratitude. We would have lost Gareth today but for you. And we'll give you some food to take along so you don't have to spend all your time hunting. And at least a pair of pants. You'll be better received."

He grinned. "Perhaps so. May I sleep in your haymow overnight? Waking up in the wilderness to face the teeth of something trying to eat me makes it hard to go back to sleep."

"Of course," she smiled. "There are things in the haymow that will scurry over you, but at least if they try to eat you, it will only be a little at a time."

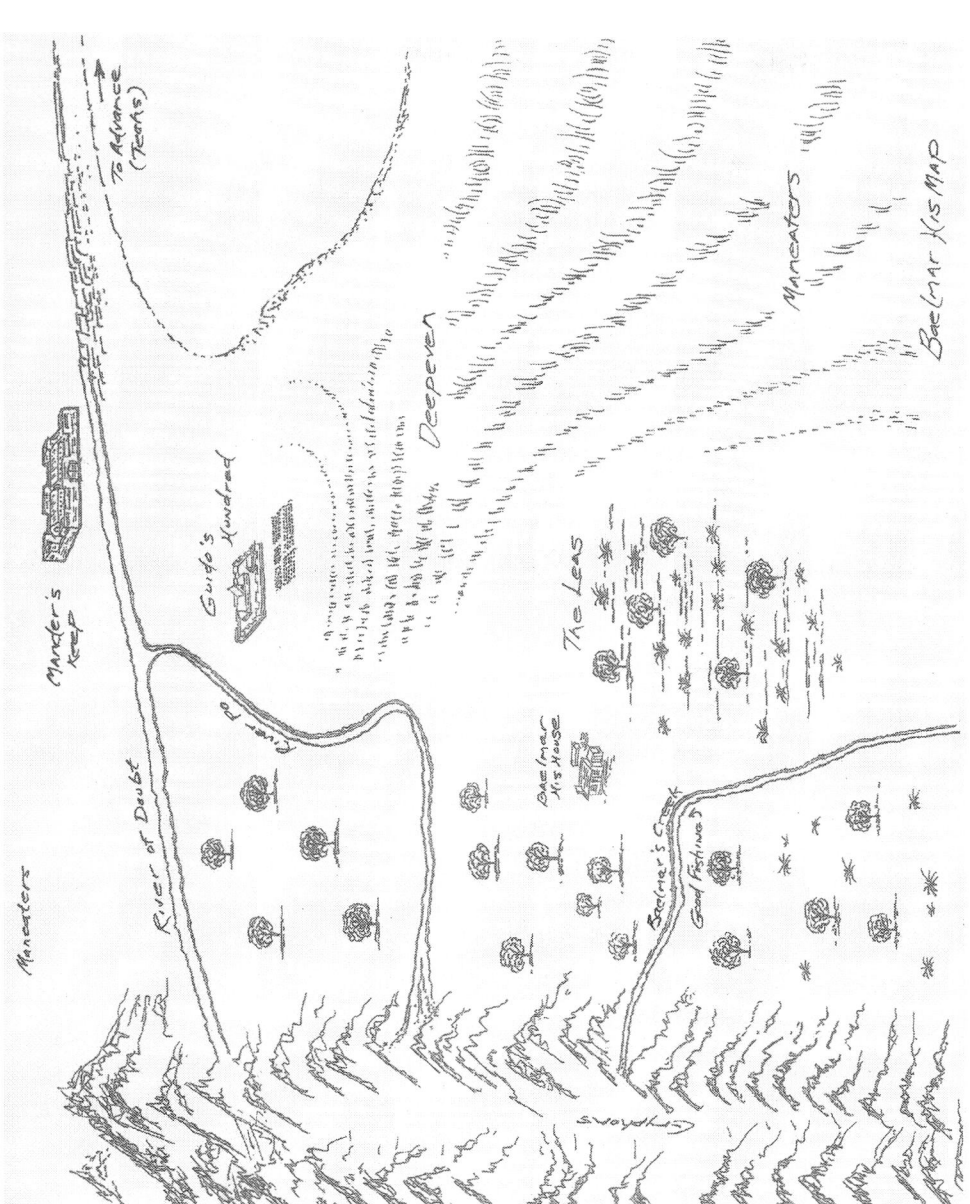

CHAPTER THREE

The Wider World

Khan slept better than he had since being dropped on the planet. There were indeed scurryings and scratchings in the haymow during the night, and bone-chilling screeches in the distance out the gable door. But there was no need to be on watch for large predators. He had closed and barred the trap door in the haymow floor. And any predator coming in through the gable door would have first faced a sheer climb, then a transverse move across the outside wall over the open barn door below. Unlikely. He thus awoke feeling itchy but refreshed and hopeful, and with only a little pain in his arm. It seemed to be healing well.

As promised, Maruil sent him on his way with a hand-drawn map – but also a pair of pants, a full belly, a bag of dried meat and dried fruit, and a water gourd. There was as well an unexpected boon: Baelmar's bow and a quiver full of steel-tipped arrows. – And a warning: "Don't come back unless you bring Baelmar back."

She held his eye. He said nothing. He owed this woman. And she was opening herself enough to ask a huge favor, though too proud to ask directly. Certainly, it meant a change in plans: go into the realm of the Lords and rescue Baelmar before journeying to the realm of the Techs. But serving the good was more important than serving oneself. And it was pretty clear. These were good people, and the people oppressing them were bad. He could still hear his father's voice. *"Duty comes first, son. Your duty is to improve the lot of humanity. When you're done with that, then you can serve your own needs."*

He looked her in the eye for a long moment and saw steely resolve, but also a hidden spark of hope. She trusted him.

"How will I know him?"

"He is large, like you, but has golden hair. A scar on his neck and chest from a dead Lord's sword." She smiled grimly at a private memory and traced the course of the scar down her own neck and chest. "And a ready smile. He will be with the horses."

"I will do my best. But I have one question whose answer will perhaps tell me something important about both Baelmar and the Lords. You elves are stealthy and skillful in the wild. You could easily hide from the Lords until they went away. How did Baelmar let himself be captured? "

Maruil smiled wryly. "You deserve your reputation as a crafty hunter of people. What I have come to understand is that the Lords released a beautiful dark, feed-trained but unbroken stallion in the Leas knowing that Baelmar could not resist capturing and taming it. Then they hid and waited until he appeared. And, as I am told by my neighbors who saw it happen, once he mounted, they whistled in the horse and captured Baelmar. He didn't jump off soon enough. Knowing him, he probably believed he could control the animal if he only tried harder."

Khan smiled. "Ah. This tells me much about both Baelmar and the Lords."

She smiled as well. "Yes, the Lords are not stupid. And Baelmar is as proud as he is strong. Or wise."

Gareth showed him on the map roughly where Mander's Keep was. The concept of scale appeared to have some elasticity on the map, but the Keep looked to be about five or six hard days' journey. More like ten at a leisurely pace. He would know it by its location on a bluff in the bend of a river. – A thoroughly defensible position in a world of bows and arrows, he noted, and probably no cannon or trebuchets.

He took his leave, thanking all three of them. "Before I found you, I thought I might be alone on the planet," he said. Then he tousled Gareth's hair. "And while you did try to kill me, you also gave me help and hope. I will try to return the favor."

The first two days' journey was uneventful. The weather was mild, with no rain or snow, so he was not cold as he had been in the mountains.

And because no large predators made an appearance he was able to sleep reasonably soundly, though he felt exposed in the open.

The ground cover was alive with small furry animals darting in and out of the grass at the edge of vision, taking little notice of him, going about their timeless business of eating and trying to avoid being eaten. Raptor birds swooped in at times and took away such creatures, hardly breaking the rhythm of their wings as they made their snatch. And animals like Dog showed themselves brazenly, apparently because they were the largest predators in the area. But they were after rabbits and other small furry delectables, not large, difficult prey like Khan.

In any case, he was now well armed with Bolodan's sword and Baelmar's bow. He had nothing to fear from large predators if he stayed alert and saw them coming. – Unless they were the size of elephants. But Maruil and Gareth had mentioned no large predators other than gryphons, which they said preferred the high country. So he felt reasonably safe.

After a day and a half of low, semi-boggy meadowland, which he took to be the Leas, the land rose slightly into mostly open, gently rolling grassland with prairie grasses and copses of trees. The local sun shone unobstructed by clouds. The air was crystal clear, blue overhead, and pink nearer the horizon. Visibility was at least twenty kilometers. Nights and mornings were cold with a frost, but middays were nearly warm enough to shuck his fur cape. But he normally kept it on because the prairie grasses were sharp.

On the third day he saw a balloon five or six kilometers away. Excitement fluttered briefly in his chest. There was no way of telling whether it was a hot air balloon or a gas balloon, like hydrogen or helium. In either case, it implied the ability to capture and compress gas – for fuel in the former case, and for lift in the latter case. And it indicated that Techs ranged into Elf and Lord country.

Another surprise came on the afternoon of the fourth day. He was walking along enjoying the white, purple, and yellow spring flowers scattered through the grass, for it was indeed spring, he had decided, or something like it. But of course, local seasons would depend upon axial tilt. If there was none, he might be in eternal spring here on the plain. The day's length seemed close to Earth's twenty-four-hour cycle, but it was hard to tell whether it was getting longer or shorter. His experience on other planets was that the human body quickly adjusted to local diurnal cycles, and almost any day length felt natural after a few days.

He was on one knee to pick one of the purple flowers to smell it when he heard a rumble in the distance. Instinctively staying in cover, he peeked his head slightly above the prairie grass to peer in the direction of the sound. Nothing. Maybe a dark smudge on the horizon. But as he watched, the smudge moved toward him. Straight toward him. And as he watched further, the smudge resolved itself into a herd of animals perhaps half a kilometer away, moving toward him at a speed that would bring them to him in half a minute or so. He looked for a place to hide but there was none. Which was a problem, because they were clearly large animals, visible above the top of the shoulder-high prairie grass. His only choice was to make himself visible and hope they would avoid him.

He rose to his full height, and feeling slightly ridiculous, he pulled Baelmar's bow off of his shoulder and nocked an arrow. There were perhaps two hundred animals, and the arrow would at best wound one of them, but it made him feel slightly less vulnerable. Then as he watched the herd grow closer, the unknown animals resolved themselves further into horses.

It was a herd of horses on this strange, Earthlike prison planet.

He had little time to reflect on this as they bore down on him, unaware of his presence. However, he knew horses. No Khan child grew to adulthood without becoming an expert horseman. He simply needed to make himself visible and threatening. Thus he dropped the bow and spread his cloak wide to make himself appear bigger than he was.

This did the trick. The herd divided three hundred meters away and flowed in two thundering rivers around him. As they did he got a good look at them. They were beautiful, healthy animals of all colors – white, brown, and black – and large, looking to be in the sixteen-hand range. Then they were gone.

Except for one, a large dark stallion, who fearlessly turned back to investigate him. The animal approached as if it owned the planet, and Khan knew that if the animal wished, it could kill him in seconds. – If he were not armed. He had Bolodan's sword if he needed it, but by instinct he left it hanging in its scabbard.

The stallion approached and sniffed him. He made no move to avoid this. The animal sniffed his cloak, then nodded his head and neck vigorously, after the way of horses. Then it sniffed his head and backed up, whinnying slightly. Khan held out his hand with a piece of dried fruit that Maruil had given him. The horse took this as its due. – Without biting his hand, which was always a risk with horses. Slowly, he raised his hand to touch the side of the horse's face. The horse let it happen, then snorted and raised his head away. No easy mark, this one. Khan smiled and said, "Easy, Boy. You know humans, don't you?"

As if to answer, the horse nodded his head and neck up and down vigorously, then put his head down to graze on tender grass at Khan's feet. This left the animal's left flank exposed, almost like an invitation. Khan took it and leapt onto the horse's back. For just a moment, there was no reaction, and he thought the horse might be accustomed to being ridden. Maybe he was an escapee from one of the Lords' fiefdoms. But then the horse made it clear he was nobody's patsy.

It was like sitting on top of an explosion. First the animal sprang two meters straight up. When it came down it threw its hind legs as high in the air as it could, virtually standing straight up on its forelegs. Khan gripped with his legs and hung onto the mane for dear life. He knew if he went over forward the animal would kill him with its front feet. But he had caught a glimpse of the stallion's dark eye looking back at him in challenge. "OK, Big Boy," he thought. "If that's how it is." He tightened his grip.

Barely staying mounted until the animal came back down, Khan was prepared for the next move: the reverse of what it had just tried. This time it stood on its hind legs, an easier move to counter as long as he didn't lose his grip on the mane. The animal snorted and bicycled its deadly front legs as if to scare him with what it would do to him if he were on the ground.

These maneuvers having failed to rid it of its tormentor, the animal took off at top speed and then planted its forelegs in a sudden sliding stop, trying to throw Khan forward. Prepared for this as well, Khan was nevertheless barely able to hold on. His arm was hurting and he was panting, and the animal was unbelievably powerful. If it didn't calm down soon, Khan realized he was going to have to make a jump for it. And maybe not get too far on the ground.

But after a kilometer's gallop, the stallion finally slowed to a walk, obviously tired, and contented itself with trying to bite Khan's feet. This was relatively easy to avoid, but alerted Khan to the fact that this horse was not going to easily accept him as master, and would lie in wait for an opportunity to get him.

"That's fine, Boy," he said. "I can accept those terms."

And with that he turned the animal toward Mander's Keep and set off across the grassland. In the distance, perhaps five hundred meters back, the entire herd followed.

Khan figured he could at best get a day's ride out of the stallion, which he resisted naming, given the horse's desire to kill him, so he persisted until the light was almost gone. He figured he had traveled twelve kilometers on the horse, probably twice as much as he could have done in the same time on foot.

He found a small, nearly vertical bluff with exposed limestone shelves where he could climb out of the reach of horses and large predators, and dismounted, giving the stallion plenty of clearance. The horse turned and offered a two-footed rear kick, a killing blow if Khan had not expected it and moved out of range. "Thanks anyway," he said with a snort, and climbed into his intended lair for the night. Finding gratefully that there were no nests or small animals to remove, he settled in quickly for the night and dozed.

During the night a radiantly beautiful, glowing woman appeared and spoke to him quietly, and he couldn't hear. She wore a white, leathery, form-fitting uniform of some kind that emphasized her mammalian nature, but the wide set of her eyes, her extra-long canines, and her pointed ears strongly suggested alien origin.

His consciousness rose to near wakefulness. Why would he dream of such a creature? Certainly, her femaleness was interesting, and it had indeed been a long time. But he had not had such dreams since he was a fevered boy. And she seemed to be trying to tell him something. But in the way of such dreams, no matter how hard he tried, he couldn't quite hear her. It was almost as if she were trying to speak directly into his mind. She seemed to be trying to warn him about something in his body; something just under his skin. Then an image of his left armpit filled his head, and a small lump under the skin. This made no sense at all, and he turned his back on the image and tried for more sleep.

Finally the dream ended and he gratefully sank into deeper sleep, thinking vaguely as he did that maybe some of the greens he had picked and eaten with his dried meat had had something unusual in them.

He awoke in strong sunshine feeling semi-rested, but still aware of the strange dream. He had certainly had more restful nights. The stone shelf on which he had slept had left its impressions on him, too, and he rubbed the shoulder on which he had been lying. Idly, he trailed his hand under the same arm and felt his arm pit. There was a small flat lump under the skin about the size of a kernel of corn and half the thickness. It was so small that he would not have noticed it without the dream, or if he had, he would have thought it was a skin anomaly and forgotten about it. The hair on the back of his neck stood up. He felt it some more and noticed that he could move it slightly under the skin.

Now his suspicions were aroused. He took his stone knife from his bag and poked the tip of it under the lozenge-shaped lump, piercing the skin. Out fell a small metal device that he quickly recognized: a tracking transponder. Anger welled up, but he quickly throttled it, sliding back into professional mode for just a few seconds. Anger was an energy source only; it was never to be permitted to flow out.

Now he was wide awake and his mind was racing. So. Earth Central Government wanted to track him. Interesting and disturbing. To his imperfect knowledge, ECG operatives had never set foot on Prison Planet. He had always thought once prisoners were sent down, that was the end of their lives as far as ECG was concerned. It was hard to see what good a tracking chip would be.

Unless they wanted him back at some point. Unless they planned to send down operatives to snatch him, or unless they wanted to do something to him from orbit based on his location.

The only thing they could do from orbit was observe or destroy. It was possible to transport based on a tracker chip, but was not considered safe and was normally done only with freight. Normal practice was to transport based on the signals from a communicator.

So what did they want? If they wanted to destroy him, they would have done so already. It had to mean they wanted him back for something.

Suddenly he felt as if he had taken a whiff of pure oxygen. Clearly they wanted something from him, so the tracker was a kind of power. A ticket. A means to get off this planet, get revenge on Nathan Fox, and redeem his father's name. At some point, he would encounter an ECG operative trying to snatch him, and he had to be ready. The question was, would it be obvious, or would the operative be undercover, posing as an Arcadian?

Thinking furiously, he put the tracker into his shoulder basket, gathered his things, and climbed down from his stone shelf. He was so preoccupied he almost missed the footprints. In a patch of moist soil in the shade of the bluff, there were small bootprints. Very light, but unmistakable. With heels. Elegantly shaped like a woman's boot. The hairs on the back of his neck stood up. His mind raced. Someone had gotten close to him without his waking to defend himself. His discipline had gone lax. But she had known about the tracker. She had been real.

And she had not been human.

As a naval officer after leaving the academy, he had patrolled human space – roughly two dozen quasi-habitable planets in fifteen systems – to protect it against the alien threat. ECG policy was to preserve the planets for future colonization, but not to allow such colonization until the alien threat had been eliminated. And more importantly, not until the Great Equilibration, the event preached by ECG as the eventual result of its global efforts to make everyone equal, to defeat poverty, hunger, crime, ignorance, and despair, and to perfect living sustainably in a closed system. Then and only then would humanity be fit to thrust itself upon the cosmos, after it had been perfected by ECG.

During seven years of such patrols, Khan had seen no evidence of such an alien threat. No alien vessels of any kind. – Which, in an impolitic moment, he had once verbalized in front of his commanding officer. Despite his family's huge influence – or perhaps because of it, he now realized – this indiscretion resulted in immediate reassignment, out of the regular Navy and into ECG Internal Police as a colony buster.

As an Internal Movement Control Officer, he had been surprised to learn that many of the planets had sprouted illegal colonies – a fact kept secret by ECG. Disaffected scientists, military people, freighter pilots absconding from the Mars run – anyone with access to a gravity drive

– had apparently been fleeing the socialist paradise of ECG for several generations and setting up colonies that had to be stamped out. And he had loyally done that job for four years, sometimes literally vomiting at the crimes against humanity he had to commit. Invariably, the colonists fought to the death to avoid Return. Finally it had become too much, and when precipitated by what ECG had done to his father, it had pushed him to the act that had sent him here.

During those four years of colony busting, he never saw or heard of an alien. He had come to believe humans were alone in the galaxy. Here was – proof? – that he had been wrong. What was not clear was whether ECG had ever had evidence of aliens, or had only been using them as a bugaboo to maintain the slavery of the people of Earth.

Didn't matter. He had a mission and now a mystery to deal with. But it was clear he was going to have to be careful. And it was clear he was going to have to have a strategy to deal with whoever in ECG was tracking him.

Still, the game had changed. The chip was a kind of power. Hope for the larger mission remained. But first, Baelmar.

It was too much to expect that the horses would have remained nearby, but he gave a whistle in any case to see what would happen. Nothing did for several minutes, so he gave another shrill whistle. Soon he heard the thunder of hoofbeats, and when he climbed to the top of the bluff to see across the grassland, sure enough, there came the entire herd, with the stallion in the lead.

The stallion didn't make it easy, and several of the other horses did their best to kill him, but he managed to lure the beast with a dried apple, and repeated the mounting exercise he had done yesterday. The effect was the same, but didn't last as long, and he was able to stay on his mount. He turned the animal to the northeast, and he and the entire herd set off for Mander's keep.

After two days' travel, he and the herd came to cultivated fields of beets and turnips with well-fed but poorly dressed people, mostly small children, pulling weeds. They eyed him suspiciously. The herd stayed behind when they saw the children, which was a good thing. He didn't want their crops to be destroyed.

"Which way to Mander's Keep?" he called to the nearest boy.

The boy pointed wordlessly behind him, in the direction of a large, light-colored building on a distant hilltop. It was a rambling affair that appeared to have battlements and crenellations, but was too far away to tell.

"That is Mander's Keep?"

"This is the Guido Hundred Big House," said the boy. "You're not one of Lord Ruggiero's men, so you have to get his permission to cross. You must go there and ask." He pointed again at the great house in the distance. "If you were one of Lord Mander's men, you would know how to get to the Keep. You have Elf pants, but you also have a sword, so you look like a Maneater that's killed people and taken their stuff. Are you a Maneater?"

"I've never been that hungry yet, but I suppose there's a first time for everything. If I were going to start, I'd probably want a victim with more meat on his bones than you," said Khan with his best smile, and set off toward the big house on the hill.

He was not surprised to be met by a horseback patrol at least a kilometer away from the house. Three men in similar livery, all armed with broadswords, shields, bows slung across their shoulders, and crossbows slung from their saddles, converged on him from three sides on horses at least as big as the stallion he rode.

"State your business, Stranger," barked the one in front. "You are not one of Mander's, and you're not one of Laberteaux's, and you travel alone. What trouble do you bring?" He was a large but lean fellow who looked as though he knew what he was doing with every weapon at his disposal.

"I only mean to cross the Guido Hundred on my way northeast. A boy in the field tells me I require permission."

"That way lies Mander's Keep. What business do you have there?"

"It's my business, and none of your own. All I require from you is your absence from my path. No offense intended." He gave his best smile.

"What you require," said the man affably, "is better manners. You look able-bodied enough. We'll put you in the stockade for a couple of weeks to soften your tongue, then put you to work in the mine. Dismount and follow me."

"I only follow men I respect, which is generally men who can fight better than me. You don't appear to be one of them. You look a little womanly."

The man grinned raffishly. "Not only a loose tongue, but a smart ass, I see. One who's about to get the ass whipping of his life. "He slung a leg over his saddle pommel and slid to the ground. "Give Elbert your reins and jump down for your beating." He took a closer look. "You don't have reins. Where did you steal that horse? He's too fine for you." Then his eyes widened and he turned to one of the other men. "Elbert, who does that horse look like to you?"

"It looks like Il Mostro," said the man with reverence, "but nobody's ever ridden him, and then lived. Except maybe the Elf Baelmar." He turned to Khan. "Where did you get him?"

"The edge of the Leas," said Khan, declining to say more.

"You have a strange way of speaking," accused the leader. "And the 'Leas' is an Elf word for the West Riding. But you are no Elf. You look more … dangerous. And you are carrying a sword from Mander's Keep. Bolodan's sword, unless I am mistaken. Get down and declare yourself."

Khan sighed. "Your word of honor before I dismount that your men will not try to harm the horse or me. Only you and I will fight. Else I will have to kill your men too, which I don't want to do. Alexander Khan," he said, making a mock gesture of obeisance. "At your service. As soon as I kick your ass." He raised a leg to dismount.

"Whoa!" said the leader. "Keep your horse. *The* Alexander Khan?"

"You are the second person on this planet who has asked me that question in that way. I know of only one Alexander Khan. I am he. I am what I believe you all call a New Arrival or a Newby. I'm afraid I committed an indiscretion on Earth that cost me my place there."

"You are not here to kill us all? I have heard that is what you do."

"I am not. I am now one of you. You may view this as the inevitability of justice in the universe. Besides, this is not an illegal colony. It's a prison planet."

The leader made a motion similar to a salute. "Let us not fight. Your family's repute overweighs your own actions, which all have known were necessary to maintain your family's position."

"You know of my family? You know of me?"

"Of course. We get news from New Arrivals. Everybody in Human Space knows of your family, I suspect, and its enterprises' contributions to human freedom. Come to the Big House and meet Lord Salvatore and tell us the News. We haven't had a New Arrival for months. I think they're all being dropped in the Deepeven and picked up by Techs. Elbert, go and alert Signor Ruggiero." Elbert trotted up the path to the castle.

Khan was interested by the use of the term "human space," and revised again his assessment of the knowledge level of people on the planet. Clearly they knew of the illegal colonies, even though he was pretty sure no one from those planets had ever been brought here. He had long suspected that, despite the talk of re-education, most of his returnees had simply been exterminated after he delivered them back to Earth.

As always when going into an unknown situation from which he might need to escape, Khan took tactical mental notes. The Big House was a well-built, rambling limestone castle of thick, six-meter-high walls and remarkable extent. It stretched at least seventy meters in each direction from the main entrance, which if the castle were square would encompass close to two hectares, or nearly five of the old-style acres that Earth's big landowners still used. In place of a wet moat was a four-meter-deep ditch lined with sharpened abatis. Guards armed with crossbows watched from crenellated towers. To properly defend five hundred and sixty meters of perimeter would require from one third to half that many well-armed and well-trained bowmen. Make it, say, a three-to-one ratio of peasants to fighters, since the Lords probably didn't farm, and you had an operation of around a thousand people. No small thing to manage. Despite the fact that he was expecting to meet a warrior chieftain who was in charge because he could kill any opponents, Khan was grudgingly impressed. It looked like a well-managed operation.

A massive drawbridge with arm-thick iron chains led across the dry moat and under an equally ponderous iron portcullis. At the approach to the drawbridge Khan's mount rebelled. No way was he going to cross the bridge. Khan started to dismount.

"Gentlemen, give clearance, or somebody will get hurt, most likely me. I'm going to have to let him go."

"We can put him in the stables overnight," said one of the guards.

"Not likely," said Khan. "I don't think we could get him there, and if we did, he would destroy his stall. He's given me three days of service, for which I am grateful. If he sees fit to come back when I call him, so much the better."

The mount did indeed try to kill him when he dismounted, but as before, he was ready, and he watched the stallion tear off in the direction they had come, raising a cloud of dust.

"He would be a fine mount if tamed," said the leader with a grin. "But he seems to be holding a grudge. Maybe something you said? Your smell?"

The living quarters within the castle bore signs of refinement and taste. Furniture was skillfully crafted. Tapestries and paintings lined the walls. Books were visible everywhere. And Lord Salvatore Ruggiero turned out to be anything but the warrior chieftain. He was sixty if a day, with thick gray hair and an expressive face lined by experience. True, he loomed over his men by several centimeters. Heavy shoulders and forearms gave the impression that he could handle a sword and a bow, and despite a prosperous paunch, he looked as though he could handle himself in hand-to-hand as well. But the dominant impression he gave was of a man with a lively intelligence and a keen interest in the world. He clothes were well-made but modest: wool trousers, linen shirt, natural-finish riding boots that looked as good as any Khan had ever owned, and a tooled belt with a finely-wrought solid brass buckle. He looked more like a swashbuckling CEO than a warrior.

"Major Khan!" he boomed, extending a welcoming arm. "Come and tell us the News. We will prepare a feast, and you will tell us of happenings on Earth and on the colony worlds."

And with that, Signor Ruggiero led him into his study and pumped him dry of every piece of Earth and colony history since the gravity drive.

"I have heard much of it before, but I always like to hear it again from different people to see how the stories change. It tells me much about Earth, but about the people as well."

After a couple of hours, they moved to the formal dining room, and Khan had to admit he was surprised and impressed. The table was finely done, and set with white linen, real flatware, and hand-blown wine glasses. Perhaps Prison Planet was not going to be such a primitive place after all.

Salvatore wined him and dined him at a long table full of his men, and wanted to know why he was going to Mander's Keep. It seemed Salvatore was a peaceable man who had learned the arts of war to protect him and his. The grandmotherly serving woman who brought in the food did not seem cowed, and in fact carried herself with the dignity of a lifelong school teacher who just happened to be filling in as table server in a pinch. Khan noted her spectacles, which implied not only reading, but local lense-grinding technology, or trade with the Techs.

"Mander is a mad dog who loves only power and war, like his predecessor, and his predecessor before him," said Salvatore. "Something about the Keep and its location makes them all power-mad over there. They succeed each other by killing their predecessors. They build nothing except fortifications. I on the other hand am like Cosimo Il Magnifico." He spread his arms wide to indicate the grandeur surrounding them. "I commission paintings, stories, music, and invention. Guido's Hundred always has at least ten artists and scholars in residence. Of course, they too have to pull weeds and sweep, but only for half a day instead of a full day."

Khan had noted the rather pedestrian landscapes and portraits on the walls but mentally gave credit for trying.

"Actually, it was Lorenzo who was styled 'Il Magnifico.'" he said. He then gave a brief history of Cosimo De Medici, and his grandson, Lorenzo, and their importance in fourteenth and fifteenth century Florence. "But both were patrons of the arts."

This slowed Ruggiero not at all. He gave an expressive shrug.

"They send animals to populate this world, who knows whether for us or for some future colonization plan, but nothing else. No books, no supplies, no tools. They send us naked to survive or starve. My great-great grandfather, Guido Salvatore Ruggiero, arrived naked with only a knife. So history is what we make of it out of our collective memories. It is part myth, which is not a bad thing. Is it different with you?"

Khan savored a bite of what tasted like beef in an excellent broth, and chased it with a sip of wine. If he wasn't careful he could be seduced by all this.

"Not really. It's always difficult after a hundred years or so to tell what really happened. Politicians and mythmakers rewrite history. And in my case, I arrived naked, without the knife, in the middle of a snowstorm in the mountains."

Salvatore boomed laughter and reached across the corner of the polished table to clap Khan heartily on the back. "Ah, you merited special punishment! Usually they drop them near a fief in the Realm or with the Techs. What did you do to provoke them?" And why Mander's Keep?"

Khan could see he wasn't going to be able to get by without giving up some information. He cleared his throat uncomfortably.

"They executed my father. Brought Khan Industries down to near collapse. Probably expropriated it by now. Then the little bastard that killed my father bragged about it to my face in a public reception of ECG cadre. Described the pleasure of shooting my father in the back of the head. He was feeling safe because we were in a gathering of high officials, and because my position as an officer in the Internal Movement Control Forces depended on my not reacting. I did not react. Three days later he was brutally murdered in his apartment by an unknown assailant who left no clues. The assailant broke his neck and kicked his corpse downstairs onto the floor below. The surveillance cameras all malfunctioned simultaneously, and no one saw the assailant come or go. Three days after that I was arrested for the murder, despite a total lack of evidence."

Quiet fell around the table. Khan cleared his throat. No emotion showed on his face, but he didn't trust his voice to speak further. Ruggiero spoke gently to break the silence.

"Of course the man who ordered your father's execution also planned your encounter with his killer. And he knew both of you well enough to know what would happen. Had the, er, unknown assailant not killed the man, the man who ordered your father's killing would have had your father's killer killed in such a way that he could blame it on you. Clearly, the government had decided to take down your family. A major blow to human civilization, given the technology I'm told Khan Enterprises produced: everything to make a man free of central control."

Khan mastered his voice. "Yes, I believe you're right. About the decision to bring my family down, and about the man who planned the encounter.

Nathan Fox. Director of Technology Control. Been after my family for twenty years, but my years of loyal service to ECG military and later the Internal Movement Control Directory kept them away. For more than a decade. It might have been better if several months had passed after my father's murder, then an unknown assailant had taken out Nathan Fox himself first, followed by my father's killer."

"That would have been hard," nodded Ruggiero. "I don't know anyone who could have controlled himself that well. But ECG would have found another way to bring you down if ... things had not gone as they did. It seems they must be struggling to keep control."

"I've seen no signs of it. I think they were simply removing the biggest remaining threat to their primacy. Insuring and perfecting their total control over the people of Earth and the Mars and Lunar Stations."

"We have of course heard of you. You are notorious, and in fact might not be safe among the Techs, unless they understand the game you and your father were playing with ECG. You have a lot to answer for personally, but as I said, some of us see a larger picture. But tell me. You've been to several planets. How many colonies? We've heard of nine."

"Twenty-four."

"Twenty-four! And you wiped them all out? Killed all of the colonists?" An edge had entered Ruggiero's tone.

"Always. . . accidentally left a few escapees. With some new technology that we would ... accidentally lose during clean-up operations. Took the captives back to Earth for re-education. Never saw them after that. Was told they spent six months in re-education camps, then were released after a selective memory wipe. Always suspected they were turned into fertilizer."

Ruggiero's stern expression changed to shock at the use of the term 'fertilizer,' then softened a little. "I am not your judge, but I am human. Didn't you feel guilty?"

"Of course. Every day. Even now. But I'm sure that as Lord of Guido's Hundred, you sometimes have to do things that, on their face are evil, but when interpreted in the larger sense for the good of the whole fief, are positive." He heard his father's voice: *Sometimes a leader must do things for the sake of the people that he would hang a private citizen for doing.*

Ruggiero's expressive face went through several changes as he obviously remembered just such a thing. "Yes, it is true."

"And that's how my father and I saw it. For the greater good of humanity, it would be better if he continued infiltrating freedom technologies into earth society, even at the cost of some of the illegal colonists' lives. Of course it didn't feel good. None of my men liked it either. The hardest thing was to discipline them when they were insufficiently. . . vigorous. A soldier's life is, after all, following orders. Without that, you have no discipline or self-respect at all."

Ruggiero mulled this for a moment, looking Khan in the eye, and then finally nodded. He didn't fully understand, but could accept what Khan had said. Then his manner changed and a light came back to his eye. "And during your travels, did you see the aliens that ECG explorers encountered three centuries ago? The reason for colonies being forbidden?" He was eagerly curious like a boy.

Khan felt a pang in his stomach as he thought of that bootprint at his campsite two nights ago. Had he actually seen her? "No. I have never seen an alien on any planet, and I have long assumed they don't exist. – That ECG is simply using them as a bugaboo to keep humans on Earth and under their control. – The way parents scare small children into proper behavior with monster stories."

Ruggiero shook his head disgustedly. "This is what people of affairs here have long thought."

"People of affairs?"

"Yes, people like myself who believe that only if we form larger relationships here on Arcadia through trade and education, relationships among all the people, can we advance. I can run Guido's Hundred for the good of its people, but we are limited in the small things we can manufacture, in the number of things we can grow for food, in the types of clothes we can make, in the books we can get. We need to promote trade. I have started a regional council for the purpose of information exchange and have been inviting all the fief lords in the area, as well as Elves and Techs. But few come. Success has been meager because of distrust. They think I want to be king. And then after the last council, Mander's men attacked, robbed, and killed several groups journeying back to their homes.

So we have a long way to go. That's why I asked why you were going to Mander's Keep. The man is a dangerous animal. Why would you go there?" Then he nodded at the hilt of Bolodan's sword, which Khan had declined to forfeit upon entry to the castle. "And how did you get that?"

"I was taken in and fed by a kindly Elf woman named Maruil. While I was there, Mander's men, including two of his sons, attacked and tried to take her son for a horse caller, and her daughter as well for … darker purposes. I'm afraid I had to kill Bolodan in a challenge battle, which is how I got his sword."

There were appreciative hums, grunts, and nods around the table from Salvatore's dangerous-looking men. They knew of Bolodan and what this meant. They looked at Khan with renewed respect.

"I'm afraid we also had to kill two of his men as well." More nods and sounds of approval and being impressed. "I am now going to Mander's keep to find and free a man named Baelmar, Maruil's husband, who has been enslaved by Mander to train his horses. I suppose the reason he doesn't escape on his own is fear of reprisals against his family. So it is not a simple mission. Taking Baelmar will be easy compared to preventing reprisals."

Salvatore nodded, using a large hand to wipe his mouth neatly with his linen napkin and lay it carefully beside his plate. "After you mentioned Maruil, I thought it might be something like that. We know of Maruil and Baelmar. Good people, if a bit strange, as all Elves are. Communicate with nature spirits and animals, things like that. But devoted to learning, of a particular kind. They are the best archers for ten days' riding. We paid them with books for training our men, but they are too far away for us to protect. I offered to give them land at the edge of Guido Hundred, but like all Elves, they are independent and prefer to live alone in the forest or the Leas. But they make the world's best bows, the best dishes," and here he raised one side of his colorful earthenware plate, "and they are skilled at the healing arts. If you are wounded, the best person to take care of you is an elf."

Khan touched his wounded arm. "This is true. I was fortunate." And he related the story of the gryphon. More sounds of appreciation came from around the table.

"You have had a challenging time on our beautiful planet, and experienced perhaps the worst of what it has to offer. At least you were not surprised in your sleep by a roving gang of Maneaters. That would likely have been fatal. We try to wipe them out, but they breed quickly."

"Maneaters? How can they prosper without wiping out huge slices of the population? By eating them."

"They are simply savages who live off of the land. Mainly they eat roots, flowers, nuts, and animals of the campo. The problem is that they see people as simply other animals to be hunted down and eaten."

After dinner, the dishes were cleared by a plainly dressed but clean and well-fed girl of twenty or so who also did not look browbeaten or slave-like. She gazed levelly and curiously back at Khan. Salvatore saw him looking and smiled. "My daughter, Olympia. You were expecting a slave?"

Khan deflected the gambit with a smile. "She is beautiful. At the risk of sounding ungrateful for that wonderful meal, she must favor her mother."

Salvatore acknowledged this traditional friendly insult with a wistful smile. "She does indeed. And she is all I have left of her mother. Died in a plague fifteen years ago. Kills in a day. Still no one knows how to stop it."

This was a reminder to Khan if he needed it that he had been plunged back in time several centuries. Arcadia might be nearly Earth-like, but conditions were medieval.

The group moved into a parlor-like room with many upholstered chairs sitting in conversational groups with small tables between them. First there was music. One of the guards played something approximating a violin while a young man who had not been at table sang a long ballad glorifying the history of the Ruggieros. Then Olympia and her father sang a lively harmonic piece *a capella*. Both had good voices, and on choruses, the guards joined in. And finally, out came the game boards – made of wood, not cardboard – and games began all round among Salvatore's men: chess, checkers, Go. Khan marveled at how much of Earth culture had been brought here in memory alone.

He found Salvatore to be an extremely challenging chess partner, and was quickly in trouble. "No dishonor," said Salvatore. "I suspect that in your life, you have not had a lot of time to play chess. I play every night." He sighed and looked at Khan under his eyebrows. "I was hoping for a more challenging partner, though. The only one who can stand up to me is Olympia."

"Ouch," said Khan. "So, if I come this way again, I should avoid playing chess with Olympia as well as yourself. But I confess that my heart has never been in games. When it's life or death, I get serious. Otherwise I can't make myself concentrate."

"A plausible excuse, which I will accept." Salvatore stood and raised a hostly arm toward the back of the house. "Come. It is late. Let me show you to your quarters. The least we can do is give you a night in a decent bed before you go off and get yourself killed. I suspect you might also like a bath, so I'll have some water heated."

The stone-floored bedroom was spartan by most standards except perhaps those of a medieval castle, but after two weeks of sleeping on the ground, or once in a haymow, it might as well have been the fanciest resort hotel on the beach in Hawaii or the Wonderdome in Tycho – ECG's sop to civilian space travel. Though sprung by ropes stretched between thick planed side boards, the carven four-poster bed was a generous two meters wide, and made up with sheets of buff-colored linen. Apparently nothing like cotton existed on the planet. The mattress stuffing was a bit lumpy, suggesting old rags, and the quilt was too thick by half, but to Khan it looked like a bit of heaven. A heavy armoire of dark, hand-worked wood stood against one wall, and a writing desk and chair of lighter wood with dark inlay stood before the room's sole, unglazed, window now closed by shutters. He was not surprised to see a stoppered ink pot, an assortment of quill pens, and a small sharp knife. In the desk drawer lay three sheets of precious writing paper awaiting the thoughts of Salvatore Ruggiero's guests.

Khan wanted more than anything else to simply climb into the bed and rack out, but he suspected that Salvatore's comment about the bath meant that he stank, which meant he should wait for the bath. When he was about ready to exit the room and start searching for the bath facilities, a light knock came at the door.

"Come."

Olympia entered the room and looked him up and down demurely. "Your water is ready, Signor Khan. If you would follow me."

He followed her down a dark hall lighted by too few candles into a stone room with a tub-sized pool in the middle. "The water in the bath will stay warm for twenty minutes," she said. "But the rinse water gets cold much faster." She pointed at a shower-like arrangement with a wooden tub above and a pull rope and gave a mischievous grin. "Give me your clothes and I will clean them while you bathe. You really need it." She wrinkled her nose.

"Perhaps you could go outside the door and I could hand you my clothes without your seeing me naked?"

Her eyes flashed in the dim light, and she cocked a hand on a hip. "I suppose you think I've never seen a naked man before?"

"That's exactly what I think, young lady, and exactly how I imagine your father wants to keep it. Out. But before you go, where and when will my pants reappear? The fur cloak stays with me, by the way."

Her shoulders sagged exaggeratedly. "I'll hang them in your room to dry. You're no fun."

Khan threw his pants out the door and slipped into the blessedly warm water. A rough, smelly bar of soap with grains of sand in it helped wash the grime off, and he made the best of his first bath in two weeks, soaking for a good fifteen minutes. Of course, as he had suspected, as he was rinsing off under the much cooler water of the gravity shower, he heard small noises behind him. He was tempted not to look, knowing that he would catch Olympia ogling his behind, but a lifetime of caution prevailed. He took a quick look over his left shoulder just in time to avoid a knife thrust aimed at his kidney. It was one of the guards who had sat at the table during dinner.

Khan raised his knee and broke the man's extended arm over it. The man screamed. An elbow to the man's nose, followed by a foot to his testicles produced something more akin to a high-decibel groan, and Olympia appeared wide-eyed at the door to see the man writhing on the floor.

She took in the whole picture, including Khan. "You are a remarkable man, Signor Khan. It appears you have caught a spy. We knew we had one.

Father will be glad." Her eyes drank in his form, then came back to meet his eyes. She smiled impishly. "Those blue eyes are rather startling."

"And you are a persistent young lady, Signorina Ruggiero. Are those my pants?"

"Yes, they're as clean now as I could get them. "

She tiptoed across the wet stone floor and handed them to him. He put them on wet, and only then did she raise her gaze.

He looked her in the eye and thought to chastise her, but what he saw there was no girlish expression, but a cool, level regard. "Best get your father," he said. "He'll want to talk with this gentleman. I'll make sure he doesn't go anywhere."

Salvatore appeared in a few minutes with his captain of guards. Retribution was swift. Rough questioning confirmed that the man was Mander's spy, working for money. Yes, he had been a spy all along, and had given Mander details of the groups' plans for returning from the council. Yes, he had taken action now because Mander was unsettled and maybe a little frightened by Khan's killing of his son. No one should have been able to do that. He had been told by a Maneater fortune teller woman that Khan would come after him. He wanted him killed first. Ruggiero extracted every scrap of information that the man had ever passed to Mander, and then, as casually as he would gut a fish, he slit the man's throat from ear to ear, then wiped the knife on the man's shirt before the man's dimming but still-horrified eyes.

"Well, Signor Khan, it seems clear that Mander knows you are coming. You might want to consider your strategy carefully."

CHAPTER FOUR

FACING EVIL

Khan left in the morning with a heavy heart and as many weapons as he could carry. Lord Ruggiero had been generous: a crossbow with twenty steel-tipped bolts, a muzzle-loading flintlock pistol with enough powder and ball for ten shots, and a fine mount with saddle and bags, one stuffed full of dried meats, fruits, and vegetables. As well, at Khan's request, there was a coil of rope and a grappling hook. And there had been a good pair of used boots and hand-knitted wool socks beside Khan's bed when he awoke. They fit reasonably well.

"It's the least I can do for you," said Salvatore in the courtyard as Khan mounted and made ready to leave. "What I can't do is help you in any open way. I cannot risk war with Mander. We would not lose, but we would not win, either. Last war, both sides lost a hundred or more people. You are one man, Khan. Win and the world will love you. Lose, and the world will not miss you. Sorry. But be prepared, too, that if you win, you will still not be safe. Mander's men will want revenge, and if you deal effectively with that and become Lord yourself, other Lords will fear you."

Khan's mount pranced and turned, forcing him to swivel in the saddle to keep eye contact with Salvatore, and finally to rein the animal in. "There is no safety in this life, Signor Ruggiero." He did not feel comfortable calling any man 'Lord.' "We have only vision, duty, and honor."

Ruggiero grabbed him by the right hand and forearm in a manly handclasp. "May the Great Lord go with you, Signor Khan. You are a man of courage. You may yet balance your personal accounts."

And with that and a salute, Khan set off into the northeast regions between Guido's Hundred and Mander's Keep.

The land changed quickly from open savannah and agricultural land to upland scrub and partial forest. He seemed to be climbing into another mountain range, though it didn't show on Maruil's map. It turned out to be a ten-kilometer-wide hogback ridge running east and west, with substrate limestone so close to the surface that vegetation had difficulty getting a purchase. Here and there, scrubby cedar-like and pine-like trees thrust root fingers into cracks between the layers, and small clumps of silversword appeared like surprises on the dry soil. But beyond that, there was little but scrubby grass and snake-like creatures with multiple sets of very short but very quick legs.

The north side of the dry ridge descended by cliff and talus slope into a broad river valley. The sudden fertile greens and ripe golden hues pleased Khan's eye. It was ironic that the lord of this peaceful-looking valley was Mander.

Far in the distance, on the other side of the river, stood Mander's Keep, just as described: a massive, forbidding fortress on a bluff in a bend of the river. Ten-meter-high crenellated walls separated fifteen-meter-high guard towers clearly built to defend against both outside attack and internal attack from the battlement. On the three sides away from the river, slopes fell away from the walls into a dry moat, making siege ladders nearly useless. The place was virtually impregnable. But green and gold cultivated fields surrounded it like a quilt, taking some of the edge off of its evil appearance and giving his heart a small lift. Ant-like figures unloaded freight from five large rowboats tied up at docks below the castle. Two small sailboats also rode beside one of the docks.

Clearly, frontal assault was infeasible, even if he had the troops and siege engines to do it. It would take a thousand men or modern arms to crack that nut. And since at least a couple of Mander's men knew him by sight, posing as someone else would serve only to get him into the compound, then imprisoned or worse. Thus, tactical surprise was in order, which required detailed situational knowledge. He made camp in a copse of trees the better to observe awhile.

An afternoon and evening's worth of watching showed a lot of river traffic to and from the Keep, and much less ground traffic. There was no ground traffic on the near side of the river. A ferry lay beside one of the docks, with long sweep oars racked along its sides, but while he watched, it was not used.

The river traffic was all on the upstream stretch of the river. During the afternoon, five more large rowboats arrived and unloaded, and the previous five loaded and departed. He couldn't tell, but it looked like bottles and dry goods coming in, he assumed from the Techs, and lumber, potatoes and beets going out, probably to the Techs. He consulted Maruil's map. Indeed, there was a Tech settlement named Advance forty or fifty kilometers upstream. Hard to tell with the map's elastic scale how far it really was, or how big it was. But it looked as though it was trading with Mander. Another look at the map explained why Ruggiero and Mander were natural enemies. The river before him was the River of Doubt, and downstream from Mander's Keep a tributary named the Po joined it, after passing just northwest of Guido's Hundred. Salvatore could send goods down the River Po, then up the River of Doubt to both the Keep and Advance. However, Mander controlled Ruggiero's water route to and from Advance. Probably collected "duty" on Ruggiero's goods each way.

The view beyond the castle was partially obstructed, but he could make out a single road, consisting of two wheel tracks worn through the grass. Nearly all its sparse traffic was horse patrols of three or four men-at-arms heading out or heading in. Nearly no wagons –with the exception of hay wagons. He watched two appear from around a distant bend in the road, then approach the castle and disappear behind the walls. As far as he could see, they were not checked by the horse patrols.

His best bet was to cross the river downstream. No traffic had come from that direction. And if any surprise traffic did come upstream it would be mainly focused on fighting what appeared to be a stiff current, not killing him. Once across, he would circle back up to find the haying areas and hide himself under a wagonload of hay. That would put him inside the castle and likely as close to Baelmar as he could get, since the hay was likely to go the horses, and Baelmar would be nearby.

There would then be two remaining challenges: how to overcome the reasons Baelmar had not left already – as he had surely had a chance to walk away if he wanted – and how to escape without the two of them being seen. – And into the bargain, how to avoid losing his fine mount. They would need it to escape. The horse would remain staked in the wild for only a day or so before pulling loose to look for water. The beast owed Khan no loyalty as of yet and would likely strike off for Guido's Hundred for easy food and water.

Though the sun had nearly set, he decided to cross tonight and make his move tomorrow morning. This would give him time to dry off from the crossing, and to find the haying fields. No hay would be loaded into wagons until the sun had dried it, meaning that the haymakers probably wouldn't show up until mid-morning. Thus, he would have time to hide himself in a partially filled wagon before the dew dried off of the windrows of hay. – Assuming there was a partially filled wagon. If not, he would have to hide and insert himself when no one was looking. Tonight he would water the horse, cross, and make a cold camp so he wouldn't be detected.

He rode his mount back up and over the top of the ridge, careful to stay in cover as much as possible. Then he cut northwest on the back side of the cover and rode in the downstream direction for more than a kilometer. When he judged he was out of sight of the castle, he cut back over the ridge to find the river again.

Up close, it turned out to be a dangerous river: cut banks and a stiff current. He began to understand its name. It took half an hour to find a gravel bar that showed on both sides of a broad bend of the river, making it look like a decent crossing.

When the horse stepped off the dry gravel bar and into the channel, it plunged deep beneath the surface. With his head just above water, Khan could feel the horse trying to swim back up. There was no bottom. It wasn't a gravel bar at all, he realized. It was gravel that had washed down from upstream onto the walls of a stone cut. The bottom dropped away like a cliff.

Then the current swept Khan from the horse's back and under the turbulent brown water. He rolled several times, and for several seconds couldn't tell which way was up. He barely managed to keep hold of the twisted reins. Then the horse gave a huge snort and he moved to that sound. His head broke the surface beside the struggling horse's wild eye. He spoke soothing sounds to the animal though he too was terrified.

The horse calmed, and they settled into a rhythm, he paddling vigorously with his left hand and kicking fiercely while he held the reins with his right, and the horse doing its instinctive bottom-searching, fast-walk swim. For what seemed like half an hour but was probably only sixty seconds, the two swam side by side for their lives, panting with effort, being swept downstream three meters for every meter of progress they made toward the far bank.

Finally, with great effort, just as they were swept past the end of the targeted gravel bar on the far side, they were able to make their way out of the current and into an eddy on the bar's downstream side. The stone bottom felt like salvation. As they climbed out, he noted that downstream, there was nothing but three-meter vertical cut bank as far as he could see. Even though the water had been cold, sweat broke out on his forehead. It was clear that if they had not made the gravel bar, they would have drowned downstream, unable to climb the vertical cut banks.

"Boy," he said to the horse, "I don't know how you feel about boats, but I suggest using one for our return trip." The horse rumbled its agreement, and Khan rewarded it with a soaked piece of dried fruit.

They passed a miserable wet night in a copse of trees on the river flat, bitten mercilessly by insects he couldn't identify. Finally, near morning, they moved to higher ground to get away from the bugs, and Khan dozed fitfully until sunrise with his back to a tree.

After drying out for an hour or so in the sun, Khan turned upstream and quickly found men pitching hay onto wagons. He was late. They worked with large pitchforks in a raggedly mown pasture with windrows of dried hay. He watched from behind a tree line for fifteen minutes as they walked lazily along – one man leading the horse pulling the wagon, and one man on each side manning a fork. They took liberal rests, from which Khan concluded that these were bondsmen of some sort, though he saw no overseer. But in watching, he quickly realized another flaw in his plan of hiding under a load until it was pulled into the castle. Five wagons were already loaded and waiting, some clearly since yesterday. It looked as though one crew was loading the wagons, and another even more casual crew, was hauling the wagons from the hayfield to the castle. There was no way to tell which wagon was next, and there was no way to get to the wagons unobserved. He might wait under a load of hay all day and never make it into the Keep.

He was going to have to trust these men. He took a gamble that they were slaves and would not betray him to their masters. He rode out of cover.

"Hello, men," he called cheerily. "A fine day to you."

"And you, m'Lord," they said, taking him in and dipping their heads a token amount.

Khan realized they thought he was a Lord because he was armed, wearing boots, and riding a horse. "Any way I could sleep in your stables tonight before I continue my journey tomorrow? Without the local lord knowing I am here? I only want a place to sleep in peace. Don't want to go through the whole hospitality thing."

There was a long silence as they moved closer and examined him from top to bottom. The elder of the three, a man of fifty or so with an intelligent face, looked at the hilt of Bolodan's sword, then at Khan.

"I don't imagine you would like the hospitality you would receive, m'Lord, should Lord Mander know you are here." He nodded at the sword. "We've all heard about Bolodan, you know. But given as how Mander and his murderous band killed my entire family, and the loved ones of each of these gentlemen, I don't see why he should find out about your ... sleeping in the stable. May we know your business so we can help?"

Khan looked long at the man, searching his face for deceit. He saw nothing, only a clear, steady eye. Huge risk, but it would be helpful to have confederates. And the hairs on the back of his neck were not standing up. He slid down off his mount so he could face the man closer to his own level. "I seek Baelmar," he said finally.

"And may we ask what business you have with him?" said the man. "Not to be impertinent, but you are asking us to risk a beating or worse for a total stranger."

Khan continued to look the man in the eye. He still saw no deceit or calculation, only perhaps a kind of hopeful interest. And the comment about the beating hinted further at a potential alliance. If he could get the slave network on his side, his chances of success were much better. Of course, if they betrayed him, he was probably dead. He decided to take the risk. "I am going to free him. At the request of his wife. "

There was a shocked silence. Then all three nodded warmly. "Baelmar is the finest of men," said the elder. "Were he not an Elf, with their strange ways of peace, he could have killed Mander and most of his Round Table, as he calls it, many times over. He is a bull of a man. But he is an Elf and a man of peace. And he fears as well what Mander would do to his family if he walked away, which he could easily do. He is the Horsemaster, and could easily just ride away. But Mander is the cruelest of men. He kills to control. He kills for practice. He kills for pleasure. We would all have walked away long ago except for his threats to kill all our friends both inside and outside the Keep. You'll find none of his slaves with a liking for him."

"I see." And Khan did see. He had suspected it at Guido's Hundred. To really free Baelmar, he would have to kill Mander and all his loyal men. Wipe out his operation. And Maruil had known what she was asking. And she had known that he did not know. She had foxed him, playing on his sense of honor. He quickly saw that without an army, there was only one way to do something like this: a challenge battle. He would have to call Mander out, personally, and challenge him to mortal combat. And to succeed in that required that Mander's men's sense of honor forbade reprisals after he killed Mander. Assuming Mander didn't kill him. But honor among people like Mander and his followers was chancy in his experience. So he might need some help.

"Is there an arms room in the castle where arms are stored for the larger army, beyond the twelve I assume sit at the Round Table?"

A flicker of hope, like a stubborn flame overcoming dampness, appeared in the elder's eye. "There is."

"With arms for how many?"

"At least a hundred fifty. The castle guard is three hundred, with half on guard during the day, and half at night. They store their arms there."

"How many slaves and serfs inside the castle?"

"We are all slaves. There are no serfs. We breathe at Mander's pleasure. Maybe eighty men and as many women or more in the castle. Probably that many again outside the castle living in huts in the fields. Not counting children."

Khan looked all three men in the eye. "Are you ready to risk death for freedom?" Images from his study of Earth history of the Bauernkrieg, the German peasants' catastrophic uprising in 1524 and 1525, came unbidden to his mind. He hoped this turned out better for the peasants.

The elder looked at him long, weighing, measuring, assessing. Finally he took a deep breath and let it out slowly. "'There is a tide in the affairs of men—,'" he intoned in a sonorous voice.

Khan nodded at the familiar quote. "—Yes, 'when taken at the flood —'"

"'—leads on to fortune.'"

"Let's stop it there and not tempt fate," said Khan. "You are a learned man. First Generation on Prison Planet, I assume, as I've not heard of anyone being sent down with a copy of Will Shakespeare."

"Indeed." The mean reached out his hand. "Dr. Stanhope Greis, lecturer in literature at Oxford, until the impolitic public comments that got me sent here. Also philosopher, iconoclast, gadfly, and raconteur. I have studied philosophy, medicine, law, and unfortunately, also theology. I cannot claim wisdom, but I am at your service. And I'm sure I can speak for my companions when I say they will fight for their freedom, too." They nodded nervously.

Khan smiled and took his hand. The palm was hard as leather. "No need to explain why you were sent to Prison Planet. Dr. Greis. In ECG society, your titles sound like a court docket charge count. Alexander Khan, at *your* service."

The man was taken aback. "*The* Alexander Khan?"

"The same," said Khan, by now accustomed to this reaction. "Perhaps we can trade stories later, once I've achieved my objective. Now a couple of key questions: how many of the slaves will rise at a signal, and take up arms, and how many will betray us?"

Dr. Greis's face fell in a sad way. "You are obviously deeply familiar with human frailty, Major Khan. It would be about half and half. But we know which half is which. And nearly all of the betrayal half would act out of fear. There are only a few stupid enough to believe they could get into Mander's good graces by informing."

Khan nodded. "This will involve bloody killing, Dr. Greis. I plan to call Mander out personally and kill him in a challenge battle. But if there is no honor among his lieutenants, and they do not abide by the outcome – which I strongly suspect – we'll have to kill all of them too. Pretty much in cold blood. Only fools fight fair fights. But there will be dying, too. I assume the slaves are not experienced fighters."

"We are not. But we have deep reserves of anger upon which to call. What about the Sons?"

"The Sons?"

"Yes, Mander has around forty sons of all ages from ten to thirty by around twenty different women. At least six of them sit at the Round Table. I hate to say this, but unless we completely destroy his entire family and one of us – you – takes over as head man to control the rest of the garrison, then we will just be pulling the top off the weed instead of pulling it up by its roots. It will regrow."

This was getting harder and harder. Khan had no desire to kill Mander and set himself up as the new lord. He certainly had no desire to kill ten-year-old boys. But he saw that in a lawless world ruled by pure ruthlessness, there was no substitute for strength.

"We will kill the ones that take up arms against us. The others will be given a choice: join the new community or be exiled."

"And who will become Lord?" Dr. Greis looked at him for the first time with open suspicion.

"You all will. Jointly. In a democracy. When not working in the fields or the smithy or the leather shop, every one – man and boy and woman and girl – will train day and night at arms. You must train for the rest of your lives to protect yourselves against bandits, brigands, parasites, and knaves who produce nothing, but set themselves up as a warrior class living off of the work of slaves, simply because they're good at killing. You all have to become good at killing, too. I will teach you. "

Khan could see doubt and fear growing on the men's faces, but a kind of gritty resolve and hope at the same time. "Are you still with me, then?" he asked.

Adam's apples bobbed, eyes darted back and forth looking for escape, and sweat dripped down brows. Finally, the youngest of the three straightened his back and spoke. "We are with you. Freedom is worth fighting for."

"Well said," said Khan. "In fact, it always must be fought for." He looked to the other man.

He nodded grimly.

"All right, then," said Khan, scuffing the ground with his new boot to create a large bare spot in the soil. "Draw the layout of each floor of the castle, show me the places that are guarded day and night, and I'll tell you the plan."

Dr. Greis explained that he would arrange entry into the castle. First he would go himself to prepare Baelmar for Khan's arrival, using Maruil's name. Then he would take Khan in under a load of hay, directly into the covered stable.

Under the hay on the ride in, Khan entertained dark thoughts of betrayal, but when the horse stopped, a friendly voice boomed out. "Come out, Major Khan. I know you're there."

Just in case, Khan crawled out the opposite side from where the voice had spoken, only to find waiting for him a large, good-natured bull of a man in rough linen pants and shirt, leather vest, and golden hair tied behind his head. He crushed Khan's hand, pounded him on the back.

"Welcome to my stable, Major. You are not very good at stealth and deception, but you are safe here." He gave a brilliant smile.

In his tack room, he offered Khan a bench, took a facing bench, and pumped Khan for news of Maruil and the children. Saddles in various stages of repair sat on saddle trees, bridles hung along one wall, and smelly unguents for sore pasterns broadcast their presence from clay pots on the back of a workbench. And down a long row of wood-front stalls, horses stuck their necks out and looked curiously down the stableway at Baelmar and Khan. "Mander's and the Round Table's horses," Baelmar explained. "The rest of the remuda is kept outside."

Khan nodded his understanding and told all he knew, careful to emphasize Gareth's and Branwyn's bravery and Maruil's hospitality. – And his sleeping in the barn. And why he was here. Baelmar lapped this up like a dog drinking water. But a cloud came over his sunny face at the last.

"I have been here over a year. I want to go home. But I am a peaceful man who doesn't believe in violence," he explained to Khan. "What you propose will cause a bloodbath. And to be honest, I don't know that I can trust you. Your reputation comes before you. From what we've all heard from Newbies, you're something of a notorious. . . bastard." Then to soften the blow, he smiled big with white teeth. Because of his size and good nature, he was clearly accustomed to getting away with saying things like this and slipping them through with his winning smile.

Khan regarded Baelmar while he mulled this speech. The man looked like something out of a Norse myth. Only slightly shorter than Khan, he outweighed him by at least twenty kilos, all muscle. His shoulders were broad, and his massive, ropy arms looked as though they could crush a barrel. Whether he sat or stood, his thick legs looked to be planted on Arcadia like oaks. Yet instead of stout boots with heels, he wore soft elf moccasins. Khan took a chance.

"You don't use saddles and bridles, do you?" he said, nodding at one of the saddles in repair, then at the moccasins.

Baelmar's forehead wrinkled in momentary confusion, then flattened into its normal sunny smoothness. "The horses are my friends," he said with quiet pride. "They take me on their backs as a favor. People who don't understand horses, violent men who like to control other beings, they are the ones who use saddles and bridles. I only teach the horses not to kill so these men" – he gestured toward the upper parts of the castle – "can put saddles on them and ride them. I do not approve. But I do it for my family."

"Yet these men attacked your family anyway."

"So you say. But you are here, and you know of Maruil and Gareth and Branwyn, and it is true that someone killed Bolodan. It is the talk of the Keep. There must be some truth in what you say."

"And have you ever killed animals that were harming your horses?"

"Of course. Many times. A gryphon once. Took all my arrows. Also many wolves."

"There are wolves here on Prison Planet?"

"I understand they are a mixture of Earth dogs and a local animal with a longer mouth. People make pets of them, but they can be dangerous in the wild."

Like Dog. But Khan stayed on the thread. "So you will kill animals that threaten your horses, but not men who threaten your family?"

Baelmar looked momentarily peeved. "You are a smart man, Major Khan, with a quick mind and a smooth tongue. I see where your words will go. But if we go on as now, there is discomfort but not much risk. The sun will come up tomorrow. We will eat. We will ride horses. We will steal some wine from the Lords and tell stories at night and sing. Yes, we might get a beating if we do not do what the Lords want, but we know them well, and we know how to avoid the beatings. Usually, though some of them kill us for their sport. If we do what you want, we might be free, but we might all die. But you, a stranger, offer to lead us, and tell us we will be free."

"Yes. The dilemma of slaves everywhere," said Khan. "Dr. Greis and his friends are ready. I am told that if you commit yourself too, most others will follow. It is your only hope of freedom and reunion with your family. There is never safety in appeasement."

Baelmar screwed up his mouth, shook his head, and snorted. Then he looked down the stableway, at all his farrier tools, his comfortable shop. It had clearly not all been bad. He was Horsemaster, after all. But his head started shaking involuntarily from side to side in a kind of denial. There was clearly an internal dialogue going on. Finally he said, "All right, damn it, Maruil, I'll do it." Then he looked at Khan. "Ehh, Major Khan, I mean. I suppose there's a point in every man's life like this."

"Usually more than one."

Khan and Baelmar waited in the stable until nightfall when Dr. Greis brought word that the guard had changed, and Mander's banquet had started in the great hall. He had also spread the word among all the denizens of the castle, and had even gotten word to many of the bigger men from outside the castle. The air was electric with expectation.

In a few minutes, key participants – banquet-hall servants, stable boys, washer women, and courtesans – began gathering in the stable for the pre-battle briefing. They gawked and throat-cleared and tittered and shuffled and found excuses to get as close to Khan as possible. He knew from long past the effect his size and demeanor had on both men and women, so he expected them to follow him. But he also knew that many probably just wanted to see the tall, dangerous-looking man who came in from nowhere to promise freedom if they survived a night of battle.

In the stableway lay the bodies of two traitors whose throats had been slit by other slaves as they attempted to sneak upstairs to report to Mander. So speed was of the essence. Khan explained the plan and the timing, and then set the hook: "I know you don't know me, and you don't know if you can trust me. So here's how you can know: I'm putting myself on the line first. When I've killed Mander, I will yell 'freedom' as loudly as I can. Serving boys will be there with me, so there's no deceit involved. That will be your sign to set the plan into motion. Let's move."

When Khan slipped between the massive wooden doors of the banquet hall, his heart was pounding. How had he managed in less than a month on this planet to get himself into this situation? But he knew the answer. Honor. Duty and honor. Those old killers. But as Pierre had always told him, and as he knew from experience, fear does not stop you. In fact, it doesn't even show on the outside of you if you move with deliberation.

He stood quietly just inside the doors for a few moments to get his bearings. There was a raised dais at the far end with the man he instantly pegged as Mander at the back of a semicircular table, with six young men seated on each side. The effect was that no one's back was to the room. Below on the main floor was a long, central table with at least two dozen men sitting along it. Food was arriving on giant platters carried by young serving boys and girls.

Mander, a smaller, meaner-looking man than Sillion or Bolodan, was bullyragging one of the servants, who had apparently slopped some broth onto one of his men. The boy, probably no more than twelve, stood terrified, head down, struggling not to cry.

"What should I do to you to demonstrate to your colleagues what happens to an associate who doesn't know how to treat his betters?" Mander asked reasonably, his purring voice like the rasp of a snake in dry grass.

The boy said nothing.

"I'm speaking to you, boy," said Mander, now in a silvery voice intended to sound paternal. "When I speak you must respond. I am your superior in all ways. I can kill you for no reason. In fact, I may do that as an example to the others. What do you think of that?"

"No, wait, Mander!" said one of the men at the high table, in a mocking voice intended to sound like a boy. "That would hurt my feelings. I'm just a boy after all!"

The others at the high table laughed uproariously, and the men at the lower table chuckled perhaps a bit uneasily. Mander drew a dagger and tested the tip on his forefinger while smiling at the boy.

"Come here, boy. I want you to feel the tip of this dagger. Tell me if you think it would go through you, or do I need to sharpen it more?"

The boy was now shaking uncontrollably, his head shaking back and forth in denial, and as Khan watched, a dark puddle appeared around his feet.

"Disgusting!" shouted one of the men at the high table. "In our dining room! He leaped up, drew his sword, and in two great strides grabbed the boy by the hair in preparation for cutting off his head.

Just in time, Khan heard the prearranged bird sound come down from the great beams overhead. His rage had nearly overmastered him before they were ready. Now they were ready.

"Coward!" he boomed, and stepped fully into the great hall. "Unhand that boy and fight a man, you dung-eating dog!"

Silence fell in the great hall, and all faces turned toward Khan. One of the men at the high table leaned over and whispered to Mander. It was Sillion, Bolodan's brother, and the leader of the raiding party at Maruil's house. Then Mander spoke.

"You will not like what I'm going to do to you for killing my son, stranger, but I assure you, it will entertain us all for a week or two to come. You look as though you can last for at least that long with your guts wound around a spindle in front of you."

"I came here to kill you, Mander, but I have heard that you are a coward who is afraid to fight, and who sends others to die in his place. Is that true? Frankly, you look like a coward."

"Kill him, Hoke," he said to the man holding the boy by the hair.

"A pleasure," growled Hoke, throwing the boy to the floor. He leapt from the dais and raced down the main floor toward Khan, two-edged sword forward in attack position.

Khan stood his ground, taking deep breaths, moving into the battle zone where all slowed to a crawl, and he saw every detail: the watch (where had it come from?) on Mander's wrist, the tattoos on the massive forearms of the charging knight, the poor workmanship in the eagle design hammered onto his polished breastplate, his grip on the sword indicating that he was going to swing it at the last minute instead of stab it, as his attack suggested.

At the last second, when the man's running approach should have changed into the ballestra, or fencing-lunge attack appropriate to a thrust, but didn't, Khan made his move. In one motion, he drew Bolodan's sword, spun clockwise, and fell to the stone floor, sweeping the sword around him twice at knee height. Simultaneously, the man made his own move, spinning to his left and sweeping the air at waist height in a deadly circle, with both hands on the sword hilt. The difference was, his sword swept above Khan, meeting only air, while Khan's sword met his legs, cutting through linen trousers, skin, flesh, and bone with little slowdown. Cut off just above the knees, he fell to the stone floor with a grunt of surprise, then looked in dismay at his missing lower legs. Blood hosed out of his femoral arteries in squirts, quickly creating a meter-wide pool on the floor. "AGGHHHH!" he cried. "My legs!" Then he sank slowly back to the floor and the oblivion of no blood to the brain.

Khan got up and dusted himself off. There was a stirring among the men at the tables, with several of them standing up as if to take care of this intruder who dared invade their banquet and kill one of their own. But Khan cut them off. He pointed at Mander with his now-bloody sword.

"Coward!" he boomed. "As I said. You are afraid to fight. You send others to die for you. I am here to kill you with your own son's sword. Will you accept an honorable challenge, or will you show your cowardice again?"

Suddenly there was the sizzle of an arrow cutting the air from above, and a thump as it hit its target, a guard Khan had not noticed on the left side of the room. The man's crossbow fell from his hands and struck the floor, releasing its bolt to skitter across the floor and punch through a soldier's calf. The injured soldier bellowed, and the shocked guard fell dead with Baelmar's arrow through his neck. Khan did not look up. So far, the plan was working. Baelmar had entered above by a way known to servants and hidden himself in the darkness on one of the huge beams that crossed the hall.

At the lower table, this produced angry shouts and the hiss and clank of swords being drawn, with men looking desperately around at the dark area above to try to spot the assailant. But at the high table, it produced interested glances toward Mander to see what he would do. These men were just a vicious as he, and if he showed weakness, they might kill him themselves. He looked back and forth among them and bowed to the inevitable.

"I will feed your liver to my dogs!" he bellowed, standing up and dumping his chair over backward. "But only after I cut pieces off your body every day for a week, fry them, and make you eat them. And I'll start with your balls, you impertinent son of a bitch!"

Then with speed like a cat, he threw something shiny overhand with his right hand. Too late, Khan realized that Mander had also undergone genetic modification and received the same quickness in battle he himself possessed. The thing flashed at unbelievable speed through the air directly toward his groin. With great effort he sidestepped just far enough to avoid being unmanned and took the object in the hip.

Pain exploded upward instantly, and he knew that the level of pain was only preliminary, as when a finger touches something red hot. The real pain would come after a few seconds. Before that happened, he assessed the situation: a seven-pointed throwing star protruded from his hip. He grasped it carefully with his left hand, cutting himself slightly by simply taking hold of it, and pulled it from his body. Blood gushed out. He ignored the pain and willed the bleeding to slow.

This would be a harder fight than he had thought. Mander didn't have to fight his own fights because he had long ago proved to his men that he was a much deadlier badass than any of them. Probably former federal police or crime syndicate operative. But Mander probably didn't know that he himself had been genetically modified. So he faked more pain and disability than he felt. He staggered a little, looked at the wound in exaggerated dismay, and allowed a groan to escape his lips. Nevertheless, below his brows, he watched Mander carefully as he approached, swaggering confidently, his drawn sword at the ready.

"Not so tough now, are you, Asshole? You come to my planet, invade my fief, screw around with my Elves, and kill my son, and you expect to come into my keep and kill me? Just who the hell do you think you are?"

Khan acted as though it was agony even to raise his gaze to face Mander. "Alexander Khan, at your service."

Mander had just enough time to register shock before Khan threw the star backhand with the same blazing speed with which Mander had thrown it. The difference was, Mander was only three meters away and had much less time to react. The problem was, though Pierre had schooled Khan in all forms of combat, including the use of throwing stars, in his injured state his aim was a little off, especially since he had thrown with his left hand. The star missed the aimed-for larynx and cut a furrow through the right side of Mander's neck. Unfortunately it also missed the carotid artery, but the wound was enough of a surprise to make Mander raise his left hand to investigate. Though there was no arterial pumping, the bleeding was profuse. Mander's hand came away covered with blood. Now it was his turn to be dismayed. Perhaps he thought his carotid had in fact been cut. In any case, his guard was down for a few split seconds, and Khan struck. Sword high, he did two classic ballestra lunges, each one shooting electric bolts of pain up his hip. Too late, Mander saw his mistake in losing focus, and Khan's sword entered his throat in front and came out the back of his neck, severing his cervical vertebra. He was dead before he hit the floor.

"Hooo, hooo!" said the men in the hall. It sounded like some kind of cry of alarm or rallying cry.

Khan didn't have to wait long to find out which. As one man, they rose from the banquet tables with drawn swords and made for him. So much for the honor of a challenge match. He prepared to go down fighting. But he remembered to give the signal: "FREEDOM!" he bellowed. "FREEDOM!"

At that moment, a swarm of arrows and crossbow bolts descended from the darkness above like angry hornets. The charging men fell in groups. At the same time, the huge wooden doors to the banquet hall boomed open, and a crowd of slaves rushed in brandishing lances, pikes, swords, battle axes, daggers, pitchforks, scythes, tree-felling axes, meat-boning knives, and one bow saw.

This enraged Mander's men even further, and they fell to with a vengeance, killing six of the slaves in a matter of seconds. But years of pent-up rage, along with the slaves' raw numbers, quickly began to tell. Khan used the moment of surprise to his advantage, beheading several men-at-arms while they were distracted. It was bloody mayhem, and at one point, one of the Round Table knights, who looked like a son of Mander, yelled, "Call in the Guard!" But anyone who tried to get out the door was hacked to pieces by enraged slaves gone mad with revenge. Curses and grunts, the clash of metal on metal, the thump of metal on bone, and the shrieks of the dying filled the hall.

In five minutes, it was all over. Fifty corpses lay heaped around the hall, often two deep: the initial killer was subsequently killed and fell atop his victim. Arms, legs, and heads lay separate from bodies. Blood covered the floor in a single great, dark, slick pool. The smell of blood and shit and hot unwashed bodies was thick in the air. Fifteen slaves lay dead, including Dr. Greis's two companions from the hayfield. Khan's gut twisted. Just boys, and he had guilted them into it. But as of old, he stuffed down such after-battle feelings mercilessly. They had fought for freedom and lost their lives, but maybe won freedom for their friends. It was a fair trade in the larger scheme of things. But it wasn't over. Not quite yet.

Four of Mander's men remained alive and had thrown down their swords and daggers and raised their hands in a terrified bid to say alive. Caught up in a fit of violence and vengeance, the slaves crowded in to slaughter them.

"No!" boomed Khan. "Don't be like them! Tie them up until we're finished outside. Throw them in the dungeon. There must be one around this place."

Grudgingly, the slaves complied. Dr. Greis started to follow, but Khan called him back.

"What about the Guard barracks?"

"A horrible scene, I think. I don't think I'll ever be able to forgive myself for this slaughter. As you suggested, the washer women and serving girls who ... serve the men devised their own plan. They filled large earthen water jars with oil and set them around the barracks beside the water jars as if they were extras. Then they placed an extra oil jar just inside each door. One side of the room has no windows, and the other side's windows all give out over a twenty-meter drop. When you gave your signal, they opened the doors and knocked over the jars just inside. Then they threw in torches and barred the doors. Naturally, the men picked up the other jars of oil thinking they were water to put out the fires. If you listen, you can hear the men screaming. A hundred fifty men burning alive."

"Good," said Khan. This was no time to go soft. "That leaves only the guard on the battlement."

"'Only'?" snorted Dr. Greis. It's another hundred-fifty men. Humans like us. Some of them never did anything evil to the slaves. This is sickening. And by now they've probably been warned. They could kill us all."

"Has to be done if you want your freedom, Dr. Greis. It is precisely the capacity to use violence that allows men to enslave others, and the unwillingness to use it that keeps slaves in slavery. Baelmar!" he called out, turning his face up to the darkness. "Are you ready?"

Baelmar called down from above. "The left battlement! Give us three minutes and we'll be ready!"

Suddenly, where before he could see only gloom, Khan could see indistinct shapes moving in the rafters above, climbing over the edge of the banquet-hall wall and disappearing into the rafters above the barbican.

The plan was simple: Counterclockwise from an outward-facing perspective, Baelmar would lead a group of nine archers – or at least men who knew roughly how to use a bow – around the battlement from the left side of the barbican that housed the portcullis. Khan would lead a second group around from the right.

Given his reasonably experienced bowmen, Baelmar had elected a fast-moving cover-and-fire approach, in which pairs of archers would run forward to new cover, behind a barrel or a buttress, while the men in the rear kept up the rate of fire to cover them. Khan had only men who had no experience with weapons or fighting of any kind, so he elected Philip of Macedon's phalanx approach, with a shield wall in front, but with very long lances poking between. This gave the men a sense of security, partially false as Khan was at pains to point out, because while bowshots would not fully penetrate the steel-clad wooden shields, crossbow bolts certainly would. Thus the need to move right along with no dilly-dallying. The men got his point when he stressed the importance of picking up and manning the shield or lance of the man in front if he fell.

Mander's guards were trained, disciplined soldiers, so the plan quickly fell apart. First and foremost, it was dark, so it was difficult for Baelmar's men to select targets. More importantly, while Baelmar accounted for a guard with nearly every shot, his men were amateurs by comparison. But the guards were not. Their fire was disciplined, well-aimed, and deadly. Baelmar lost three of his nine men within minutes, and the battle on his side of the battlement turned into a stalemate, with each side firing from cover to no effect, and unable to advance.

On Khan's side of the castle, the guards wasted no time in bringing up men with crossbows to replace those with bows. And guards on the far wall took to firing high, parabolic bow shots to fall down on Khan's men. The effect was disastrous: four of his front line of five shield bearers went down. "Pick them up! Pick them up!" he shouted at the second rank, but they were starting to fall as well. They turned and ran, leaving the men with the lances uncovered. "Charge, Men!" he bellowed. "Full speed! They can't stand against your lances! If you run, they'll shoot you in the back!" While he spoke a lance carrier took a bolt to the face and fell, dropping his lance to the stone battlement. There was a moment of pause as each side took stock. What would the slaves do?"

"Damn right," growled a skinny man in his fifties, picking up the lance. "What's a man like me got to lose?" He turned to his fellow lancemen. "Come on, you lazy, cowardly bastards! Let's at least die like men, and take a couple of these parasites with us!" And with that, he roared "FREEDOM!" and charged straight for the nearest guard, who while he watched to see what would happen had failed to recrank his crossbow. He moved desperately from side to side to try to avoid the lance's point, but there was no place for him to go. Even a crossbow bolt through the shoulder from another guard did not stop the slave as he drove the lance a good meter through the guard. The guard looked down in surprise at the lance through his solar plexus, then sat down in dismay. Undeterred by his wound, the slave backed up to pull the lance from the guard's body, and charged another guard. This guard put a crossbow bolt through the slave's heart, but too late to save himself from the lance.

This show of the guards' vulnerability was all the other lancemen needed to get them to charge forward. The crossbowmen retreated, because cranking a crossbow takes time and can't easily be done on the run. The regular bowmen advanced and started firing, but now the slaves saw the strategy, and they picked up the shields to protect their formation from the arrows. The difference was speed. If they moved forward at speed, the crossbowmen had to retreat before their lances, and the bowmen's arrows couldn't completely penetrate their shields. Once they understood this, a loud "HOO HOO" went up, and they moved forward with a vengeance, their blood lust up. The slaughter began.

Seeing their fellows on Khan's side in retreat, the guards on Baelmar's side started firing across the castle at Khan's men's flanks. This exposed them enough to Baelmar and his bowmen that they could be picked off in twos and threes, thinning their ranks before the lancemen got clear around the castle.

Khan manned a lance himself when a slave fell and accounted for five guards before the remaining guards threw down their weapons and threw up their hands. "Mercy!" they cried. "Don't kill us all. Tell us what you want and why you are doing this!"

The slaves ignored this and continued to kill them until Khan bellowed "STOP!"

Battle blood up, eyes looking like the eyes of crazed beasts instead of humans, the panting slaves reluctantly stopped and looked back at Khan.

"Set the standard now for your new society!" said Khan. He realized he was speaking to people who had no tradition of democracy. "Mercy for those who ask it. Justice. Fairness for all. You have beaten the tyrants. Don't become tyrants yourselves."

Grumblingly, the slaves lowered their lances but not their shields.

"Men!" said Khan to the remaining guards. "Mander lies dead inside. Your leaders are all dead. You have two choices. Leave now, this minute, and never come back on pain of instant death, or join these men and women, these former slaves, in a new community that runs itself."

"I'll come back, by God, with an army," said the senior man, as evidenced by his polished copper gorget. "I will sell my sword to Poikonen or Nakagawa, by God! They'll know how to deal with scum like you and your associate friends!" His eyes blazed.

"Are you certain you'll be back with an army?" Khan asked.

"As certain as I'm standing here looking at a jumped-up slave who needs to learn his place," said the man, red-faced.

With an economy of movement, Khan drew the flintlock pistol from his belt and shot the man in the face. The man fell backward on two of his men, who protested in dismay while letting him down slowly onto the stone battlement.

"Now, back to the choice I offered," said Khan, and backed away with a please-this-way gesture to give the guards a route toward the nearest stairway. "Or if you prefer to stay, the first task will be to bury all these bodies and clean up this mess. After that, I'm sure you'll be able to run for elective office the same as anybody else, but I'm guessing your chances of success are not the best."

Without a word or a final glare, all the remaining guards filed humbly past Khan, descended the stairs, and entered the passageway below that led to the stables.

"We'll hear from them again," said Dr. Greis grimly.

"I'm sure of it," said Khan. "But they're just a few more. First you'll hear from other Lords looking to fill what they will see as a power vacuum. So your first task, after reorganizing yourselves, is to fill it first. You are now free men. Welcome to the terror of being truly free. What will you do next?"

CHAPTER FIVE

DEA EX ERIDANI

"Go with your gut, Lexy. You get too analytical, you kick yourself when you're wrong. You feel bad. 'Where did I go wrong?' All that shit. Go with your gut. You'll be right nine times out of ten. And when you're not, you'll say, ah, so what?"

Great Grandfather Culpepper Conn, *Khans to Khans*

"At some point, Son, you have to produce an heir. This strongly implies the need to find a good woman."

Lucian Khan, *Khans to Khans*

After a month at the Keep, Khan was ready to move on. The Tech town of Advance drew him like a magnet, because he knew if there was anywhere he could advance his goal of getting back to Earth, it was there. But he had a duty to help these slaves learn to face their freedom, so he had stayed to help.

He had now taken every capable person at the Keep through four intensive weeks of martial arts training, helped significantly by Baelmar. There was physical conditioning, swordsmanship, the long bow and the crossbow, and the lance. There was hand-to-hand, the small knife, and the throwing star. There were also classes in battle tactics for those who showed an aptitude. And to support an ongoing requirement for training, he had developed trainers for each of these fields. Some weren't very good, but they would get better. – Or their trainees would die. Then the trainers would get better.

But this wasn't enough. He had schooled the citizens of the Keep also in the importance of having a leader they all supported. He had supervised the storing up of sixty days' food in case of a siege. And he had insisted as well on the making and storing of large quantities of arrows and crossbow bolts, which were in surprisingly short supply. In short, he had done all he reasonably could for Mander's former slaves, and wanted to leave before Sunrise Keep, as the people had restyled it, decided he was their new natural leader.

Dr. Greis had been elected head of the Keep council and had appointed able people to several key responsibilities, including wisely subjecting the appointments to ratification by the whole Keep. Farming operations were running smoothly, and without the parasitic weight of the lords, surpluses had quickly developed. Daily military training was an unquestioned requirement for everyone of all ages, with no exceptions except infants and the bedridden. And a contingent of elite horse guards expert at all weapons was being rapidly developed in order to conduct ranger operations to prevent military surprise. Significantly, all military activity took place under leaders elected by the troops themselves. They weren't necessarily the best military minds, but they had the support and obedience of their people – both male and female citizen soldiers. Khan had done his best to drill the leaders on tactics.

Despite the slaughter that had brought all this about, Khan was proud of the changes. He was worried that two or three other lords might gang up on the Keep to show their own slaves that such a rebellion would never be tolerated. But he had received a visit from Salvatore Ruggiero and a promise that Guido's Hundred would help defend Sunrise Keep if the need arose. "If it comes to that, I can share governance with my own serfs," said Salvatore. "It will come to that eventually or we will never advance."

So it was time to go. His moves so far had been reactive. He had done the necessary, the logical, the dutiful. Now it was time to figure out how to use the resources of this admittedly charming planet to gain his revenge on Nathan Fox, and to break ECG's grip on the people of Earth. He refused to accept that he was on Prison Planet for the rest of his life. He refused to accept a lifetime of the reduced circumstances in which he found himself.

Arcadia was charming, beautiful, even seductive. But he didn't want to be seduced and imprisoned by it, like Odysseus by Calypso. He still had the tracker chip in his bag. Somehow it was a thin grip on power. He just hadn't figured out exactly how yet. But his gut told him the key to that power lay with the Techs. He was no scientist or professional engineer, but he did have a degree in military engineering. He could be useful to the Techs, depending on the level of technology they had achieved. And they could be useful to him. Certainly, he did not want his primary contribution for the rest of his life to be as a military leader in medieval warfare. Since his family's mission had always been to bring technology to the people, Advance seemed the logical place to go.

"I'm coming, too," Baelmar said with a big grin. "I have to keep you out of trouble."

"You're joking, right?" said Khan. "I risk my life to save your sorry ass so you can go back to your wife and family, and you're not going to go home? Maruil will kill us both when she hears about this."

"She knows. I've already sent word. We both owe you. A lot of people owe you. More than you can realize. You've brought the Western World a big, good change for the first time in memory. And you did it without knowing what you faced. You are brave, Mr. Khan, but ignorant about our world. It's amazing you have not been killed so far." He flashed a big smile. "You require protection. I'm going with you to the Techs so you get there alive. You will get yourself into trouble along the way, and I will be there to save you. Again, like in the banquet hall." He grinned again, then looked thoughtful. "Many wise people think you are destined for big things. That you will make more big change to make up for your past sins. So we all want to see you survive."

"Destiny," Khan snorted. "You have addled your brain by breathing the herb potions you use on your horses. I've just been trying to survive. Honorably. Look, it's true you're passable with horses and a bow, and yes, you helped a small amount in the banquet hall fight, but I have no need of a minder between here and Advance."

Baelmar crossed his arms. "How many streams must you cross between here and Advance?"

"Well, I don't know. I'll cross them when I come to them."

"Like you crossed the River of Doubt?"

Sweat rose on Khan's brow as he recalled that crossing, but he said nothing. Baelmar bored in.

"The word is, you crossed at Dead Man's Crossing. You are the second person in a hundred years to survive the crossing there. If you had gone farther downstream, you would have found a rope bridge strong enough for a horse. Bridges are useful things for crossing streams, my friend. If you know where they are."

"It is true, a bridge would have been useful, had I known about it, but exercise does a man good."

Baelmar nodded his amusement. "And if you don't drown on the way to Advance, you'll likely get plenty of exercise for your sword arm. How many fiefs between here and Advance?"

"Two, maybe. Hard to tell." He pulled out Maruil's map. "You should recognize this map."

"Yes. I made it. For Gareth when he began to roam. The other version names two fiefs. But neither version shows how to avoid horse patrols, which you will want to do, since you are now a marked man among the Lords. And neither shows that between the Leeward Hundred and the Godfrey Mark is a wild area controlled by neither lord, and often roamed by Maneaters. They come, set up their tents, stay awhile, hunt and fish, then fold their tents and go. The problem is that, for them, hunting includes humans. Very few escape once captured by Maneaters."

"I see. So you're going to protect me from these Maneaters?"

"I'm going to show you how to avoid them. Give up, Major. You can't avoid me going along." Baelmar flashed a big grin with white teeth.

Khan sighed. "I'm probably not coming back, you know. How will you get back to Maruil without me protecting you?"

Baelmar boomed laughter. "You will be back many times. And I was born here, Mr. Khan. Do not worry about me."

"Right. Until somebody suckers you with a big dark stallion again. All right. I suppose I can use somebody to share guard duty with. Let's go see what it's like among the Techs."

Baelmar gave him a thoughtful look but said nothing.

They used the ferry to cross back to the southwestern bank. Baelmar explained that, while parts of Advance lay on both sides of the river fifty kilometers upstream, the southern bank was less frequented by Maneaters. Khan rode the horse from Salvatore that had brought him this far, and Baelmar rode a huge chestnut stallion bareback. Khan had stuffed his saddlebags with provisions and crossbow bolts, and he carried three bolts in his belt. Baelmar wore a backpack with his provisions, and had a full quiver of thirty arrows slung across his back.

Khan wanted to climb the escarpment and follow it, but Baelmar said it only followed the river for half a day's ride or so. He recommended one of them following the fairly well-trodden riverside path, and the other moving parallel and behind, but silently through the woods. He suggested himself for the latter role. "No one would hear me in the forest," he smiled. "But a Newby like yourself? Well, you would crash around like a cow."

"Fine," smiled Khan through his teeth. "We'll ride the escarpment for as far as it stays close to the river, staying in cover where possible, and observing the river valley. There's less chance of ambush in the river valley cover that way."

"True," nodded Baelmar. "But sometimes we will be outlined against the sky and visible from the river valley. That will give ambushers a chance to plan."

"—Which means we need to do something unpredictable after we enter the valley's cover."

Khan could see that Baelmar was going to be no pushover. But he couldn't afford to give up control. In the event, they combined both plans, and the last kilometer before the escarpment ended, Baelmar dropped down into the woods. When the bluff swung away from the river valley, Khan found his own way down and, true to Baelmar's prediction, crashed through the woods until he found the riverside path. He assumed Baelmar was behind him. His crossbow was cocked with the safety loop holding in the bolt, and his flintlock was loaded as well.

Within minutes of starting down the path toward Advance, he began to hear sticks cracking in the woods. Then a voice came from the cover.

"We saw you coming down the ridge, Mr. Khan. You might as well give over your goods now. Throw them on the ground, and no one will be getting hurt, you see."

"My goods are my own, my invisible friend, and for all I know, this "we" you speak of is just you. Besides which, I have no goods of value."

"Your sword is a beauty, I must say, and your crossbow, and that pistol you have. Not to mention your horse and saddle. All these will look good among my possessions."

"Show yourselves, and we will talk like gentlemen."

"Aye, it's no gentleman you are, Major Khan. Murderer, more like, and dangerous. If you need proof that we are many, we'll put three arrows into your saddlebags. We don't want to harm your horse."

Three sudden zipping sounds ended in thunks as three arrows appeared in his right-hand bag. He hoped they hadn't pierced the precious black-powder bag that was in there. The horse hadn't reacted as though wounded, so they probably hadn't gone through all the layers of leather.

"Weapons on the ground and hands up. The pistol first, if you please, then the crossbow, then the sword."

"OK, you make a persuasive case," said Khan and complied slowly and deliberately, giving his best smile.

Four loin-clothed bowmen in rawhide leggings melted out of the shadows on moccasined feet. Their bows were short but recurved and skillfully made with polished wood, bone, and sinew. Each man wore a knife and a bola hanging from a rawhide belt. All were shirtless with brightly beaded leather vests, and tattoos over the entire chest and face. Each wore a beaded headband with various colorful symbols running across the forehead, and with hair pulled back and tied neatly behind the head with a ribbon. All were clean-shaven, and wore leather vambraces with fantastical designs. Two wore necklaces of what appeared to be human teeth. The one Khan took to be the head man wore a bronze gorget. All in all, the effect was: healthy, relatively clean, prosperous, but dangerous savages.

"A smile gets you far," smiled the head man, exposing sharpened canines, "but a smile and a weapon get you a lot further." He picked up Khan's crossbow. "Nice weapon. By Lord Ruggiero's armorer, I see, it is.

He's provided us with some of our best. Not willingly, of course." The tone turned slightly less cordial. "Dismount. You're on my new horse."

"Actually," said Khan reasonably, "it belongs to Lord Ruggiero, and must be returned. May I take it you're going to return it to him?" He slid off the side of the horse closest to the man, in such a way that his sword was only centimeters in front of his toes. "And that you four would be what everybody calls Maneaters?" Khan smiled as charmingly as he could.

"We are the Dawn People," said the man, not offended. "We eat our strong enemies. People like you, Mr. Khan. Their strength flows into us and makes us stronger." He smiled to show off his canines again and started to pick up the sword. Realizing his mistake, which would have put him close enough for a kick to the head, he straightened. "Your sword, Mr. Khan. Pick it up and hand it to me, pommel first, if you will."

"Certainly, Mr. –. I'm afraid we haven't been properly introduced. I don't know your name."

With that he thrust a toe under the sword, flipped it up to hand height, and in one motion drew it from the scabbard, beheaded the man to his right, then spun on around and beheaded the man to his left, leaving the leader and one man now drawing a bead on him with his bow. With his left hand, he pulled Mander's throwing star from the special leather pocket he had put on his belt for it, and back-handed it into the solar plexus of the bowman. The bowman collapsed, plucking at his belly to try to remove the thing that had nearly disappeared into it.

At that point, Baelmar materialized out of the woods on his horse with drawn bow pointed at the leader. "I'll do the introductions, Major. Major Khan, meet Seamus Branchrunner. Seamus Branchrunner, meet Major Khan. Seamus, it seems you're out of your normal area. Your weapons on the ground, if you please. We elves don't like violence, as you know, and it would be a shame to have any more."

The Maneater dropped Khan's crossbow and raised his hands. "Your friend has just killed three of my kinsmen, and ye talk of disliking violence?" said Seamus.

"The knife you keep in the sheath on your back, too," said Baelmar cheerfully.

Seamus reluctantly pulled out a large throwing knife from behind his back and tipped it into the soil.

"You're forgetting the part where you and your kinsmen were robbing me and talking of eating me," said Khan. "Killing you all seemed perfectly legitimate." He turned to Baelmar. "You know this man?"

"I'm afraid I do. Seamus was born an Elf in the far north but went over to the dark side. It is rare but it happens. We met as elves in boyhood, and our paths have crossed a few times since. Remember last time, Seamus? You promised to make my death painless, and to make sure my meat was distributed as widely as possible, and only to the best people? Remember?"

"Aye, and I make the same promise now. To you. Not to him." He cast a dark look at Khan. "He will die a painful death."

"But you appear to be at a disadvantage, Seamus," said Baelmar. "And I'd like to know what you're doing here. I didn't expect Maneaters for another twenty kilometers."

"That's why we're here. That, and we moved in after Mander fell. We thought the peasants would be weak, and we could take their weapons. No one will trade weapons to us, you know. Only cooking pots and other harmless things. We make the best bows, but guns, swords, and crossbows we have to steal. And it is you, Baelmar old friend, who is at a disadvantage. You can kill me, but you are surrounded, and will both be roasted tonight, nonetheless."

"Brave talk," said Khan. "But we'll be leaving now."

He bent to retrieve the throwing knife, which looked to be a good addition to his personal arsenal, and an arrow grazed his forearm and buried its head in the dirt within two centimeters of the knife. He moved quickly to the side, snatching up the crossbow, and for his trouble received an arrow through the left forearm. He dropped the crossbow, snapped off the arrowhead, and pulled the arrow out of his arm. He sincerely hoped the tip had not been poisoned, but doubted it if the Maneaters intended to eat him. He raised his hands, as did Baelmar, still astride his horse. Several Maneaters dropped from the tree canopy, and many more melted out of the undercover, bows drawn, to surround them.

"Well, Baelmar, you've done a fine job keeping me out of trouble so far," said Khan. I feel perfectly safe in your hands."

"I'll have a plan. I'll let you know as soon as I think of it."

Seamus gave an order in a language Khan couldn't quite follow, though it sounded tantalizingly like Standard. His and Baelmar's hands were bound behind their backs. Then teams of two men stripped the corpses, carefully stowing their belongings in bundles, then field-dressed the bodies like deer, slitting them from throat to anus and dumping their innards on the ground. Khan had seen many bad things in his life, but this nearly overmatched his self-control. Bile rose in his throat but he forced it back down because he didn't want to display any form of weakness. But if he had doubted the savagery of these people before, he now had no room for such doubt.

Once they were done cleaning the carcasses, three Maneaters picked up a carcass apiece, slung them over their shoulders, and headed off into the woods. The whole group moved out behind them. Khan and Baelmar were frog-marched a kilometer upstream, where they rendezvoused with the Maneaters' horses. Then they mounted and climbed the escarpment and followed it northeast, trotting easily in the gathering darkness. When the moonless sky was dark as black velvet, with only starlight, they turned east and headed out onto the plain, still cantering in the pitch darkness. The horses seemed to know where to put their feet. After an hour's ride, they came to a huge campsite with several small fires and one large fire blazing in the middle.

"It looks as though they are preparing for a feast," said Baelmar cheerfully.

"I'm hungry myself," said Khan. "I hope something good is on the menu. But just in case, have you come up with that plan yet?"

"I'm working on it. You Earth people are always in a hurry from what I've heard, and you bear that out."

"I'll try to be patient. Maybe they're into slow roasting, and you'll be first after telling me the plan."

They were taken straight to the central fire, which Seamus called the Council fire, where people were starting to gather. The three bodies of their fellows were delivered to a group of women, who immediately started to skin them, spit them, and otherwise prepare them for roasting. An imposing man of great height with animal tusks protruding outward through the sides of his nose, and wearing a long, white, beaded-leather robe appeared from Khan's right without his being aware.

"Welcome to our Council Fire, Major Khan," said the man. It is unfortunate that your fate is to roast over it, but that will wait for tomorrow night, since by your actions, you have given us much meat tonight. These are our brethren, and we must do them the honor of eating them fresh."

"I'm sorry, Sir. You have me at a disadvantage." Khan indicated his bound wrists. "I don't believe we've met, yet you know my name. And am I to consider it an honor to be roasted and eaten by your people?"

The man stepped aside in a courtly way and gestured for Khan to accompany him. "Please. Come to my lodge. We will talk of many things."

Khan followed the man to a large teepee in the place of honor at the head of the oval forming the inner ring of teepees. Half a dozen or more rings surrounded the inner ring. Khan's quick calculation, if each teepee held three people, yielded an estimated camp population of four to five hundred.

In a polite motion, the man held aside a flap for Khan to enter. He stepped inside and was shocked. Instead of the expected squalor, there was light and order. Hanging oil lamps lighted the interior, leaving no dark corners. The teepee covering itself was a patchwork of pieces of waxed linen and waxed rawhide, neatly sewn, all of it light-colored, so the dominant impression was one of surprising light. The entire perimeter of the teepee at eye level was hung with bead tapestries of extraordinarily rich imagery, including both geometric shapes and hunting and religious scenes. Furs and carpets covered the floor. Colorful pillows lay here and there. A comely young woman sat in the rear doing beadwork on rawhide. Near what was apparently the man's bedroll was a small pile of books. And overlaying the air in the teepee was an incense smell, as well as a somehow disquieting tallowy smell that Khan could not identify. He assumed it was the oil in the lamps.

"Your reputation goes before you, Major. I have a reputation myself, but it does not reach as far as yours. I am Cuchulain, chief of the Dawn People." He gestured to a spot on the ground well furnished with carpets and pillows. "Please sit. I would like you to tell me all you know of far places and other planets before we divide your strength among ourselves. And if you pass the test later, perhaps you can become one of us yourself and not yet be divided."

For lack of alternatives, Khan sat. The old tale of Scheherazade came to mind. If the man was curious, perhaps Khan could keep him entertained and keep himself alive long enough to figure out how to escape. Larger and more muscular than Khan, Cuchulain settled easily into a cross-legged posture without using hands to steady himself. Khan wondered whether this was an intentional display of physical poise, or an unconscious, habitual action. In either case, it was clear the man would be a formidable, if not deadly hand-to-hand combatant. He was not only huge; he was limber and probably quick.

"Chew this and swallow the juice," said the man, handing Khan a dried flower. He placed one in his own mouth and chewed. "It will bring our minds together and help us understand each other."

Khan made no move to take the dried flower. He had no desire to share mutual understanding with this well-mannered savage.

"You will chew it," said Cuchulain mildly, his dark brown eyes boring into Khan's. "I can make you do it myself, which will humiliate you, or call in several men to hold you. Either way, you will swallow it."

Acknowledging reality, Khan put the dried yellow blossom in his mouth and chewed. For just a moment, he tasted extreme bitterness, then his mouth went numb and he could not even feel his tongue. The numbness slowly spread down his throat. Had he been poisoned? Would he be able to breathe? He drew a deep breath and his heart began to pound.

"Of course the one I gave you is from a different plant than the one I'm chewing," said Cuchulain mildly. "But it will not kill you. It will speed your senses and make your thoughts clear. The one I'm chewing will permit me to see your thoughts."

Khan doubted all of this except that his blossom was from a different plant. Cuchulain would hardly be able to breathe, let alone speak, if he had chewed the same type of blossom. But gradually, along with the pick-up in heartbeat, his respiration sped up and became easier, and more interestingly, his mind became clear. Not just the clarity of a bright morning after a good night's sleep, but blindingly, startlingly clear. He became aware of several simultaneous threads of thought running through his subconscious, one of which dwelt on the mammalian nature of his alien night visitor on the way to Guido's Hundred, and one of which was a string of images of the things he would like to do to Nathan Fox for arranging his father's death. Simultaneously, he noticed myriad details inside the teepee: the girl was watching him with sidewise glances; Cuchulain, who was also watching him closely, had carefully trimmed but very long fingernails; the clay oil lamps were skillfully glazed, and almost certainly made by Elves; the unique smell he had noted before was coming from the lamps, and he realized in a flash that the melted tallow being burned there was rendered from human bodies.

"Yes," said Cuchulain, looking at him intently.

This broke him into a sweat for the obvious reason, as well as because it seemed to indicate that Cuchulain really could see into his mind.

"Yes, I can," said Cuchulain.

Now Khan realized the extent of his exposure, and he sought to regain control and to blank his mind. He had been trained in the meditative arts by Pierre as part of his youthful martial arts training. One exercise had been the classic, "Think of a snowy steppe in the middle of a snowstorm. Nothing is visible as far as the eye can see except deep snow. Do not think of a white wolf." Khan concentrated on this exercise now until all he could see was a snowy expanse in a blizzard – similar to his arrival on Arcadia. But then his subconscious reared its head, and his fight with the gryphon surged up out of the darkness. He pushed it back down and went back to the snowy expanse.

"Very impressive. Few encounter a gryphon and live. And few can control their minds as well as you. Your mind is more disciplined than most, Major Khan, but I can still see all its parts. I see that you have met the Witch of the Leas. Most who meet her do not think about her breasts. They count themselves lucky to have survived. She takes people away. But that is not what I want to know. Show me the worlds you have visited."

Khan found it interesting that a cannibal savage was curious about other worlds, but he saw no reason to deny Cuchulain this request. He replayed in his mind his visits to the twenty-four colony worlds, as well as worlds that had not been settled. Cuchulain closed his eyes and drank in the images and remained silent for a long while.

"The World is many worlds," he breathed, breaking his silence. "Beautiful worlds. And the boat that floats from star to star is magical and powerful. And yet men are still men, evil and good and cowardly and brave. And no world is more beautiful than the Great Mother. Your kind call it Prison Planet. Elves call it Arcadia. Techs call it Earth 2.0. But the Great Mother is more beautiful than Earth itself." His eyes closed for a long moment, then he opened them. "You think me a savage," he said. "Yet the things you have done are far more savage."

"You eat people," Khan tried to say, but his tongue wouldn't work.

"Our ancestors did this of necessity. We do it as a sacrament. We eat our worthy enemies, and our own warriors when they die. There is a long Earth history for this. Even the main ritual in Earth's main religion is based on eating the body and blood of an admired person. We are not savages. We are philosophers of nature."

"How do you know these things about Earth religions?" Khan thought.

"You are not the first who has eaten the yellow blossom. And I have books. And we range far and wide – farther than the Techs. Lords never travel. Elves will travel a few weeks away to explore. The Techs send their balloons to explore, but most don't return because the winds always come from the west, and their pusher devices can't overmatch the winds. But we have been to the other side of the world. We are the true lords of this world. We have seen things no man has seen. We have been south to where the stars are different in the sky, and north to where there is only snow and ice. We know things because we explore."

Khan tried to form a question in his mind. "And what kind of people did you meet in these places?" but the drug was beginning to wear off, and he had to piss like a race horse. But still, Cuchulain got the question.

"People everywhere are the same," he said. "Evil and good. Cowardly and brave. Wise and foolish. Only the details are different. On the other side of the world we met survivors from a group called a commune. Most had starved waiting for someone else to do the work necessary to feed and clothe them all. The survivors became elves, though they called themselves naturists. They wore clothes only in winter time. And we met other wandering groups like ourselves, always on horses. And everywhere we saw stopped-up, fearful people like the Lords who pretend bravery, but barricade themselves into castles. And everywhere there are deniers like the Techs, who try to recreate the world that rejected them. Only the wanderers and the Elves take this world as it is. Newbies usually go to the techs if not captured by the Lords, but their children often become Elvish, and second-generation Elves sometimes become Dawn People. It is a progression of the natural. Tech life is unnatural."

Khan struggled to get up. Rolling onto his knees wasn't that hard with his hands bound behind his back, but keeping his balance was. "Affu pss," he was able to manage, before losing his balance and falling on his side.

Cuchulain looked at the young woman and hooked his head at Khan. She brought a clay jar over to Khan and made the necessary arrangements for him to relieve himself while she held everything in place. "Jeez," he said.

"This is Marna," said Cuchulain. "She will sleep with you tonight to capture your seed so your blood flows down the generations. You have disappointed your father. You have no children. This will please him where he is in the sky."

In his vulnerable position, this hit Khan in the gut. He and his father had had words about this, with his father stressing the need for him to take his place in the Khan family hierarchy, that he had done enough to appease ECG, and that it was time for him to return to the family estates and assume his rightful social and political position, all of which meant having a presentable wife. And he had said, yes, he would like a good woman, and indeed had had a few on a temporary basis, but all had been repelled by the work he did for ECG and could not understand how a good man like him could continue doing the bad things they heard about on the grapevine. And he had explained again to his father that the danger from ECG was far greater than his well-meaning but slightly naïve father understood, and that only his position with Internal Movement Control had saved the Khan family from retribution for its release of freedom technologies: PV cells, powerful batteries, solar stills that took sea water and produced oxygen, hydrogen, pure water, and mineral nodules that could be coked and sintered into gold, magnesium, sodium, and many other minerals.

"Not with a savage," Khan managed to say, as Marna finished up and took the jar outside.

"No, not with a savage," said Cuchulain. "With Marna. And when you're done, there will be a feast."

With that, all mildness in Cuchulain's face went away, and he gave a low whistle. Two huge men entered the teepee and hauled Khan to his feet. "Marna's teepee," said Cuchulain. "Bind his feet when she is ready."

And with that Khan was unceremoniously hauled off to a teepee in the third ring of tents. Inside was not so grand or well lighted, but comfortable with furs and carpets nevertheless. Marna was unselfconsciously naked, and gave instructions to hold Khan while she removed his pants. Then she pointed at his ankles. The men pushed him down and bound his ankles with rawhide strips. Then Marna made shooing motions and the men left.

"Trouble getting dates?" Khan said, trying for lightness. In spite of himself, he was becoming aroused. It had been a long time, and the young woman was attractive.

She made sure he was ready and settled onto him slowly and sensuously, nearly embarrassing him with a too-quick response. Then he reproved himself, thinking, why should he care what this woman or the Maneaters in general thought of him? But it was a matter of personal honor, so he gritted his teeth and tried for control. He tried several times to buck her off, but this made self-control more challenging. Finally, in a meditative approach he tried for total control, to avoid giving Cuchulain and this woman what they wanted. But it was to no avail. She was a skilled partner, and in very little time, she was carrying the seed his father had surely not intended for a cannibal maiden on another planet.

He groaned in disgust, turned his head away from her, and tried again to buck her off. She nevertheless stayed on, and cooed soothingly. "I will take good care of him," she said. "Long after you are dead, you will look down from the sky in the next world and you will be proud. He will be a tall, handsome warrior like yourself, with big shoulders and dark hair, and full of wisdom like Cuchulain, for I am his daughter."

"Absolutely fantastic," he said. "Son-in-law to a cannibal." He looked at her, and despite himself, saw an attractive, sensitive woman. But his stomach felt as though he had eaten street-vendor food in Calcutta and was beginning the regret phase.

She leaned forward and gently kissed him on the cheek. "You must go now," she said solemnly. "You face a test. If you pass, you and I will be husband and wife. If you fail, you will be in the next world tomorrow."

She rolled off of him onto her back and whistled softly. The same two large fellows who had brought him in came in and hauled him to his feet. They started to drag him out.

"My pants?" he said.

The men looked to Marna, who had covered herself with a thin blanket and raised her knees. She nodded. "He is a great warrior," she said. "He must have his dignity."

With feet unbound, pants on, and feet rebound, he was dragged out to a position of honor beside Cuchulain at the fire. At least two hundred people were seated cross-legged in a large circle around the fire, most in their fantastical attire, but some unselfconsciously naked, displaying full-body tattoos. Unambiguously human body parts were being turned on spits over several smaller cooking fires, where women were cutting off small pieces of meat and spearing them six at a time on sharp sticks. The sticks were being passed around the circle and the meat consumed with gusto.

Dear God, thought Khan, let me please meet the test with dignity and honor. He thought what an irony it was that the scion of the family devoted to technological advance was apparently going to die at the hands of cannibals. He had no idea what test Marna referred to, but had zero doubt that it could not be good.

When it came, he was surprised at what it was, but absolutely right that it was not good.

"Here," said Cuchulain, extending a shish kebab to him. "This is meat from one you killed. Do him the honor of eating of him so you will remember him forever. Do this, and you will become one of us. And you will live."

Khan desperately looked around for Baelmar, finally spying him at the foot of the oval, looking sick in the firelight. Based on his facial expression, he assumed he had already "passed" the test.

"I won't do it," Khan heard himself say, still not fully able to control his speech. "A man lives according to his own nature, or he dies. It is not my nature to eat human flesh."

Cuchulain apparently expected this, for he hesitated not a moment. He pulled the pieces of meat off the skewer into the palm of his hand. Then he reached over and pinched Khan's nose shut so he couldn't breathe. When Khan finally had to open his mouth to breathe, Cuchulain crammed the pieces of meat into his mouth. Then he covered his mouth with his other palm so Khan could not breathe at all.

"Chew," he said.

Khan chewed. He knew he did not have the will power to suffocate himself. Perhaps there was such a thing as becoming a cannibal, living to fight another day, and never telling anybody. The meat tasted like pork.

"Swallow," said Cuchulain.

Khan swallowed. His plan now was to poke his finger down his throat if given half a chance. Maybe they would untie him later.

"Was it not good?" asked Cuchulain. "Are you not now one of us?"

"Never," said Khan. Then he discovered that he didn't need to poke his finger down his throat. All he had to do was look at the thighs roasting over one fire, and the arms and hands roasting over another, and his gorge rose of its own accord. Up came the chewed pieces of meat in an explosion of disgust, the sight of which increased his vigor in vomiting up his guts. He felt as if he emptied everything he had eaten for a week.

Cuchulain looked truly disappointed. "You have failed our test, Khan. As did your Elf friend earlier, in the same way. Tomorrow you will both die."

Both were dragged to a teepee in the fourth ring and dumped painfully inside, their wrists and ankles bound. Guards were posted outside – they could hear them talking – and the situation indeed looked grim.

"They would have seen us on the ridge, too," said Baelmar. Our mistake was believing they would behave as they have in the past."

"Thanks for the failure-mode analysis," said Khan. "I feel much better, knowing how to avoid this problem in the future. Of course, they are planning for us to have no future."

"You are welcome," said Baelmar cheerfully. "It's always important to see the bright side. However they plan to kill us, it can only hurt for twelve hours, if they wait until morning, and plan on eating us for supper tomorrow night. We have all night to be happy." Khan could actually hear him smiling.

"Baelmar, did Maruil ever smack you when you said things like that?"

"Frequently. She was always the serious one. She would tell me I was a good-natured idiot. Then I would make her laugh. Then we would kiss and make up, if you know what I mean. That was always the best part."

"Look, I can barely feel my hands, but while I still can, let's back up to each other and see if we can untie each other's hands. "

"I was going to suggest the same thing myself."

It turned out to be no use. The rawhide had been damp when wrapped around their wrists, and the knots were hard, double-overhand knots pulled tight, with no intention of being untied, only cut.

"Was there anything else you were going to suggest?"

"Prayer," said Baelmar. "But it seems to help only those who are helping themselves. We are not doing much."

"Can you get your arms down over your ankles so your hands are in front of you? If we can do that, maybe we could then chew through the rawhide."

Both tried this maneuver, but neither could get his bound wrists over his buttocks.

"All right," said Khan. "Let's see if we can chew through each other's bindings. It means we'll have to back up to each other's face."

With that, Baelmar gave a gigantic fart. "You do my knots first," said Khan, and they both broke into laughter despite the situation.

This didn't work, either. The rawhide was too tough for Baelmar. After a no-farting promise from Baelmar, Khan tried to chew through Baelmar's bindings, and could not do it. They rolled away from each other and stared into the darkness.

"How did you meet Maruil?" said Khan. "She seems a fine woman."

"We grew up on the Leas together, picking berries, hunting, and playing games in the bushes that we were too young to play. It was a wonderful time. The Lords didn't use to come so far into the West Riding, and we and our families lived in a wonderful, peaceful world. We married as soon as our families would let us and started having children soon after. Did you ever have a woman who stayed with you?"

"No, never. There have been women, of course, but never serious." He exhaled, not quite a sigh. "There was actually a girl when I was a boy. Chloe.

The daughter of one of our estate keepers." He smiled at the memory. "We were maybe fifteen. We were going to run away and live together forever beside the ocean far away. I think part of it was avoidance of the Khan family responsibilities I saw coming my way. But our fathers explained the facts of life to us: we were not meant for each other, because we were not of the same class. And I would have to assume leadership of Khan International when the time came, or see three generations' worth of building fall to nothing. As it happened, they've murdered my father, done their best to destroy the corporation, and exiled me here on Prison Planet."

"Arcadia. It sounds more beautiful than 'Prison Planet.'"

"It is beautiful, but deadly. It's determined to kill me, and it looks as though it might succeed this time."

"Hoo, hoo," said Baelmar. "Until the last breath, there is hope."

"I suppose," said Khan. "And despair is the most unforgivable sin. But for once, I'm out of ideas."

Baelmar yawned audibly. "I, too, have no ideas about how to escape. But I am sleepy. Something will come to me in my sleep."

Khan did not reprove his companion for this. Sleep might be a welcome escape. They had much to face tomorrow, and he at least wanted to face it like a man, with as much dignity as he could muster. He settled back himself and surprised himself by dozing.

The next thing he knew, he was awake and there was a cool, white light in the teepee. It came from behind him. Someone was sawing at his wrist bindings with a knife.

"Who are you?" he whispered.

"A friend," said the female voice, in a strange accent. "We cannot permit you to die this way. Much is expected of you."

His hands came free and he rolled over to see the woman from his dream on the way to Guido's Hundred. She had the same white-blonde hair, pointed ears, tight white jump suit, and attention-drawing mammaries, and she glowed all over with a slight fluorescence. She wore a kind of utility belt with several attached pouches and tools.

He went to work untying his ankle bonds while still looking at her. She stood up to a height that appeared to be nearly his own. "How did you find me? My tracking chip is in my basket, which was taken from me. "

"We track you, not your chip." It was then that Khan realized that her lips were not moving when she talked. Her voice was somehow inside his head. And her eyes bored into his with an unsettling intelligence. The hairs on the back of his neck stood up.

"The guards?"

"Asleep." Again, no lip movement, though if he were to close his eyes, he would swear that she was speaking audibly to him.

"Who are your people, and why are you glowing like that? Is that a personal force field?"

She smiled slightly. "I'm sure you can surmise who we are, Major. You found our outpost in what you call the Epsilon Eridani system three hundred of your years ago. Your leaders later misrepresented the encounter. We scared them. But we have watched and helped your race for a long, long before that meeting, guiding you to take your future place among us at the right time. And yes, it's a force field. Our technology is far ahead of yours. Hurry. No one must see me." She handed him the knife.

He cut his ankle bonds and moved to cut Baelmar's bonds. "They already know about you. They call you the Witch of the Leas."

"Those who think us such should not see us." She made no-no hand signals at Baelmar, who snored the sleep of the blessed. "He must not know about me," she whispered. "You must leave him to his fate."

Khan never hesitated. "Can't do that. It's both of us or neither. Can't you memory-wipe him?"

"It might permanently damage him. Your brains are primitive compared to ours."

"Better than being the main course for dinner." He cut Baelmar's wrist bindings and started on his ankle bindings. Baelmar came awake as he did.

"Where did you get that knife? He's a beauty. Whoa! Who is your friend, Khan? She looks like a dream creature. She looks like the Witch of the Leas. There are stories."

The alien woman's mouth crimped slightly at one corner. "We must go before they wake. Quietly."

Baelmar and Khan required no urging, though Khan was pretty sure Baelmar could not hear her in his head as he did. Both crept out silently. The guards outside were breathing loudly, but their seated postures looked so unnatural that Khan assumed the alien had rendered them unconscious in some manner. No one else was out and about, so they were able to make their silent way to the horse grazing area with no problem. Baelmar found his giant chestnut, and Khan found Ruggiero's stallion with his gear still hanging on him. Baelmar took the reins of both horses and put his finger to his mouth in the universal "quiet" gesture. Khan instantly understood and agreed: Baelmar could lead the horses quietly away from the camp, where Khan would certainly make noise. No pride lost there. He acknowledged Baelmar's superior skill.

He turned to the alien woman to thank her and she was gone. Yet her voice sounded inside his head. "Keep yourself out of trouble, Major Khan. You are lucky this time. I am not always in the system. Go to Advance. Learn all you can of the Techs. Then you must return to Earth to free those who want to be freed and capture the technology that will accelerate the Techs' advance. Earth itself may be a hopeless case, nearing collapse, convulsion, die-off, and regression to hunter-gathering. But your race can be saved as an advanced race, and you are the human best situated to save it."

"Easy for you to say," he mumbled, trying to imagine how he would do any of those things, not least, get back to Earth.

"Ssshhh," said Baelmar. "I didn't say anything. You'll get us caught again."

And with that, they crept away into the darkness.

CHAPTER SIX

"Horseshit, Lexy. These are the same morons who tell you not to kill a charging bear because he's an endangered species. Perfect example of Darwinism in action. This 'One People, One Planet' stuff is horseshit. ECG doesn't even believe it themselves. They just want to keep us all prisoners. But some with guts will find a way. They always do. They will escape to the stars, Boy, and rape, and plunder, and build and develop, like real men always have, and make their ancestors proud."
Great Grandfather Culpepper Conn, *Khans to Khans*,
on ECG's One-Planet policy.

"Mankind's destiny is to explore and settle every habitable planet in the galaxy. Khan family destiny is to enable that to happen."
Grandfather Quintus Khan, *Khans to Khans*

"We will free humanity from the commissars in your generation, Alexander. —The ones who want to be freed, that is."
Father Lucian Khan, *Khans to Khans*,
shortly before his murder.

The journey to Advance took longer than the expected three days. The reason was the circuitous route they took through open, grassy upland country to avoid Maneaters in the tree cover along the River of Doubt. The trip was uneventful, with no bad weather and no attacks by man or beast, but after becoming acquainted with Cuchulain, Khan and Baelmar never let down their guard. They doubled back frequently to see if they were being followed, and one always kept watch while the other slept.

Now, after six days and nights, according to Baelmar they were nearing Advance. They had circled back to where they could see stretches of river through the trees half a kilometer away, and they approached cautiously. Signs of civilization – cultivated fields, well-crafted sheds, split and stacked firewood – had begun to appear. This close to what Baelmar described as a civilized settlement, Khan expected no trouble, but they remained wary. In overthrowing Mander, he and the people of Sunrise Keep had upset the regional balance of power and made themselves unpopular with the remaining Lords.

They were still at roughly twenty meters of elevation above the river when they heard an odd sound. Both stopped to listen. A steady, rhythmic, thump, thump, thump came from below near the river, but they couldn't see what was making the sound. They had come to a large field of squash, planted in rows with shallow irrigation channels beside each row. Then Khan saw it: near the edge of the field, water gushed out of a large pipe in syncopation with the thumping sound below and flowed out through distribution ditches and down the rows of squash.

"A hydraulic ram," he breathed. "They have a ram gate down by the river and are pumping water up here with it." Just the sight of even simple technology being used to make work easier lifted spirits he had not realized were low. He knew ECG satellites in orbit would fry any source of radio signals, including alternating current generators. But this was technology that worked for the situation.

"It's Tech magic," said Baelmar. "I have seen this before, and there is never anyone here pumping the water. It's some kind of spell."

"It's a spell you can learn," said Khan. "It's repeatable. It's magic anyone can do. Where is the actual town?"

"We are still at least half a day away. Their farms spread farther outward with each passing year. They cut the trees for burning in their houses and factories and plant food in their place. Soon they will have no wood for cooking. They are like locoos, which eat everything in sight and then starve. They are not bad people, but what they do to Arcadia is not natural. "

Khan was pretty sure "locoos" descended from "locusts," so he got the message. It was the old story. Better life required better tech. Better tech required continuous growth. Continuous growth required more resources.

Khan dinner-table discussion during his boyhood had been lively on this recurrent subject. "Civilizations consume resources until they're gone," Grandfather Quintus would say. "Then they find new resources or die from overreach, like Rome. Rome grew until it couldn't get new slaves and new farmland, then all of a sudden it couldn't defend the overstretched empire." And his father would say, "Evolving technology, Son. That's our saving grace. But it requires constant growth." And then Great Grandfather Culpepper would weigh in. "More planets, Boy! That's our only future." Then all three generations would look at him with expectation.

He had sacrificed himself in years of service to ECG to enable Khan International to work toward that vision. Indeed, ECG's main condition for permitting colonization was that humanity first develop self-sustainable, high-tech, no-growth civilization on Earth: the Great Equilibrium. Else, the theory went, humans would ultimately end up in resource wars with other races, and perhaps get wiped out by a more advanced race. Thus: sustainability before panspermia. The direct opposite of the Khan philosophy. ECG called this the "One-Planet Policy." But so far, conveniently for ECG oligarchs, this goal was not even close. So they had to stay in power to keep working toward their goal. And population grew and resources diminished, just like Grandfather Quintus said.

In the case of Advance, according to Baelmar, other than modest trade with the Lords, and much more modest trade with the Elves, the town was on its own. This meant, Khan concluded, it would rise to the ceiling of its resources and no further until it could trade widely across the planet.

They passed farm after farm, some with horse-drawn cultivators working, one with an honest-to-god steam tractor drawing a chisel plow, though the tractor looked primitive even by Steam Age standards. The driver waved. "Do they not fear attack?" Khan asked.

"No. We are being watched by Techs in balloons," said Baelmar, nodding toward the horizon in the direction of the town. Two balloons hung there in the light haze. "They keep them in the air at all times, and they have a way of sending messages down thin strips of metal. If they see a threat, their town guard will ride out in large numbers. They all have guns and crossbows, and some of their guns can shoot more than once. Maneaters and Lords all know that to attack the Techs means death. Techs are weak warriors, but they are many, and they have good weapons. And they hunt down attackers and wipe out their whole group."

Telegraphy, Khan realized. They were using telegraphy based on DC battery current. And they had enough chemical knowledge and fabrication technology to produce primer caps or rim-fire primer, and enough machining capability to produce revolvers – perhaps revolver rifles. They were probably using black-powder paper cartridges in revolvers with primer caps. Throwaway brass casings would be a terrible waste in an early culture like this, and the dies required were probably still beyond them. Thus, lever-action or gas-action weapons were surely still beyond them as well.

There was no city wall, but there was a fortified picket line with observation towers and earthen embankments fronted by wooden abatis and concertina wire. The city itself, looking more like a one-to-two story country town, stretched across the river valley below them for at least two miles, and up the slope on the far side of the river. In the distance, two wooden-truss bridges crossed the river on piers, one bridge on each side of the town.

They were met by a twelve-person horseback patrol a couple hundred meters outside the picket line. All the men and a few women wore identical green linen uniforms, which looked slightly shoddy and of only a couple standard sizes. All had rank blazons on their sleeves – the familiar system used for the last five hundred years on Earth. All wore revolvers on their belts.

Khan addressed the most senior. "Good afternoon, Sergeant. We are here to visit your fine city, and in my case, to offer my services wherever they may be used. My friend is an Elf, and will ultimately be returning to his people."

"Newby, uh?" growled the man. "Hungry? Maybe an engineer back on Earth?"

Khan nodded to both.

"We get dozens like you. Most are working in the coal mine. Ain't much call for Double E's here. But we can use more coal diggers, wood splitters, stone masons, carpenters, and foundrymen. Short of blacksmiths, too. Got any skills?"

"Not at any of those, though I have no doubt I can dig coal and split wood. My experience is mainly military."

"Got a name?"

"Alexander Khan," said Khan, bowing slightly from the saddle.

The sergeant's eyes narrowed, and his hand moved toward his revolver. "*The* Alexander Khan?" he said.

"The same, at your service."

"You son of a bitch!" shouted the sergeant, pulling his revolver. "I thought you looked familiar! You killed half my family on Luyten Four and took the rest of us back to Earth to prison camp!" He cocked the weapon and raised it to fire.

"Chet," warned one of the sergeant's men.

Khan never moved. "If we killed your family members, it is because they tried to kill us first," said Khan calmly. "Our mission was always to round up illegal colonists and take them back to Earth. That is what we did. I regret the deaths. And I regret the roundups. But both were part of a larger picture intended for the good of all. But that didn't work out, and I am now one of you, sentenced to life on Prison Planet."

The man was unnerved by Khan's calm in the face of death. He blinked, hesitated, and came to his senses. The moment was over. He uncocked the weapon and reholstered it. "You gotta know you're gonna run into hundreds of your former victims here. One of them is likely to kill you."

"I am aware. Yet I believe I can be of value to Advance, and Advance can be of value to me."

"Sure, you want a meal ticket. But other than being a digger, I can't see how a police-state honcho can help much. We don't have much call for Internal Movement Control here, and we aren't Mander's Keep, in need of a mob leader. We heard what you did there, and that's the main reason I didn't kill you. Other than the fact that it would set a bad example for the men. No one liked Mander. But we aren't Mander's keep, and we don't have a military problem. We can kick the ass of any potential enemy out there on Earth 2.0. We don't need you to show us how."

"Fair enough. I'll be happy to work as a digger while I figure out how to help in a more substantial way."

"Not that easy. We got a Citizenship Committee that decides on every

Newby. Run by Estelle, our Mayor. She'll decide. If she likes you, you're in. If not, you can go back to Mander's Keep."

"Fine. Would you be so kind as to take me to your mayor?"

"Citizenship sessions are held on Tuesdays," said the Sergeant. "Today's a Monday, so you're in luck. You'll only need to spend one night in jail waiting for the meeting." He smiled an unfriendly smile.

Khan realized he had been naïve. He had expected a better welcome, but realized the sergeant probably didn't represent the best thinking about Advance's immigration policy. Especially given his history on Luyten Four. But it still seemed right to throw in with the Techs. He would take his chances with the mayor.

"Tell you what," he smiled. "We're not partial to confinement. We'll sleep free tonight and come back tomorrow to present ourselves to the Citizenship Committee. If you don't mind."

"Fine with me. Take your chances with the Maneaters. They've gone kind of crazy since Mander's Keep changed management. That new group is kind of shaky, and the Maneaters are swarming 'cause they think they can take them. At least Mander killed off a few Maneaters now and then to keep them in line."

"We've already been guests of Mr. Cuchulain, thank you," said Khan. "And don't intend to be again. And Sunrise Keep, as they now call themselves, will be just fine. They'll keep the Maneaters at bay just fine, and still deliver on their contracts with you for lumber and beets. And they'll expect that you honor yours with them."

If the sergeant was impressed by this, he gave no sign. He simply said, "Fine," and wheeled his horse and headed back down the circular, beaten-down patrol road around Advance, followed by his detachment.

"You see why I fear you might be disappointed by the Techs," said Baelmar. "These are people who do not smile, and for whom there is no magic."

They passed most of the night uneventfully, without a fire to draw attention, trading off guard duty as they had done for the past several nights. But then, toward dawn, while Khan was standing guard and Baelmar was snoring like a goat, the hairs on the back of Khan's neck prickled. He instantly drew his sword and turned around, ready to decapitate a creeping Maneater. What he saw instead was the alien woman, glowing as before, but floating a few centimeters off the ground.

He sheathed the sword. "A hologram?" he said quietly, so as not to wake Baelmar.

"Yes, this time," she said in his mind, as before, without her lips moving. "I'm actually in my ship, in orbit."

"Are we in danger? Both times you appeared before, it was to warn or save me."

"Of course you're in danger. But I came to share some history before you meet the Techs. We have been helping humans at key points throughout your history on both planets, but more directly here. For three centuries, I have brought Earth animals and plants to this planet. And so, by the way, has your government. Three hundred years ago, I showed a new arrival an iron-ore deposit and gave him a forge design in a dream. Ten years later, I gave him a treadle-powered lathe design. Ten years later, I arranged that a prisoner arrive with a copy of an old Earth book entitled "How Things Work." That was all it took to get them started. And in the years and centuries since, I have visited and helped key people working on key problems. Always in such a way that they think they could have dreamed it. Your species is amazingly resourceful at self-deception."

"Why are you helping us like this? And how am I to get back to Earth, as you said last time I should do?"

"We want your race to survive. That means, grow beyond your planet. For thousands of years, the Ten Races have had a rule: help promising races achieve star travel, but remain invisible until they do. Your race has achieved it but does not use it. The people of this planet are the same race, but superior in many ways to the people of your home planet: more spirit, more drive, more curiosity. They will in the end represent the human race. Your home planet will experience collapse, die-off and re-primitivization unless the people there rejuvenate their world view. But they won't. We have seen it before. Once a people lives in passive symbiosis with a repressive planetary government, collapse is near. We want the best from Earth to escape. And we want you to be the catalyst for change on your new world and the old. Your life has prepared you. You have it within your power to go back to Earth without my taking you there, which would break our law. Think and a way will come."

And with that, the hologram disappeared.

"You are talking to yourself again," mumbled Baelmar without rolling over. "Planning what you are going to tell the mayor? How you are going to sweet-talk her?"

"I think I would need a bath before she would recognize it as a sweet-talk attempt," said Khan.

"Yes," said Baelmar. "I have been meaning to talk with you about that."

They broke out their rations and had a cold breakfast.

Estelle Workman – Madame Mayor to her people – was a rangy, medium-height, thin-faced, sharp-eyed woman of few words in her late thirties. Dressed in loose work pants and high boots as if she was constantly on horseback, she had a small but thick notebook in a holster on her belt, and gave the impression that sitting down was an indulgence, when she could be moving on to her next objective.

"Yes, Mr. Khan, I know who you are," she said, fiddling with a paperweight as she paced behind her desk. She kept glancing at piles on her desk as if she would like to get back to work. "And what you did at Mander's Keep. By the way, *he* always delivered goods and payment to contract, so I hope your new commune doesn't screw that up. So far, so good. But, to you. Your dad. His company. I used to work for your father's company." Khan noted that she hadn't said *your* company. "I headed up the solar-electrolysis still team. Director … Fox and his Office of Technology Control assholes sabotaged that team. Free electrolysis loose in the public square scared the shit out of them. Hydrogen. Oxygen. Fresh water as a waste product. They put a mole on my team. Set me up and made it look like I was trying to free-release the technology on the net, instead of going through the normal license-control bullshit. Kangaroo-courted my ass, wham, bam, screw you Ma'am, all in a week. Your dad tried, but couldn't save me. Been here eight years. I assume you also have a story to tell, particularly given who you are, but I'm too busy to give a shit. I don't see how you can help us much. Rich boy, well educated, no experience except military and police. But …, I can't see you'll hurt us, either. You want to dig, dig." She turned to a clerk taking notes. "Record him in and issue him a dog tag. His Elf buddy, too, though I know he won't stay. Next!"

And that was that. Several other supplicants in line behind Khan shuffled forward. He and Baelmar received metal tags stamped on the spot with their name and a date: 11.14.302. They signed their names in a large ledger book containing thousands of other names, a few of which had notes saying "deceased," or "banished." Then each received a leather lanyard for the tag, a map of Advance with a list of laws and penalties printed on the back, and a gesture toward the door. They also were given chits good for a week's worth of bunking in Mama Ilse's Pension on the north side of the city, and two meals.

They took the hint and stepped out into the busy, sunny street while Khan perused the rules. It appeared the Techs had a no-nonsense view of maintaining public order:

* Theft or suspicion of theft   Banishment
* Murder or suspicion of murder   Banishment
* Counterfeiting   Banishment
* Violence against an Advance citizen Banishment
* Begging   Banishment
* Lying   Banishment
* Sleeping on the street   Banishment
* Failure to pay 10% income tax   Coal digging till paid, then Banishment
* Failure to vote   Banishment

"It looks as though we'd better find Mama Ilse's place before nightfall," said Khan, "or our citizenship is going to be revoked. But let's try the coal mine first, to see if we can find work. How bad can it be for a few days until we find something better?"

Baelmar gave him dubious glance but said nothing. "I am with you, Brother Khan, until you find your destiny, but I think my work will lie with horses instead of a hole in the ground." Nevertheless, he went with Khan as he followed the map in the direction of the coal mine on the northern outskirts of the town.

On their way, Khan took in the town. The streets in the center near the town hall were flagged with limestone river rock, and played host to many businesses. Several busy restaurants broadcast inviting smells, conversations, and clinking sounds into the street. Khan's stomach growled. A couple of general stores displayed gardening tools, gloves, buckets, and such on the sidewalks. A clothing store had piles of ready-made pants and shirts, all either light brown or blue. A pleasant-smelling leather-goods store offered racks of ready-made boots. And there was even a small, dimly lit and very meagerly stocked book store. All the store windows were paned and mullioned, glazed with panes no more than twenty by thirty centimeters. Most of the panes were ripply bulls-eye glass, blown and spun into a disc, then cut into squares. There was little plate glass, and only in small pieces, which said Advance could not produce or machine large pieces of metal plate or metal rollers.

A few buildings in the center of town were limestone and mortar, or brick and mortar, but raw-cut wood buildings predominated. Some of these were painted white or yellow, but most were weathered wood, though with no signs of rot. A few roofs were slate, but most were split wooden shingles. Some were painted white.

All in all, it was rather more than he expected, and he began to look for signs of technology. Wooden utility poles carried two and three uninsulated wires into some of the buildings near the center of town, but none surrounding. Near one building with ventilation louvers, Khan smelled sulfuric acid, and concluded it housed a large battery for running telegraphs. What he presumed were telegraph wires led off in every direction and disappeared in the distance. Internal to the town, they were probably in good communication with one another.

A clay-pipe aqueduct on masonry piers led into the center of town from the northeast, or upstream direction, and emptied into a raised water tower whose black legs and tank appeared to be cast iron. Excess water flowed from a pipe in the top of the tower into a concrete central distribution pool that fed a system of stone-lined ditches that ran alongside every street. Most of these ditches were open and presented a hazard to the unwary pedestrian, but in places they had been slabbed over. Advance's sewage system, Khan surmised. Almost certainly flowing into the River of Doubt and sending any pathogens downstream to Sunrise Keep.

Concrete was present but rare, so he concluded they probably found the lime manufacturing process difficult in some way, possibly the getting and hauling of the limestone. They probably didn't feel it was worth the trouble to kiln the stone when they could just use it to build with.

Away from the center of the town, housing predominated, nearly all one- or two-story plank-built wooden structures with mild slopes to the roof, probably to make repair easier. The surprise was the number of multi-family dwellings built in the ancient Roman-villa style, around a central courtyard, with each family apparently occupying two or three rooms but sharing common space. Nevertheless, there were a couple of conspicuously luxurious homes of brick or stone, with two stories, eight or ten rooms, a porte-cochere, and picket-fenced yards. Their grass was ragged, as though cut with a scythe, but by comparison with the rest of Advance, they passed for luxury.

Baelmar found work in the first stable they came to, where they also arranged to keep their horses, so they agreed to meet in the evening at Mama Ilse's Pension to decide: share a meager supper from their stores, or use up one of their chits? Certainly, they didn't have any money to dine in restaurants.

Khan set off on his own to find the coal mine and report in for work. Though penniless and hungry, he actually felt pretty good. Everything about Advance looked organized and taken care of. Buildings were well-built and maintained, if impermanent, dirt streets were clean, no rubbish, and citizens were clothed and clean. But there was a sense of grim urgency about everything everybody was doing, from a crew of men building a bridge over a ravine to the teamsters hauling loads of goods through the dirt streets. Nobody smiled, all had a grim set to their mouths, and nowhere were there children playing. Even if most were in school, he assumed some would be too young and would be playing outside.

This question was answered when he passed a nursery school with a play yard full of toddlers to five year-olds, all receiving al fresco alphabet instruction on a blackboard. One of the teachers admonished a busy young lad that play had to wait for work to end, and after they had helped their Mommies and Daddies when they both got home from work.

The grimness question was answered by the equally grim foreman at the coal mine, a sour-looking man in bib overalls of dirty blue linen canvas, with bulls-eye spectacles, a two-day-old shave, and a large hairy mole on the side of his nose.

"No special treatment, Major Khan, no matter who you are. Twenty credits per ton. Exchangeable for gold coins at the central bank if you want, but everybody takes the scrip. Your hours are your own – during your shift. Your face is your own to dig. But if you don't work at least eight hours a day, we'll give your face to somebody else. You lose a good face once, you'll go back to eight hours a day pretty quick. Your pick and shovel will come out of your first week's pay. Any questions? "

"Two."

"Your kind always has them. Shoot."

"Am I limited only to pick and shovel, or can I bring in other tools?"

"Ah, jeez, another engineer. Sure, you can bring in all the power tools you like, Mr. Khan. All you have to do is go back to Earth go get them. What's your other question?"

"Why does everybody in Advance look so grim? I haven't seen a smile since I've been here."

"Life is hard, then you die. What do you want me to say? It really comes down to resources. We got ten thousand people in Advance, and we stay about twenty days ahead on food. Sometimes down to ten. Estelle was a pretty girl when we elected her. Now she's skinny and wrinkled. But it's enough to worry the shit out of anybody. We got our own farms and sheep ranches, but it's not enough. Sometimes crops fail. And when they're good, we can't guard it all until harvest. Maneaters, rabbits, deer and coyotes. Coyotes get two thirds of the lambs. And the poison mold gets most of the dried food. No salt, see. We do trade with the Lords, but they only trade their surplus, which ain't much. So it's always tight."

"Who owns the farms?"

"We all do. They're owned by the city. Farmers are paid a salary."

"Ah."

"'Ah' what?"

"Just 'Ah.' How about the coal mine and the factories?"

"The same."

"Ah."

"Look, Smart Ass. You take your 'Ah' in there and produce half a ton of coal in the next two hours, you'll do a lot more for Advance than with any bright ideas you're harboring. We see your kind all the time." He shook his head. "All the time. Come here and gonna change everything for the better, and end up working their ass of just like the rest of us." He took a pick and a shovel from a rack behind his plain wood work counter and handed them to Khan. "You're face number twenty six. Bring me three full carts out by time the gong goes off."

"You bet," said Khan, and took the tools in the indicated direction – into the dark hole in the rock face, barely lighted by candles. He immediately got a case of chills thinking about coal-dust explosions. He didn't want to know what had happened to the person who had been assigned coal face twenty six before him.

Other diggers, stripped to the waist, sweaty, filthy, largely ignored him as he found his face and started digging. Based on the sundial in the dirty office window, it took him the better part of an hour to fill a wooden cart marked "1/6T when filled level" and roll it out to the smirking foreman. When the gong sounded he had delivered another, but was only halfway through his third. He continued working only to be told by a strapping young man who showed up immediately afterward with his own tools that the face was now his for the next shift, including any partially filled carts. He shrugged his shoulders as if to say "sorry" but said, "Happened to me my first day, too. Don't mind Farley. He'll still pay you for any full ones."

With no reason to think the young man was deceiving him, Khan returned to Farley, who marked his production in a book with a quill pen, and paid him six credits – small paper bills with a bad drawing of Estelle on them and stamped with the legend: "Good for all debts, public and private. Exchangeable for gold at Advance Central Bank."

"That there will pay for your bed for a day, but not for any food. You'll have to get better than this to survive, Mr. Smart Ass."

"Thanks for the tip, Mr. Farley," said Khan, and walked out leaving Farley to wonder how he had learned his name.

The evening was cool and the air good, smelling of jasmine from somewhere, as soon as he blew out his nose and coughed up black dust from his lungs. Clearly this existence was not sustainable. On his way to the river to wash, he gave himself a week to come up with a better plan.

Mama Ilse's was a double-wing barracks with a mess hall in the middle. The men's barracks was on one side of the mess hall, and the women's on the other. Double-decker, rope-sprung bunks with a straw-tick mattress and one linen sheet filled each barracks room with only narrow scurry paths between. Rules posted on the wall forbade double-bunking with anyone of either sex, as well as fighting, eating in bed, and talking after lights out. They also forbade gambling on the premises, in bold capital letters.

When Baelmar and Khan entered the men's barracks to check the place out, several vigorous card games and two dice games were in progress, with stacks and wads of money visible on the floor between men seated cross-legged in circles. The men looked up only briefly, to register that Khan and Baelmar were not a threat.

"Enforcement must be lax," said Khan.

"I have seen this before," said Baelmar. "Maneaters do it all the time. They use bones with numbers instead of cards. The quick eat the slow if they cannot pay." He surveyed the dismal surroundings. "I don't want to live like this, Khan. It is not an improvement." Uncharacteristically, the sunny smile slipped for a moment from his face.

"Agreed," said Khan. "A week. We'll get out of here. Mama Ilse's, at least. But there are people and resources in this town that can't be found outside. I'm beginning to have a few ideas."

Drawn by the smells, they used their chits from Estelle to get into the mess hall. There they ate a cheerless supper whose only advantage over the dried supplies in their saddlebags was warmth. There was a reasonably appetizing selection of foods on the serving line, including stuffed peppers, stuffed eggplant, ratatouille, beets, mashed potatoes, green beans, mounds of a boiled brown grain with a few pieces of onion and vegetable in it, stewed rabbit, fried fish, and mutton. Even fresh apples. They quickly found, however, that not only were all meat and fish dishes ten times the price of the vegetable dishes, they were not permitted on the chits. The only thing their chits proved good for was the brown grain.

"Booley," Baelmar had said, shaking his head in simulated despair when they had finished eating and gone back to the dormitory. "We eat booley only in bad winters when the summer's crops were bad and all the food has run out. We also call it fartley."

"OK," said Khan. "You sleep in the top rack. You've shared your farts before."

They traded grins on this. "I will sleep in another rack where no one has been eating booley. My own farts, I cannot smell. Your farts, even the dead can smell."

And so on. Khan showed Baelmar his six credits earned for coal digging. Baelmar had also been paid a similar amount and showed his bills. "We need a faster way to get money, or we might as well go back out and hunt and fish," said Khan.

A nearby card game ended with multiple groans and one gloating sigh of triumph. The winner saw their money. "Hey Elf," said the man, a smallish but capable-looking fellow who looked to live by his wits. "How about a little game of chance? You too, Digger." He flashed a wad of cash. "My luck is about to turn bad, for sure, and you can be the beneficiaries."

"I don't want to take your money," said Baelmar with a smile. "It is not right to take advantage of the less intelligent."

This produced a round of raucous laughter from the man's victims, and a good-natured, raffish grin from the winner himself.

"I like a man with spirit," said the man. "But from what I've heard of you Elves, you live all by yourselves and probably have never seen a deck of cards."

The losers made room and Baelmar and Khan joined their circle. "What is a deck of cards?" said Baelmar with his winning, naïve smile.

Khan watched with interest as Baelmar began by asking the rules of the game, which the man patiently explained, barely able to keep from salivating. Then Baelmar asked to see all the cards face up one time before the game began. Again the friendly but slick man accommodated him, clearly assuming Baelmar had never seen cards. And then while Khan played cautiously, missing the Universal AI link for not the first time since being exiled, calculating odds in his head, Baelmar smilingly took the man to the cleaners. It was amazing. Either he could do odds in his head or he truly was telepathic. Within an hour, the pile of cash had moved from the man to Baelmar, with Khan having merely tripled his six credits.

The haul was over two thousand credits. A hundred tons of coal. Fifty or more days' digging or working in the stable.

To his credit, the man did not lose his good cheer or accuse Baelmar of cheating. But he did say, "You know, I've heard you Elves are telepathic. I think I've just seen it in action. I'll never play poker with another Elf. Buy my supper for the rest of the week? Otherwise I'll go hungry."

"Of course," said Baelmar.

They thus they acquired a friend and contact – Ernie – who Khan hoped could introduce them to the ways of Advance. And who, of course, showed every evidence of wanting to stay close to Baelmar to get his money back. And Khan learned that Elves – at least one Elf – could do math. "It was only a matter of thought," said Baelmar when quizzed. "If there are only four of each kind out of 52, and two players have each taken eight cards each, though they hold only five, the chances that one will have three of a kind are one in fifty. If you have that hand, the chances that your opponent has better cards are many fewer. So you bet. It is simple thinking."

Khan gave him an assessing, sideways smile. "Remind me never to play poker with you, my friend. You are a wolf in sheep's clothing."

Using Baelmar's new-found wealth, they rented themselves a large room in a multi-family house and began eating in the various cafeteria restaurants around town. Nearly everyone ate in these cafeterias rather than cooking at home because it was more efficient for the entire community, both in terms of fuel use and food waste.

Both he and Baelmar continued working their jobs in order to gradually blend in to the society of Advance. They also began going to public meetings, as well as getting Ernie to give them tours of the town.

From these tours, Khan began to form an overall view of the level of technology and what next steps the town could take. Advance had a coking furnace and a foundry, for example, and could produce both cast iron and cast steel. But it had no rolling mill and no extrusion capability. The people had half a dozen hand-built working steam engines and were working on a steam-powered riverboat. But this would facilitate trade only along the river. Land or air transportation via steam engine remained impractical. They had sulfuric acid and primitive batteries, and could produce hydrogen to float balloons, but had no practical way to drive them against the wind. They had tried compressing hydrogen for use as fuel for a steam engine in the gondola to drive a propeller, but they couldn't haul enough fuel to go far. And the thick tank and the steam engine were too heavy.

But Ernie forestalled any easy condescension. "Lotta people get here, they ask why the hell we haven't advanced more. Got all these engineers. But all knowledge comes in people's heads. No pads, no UAI, no databases, no books. And there's only 10,000 of us. Takes a certain number to raise food, a certain number to protect us, so many to dig coal, so many to make clothes. All that stuff. Not enough people to specialize. Lotta what we make is one of a kind. And then there's those damn satellites. Wanna get killed? Build a generator and start it up. You won't get five meters away. So, not even any old-fashioned electrically fired internal combustion engines. No AC current. Nothing that runs off of it. Nothing that makes EM signals, even weak ones. Telegraph is about it."

Khan got it. Until they could do something about those "damn satellites," probably even after, they were up against a technological ceiling based on several constraints. Mainly, scarce capital, both human and otherwise. And low productivity. It called for a businessman's perspective.

He had never run a business. He was a soldier. But he was a trained engineer and a fourth-generation Khan. He had sat in Khan Venture Capital Board meetings and heard dozens of pitches for allocating capital to projects. There was always a sweaty, wide-eyed dreamer, terrified of the men he was trying to get money from, but eaten up with the wonderfulness of his idea. There was usually the dreamer's partner, who against his better judgment had allowed the dreamer to convince him. And there were the poker-faced Board members, who had seen it all before. They had seen hundreds of sweaty young dreamers come and go, and they would quietly let the men expound and sweat, then quietly make their decision. Could it make money?

And Khan had known even then that the Board members couldn't let the often uncouth entrepreneurs and dreamers know that they were the one percent. They were the layers of the golden eggs. They were the source of the fire that drives all leaps of progress. And he had understood then, too, that the Board members' job was mundane and even sometimes seemingly parasitic, but nevertheless indispensable. It was to bring the ingredients without which ideas alone are worth nothing: judgment and willingness to put money at risk.

Those discussions had been sleep-inducing at the time, but they now came back to mind with a rushing clarity. He was pretty sure there was nothing like a private capital market or any creative banking in Advance. He was pretty sure the town ran close to the edge, on a communal survivor mentality, with all risks mulled over by dozens of people until both risk and reward were minimized.

He was pretty sure he could change that. There were always dreamers. Could he find private capital and match them with it? Could he change the culture? He was pretty sure he could, but realized he might initially have to play both roles – dreamer and capitalist – to get things started up.

With Ernie's help, he made a list of the businesses in Advance to see if his suspicions were confirmed. They were:

Factories	Ownership/ Mgmt	Small Businesses	Ownership/ Mgmt
Coal Mine	Communal	Machine Shop	Communal
Coking Furnace	Communal	Blacksmith's Shop	Communal
Foundry	Communal	Mechanic's Shop	Communal
Glass Plant	Communal	Wagon Builder	Private
Textile Mill	Communal	Bicycle Shop	Private
Clothing Factory	Communal	Harness Maker	Private
Boot Factory	Communal	Brass Foundry	Communal

Grist Mill	Communal	Pottery	Private
Bakery	Communal	Newspaper	Communal
Jerky Factory	Communal	Food markets	Communal
Lumber Mill	Communal	Restaurants	Private
Brick Kiln	Communal	Hostelries	Private
Paper Mill	Communal	Furniture/Cabinet Maker	Private
Brewery	Communal	Clothing/General Stores	Private
Gold Mine	Communal	Medical Clinic	Communal
Copper Mine	Communal	Undertaker	Private

"Communal" almost certainly meant too much time spent in group consensus building. According to Ernie, "town" projects were generated in group settings, and significant resources were committed only by town consensus. – Which almost certainly meant outlier ideas were killed at birth by peer pressure. The sweaty young men and women didn't just have to convince the money men; they had to convince everybody in town. There was no venture-capital function, no dreaming up of ideas by individuals and selling them to private individuals with money to invest. After watching for a few weeks, Khan concluded that everybody was so used to the ECG governance model that no other way occurred to them. He resolved to take it up with Estelle.

Beyond the dead-hand legacy of ECG organization, too deeply ingrained for people to recognize it, there was the huge, fundamental, underlying problem Ernie had put his finger on. The level of technology was limited by the number of people in Advance. There weren't enough people to specialize. They needed friendly contact with other Tech communities. Assuming there *were* other Tech communities, Advance needed faster travel to find and trade with them, and faster communication as well, so they could share specialization.

He remembered the balloon he had seen from the grassland, and he had an idea. He thought it over for a couple of days, and the more he thought about it, the more he was sure it would work. It was feasible with Advance's technology level, and it would transform life for the people of Advance. And it could turn the tracking chip into the get-back-to-Earth tool he intuitively knew it was. But he needed political help to make it happen.

He nailed Estelle at breakfast in the Ralph's Downtown Diner next to city hall where she always ate. She was eating alone, running a hand through her short hair, preoccupied with something.

"May I join you for a couple of minutes?" he asked.

She sighed. "A proposal, Mr. Khan? Most people know to leave me at peace for my breakfast. It's the only peace I get during the day. And most geniuses take at least a month to figure out how to fix it all."

"In that case, how do I get on your calendar? I can help you and Advance, but I need your political support." Then he flashed his best smile. "Or, I'll buy your breakfast and you can listen now."

She sighed again. "Yes, I've heard that you and your Elf friend are flashing money around. Mysterious money, I might add, given the short time you've been here."

"Elves have mysterious powers," he said, playing along.

She gave a grim, one-corner-of-the-mouth smile and wiped her lips with a napkin. "Yes, involving the laws of chance, as I imagine, but we have no actual laws against gambling. Only house rules at Ilse's. Tell me, Mr. Khan. What panacea have you come up with? Bear in mind that we have several hundred engineers in Advance, a couple dozen chemists, a few microbiologists, two metallurgists, and one geologist. I've heard it all. What we've never had is a fix-it-all proposal from a cop."

"—Who sat on the Board of Directors of an international corporation. Because he was going to inherit it all before ECG murdered his father and destroyed it."

She looked him in the eye silently for a moment, long enough for the smirk to leave her face. "I'm sorry. I didn't know about that."

"I'll make them pay, somehow, but that's not what I came to discuss." He showed her his list of businesses. "I'm proposing a small, evolutionary change in how Advance is organized. It's an ancient, simple idea."

"Which is?"

"Private investment. A pilot effort. A trial."

She exhaled in disappointment. "For a minute there, I had my hopes up. The reason everything critical is community-owned is to minimize risk, not because we all grew up loving the ECG way of doing things. We run close to the edge a lot, particularly during dry season."

"There's a dry season?"

She rolled her eyes. "Jesus. You are a Newby. Yes. No axial tilt, so no solar seasons. No winter, no summer. But, there's a moon in elliptical orbit, which we believe causes changes in ocean currents at pericadia – that's its near approach –"

"—Got it," said Khan drily. "Done some celestial navigation –"

"—which causes air-mass changes which cause a dry season. So my point is, we have to make only the best decisions with our resources. We can't afford to gamble."

"And you don't have to, as a city. No need to change your process, except in one small regard: if a private capitalist comes up with an idea and implements it with his own money, not town money or town labor, he keeps ownership, no matter how rich he gets with it, or how central it becomes to the life of Advance."

"Not if his enterprise competes for resources with other, ongoing, Advance-owned enterprises."

"He would buy his resources on your existing open market, like the existing coal or steel markets in town. These things can be bought today by anybody, right?"

Her eyes narrowed. "Yes, though public orders come first. That's the law. Why don't you tell me exactly what your idea is?"

"Legal status for the sale to the public of shares in private ventures. Joint stock companies. Plus a physical private enterprise zone with some official support. I'm going to propose both in the next town meeting, and would like your support."

Her eyes narrowed further. "I understood the private ownership angle. What I mean is, what is your *idea*?" Exactly what are you cooking up?"

"Just think of it as Khan International's new operation on Earth 2.0," he said, using the Tech name in a blatant attempt to ingratiate himself with her.

She shook her head and crimped her mouth sardonically to let him know she knew what he was doing.

"You're nothing like your father," she said, squinting him in the eye. "I met him a few times, though of course he was far above me. But he was straight up. An open book. You, on the other hand, are much more devious." She sat back, put her palms on the table to show the meeting was over, blew out her cheeks, and exhaled. "All right, Mr. Khan. I'll give you a short string. But if you start to screw me, I will jerk it fast. You're on at the next town meeting."

With that she stood, tossed him the bill, and left. He watched her go. Her loose clothes were mannish and unflattering, entirely utilitarian, but she was nevertheless not entirely unattractive if you appreciated intelligence in a woman. But intelligence aside, hadn't she cocked a hip ever so slightly as she walked away?

CHAPTER SEVEN

*"Duty comes first, son. Your duty is to improve the lot of humanity.
When you're done with that, then you can serve your own needs."*
                                        Father Lucian Khan, *Khans to Khans*

Khan stood in the bottom of the grassy amphitheater used for town meetings, looking up at the crowd. Estelle stood a neutral distance away, looking up too, maintaining an impartial silence. The crowd mostly sat cross-legged, with picnic baskets. One young man was on his feet making his objection to Khan's plan.

"What if some capitalist buys up all the resources and starves everybody to death out of sheer meanness?" the young opponent wanted to know. "Or maybe one of the Lords works through a traitor, buys everything up, then forces us to do business with him on his terms? I don't like it! Private property is dangerous! We're doing fine the way we are. We don't want to put ourselves at the mercy of a few who happen to have money! What's in it for us?"

The young man remained standing and looked around at the other citizens as if to challenge them to disagree, tugging on a single tuft of whiskers he cultivated on his lower lip.

Khan looked up from the grassy pit. It could easily accommodate twice the ten thousand citizens of Advance. This evening it held maybe seven hundred. The banishment-for-not-voting law was for general elections. For issue votes, the rule was, a quorum was whoever showed up. If the others didn't care enough to show up, tough. They could live with the results.

It was a bad rule for sure, because apathy dictated that people more generally only show up to vote against something rather than for it, meaning – initiatives were probably tough to launch in Advance. But it was the rule. He would just have to be persuasive. Several citizens were looking thoughtful at what the young man had said. Khan had to wonder what had gotten the young man sent here. He behaved like a neighborhood ECG political operative.

Estelle was essentially an elected dictator, Khan had learned, but when major changes were proposed, she called a town meeting as a matter of course to make sure people were on board. Beloved by the citizens, she mostly ruled by consensus. She often said Advance couldn't afford to have people undercutting initiatives. People had to be on board. She stood in the grassy flat scanning upward into the faces, hands on bony hips, and nodded her head noncommittally, to acknowledge that the young man had spoken.

"Anyone else?" she said.

"Yes," said a woman with a haggard look. She looked like she did physical work from morning until night and did not get enough sleep. "That man," and she pointed at Khan, "is the reason I'm here. We had a nice colony going on Procyon Two, started by a mutinied patrol cruiser crew sixty years ago. I was born and raised there. This man and his goons came in and in two days rounded us all up and shipped us to Earth. Most of us had never even been there. We were imprisoned, treated like criminals, sentenced to deportation by some asshole calling himself a judge who thought he had some right to pass judgment on us, and sent here. This is actually better than Procyon Two in some ways, the soil is better here, but I want everybody to know who that man is: Major Khan of Internal Movement Control."

A series of hoots and cries went through the crowd, and shouts of outrage. Estelle let this go on for a minute or so, then raised her hands for silence, nodding her head as before to acknowledge the woman's input.

"Anybody else?" said Estelle.

An owlish, academic-looking man who looked uncomfortable speaking in public stood, steeled himself, and spoke. "If I understand what Mr. Khan is proposing, it is pure capitalism. Unregulated capitalism of a type not permitted since the Nineteenth Century. I am an economist, sent here because I proposed a growth theory whose corollary was the need for spaceward expansion to provide new resources. I still maintain that even good socialist economies need growth. But in our situation, where even food supply is not certain, with our limited resources, I don't think we can permit any of them to be deployed at the behest of a single individual who happens to have them. Ahem. Thank you."

At this point, all eyes turned to Khan. He had been prepared to be cast as a villain, but had expected at least one or two people to speak in favor of his proposal just because it was new.

"Anyone else?" said Estelle.

There was no one else. She cast him a sidewise sardonic glance as if to say, "Get out of this one, Big Boy." What she did say was, "Mr. Khan is a citizen of—"

"—Wait!" several people shouted. "Someone else wants to talk! It's the Elf!"

Baelmar stood in the middle of the crowd, dwarfing those close to him, looking odd in this gathering in his braid, vest, and buckskin pants.

"I wish to speak," he said. People got quiet for this interesting diversion. Elves never came to live as Techs; Techs went to live as Elves. And Elves were known not to say much.

"This man killed a gryphon with a rock." This blunt opening statement reverberated through the crowd. Baelmar waited while some explained to others what a gryphon was. – And while the question was posed: why was the elf bringing up something like this?

"He saved my wife and children from attack by Mander's men." He paused again to let this sink in. This time there were acknowledging nods.

Baelmar continued in a strong voice that carried throughout the amphitheater. "He swam the River of Doubt. He set me and the people of Mander's Keep free." More nods. "He survived capture by Cuchulain. I was there. He speaks with the Witch of the Leas. I have seen this. He does kill people with alarming ease, but only bad people who are trying to kill him. I have seen this. He carries guilt from his past, it is true, but it is for things he was ordered to do. And it drives him to do good. I have seen this. And he wears good luck like a shirt. I have seen this, too. Nobody escapes from Cuchulain, but he did."

Baelmar paused again. Then he went for his closing argument. "To an

Elf, these things mean, follow this man. He is strong and brave. We can trust him. And I speak as a man of the Leas when I say, he has destiny about him. He is good for Arcadia. We should help him. But I know Techs do not think this way. You make rows of numbers and facts, looking for a way to appear. It is a powerful way to think but it is not complete. It tells only what *not* to do, not what *to* do. Someone must always suggest the way. I am asking you one time to trust your heart. Give this man a chance to help."

With that he sat down. Khan waited through the long silence as people tried to process this. A few japes were quickly quieted by neighbors. He could read in their faces and even overhear a few comments to the effect that, while the speech was not entirely coherent in their way of thinking, its earnestness was undeniable. And he knew that even Techs had their sneaking suspicions about the mysterious powers of the Elves. And a belief that when an Elf told you you could trust somebody, you could take it to the bank. So Baelmar had helped to counterbalance the opposition, but the jury was still out. It was up to him.

Finally Estelle spoke. "Mr. Khan?"

Khan blew out his cheeks and let air escape. He reminded himself that he had expected challenges. But the stakes were high. Those who did not know him or his family would think him arrogant to say so, but he was bringing a unique perspective and a unique opportunity. And he was thinking of the Alien's charge: be the catalyst for the next phases of technological advance. – For humanity, not just for Earth 2.0. It was a moment of truth for him and for extra-solar humanity. Could humans grow and prosper and leave Earth behind, or would they choose mere cautious survival, perhaps to devolve, wither and die?

First he took three minutes and told his story. Briefly, and without emotion, until he got to his father's murder and his exile. He paused for a moment to unchoke. Then he told them he didn't expect them to understand the amoral political calculus of his deal with his father: that he play the role of loyal and well-connected ECG operative to give cover to his father and Khan International operations. But he told them about it anyway, and about Khan International's mission: to release freedom technology to humanity to free them from the commissariat in his lifetime. Ultimately to free them from Earth.

He saw a few hostile looks as he explained the rationale for his ECG service, but also quite a few thoughtful nods. That was enough encouragement to move into the vision.

"According to what I've been told, you have twelve laser satellites in Arcadio-stationary orbit around this planet, tasked with taking out the source of any EM signature. They communicate with each other, and also send regular tachyon transmissions back to Earth."

"We know, Asshole!" said someone.

"But ECG never actually comes here to look. Even when they beam Newbies down into the wilderness, they don't land and look. I heard this before I came, and I've heard it here, too. They don't survey the planet except from orbit. They haven't for three hundred years. They may not know whether we're all alive or dead. So. That leaves us every technology up to Tesla and Marconi." He stopped to see what the reaction would be. The crowd got quiet. They had heard the 'us' and the 'Tesla.' Most of these people were educated and knew some history. The exceptions were the few who had been actual criminals – thieves, murderers, and such – and he was guessing most of those had become foot soldiers for the Lords and were not in the crowd.

"The Romans did quite well for a thousand years with only water and wind power," he continued. "Also slave power, but we can rule that out. And the Brits ruled most of their world for three centuries with the same, plus finally steam in the last two thirds of the Nineteenth Century, before alternating current and radio changed everything." The crowd got quieter still. He read their faces. Attention, but some wrinkled foreheads. "Steam helped a lot. Development happened fast after steam, but it hasn't happened here. Why not? I'm told we've had at least one steam engine here for fifty years. Where's the leverage? Why hasn't it gotten us anywhere?"

Two or three people nodded and said, "Yeah."

"Part of it is, we don't have enough people here to specialize so we can reach tech-development critical mass. And we can't do much about that until we develop trade with other Tech towns worldwide – which we have no way of getting to. If they exist." Khan realized only at the end of this sentence that he had said "we." Good. It felt right.

"Hear, hear!" said the owlish looking economist who had spoken before.

"And another part of it is, we're not getting the best fruits of everyone's creativity." He paused to see if there was any reaction to this. Only more attentiveness.

"And the reason for that is, all capital decisions – decisions to commit resources -- are made first by committee consensus, then by total citizen consensus. Nothing wrong with that for reducing risk. Risk-taking is minimized to the lowest possible level. But since payback is correlated to risk, we are sub-optimizing our development decisions. We're never betting on the big-payback, long-shot idea because it's suppressed at the start. Our river-boat and rolling-mill projects are good, medium-leverage projects, but we need more, faster. Those projects are the straight-line development slope. We need the exponential curve."

The crowd remained quiet, some looking seriously doubtful. The economist, on his own turf, looked as though he were about to pounce. He was just waiting for the right opening. The fellow with the lip tuft was also waiting another chance.

"So, what change am I proposing?" He let the question ring in the silence for ten seconds. "No change whatever to processes." He let that simmer for a moment. "But the addition of two things: legal sanction for private stock companies, and for a town-affiliated development zone outside Advance. Property there would be privately owned."

"Hoo, hoo," yelled the young man with the lip tuft. "I knew it!"

Khan let the silence reassert itself. "There's nothing today to stop private stock companies except uncertainty about what would happen if the Town Council decided to expropriate their ideas and property. This would protect them. And encourage private investment in high-payback ventures the town would never take up."

"Just like I said!" shouted the young man.

Khan continued. "Developers in the proposed Zone would pay Advance a nominal sum per hectare, to be set by the city council, even though Advance does not now own or control that property. Both agricultural and industrial developers would receive transferable, unrevokable title to their property, recorded in City Hall. They would own it. Industrial developers would also receive water and police services in return for an annual fee, to be adjusted based on usage. Businesses developed there would be entirely developed with private capital, and their profits would remain with the owners and their shareholders, less Advance's normal income tax."

He stopped to gauge reaction. He could tell they didn't see it yet, but that was OK.

"That's it?" said a young man who hadn't spoken yet, whose two children sat beside him. "Leave Advance alone? Growth outside Advance based on private ownership? I don't get it. What's the downside? We get tax money from people who want to go do that, and we have to provide water and guard coverage to new factories. Looks to me like we come out ahead."

"There's a catch," said Khan, knowing that using the expression first would disarm critics.

"There always is!" shouted the young man who opposed private property. Estelle herself crossed her arms in his peripheral vision. Baelmar looked slightly doubtful. Ernie, sentenced to Prison Planet as an incorrigible con operator, gave a shit-eating grin. Khan suppressed a smile. Ernie had once run down for him the phases of a con, and was probably interpreting this pitch as the Hook, and his "catch" comment as a modified version of the Stall. He would now be waiting for the modified version of Telling the Tale and the Setting of the Hook.

This was no con, but Khan did not disappoint. "The catch is, such businesses will want to hire people. To get good people, they may compete with high wages and create some brain drain. The upside is, private businesses might develop key new technology faster than businesses funded by Advance City Council."

Estelle stirred uncomfortably but said nothing.

"That's my proposal," said Khan. "I'll appreciate your support." He decided against saying, "And if you vote it in, I may want to hire you." Of course he wasn't telling the whole story. Of course he already had plans he wasn't going to share in this forum. But if his gambles paid off, the plans would quickly ease some of the resource risk in Advance.

Estelle moderated the resulting discussion for the regulation fifteen minutes. And did she carefully select the people she called on to speak? Khan was surprised. He had half expected her to torpedo him using the townspeople as the weapon. But in fact, unless he had been more persuasive than a proponent normally can be in the face of a group – groups being naturally inertial to change – she was picking people to speak she knew would speak in favor. Of course, she picked the young private-property opponent first, giving him just long enough to go too far, and lapse into emotional argument, non-sequiturs and ad-hominems. The economist as well got his turn, and voiced the concern that private-capital demand for goods and services would drive up commodity prices, but surprised Khan by adding that competition in the ideas realm might have an invigorating effect. Finally, she picked several people who replayed a common theme: 'Khan may be an asshole, but he was an effective asshole. Now he's our asshole. He's got to have learned some business at his Daddy's knee. Let's give him a shot.' Then the economist raised what he surely saw as his voice of reason and said, "Let's not do anything permanent. Let's give it one year and take another vote. One full wet and dry cycle. Then we'll see if our lives are better."

The measure passed with this codicil. And not only was Khan pleased the measure passed, he was pleased at the sense of connectedness he felt. These people accepted him and his idea voluntarily. They weren't after his wealth – he no longer had any – and they didn't fear him. They just gave him a shot because he was one of them and might be able to help. The slaves at Mander's keep had warmed him with gratitude, and his IMC team had been fiercely loyal, but in neither case was he one of them. Here he was. It threatened to thaw his normally cool demeanor, and he solemnly resolved to do his damnedest to improve these people's lives. And of course to use this opportunity to leverage the tracking chip – to make it his ticket back to Earth, revenge, and power. – Power to help humanity as a whole, not just the people of Advance.

As he walked away struggling to deny the lump in his throat, Estelle winked.

Still living meagerly on coal-digging wages, Khan visited all the people rumored or known to have money, one by one. His pitch was simple: he proposed projects he had generated himself, and money men or women were either interested or not. In either case, before the presentation, he swore them to secrecy so enemies of the projects would remain disarmed as long as possible. Payback would come from profits in proportion to investment. He would be general manager and get ten percent of profits.

Baelmar was the first investor. His stable wages were more than enough for his modest lifestyle, but he had preserved his gambling windfall, so he had money.

"But I like feeling rich, Khan. I know it is bad for my soul. But I will offer only half of my money: one thousand credits."

"And I am happy to get it, Baelmar. I promise, you will not be sorry. I will make it grow."

And Dr. Greis: "Take what you want, Major. It's really Mander's gold, and we have no need of it. We buy everything we need from Advance or the Hundred with our lumber and beets. How does twenty thousand credits sound? It's the least we can do. The Council has already approved it."

Salvatore Ruggiero, visiting the Keep when Khan was there, pledged gold worth twelve thousand credits, saying it was a sure bet, and the first time someone had tried something really progressive. He also mentioned that his daughter was single and needed a husband, and Khan was barely able to escape the conversation with both the money and his freedom.

A week later, Sam Herman, owner of Advance's wagon-building operation, as well as one of the finest "mansions" in Advance, pledged seven thousand credits. Khan decided he had enough to start.

Next, he paid for five hectares just outside Advance on the unused plateau above the town and established this as the Development Zone. He chose this location because it was adjacent to the incoming aqueduct, and unused arable land lay close by. There on the five acres he put up, with hired help, a small frame building to serve as an office and workshop. Finally, he proudly mounted a sign over the porch saying "KHAN INTERNATIONAL – EARTH 2.0 DIVISION."

Then he hired three of the town's two dozen chemists, swore them to secrecy, and showed them to a pile of coal he had dug himself, paid for, and delivered to Khan International himself using a rented wagon and team.

"Food-grade rubber, rubber seal coating for canvas, and coal oil," he said, pointing to the coal, "and manufacturing processes to reliably and cheaply produce them. Oh, and whoever does coal oil, also do lubricating oil. A salary bonus of fifty percent to whoever can do his in two months or less. I can flip a coin, or you can decide which of you is responsible for which project, but it's one each. Now tell me what you need."

Two were flabbergasted, but one, a quick-eyed, cheerful young redhead named Maggie, simply said, "You buying us all the equipment we need?"

He liked her style. "Of course. But only if it relates."

"Of course," she said, giving a sidewise, faux devious smile. "We'll give you a list in an hour."

"Good," he said. "Here's an account number at the bank with expense money for this project. When it's gone, it's gone. Buy what you need, give me weekly reports, but we need success before the money is gone. Maggie, you're in charge."

Next he paid a visit to the glass plant with a simple, isometric drawing he had made himself. He explained the volume of business he anticipated, then got the man to sign a confidentiality agreement before he would show him the drawing.

"A glass jar with a glass lid and a wire bail to hold it on, but with a two-millimeter clearance?" said the manager, scratching his head. "Looks like a food preservation jar. What good will that do you without a way to seal it?"

"None," said Khan. "When can I see a prototype?"

"You know, we've tried food preservation in jars before. Don't have the progressive-die technology to make or use steel cans. Problem with the glass jars was, no good way to seal them. Used coal tar. Cracked. Some people died. Botulism, or something like it. Council decided it wasn't worth it. Went back to dried food for the dry season, even with the fungus problems."

"When can I see a prototype?"

"Well, it will take awhile to create the mold, and cost some money, too. The pattern shop isn't terribly busy, but I've got the pattern guys working on setting up the rolling operation. So, I'd say, right after we get a flat steel bed and a good roller from the machine shop. That's a town job, so it comes first. So far, quality has been terrible. Lotta rework."

"How much money?"

The man gave an ill-concealed smirk and named an outrageous figure.

"And then Khan International owns the mold, right?"

"Well, we've never done that before. We're owned by the city and we own all the tooling."

"But you've never had the opportunity to charge anyone the outrageous price you just gave me, right?"

The man failed to hide a greedy smile. "Well, no."

"So we'll own the tooling. No problem on the price. Two weeks on the prototype. Here's a down payment."

The paper money disappeared into the man's shirt pocket, and Khan left, feeling that he had things well on the road. However, bigger challenges lay ahead.

He also hired Ahmed, an engineer who had specialized in fluid dynamics, and gave him a written description, including a sketch, of what he had in mind.

A small, neat, proper young man, who gave the impression that even his sock drawer was in perfect order, Ahmed looked at the sketch for several minutes, going over each part in detail. Finally, he put it down and said, "This technology is four hundred years old! I read about it at university but nobody studies it any more. Where are you going to get the fuel, and how many BTUs per liter will it have? More to the point, what will its specific density be? Its viscosity?"

"Coal oil," said Khan. "Whatever Maggie can produce. Assume wide ranges and design for it. I want roughed-out design specs for the key components in two weeks. Use the existing steam engine design as much as you can so we can use existing components. But I want something pretty small – no more than twenty horsepower. And of course, it has to have a manual start. With a pull rope."

The man blew out his cheeks, looked at Khan as if so say, "You're crazy, but you're paying well," and went to work in the now-crowded offices of Khan International.

Three weeks later, looking dubiously at Ahmed's prints, the manager of the town-owned machine shop demanded a piratical sum for the fifteen pieces of a component Khan wanted, and he asked a lot of questions about the objective. "It looks like a hydrocarbon fuel injector," he said accusingly.

"It is."

"So why do you want a fuel injector? You're not going to be able to use it anywhere on this planet. Those micro-holes alone are going to force me to create new tooling. And the plunger clearances are outrageously tight. This is Earth 2.0, Mr. Khan, not 1.0. We don't have computer controls here."

"Just call me crazy," said Khan, then worked an angle he had seen his father use. "Are you saying this is beyond your shop's capabilities?"

This aspersion had the desired effect, and the man agreed to produce three of the injectors within three weeks, for a hefty price that Khan believed included some screw-you-ism as well as cost plus exorbitant profit.

"Save the process documentation," said Khan, and left.

Finally, he hired Bella, his fifth engineer employee, a halo-haired, big-boned woman nearly as tall as he was. He told her the nature of what he wanted built, and listened to the young woman, an aerospace engineer, say, "Hoe-lee shee-ut. They're going to call it Khan's Folly."

He grinned. "Fine with me," he said. "Just as long as the project flies. Hire the workers you need. I'm available for free, by the way. As long as it's not during coal-digging hours, that is."

Within two months of hiring his first people, several things happened that began to cause a lot of buzz around Advance. Khan could not go into town without being the butt of jokes or the target of job-seeking engineers.

First and most visibly, a dirigible frame began taking shape in the back lot of Khan International. Because aluminum was not available, the lightest possible hammer-forged steel rods became the ridge pole and the keel. These tied together frame elements made of laminated wood, glued together with a tree-sap-based glue of Bella's devising. "I hope this crap sticks together in the humidity," she said. "It would really suck for it to dissolve at a thousand meters."

Khan noted with satisfaction that coming out to the Development

Zone to see what was going on and to offer observations became a favorite after-work pastime for the citizens of Advance. Since there was little to see except the raw-lumber office building, really more of a shack, two three-hectare farms started by single young men who camped armed in the center of their fields to protect their crops, and the dirigible, people mostly focused on the dirigible, though they didn't know what it was. Khan could hear their commentary through the open office window.

"It looks like a gigantic snake skeleton," opined one citizen. "Except this snake has a spine on both top and bottom."

"I'd say it's more likely some kind of prototype fast housing," said another. "Probably going to cover it with canvas, like a tent."

"Nah," said a third. "It's a prototype greenhouse. I heard Khan hired some chemists, and they're working on some kind of plastic made out of coal. Remember plastic? Put clear plastic over that frame, and you'd have a greenhouse."

"No," said a bright-sounding little girl. "It's like the balloons. They're going to put hy'gen in it, and it's going to fly."

This brought general laughter. "They'll have to figure out a way to keep the hydrogen from escaping," said a man indulgently, presumably her father, nevertheless proud that his daughter had come up with this idea. "And even if they did that, the only reason they would put a frame like that inside the balloon is if they had a plan to drive it through the air. We've already proven that steam engines are too weak if small enough to lift, and too heavy if powerful enough to move them, their fuel, and the balloon. It's a greenhouse."

After a few weeks, a new development at the Dev Zone drew attention away from the slowly forming dirigible. Estelle caught him in Ralph's Downtown Diner as he ate lunch.

"OK, Mr. Secret. Give. I hear a new building on the Dev Zone has piped-in water, and that the foundry delivered five top-of-the line cast-iron cook stoves. You starting a restaurant?"

"No profit in it," he said unhelpfully, taking a bite of stuffed pepper, looking at her under his eyebrow. "Too far away from town."

"Uh huh. I also heard that the foundry delivered twenty or so cast-iron vessels with pressure-relief valves, and that coal and large quantities of fresh vegetables have been delivered. And hundreds of glass jars. And you've hired two dozen people. What would you know about that?"

He focused on his food. "Hmm. I'll have to check. I'm not personally managing that project. One of the project managers may be out of control."

"Uh huh. You know we tried pressure canning several times and it failed. No way to seal."

"Uh huh."

Estelle scraped her chair back. "Khan, if you've solved the sealing problem after all these years, I'm gonna kick your ass." She gave a frosty smile and left. This time, there was no doubt about the cocked hip.

A week later, Khan went down to one of his customer grocery stores to examine the new display. Here were jars of beans, okra, peas, beets, tomatoes, corn, indeed, all local vegetables. Customers milled around him in general disbelief, looking at the colorful paper labels saying, "Khan International – jar returnable for five cents. Do not use if jar does not suck air when opened. Use within two years."

"A cannery!" said one woman. "Using rubber seals! I haven't seen rubber since I was transported twenty years ago! Two years? How do we know it's safe, Mr. Khan?"

For answer he pulled the bail down from the top of a jar of beans, then said "Listen." He slid his knife under the glass lid and pried. A clear hissing sound came out, followed by a pop. "That's the vacuum. If there had been bacterial growth, pressure would have blown the lid off after I pulled down the bail." He reached in, took a bean, and ate it. "Want one?"

While he watched, the entire display sold out.

Ernie took to calling him "Botulism Khan" for two weeks, but it didn't happen. Sales grew so strong that Estelle sent word that it was hard to buy fresh vegetables in the marketplace, and she might have to intervene. However, the teamsters and boatmen that plied the routes between Advance and the Hundred, as well as Advance and the Keep, saw their opportunity and filled in the gap with imports. And at the same time, entrepreneur farmers in the Development Zone came on stream with small quantities of vegetables.

So, prices did rise, but only temporarily. And by all accounts that came to Khan, nearly everyone in town enthusiastically laid in canned goods for the dry season. The general dry-season anxiety level subsided. He noted himself that smiles appeared on faces in Advance. And for a few weeks, he could not pay for a drink or a meal in town. Somebody would slap him on the back and pay for him. More importantly, the doubters and naysayers about Khan International were now a minority.

Profits from the cannery quickly made Khan a hit with his investors, so he quit digging coal to work the business – and the Plan – full-time. He couldn't help indulging in some quiet pride, and wishing boy-like that his father could see what he had done. And Grandfather Quintus, and Great Grandfather Culpepper. Of course, if all worked out, he would do even bigger things.

"I don't care what you've managed to pull off," said Farley sourly as Khan surrendered his face at the mine. "You're still just another smart-ass engineer in my book. They higher they go, the farther they fall. I've seen it all before."

Khan smiled. "Thank you for the work, Mr. Farley. I'll miss you, too. If you ever need anything, just let me know. And keep that coal coming."

Then there was a setback: Ahmed reported failure at assembling the small, simple diesel engine from the custom parts finally delivered from the machine shops. "I am not a mechanical engineer!" he protested. "These parts do not fit properly together! In most cases it is because the machining is poor and tolerances have been exceeded, but I must confess to you that in some cases my tolerances were miscalculated. Without the UAI I made mistakes! The pistons will hit the head! I throw myself on your mercy." He hung his head as if expecting it to be lopped off.

"No mercy," said Khan grimly. "Back to the drawing board and get it right. At this point, you are this world's leading expert on diesel engines." He looked at Ahmed under a raised eyebrow. "Since the rods and the crank are forged – at great expense I might add – and the head is merely sand-cast and machined, I assume you will rework or redesign the head. Mill some out and fix it."

Ahmed bobbed his head back and forth gratefully and said, "I will start immediately, today itself only," and went back to work, even though it was quitting time.

Maggie on the other hand had successfully developed a process to produce oils of various viscosities from coal. She had as well hired a metal fabricator to assemble the various tanks and tubes the process required. Since Advance's rolling mill, which would produce sheet steel up to two and a half meters wide, was still not in production, this was expensive, as the existing sheet-steel capability at the smithy was half a meter. Much drilling and riveting and sealing was required. But the small oil-production operation, which used coal for fuel as well as a raw material, was up and running. Fuel was being stored in standard-size steel containers. The surplus was being offered in the town market, and had quickly found demand.

She had also developed an adhesive material that would seal canvas.

"Basically, it's coal tar, though a light tar," she said. "Waste product from the coking plant. Dark brown, not elegant, highly flammable, but it should keep the gas from seeping through. Left some outside for Bella in a keg. And if I talk sweetly with the guys at the coking plant, we can get them to start capturing the coal gas during their next few burns. Right now it's just a waste product. We can use it instead of hydrogen to fill the envelope. The diesel-fuel process creates methane as a by-product, but it has less lift than hydrogen or coal gas. And getting enough coal gas'll be a lot faster than the electrolysis required for hydrogen." And here she flashed a smile. "But the coking guys do want some investment in equipment."

"Do it," said Khan.

"Fucking fantastic," sneered Bella, listening in. "Flammable canvas dope. Fucking great. Well, at least that and the explosive gas together should make for a short pucker period if we take a lightning strike at a thousand meters. That's if the bleeding frame elements don't delaminate in the humidity first and collapse like a bad excuse." But then she went outside and went happily to work doping the canvas that now covered the huge eighty-meter-long dirigible. By now comprehending what it was, and impressed by its size, people had dubbed it "Bella's Ark."

Ultimately after a few more weeks it all came together. Bella and Ahmed nervously took Khan out for an inspection, though of course he had watched it develop all along.

The airship floated above the Dev Zone plateau tethered to several large trees. A 15-meter-long open gondola, more of a flat freight sled with railings, hung suspended beneath the gigantic envelope. A directable propeller assembly protruded from each side, capable of driving the craft forward, or thirty degrees upward, downward, to left or to right. At least in Bella's theory. The goal, as she explained, was never to have to use the envelope's release valves to release gas for altitude control, though if this was necessary, two pressure containers of coal gas were on board to permit replenishment.

Ahmed's two-cylinder air-cooled diesel engine started and ran perfectly when Khan gave the rope a test pull, as he knew it would. Ahmed had been so delighted at its first successful test that he had sat and watched it run for several hours, transfixed. Khan had watched him out the window and been reminded of Thomas Edison staying up all night watching his light bulb. And he was again filled with quiet pride, both for Ahmed and himself for dreaming all this up.

"Looks like we're ready," said Khan. "I'd say well done, but first we have to test it and survive. Tomorrow."

Bella's plan for a test run was to take a load of canned goods, clothing, and boots to Sunrise Keep, and to return with a load of raw-cut lumber. She had arranged this with the haulers who would have done this with boats, promising to give them the haulage fees to keep them sweet. The load was on and ready to go. The craft was fueled up. And she had pre-arranged for a group of men to be available at the intended landing area to catch and tie the tether ropes. All was in readiness. Khan looked out the office window and saw her pacing around looking nervous, checking and re-checking everything. The planned departure time wasn't for an hour yet, but he went out to see her. She fixed him with a gimlet-eyed stare. "You gonna go along, Asshole, or are you chickenshit?"

Ernie had told Khan that the odds in Advance betting circles were three to one that the ship would crash, and two to one that somebody would be killed. Estelle had told him in no uncertain terms not to go.

"You've proven yourself too valuable to Advance, Khan. We can't spare you. Everybody's waiting to see what you come up with next. When you came to town in that stinky animal skin I wouldn't have believed it, but we're now all believers. – Except in that gigantic floating death trap. Don't go." His response had been noncommittal.

Khan had discovered that the reason Bella was so profane was that she was actually a softy inside, insecure, fearful of others' judgments, and she used the profanity as a pre-emptive strike, a shield of bravado. But he also knew you couldn't overtly try to get inside that shield.

"If you've got the balls to go up in it, Bella, how could I do less? I wouldn't be able to show my face in Advance. Let's do this thing."

She hid a smile. "Fine, but I'm the captain. You have to do what I say or you'll end up killing me."

He saluted. "Aye, aye, Captain."

CHAPTER EIGHT

"Nobody knows you're scared, kid, unless you run your mouth, piss your pants, or turn tail. Avoid those, keep moving, and everybody thinks you're a hero. There's no difference between having courage and faking courage."

Great Grandfather Culpepper Conn, *Khans to Khans*

For someone who had spent a career sailing the galactic arm in all kinds of piloting situations, Khan found himself unsettlingly alarmed as the craft lifted off. The lift was far too great. As the mooring lines tore away, tether tenders on the ground who had untied and unwrapped the ropes, including Baelmar and Estelle, held their arms up in surprise, as if to implore the blessings of a higher power. Estelle in particular looked grimly terrified as she and the ground receded at great speed.

He quickly grew far more alarmed, even though he was firmly strapped into a seat bolted to the deck. The dirigible gained altitude so fast that the inner pressure in his ears grew painful, increasing faster than he could swallow and clear it. People on the ground quickly shrank to the size of bugs. More disturbingly, the back of the craft rode twenty degrees higher than the front, making it a very good thing indeed that all the freight was thoroughly lashed to the deck. And the propellers were apparently stuck in the lift position, accelerating the dirigible's ascent. The craft was out of control.

Still, he couldn't afford to show fear. Even though Bella was the acknowledged captain of their two-person crew, he remained the manager of this project, the dreamer-up of this idea, the leader of this undertaking, and the very personification of Khan International. He reminded himself again, as he had in a hundred previous danger situations, showing courage as a leader costs only effort. If you die, you are out only the effort, and you will have died showing courage. If you live, you will get through the danger having shown courage. The price of showing fear is high: loss of respect. If you are a leader, the price is loss of control. It is better to show courage.

He sneaked a glance to see how Bella was handling this. She was fighting the control arm, a long rod that crossed the deck and connected to each propeller assembly. A one-meter crank-style offset in the middle gave the pilot leverage and a gripping point. Each propeller assembly hung on gimbals so it could be directed up, down, to the left, or to the right. An arrangement of thin drive shafts and universal joints connected each assembly to a gearbox driven by the diesel. The pilot could push down on the hoop in front of her to tilt the propellers down, or pull up to tilt them up. Similarly, she could pull left to turn the propellers to the left, and vice-versa. Theoretically.

Straining hard, Bella renewed her efforts to rotate the control arm forward but failed. She saw him look. "Don't be shining those big moon eyes at me, asshole," she yelled over the engine. "Get your ass out of that chair and help me with this control arm. Otherwise, this fucking thing is going to put us into orbit."

He didn't react except to unbuckle his belt. "Miscalculation on the amount of lift?" he was able to manage. They now appeared to be near 1000 meters, and he could not detect any slowing in their ascent. He fastened a safety line to the control arm itself and sidled over toward her, trying not to slip toward the nose.

"That, and it looks like I forgot about the gyroscope effect of those buggering propellers. They're damn near impossible to turn, and I'm afraid the control-arm connections to the gimbals may not be strong enough." She gave him a grim smile. "Guess we'll find out, if you're man enough, along with me, to turn the arm."

"Well, since you call my manhood into question, I guess I'll have to show you how it's done," he said, giving a raffish smile he didn't at all feel. He laid to with a will, quickly breaking into a sweat, catching a whiff of her fear sweat as he struggled along with her. At first he didn't think they could do it, thinking he didn't weigh enough to put the required downward pressure on. But then he said, "Excuse me," and stuck one arm through Bella's seat belt alongside her leg so he would have leverage. He heard her say, "You're getting mighty fresh" just as he exerted a mighty pull on the rod, and it moved downward. Once moved, it didn't try to go back; it simply required a large amount of leverage to overcome the gyroscopic inertia of the propellers.

"We have to turn around and go back, so we can get help tethering," he yelled. "They're probably still there watching."

She nodded grimly and they muscled into a descending left turn.

After several tense minutes, they spotted Advance, the Dev Zone, and the crowd, and managed to set themselves up in a descending spiral. But the propellers were now canted forward at nearly a thirty- degree angle to overcome the lift, and they were going down fast. It looked to be a chancy business to control both the lift and forward motion well enough to keep from flying into the ground on the one hand, or pulling tetherers off the ground on the other.

"How about we let out some gas?" he said. "We could kill somebody fighting all this lift." He flashed a smile. "Maybe ourselves."

For the first time since he had known her, she lost her bravado. Her shoulders slumped forward and she looked defeated. "Yeah, maybe so, Boss. Hard to know how much. Give it maybe a minute."

The overhead valve was fitted with a hand-cranked impeller, since the pressure in the envelope was barely above atmospheric pressure, and it was recognized ahead of time that they might have to dump gas. In recognition of fire and suffocation danger, the gas was vented through a blowpipe extending two meters overboard. As soon as he opened the valve he could hear escaping gas, so he didn't crank, but counted to sixty nevertheless and shut the valve.

"We filled it at night," she said, pointing to the blowpipe. "That's why it's under pressure. The sun's warmed it up. Jeez. Physics 101."

"Yes," he said. "But the lift would remain the same because the volume is constant. We're going to need to determine the exact neutral buoyancy point for a given load of gas before each takeoff, and carry enough weight to maintain it. It's going to make freight hauling complicated. We'll have to haul either freight or ballast on the outbound trip when we're going out to do a pick-up."

"Yes," she said calmly, "and we're going to need to turn this wanking control arm up soon, or we're going to die."

Khan looked down to see the ground approaching at alarming speed, and their would-be tetherers running for their lives. He leapt to the control arm and pulled up with all his might, this being an easier strain, and the propellers turned up. The gigantic dirigible slowed its descent, and the nose bumped down gently into a squash patch and ripped out several rows of plants, digging a furrow as it went, since the engine and props were still running.

"Tie us off!" he bellowed, and people on the ground swarmed to snatch the tethers, which he and Bella had not had a chance to reel up and were being dragged through the squash patch. In a matter of seconds, they were secured to large trees, and the craft began to rise as it pulled on its lines. "Shut down the engine, Captain?" he bellowed over the sound of the engine and propellers, which were louder here near the ground.

"Crew, shut down the engine!"

He grinned and snapped a salute. "Aye aye, Captain!"

Shutting down the engine was accomplished by turning off the fuel valve. The engine coughed and died, and the propellers stopped. The dirigible's tail settled a couple of meters toward the ground, but stopped while the ship was still canted toward the bow, with the tail still well in the air.

He and Bella looked at each other solemnly, then burst into laughter. Both were soaked with sweat. "You didn't fool me, Khan. You were scared shitless."

Not normally given to japery, he indulged in this moment of high relief. "I'll not be submitting my drawers for inspection, but I'm sure some would say I'm just as full of shit as I ever was. You, on the other hand, have clearly been faking your resume as an aeronautical engineer." Her face clouded slightly. "Build a dirigible on a primitive planet from primitive materials and only take it to fifteen hundred meters on its maiden flight, then bring it back for a less than perfect but still safe landing. I'm sure someone else could have done better." Now her face truly clouded up "I just don't know who it would have been. In this galaxy arm, anyway."

She gave a bright smile. "Maybe move the gondola back a meter or two," she said.

"Put a clutch in the drive train so we can disengage the engine from the propellers if necessary, while leaving it running," he said. "It'll make it easier to start, too."

"Redesign the control system to multiply the pilot's leverage," she said.

"Carry more pressurized containers of gas to replenish the envelope if needed."

"Calculate the lift capacity of various loads of gas in the envelope. We didn't really even measure it this time. Just pumped in till it floated with a load, then some for good measure."

"Find the center of gravity and mount a tethering reel there with a grappling hook on it. We can't always depend on having ground crews."

"Hey!" called someone from the ground. "You guys all right?" They were invisible from the ground, being roughly seven meters above it.

"So, can you do all that in a week so we can take our maiden voyage next week? This, after all, was only the test flight."

She gave a brilliant smile. "Give it our damnedest, Mr. Honcho. Mr. Khan International – Earth 2.0 Division."

On the ground, they were greeted by a crowd of people headed by Estelle, including all Khan International employees, fifteen or twenty townspeople, Ernie, and Baelmar. The armpits of Estelle's shirt were soaked with sweat, and her look of relief was a thin veneer over the fright. For once she forgot she was a leader speaking in front of people.

"You dumbass!" she hissed, stepping quite close to Khan and talking low, directly into his face. "Dumbasses," she amended, stepping back, taking in that Bella was listening and paying close attention to her body language toward Khan. "Think what would have happened to the spirit of invention and enterprise around here if you … two had become grease spots on the Dev Zone!"

"Um hmm," said Bella, regarding Estelle with raised eyebrows, then Khan, as if she were realizing something for the first time.

"People recognize there's risk associated with big payback," said Khan.

"Jesus, men are clueless," muttered Bella.

Khan went on. "And after all, nobody got hurt. Our controls need some work, but this was really just a test run."

Hands on hips, Estelle shook her head in disbelief. "Tell me, Mr. Khan," the "Mr." being for public consumption, "that you – you two, that is – are not going back up in that thing."

He smiled. "Not for another week. Got some small adjustments to make. Then we'll make the Sunrise Keep run." He wasn't sure what had gotten into him, but he had to overcome a sudden impulse to lean forward and kiss her on the forehead.

The normally unflappable Estelle rolled her eyes, wagged her head, flipped a hand in the air helplessly, and left in a huff. Khan watched her storm down the slope, struggling with vague feelings he had never had before. At least not since he had been about fifteen or so.

"Unh hunh," said Bella quietly, with an "I knew it all along" tone. "Mmm, mm."

Khan ignored her. "Ernie! How much money did you make?"

"Lost my ass, Boss. I was sure you were gonna crash. No offense."

"Let that be a lesson. Never bet against a sure thing. Baelmar! Want to go on the next flight?"

Baelmar blanched at the suggestion and swallowed hard, but rallied. "Of course. I do not mean to offend, but I think I could control the thing better than you two did. In fact, I think almost anyone could have." He smiled a big smile.

"That's the spirit. Techs will be embarrassed not to go if an Elf goes without fear."

Within ten days Bella had made the necessary changes and gave Khan a tour. To improve leverage, each propeller assembly now had a 500-centimeter-long vertical bar bolted to its side, with an eyebolt in each end for ropes. Three meters behind each propeller assembly a new steel frame with pulleys provided leverage points for these up-down control bars. The steel rod still ran across the deck connecting the propeller assemblies, but now it connected to a second bar projecting from the rear of each propeller assembly. And now there was a new pulley and crank arrangement on a pedestal in front of the pilot's seat connected by ropes and pulleys to the new leverage bars on the propeller assemblies. A hand crank protruded from each side of the pedestal. To direct the propellers downward, the pilot rotated the cranks forward. To direct the propellers upward, she rotated the cranks backward. To turn to the left or right, she rotated the pedestal left or right using the handles on the cranks for leverage. Bella sat in the captain's chair and proudly demonstrated to Khan. All worked smoothly. But of course, the engine wasn't running.

"What happens if the pulley ropes break?" asked Khan. "Those were some terrific forces."

"Don't give me that Failure Mode and Effects Analysis crap," said Bella. "I invented that shit. I, after all, am a certified engineer, not a fucking dilettante billionaire playboy cop make-believe capitalist." She gave a mean, toothy grin.

Khan had grown used to Bella's profanity and insults by now, so he always tried to respond in kind, though he was not good at it. "Actually, somebody in the American military in 1949 invented that shit. But if you give me a good answer, I will acknowledge that you are an accomplished practitioner of that shit. – As opposed to a donkey-humping shoot-from-the-hip, dick-brained farm mechanic who damn near got us killed."

She smiled big. "Boss, you gotta do something about your language. It's deteriorating. If you're gonna cuss, you got to cuss more elegantly. But to answer your question, I haven't forgotten you stickin' your arm through my seatbelt along my leg, which must be avoided again at all costs." She leaned close and gave him a fake accusatory stare. Then she moved to one side of the deck, grasped the waist-high cross-deck control rod now connected to the propeller-assembly tail levers, and lifted. The propellers tilted downward. "We still have control, just you on your side and me on mine. The offset is bigger now to accommodate the control pedestal, but it's no longer used as a crank, only as a lateral pull point. Trust me, even if the ropes break, we'll still be able to control it. The transverse rod is a back-up. And if all else fails, we can declutch, reposition the props, then reclutch."

"Sounds good. How about center of gravity and lift control?"

"I would like to tell you I found center of gravity by calculating it."

"How did you find it?"

She squirmed a bit. "The Elf suggested a means."

"Which was?"

"Attach a board with a row of eyebolts to the bottom center of the gondola running front to back. Reduce buoyancy to just a few kilos. Tie a single tether to an eyebolt, release the other tethers, and float the ship. Continue from eyebolt to eyebolt until it floats level."

Khan smiled at the thought of Baelmar earnestly and modestly suggesting this simple method to an engineer. "And the result?"

"It worked, so we told Baelmar to go fuck himself. We moved the gondola back six hundred centimeters. We painted a black line across the deck where the center of gravity is. Freight has to be evenly distributed on each side of the line. More than two people on one side versus the other can make a difference, too. We're looking at setting up the diesel tanks fore and aft of the line with a line and a hand pump between so we can use the fuel as trim ballast. And we've added two bubble levels as an attitude control monitor. Plus we added the tethering reel with the grappling hook."

"And the spare gas?"

"Four pressure containers. Enough to handle four descents by blowing gas and replenishing. But the best is, we also added a separate envelope inside the main envelope, which we can fill with air if we want to reduce buoyancy or gas if we want to increase buoyancy." She puffed out her chest. "My idea."

"Excellent idea! So we're ready?"

"If you are. If your lady friend will let you go, that is," she said naughtily.

Khan did not respond to this but did address the issue directly by inviting Estelle to go. "You have got to be out of your mind!" she said. "I see it clearly in the *Advance Daily Page*: "Key Economic Driver and Mayor Kill Selves in Stupid Stunt.""

In the event, Ahmed, Baelmar, and Ernie went. Ahmed, a gentle soul, spent a good amount of time before departure looking peaked and kneeling on his prayer rug, but revived when Bella started in on him. "How do you even know where the hell Mecca is?" she said, gesturing in the direction he had been praying. "E2O is turning, we're light years away from Earth, it's a moving fucking target. If Allah exists, he doesn't give a damn what position you're in when you pray. Admit it: this is a situation your camel-dealer Prophet never envisioned."

"Bella, Bella, Bella," said Ahmed in a soothing way, looking around as if for lightning bolts. "You mustn't speak that way. You will bring ill luck on our expedition."

"Yeah, yeah, yeah," said Bella. "We'll bring our own luck through either preparation or lack of it. Quit your praying and fire up that engine, Engine Mate. And look smart about it."

That was the end of religious discussions. Once the engine fired up on the second pull, Ahmed was more consumed with admiring his creation than with paying attention to Bella. He hardly noticed that they had lifted off, enabled by Khan's standing on the ground and pulling the grappling hook loose, then climbing quickly aboard on a rope ladder.

Baelmar on the other hand cinched himself into a seat and began reciting a chant, to Bella's delight. Ernie turned a light shade of green as they slowly gained altitude. "Bunch of damn pussies," muttered Bella with great satisfaction.

She immediately tested out the new controls, which worked to perfection. She beamed. They had leveled out at perhaps only two hundred meters, and Khan asked if she wanted more gas in the internal envelope. "No, the relatively neutral buoyancy makes it easier to control altitude with the propellers," she said. And with that, they set course for Sunrise Keep, following the River of Doubt as a guide.

A distance that normally took boatmen three days to travel downstream and five back up, and teamsters about the same as the upstream time, assuming all stopped at night, took less than three hours at what Bella had calculated was peak speed of 33 KPH, though they cruised at about 20. The entire trip turned into a non-event, as they were able to grapple to the edge of an empty wooden river dock, and lower themselves to a convenient level for loading and unloading.

The entire population of Sunrise Keep swarmed onto the parapets and the river slope to see the gigantic airship. Boys streamed out to ogle, and a few tried to climb aboard.

"Avast, there, Laddy," roared Bella, pointing at the first group. "Climb aboard, and I'll take ye to the Maneaters."

This was enough to dissuade the boys, but they didn't go far. They peppered Khan and Baelmar and Ernie with questions, which each answered according to his own style. Baelmar had recovered his composure and rhapsodized at length about what Arcadia looked like from the air. Ernie made up stories in which he was the hero, and Khan maintained a scientific approach. The boys' curiosity was insatiable. Finally, Khan put them to work unloading the airship's cargo and setting it on the dock. This at least enabled them to board the craft so they could later brag to their friends.

After fifteen minutes or so, Dr. Greis himself made his approach down the river slope from the castle to officially greet them.

"Major Khan, you do always change things with your arrivals," he said. "Please come into the dining hall and eat some good Sunrise food while your vessel is being loaded."

"We would love to, Mr. Council President," said Khan, careful to use Dr. Greis's official title within the hearing of others. "Better next time. We have people back in Advance who will worry terribly the whole time we are gone. We must return by nightfall to avoid that. However, we will be setting up regular freight and passenger service between here, Advance, and Guido's Hundred. We have not forgotten our investors. And in fact, we can take a passenger or two back with us if desired."

A hundred boys and girls raised their hands and started jumping up and down when they heard this, and Dr. Greis smiled. "You have changed things forever, Major. I would love to go myself, but choose a child for the honor and bring him back on your next run. It will be like releasing an education virus among our people. And tell Madame Mayor I would like to discuss opportunities for closer ties, including sending some of our children to Advance's school, setting up a water-powered machine shop here, and buying some revolver rifles. There are indications the neighboring lords intend to teach us uppity slaves a lesson, and I want to adjust the kill ratio as far as possible in our favor. We would also like our own cannery." He gestured at the boxes of canned vegetables. "We can buy the jars and sealing rings from you and preserve our own vegetables."

"I will pass on those messages. And I'll make sure you get a thousand canning jars, lids, and rings on the next run."

He turned to Baelmar. "Baelmar, you know these boys and girls. Why don't you select the one who gets to take a ride with us back to Advance?"

Baelmar smiled and shook his head in appreciation. "You are smooth, Mr. Khan. You avoid disappointing the others and get credit for the one. Fine." He turned to the children. "No favoritism! I am going to close my eyes, turn three times, and walk among you. I will then put my hand on the head of the lucky boy or girl."

He did this, and his hand ended up on the head of a very happy boy. "Sandeep!" said Baelmar. "How did it get to be you?"

"Hey!" said several of the boys. "Not fair! Just because you know him."

"Completely accidental," said Baelmar. "Maybe I smelled the stable on my old stall cleaner. Come onto the skyship, Sandeep. Make sure you don't add your own manure stink to the horse stink once we get up in the air."

The trip back to Advance was uneventful as well, and Khan was again gratified that they were able to grapple their own way down, which was a good thing, because no one was on the landing field behind the office, and if they were to go exploring, they would need to get good at mooring themselves.

However, it didn't take long for the townspeople to arrive, some with wagons to haul freight, some just to gawk and ask questions. The freight was duly unloaded, questions were airily addressed, as if the world's first successful dirigible flight happened every day, and Khan was at loose ends. He had indeed effected big changes, and now it all seemed ordained. It would not be long before people could not imagine not having the diesel-powered dirigible. And four more were planned.

He decided to take Estelle out to supper to celebrate. Assuming she wanted to go. He found her still in her office, at her large wooden desk, working with a couple of large ledger books. A coal-oil lamp burned at each end of her desk. She was running her fingers through her tousled hair, looking thoughtful. She heard the wooden floor squeak and looked up. Her face lit up momentarily, then she put a lid on it and reassumed her normal ironic pose.

"Ah, so you survived again," she said, leaning back. "Did you make it past the duchies," which was her sneering word for the fiefdoms between Advance and Sunrise Keep, "or did you have to beat a hasty retreat again?"

"To Sunrise and back, with their freight. It's been unloaded and brought into town. And we brought a Sunrise boy along for the ride so he can brag to his buddies when we take him back on the next run."

"Well, well, well," she said. "This does change things. And so do those glass jars of vegetables and meat, I must say. I was just going over our foodstock reports." An appealing, unworried smile came to her lips as she turned a page, then looked up at him. "It's the first time I've felt comfortable on the subject since I've been mayor. Based on public stocks alone, we should be fine until next growing season, and citizens have laid in bigger than normal home stocks."

"You're welcome."

She snorted. "Smartass. Walk in here and fix our worst problem without raising a sweat. A problem we've struggled with since I've been here. The Food Preservation Team is our longest-standing task force. Problem is, meat needs salt to dry best, and fatty meat like mutton or pork, which is mainly what we have, goes rancid pretty soon without salt. You can lose whole batches. But every salt expedition has found almost none. Nada. So saltless drying processes are the best they've been able to do."

"I know."

Estelle continued as if he hadn't spoken, staring at a point in the air, reciting the details of the problem that had been her nightmare for several years.

"Drying works on vegetables, but then we lose most of them to that damned poison mold. Grows well even in dry season. And its mycotoxin is heat-stable, so once the mold starts, the food is lost. Cooking won't break down the poison."

"I know."

Estelle ignored him, continuing her obsessing over the details of this cursedly familiar problem.

"Every year, we lose stocks. Some years up to half, since the signs are subtle. People get paranoid and throw away good food. We also lose a few Newbies who don't recognize the signs. And then there's what happens if we have a bad growing season. Been some dry seasons when we lived on corn cakes and bread. Then even the corn went bad. We just plain went hungry. Irrigation helps, but we can't irrigate widely enough in dry season. So sure, we've tried canning. Tried coal tar and something like beeswax to seal jars, no luck. Botulism."

"I know."

Estelle persisted.

"Tried hand-made steel cans sealed with solder. No luck. Leaked. Thought of screw-top lids with rubber seals on glass jars, but don't have the stamping technology to stamp the lids out of steel. And never could develop the rubber. We were looking at plants for it."

He realized his success had made her feel guilty for not succeeding, and she was reviewing to find the place where she had gone wrong. She looked at him for the first time directly.

"How did you know about the problem?"

"Farley. Also, the glass-plant manager. Almost anybody in town. It's no secret."

"But how did you come up with the glass-lid-and-wire-bail concept? And rubber from coal?"

"I'd like to claim genius, but I can't. Family cellar junk. People used them in the Nineteenth and Twentieth centuries. Some Khan family cellars go back even further. Great Grandpa, when he got rich, would buy these great old houses, furniture, cellar junk and all. Kind of a nouveau riche thing. Immediately have the trappings of wealth around you with no effort. I remember a box of empty jars and brittle rubber rings in the cellar. One of the housekeepers explained what they were and how they used to be used. Rubber from coal was just a guess. Maggie thought I knew what I was talking about, so she was able to do it."

Estelle closed the ledger with a thump and blew air up, moving her hair out of her face.

"Well, that one change has changed everything for us." She shook her head. "Those rubber rings." She shook her head. "We had the pieces all along. We just didn't put them all together. Oh, well." She looked up at him and raised an eyebrow. "Now it's time to celebrate and turn our attention to other advances."

She paused and gave him a look he wasn't entirely sure he understood. He didn't respond.

"Speaking of ad*vances* …." She looked at him sidewise and wiggled her eyebrows.

He looked confused and did not otherwise react.

She sighed, shook her head, and put her palms flat on her desk. Then she gave him an appraising look. "Speaking of *advances*, Mr. Khan, how obvious does a girl have to be before you ply her with wine and attempt to take advantage of her favors?"

Khan was taken aback. "Oh!" he said. "Well … , maybe I'm a little distracted. And out of practice. Not that I was ever practiced at that sort of thing," he hastened to add. "What I mean to say is, my life has not been conducive …." He stopped, realizing he was digging himself into a hole. "Look, Estelle. I … did notice you right away." He stopped again. "Look. It has been a long time. And I … do confess my interest." He felt his face flushing.

"Why Mr. Khan, I do believe you are blushing like a boy." She flashed the first full smile he had seen from her, and refused to look away, enjoying his discomfort.

"Well, I did come here to ask you to dinner to celebrate our achievement. It is difficult to know what might develop."

"Yes, with perhaps only a little encouragement, something may well come up."

In the morning when he showed up late for work, he was surrounded by sidewise glances and smiles that were quickly replaced by elaborately blank looks when he looked. Bella came in to get a tool she had hidden in her desk – she didn't trust anyone with her tools – and when she brushed by his chair, said, "Unh HUNH," then "MMM MMmmm."

"Man can't make a move around here," he muttered.

"Not you two," she said as she swept out the door. "Best entertainment in town."

CHAPTER NINE

"Where there is no vision, Alexander, the people perish. Khans will always provide a vision."

Grandfather Quintus Khan, *Khans to Khans*

K han was pretty satisfied with his progress but saw that going further might encounter inertia. After the pilot run to Sunrise Keep, and the start of twice-weekly service to both the Keep and Guido's Hundred, Advancians wanted to sit back and take a breather from change. Canned foods, rubber, coal oil lamps, diesel engines, and dirigibles were huge improvements in the Tech way of life. Entrepreneur farmers on the Dev Zone plateau had created a food surplus, so prices had gone down. The three communities had quickly strengthened ties. Trade had surged, dwarfing its previous trickle. People moved from one place to another, mostly children into Advance for boarding school, but some technicians and teachers out to the Keep and the Hundred. As he had anticipated, Salvatore Ruggiero had had to give his serfs a vote on some issues to keep them down on the farm, and so far it was working out. Life was good. There was a sense of well-being, of plenty, of satiation, of no need to go further. Everybody wanted time to absorb the new.

"You going to kick back and live on the fat now?" asked Ralph, the owner and barman at the popular Downtown Pub and Diner. He was on his back under his new coal-oil-fired steam table. "Damned leaky rivets," he said, and crawled out, wiping his hands on a towel. "Look, you deserve it. Looks to me like we're good now. Focus on just living. Raise our families." He wiggled his eyebrows. "You should think about one, too."

"Been thinking some about that," said Khan, now used to the ribbing and prepared with the stock answer that would quiet people the fastest. He noticed that Estelle also received the same and responded good-naturedly and non-committally. "But no reason we can't raise families and advance even more."

Ralph wiped the bar and gave a non-committal shrug.

Khan paid his bill and started his customary morning walk up to the plateau on the northeast corner of the town where the humble, wooden, shack-like Khan headquarters buildings stood. It helped him to walk and think in the mornings, before people started lining up to ask questions. It was a beautiful, bright morning, as most mornings in Advance were.

Advancians thought they had arrived, now that they had the dirigible and the trade association, but he knew they needed more. If Arcadia was to pick up the torch for humanity, as suggested by the Alien, there was a brief window of time. Before the inevitable collapse of the too-complicated civilization on Earth. Before ECG stopped sending highly educated Newbies. There was much to learn and relearn. Much knowledge to preserve.

The little three-community trade association was only a start. It was also vulnerable to external forces: a terrible drought, sudden crop destruction by pests; a plague of the type that had killed Salvatore Ruggiero's wife, a surprise attack by an alliance of Lords; a surprise attack by an unknown Tech settlement. It had to grow. It had to improve its odds. If Advance could build dirigibles, other tech communities – which he assumed existed – could as well. Better for Advance to find them first and preemptively establish trade. Yes, Advance had made progress, but their hold on it was tenuous. They needed to explore and grow.

ECG interference was probably not a threat. Not to Advance, surely. In three hundred years, they had never descended from orbit – just beamed prisoners down. To Khan, maybe, but not looking likely. He had expected them to react to anomalous chip movement resulting from dirigible flights. That was his whole plan. Maybe snatch him up to an orbiting ship, at least for interrogation – thus giving him a chance to take advantage of the situation. He was pretty sure he could.

But apparently he had miscalculated. ECG had not reacted. He might actually be grounded here. So while he still carried it, he now seldom thought of the chip. It served mainly as a memento of high tech on the old world. He still missed the UAI and being able to ask whatever question came to mind. He missed music on demand. And ironically, given his old job, he missed the tremendous sense of freedom of being able to climb into a starship and go to another planet. But in the main, ECG had faded into the background of his mind, and he had now started to consider himself an Arcadian for life. His job was to build Arcadia.

He wanted to fire the imaginations of young men and women of the three communities with visions of the distant and unusual, with the chance for adventure, with the burning thirst for knowledge. He wanted to add oxygen to the fire of Advance's progress. He wanted to establish intellectual contact and trade with enough other advanced societies to permit specialization: to achieve developmental critical mass.

He had seen a few isolated settlements like Advance on other planets while dismantling them, and they shared a common characteristic: cultural and scientific stasis. Even if they started with all the technological advantages and equipment available, their low numbers of people limited them. They reached a glass ceiling of development defined by their numbers. They couldn't replicate the high tech they started with. They did not advance, but in fact devolved. Cultural scientists – later exiled from Earth for sharing such views – had written that, to develop advanced industrial technology, a civilization needed an intellectual and trading community of at least ten to twenty million highly educated people – plus the ability to constantly grow. So it was necessary to find other communities like Advance and set up regular intercourse with them – assuming those societies existed.

It was time to explore the planet, and Khan International (Earth 2.0 Division) would provide the means. That was how he saw the evolved mission of the Khan family.

Khan International was doing well financially, and he wished his father could see it. His father had never seen him as a spendthrift, only as inexperienced with the real meaning of money. And now here he was, a venture capitalist. He didn't have the money to build four more dirigibles, as per original plan, but he did have enough to build three. And the profits from the newly established trade and haulage fees were steadily building up. The town machine shop wanted to build and sell diesel engines. He and Ahmed would split the licensing fees. So while original projections were proven to be a bit airy, they were nevertheless doing quite well.

He would ultimately have money for the fourth airship, so he had told Bella to build three and plan for the fourth. He also directed her to find and train other pilots, and to figure out how to navigate other than by ground features. If they were going to explore, they would need to find their way back. After a couple thousand kilometers, dead reckoning would not get it. They would need sextants and compasses. Luckily, the planet did have a magnetic field. The accurate chronometer they needed for longitude would have to wait.

But as his father had once warned him, practical management matters quickly overweighed more fun things like vision. His enterprise was affecting a lot of lives and aspects of local economics. Increasingly, arriving at the office meant dealing with a lot of unexciting details that had none of the magic of exploring.

This morning was no different. After Khan had walked up the hill from Ralph's to the interplanetary headquarters of Khan International, he found a delegation of five boatmen and teamsters waiting in his office.

Most of the men were from Sunrise Keep, though they were accustomed to staying for brief periods of time in Advance until they had a return load. Their grievance was that they had lost the light, lucrative, easy-to-haul freight business to the dirigibles and been left with only the heavy stuff – lumber, livestock, farm implements, pallets of fired brick and clay pipe. Selected by their peers, these men demanded recompense.

"We only want what was already ours," said their spokesman, a large, muscular fellow named Tom with the sleeves cut out of his shirt. Several rings of dried sweat showed in the armpits. "We had steady business and steady pay, what with the vegetables and lumber going out of the Keep, and the clothing and shoes and metal parts coming in. We weren't rich, but we fed our families. And Lord Mander left us alone, and treated our families pretty good. Now we can't feed our families on what we make. Not after what you started with them blimps. They're taking the easy freight where the money is." He stopped and eyed Khan, clearly expecting to walk away with some money.

Khan eyed him back. He regarded the man's companions, all built like barrels with massive arms and legs. They stood uncomfortably in their rough clothes in this office environment, uncertain what to do with their big hands. These were hard-working men who didn't deserve the shit end of the stick, and whom it was pointless to antagonize. They were accustomed to rowing fifty kilometers upstream from Sunrise Keep with a boatload of freight. They knew what work was, and did it faithfully. They needed to be redeployed.

"Tell you what," said Khan. "I'll make up the difference, but you'll work for me, how's that? I'll pay you for your boats, but then I'll own them, and I'll make a few modifications."

Tom was not at all sure about this. "The boats have always belonged to us."

"And the jobs will still belong to you. It's just that the jobs will change a little. Khan International will charge customers for the freight, and you'll get a weekly wage. What's the best week you ever had?"

Tom swelled his chest. "Two hundred credits." He looked sidewise at his companions. "'Course I had to divide it up."

Khan could see his way through now. "I'll pay each of you twenty percent more per week than your best week. That's after you covered your expenses. He noted looks of confusion so he quickly added clarity. "Divide your best week's wages into five equal parts, and I'll add a sixth part."

Smiles broke out.

"But you'll need to learn a few things. Won't happen immediately because we can't get them made fast enough, but you'll need to learn to run a steam engine. We're going to put a small steam engine in each one of your boats. Burn coal or wood, either one. And depending on what we find with the dirigible, we could be sending you far, far upstream or downstream. Might send you down to the mouth of the Po River, then up the Po to the Hundred so their stuff can come the whole way by water."

"When does the new pay start?" one of Tom's companions asked gruffly.

Khan reached into an unlocked drawer and pulled out a wad of paper credits. "Right now. I'll pay you for this week now. But before the end of the week, you have to put up a sign on each of your boats that says 'Khan International.' And at the end of the week, I get all the freight fees, which you will continue to collect. Are we good?"

The men were uncomfortable and slightly reluctant. The change was sudden and more far-reaching than anybody could envision, but each had a fistful of paper credits, and the promise of the same amount next week. They agreed and left.

Ahmed had watched this entire exchange. "Mr. Khan, you do your ancestors proud. You are a businessman the equal of any I have seen, and I come from a part of Earth where bazaars have existed unchanged for a thousand years, with families of bazaari merchants that go back nearly as far. It is a surprise when your previous experience was police work."

"Great Grandpa Culpepper may have rubbed off on me a little. He could have held his own in the bazaar, I'm sure. It's all about role playing. My police work was a role. Kind of like the role you have to play when your boss makes promises about steam engines of a size that doesn't yet exist and you're the engineer who has to design them."

Ahmed's white teeth flashed in a big smile. "Yes, I wondered where you were going to get those, but I do have some ideas. I'll have a prototype design on your desk tomorrow evening. You are betting that there are settlements upstream or downstream whose freight will make up the difference?"

"Right again, Ahmed. – Which cash-flow-wise means I need to get Bella moving faster on the second dirigible so we can use it to find out. We don't dare risk the first dirigible on anything but the milk run, now that everybody is dependent on it. But even if there are no new settlements we can trade with, I'm sure there's coal, copper, iron ore, or lumber upstream or downstream that we can use to recoup the investment. And settlements. Likely on rivers. If the scuttlebutt I used to hear on Earth about this place is right, three million people have been transported to this planet over the last three hundred years. Any kind of survival and fertility rates at all mean there should be at least 10 million people on this planet. If a third of them are Techs, that's three million. If their settlements are the same size as Advance, that's three hundred Tech settlements around the globe. That is opportunity. It's also how I'm going to pay my stockholders' dividends: new markets, new sources of trade."

Khan was delighted that the second dirigible went faster and easier. Bella put her experience with the first to good use. But of course, being an engineer, she could not resist the opportunity to make improvements, which she was showing to Khan and Ahmed on another bright Arcadia morning.

"Internal envelopes both fore and aft, each of which can be filled with air or coal gas, as desired for elevation as well as trim. Makes center of gravity less critical, and balancing the load much easier. There's also a new repair kit for both dirigibles, including envelope patching materials, spare control cables and hardware, diesel parts, and tools. And a pedal arrangement to drive the propellers, if all else fails." She looked significantly at Ahmed.

Ahmed was offended, and uncharacteristically, couldn't resist a barb.

"I can see why you would anticipate failure in the components you designed, since some have failed already, but the diesel will run for thousands of hours before needing repair."

Bella was entertained. "Well, well. The mild-mannered Ahmed has had his pride pricked. Look, Dickhead. If I read the Boss right, we are going to take this thing thousands of kilometers from home. You want to go along with no tools and parts to fix your gold-plated fucking diesel?"

Ahmed considered this. "I would like to go along, and I suppose it might be prudent under those circumstances to take parts and tools. But if you believe the diesel is as you describe it in your expression, then you are an infidel and a barbarian."

Bella was delighted. "A personal attack! Ahmed, there might be hope for you yet! And here all this time I been thinking you were a girly man afraid to offend anyone."

"Perhaps because you are a manly woman," shot back Ahmed.

"All right, all right," said Khan. "The two of you kiss and make up. We are indeed going thousands of kilometers away from home, and I need you two to get along."

"I would rather kiss a pig," said Ahmed with all the dignity he could muster.

"And if I'm going to kiss somebody, I want him to have more than I suspect little Ahmed has got," said Bella.

"Ah, Jeez," said Khan. "It was just an expression. Now come on. I expect some professionalism from Khan International staff. That means being able to work with people with whom you might not be best friends. Shake hands."

Reluctantly, the two shook hands. Bella's hand dwarfed Ahmed's, which he withdrew as soon as possible.

"Now, let's plan our upstream and downstream missions. Upstream first. We follow the river to its source. Doesn't have to be navigable. Settlements could be beside it all the way to its source just as a source of water. We take Lizzie the geologist with us and land her wherever she wants so we can develop a first-cut mineral resource map. Then we do the downstream trip, which will likely be much longer. I figure we need to plan for at least a ten-day trip: four days out, two days with whatever settlement we find, and four days back. Four twenty-five-hour days at 33 KPH would be well over three thousand kilometers."

"No way the river's source is that far away," said Bella. "More like a thousand kilometers, max."

"That's what I think, too, but it could go a long way downstream. Just building in a safety factor to our planning. Key thing is, we need to be able to tell the crew of the other dirigible how long to wait before coming after us."

This hit Bella in the gut.

"What other fucking crew? I been doing the flying. That's my ship!"

Ahmed smiled a satisfied smile as he watched this exchange.

Khan put up his palms to ward off this blast. "We're building a total of five. Did you expect to keep the other four as spares for yourself? We have to let go and let someone else fly. You haven't been flying by yourself. Isn't there anybody in your crew that you've let fly the thing?"

"Well, yes. Sandeep, the boy from the Keep. Never got rid of him after his first ride. He's been on nearly every run, back and forth. Curious as hell, good learner. He begged and begged, and I finally let him take the helm. He was a natural. He's only fourteen, but he has good reflexes. And he's smart and takes instruction. He understands the principles involved. Good kid."

"Bit young, isn't he, for that kind of responsibility? I don't like it."

Now Bella was being challenged on her judgment. "He can do it,

Boss. I'll let him do the whole run next two times, just to watch him. But I know he can do it."

Ahmed watched as Khan pushed a little harder. "I'm still not sure I like it. What about the boy's parents? What would they think? And I think we need an older, responsible adult with him, even if the parents agree."

"I can arrange that," protested Bella. "Leave it to me." And she left the plateau to go down to the town.

Ahmed smiled and shook his head in quiet appreciation. "Mr. Khan, you bear watching. You are the smoothest manipulator of people I have ever seen."

Khan gave the slightest of smiles. "I don't know what you're talking about," he said, and went back to his desk.

Within a week, all was in readiness. *City of Advance*, as Bella had dubbed the new vessel, was inflated, flight-tested, and loaded with provisions and sample trade goods. The back-up crew was given *Enterprise*, the first vessel, and told to continue the milk runs, but to come upstream after them in ten days if they hadn't returned.

"You're taking a squad of the Guard," Estelle informed him at one of the breakfasts they now shared every other day or so at the Downtown Pub and Diner. "Heavily armed."

He protested. "That will cut way back on the trade goods we're able to take. Not only will we have the Guard's additional body weight, we'll have their weapons and food, too."

"I will confiscate the airships unless you agree," said Estelle agreeably. "They – and you – now constitute a key part of our development strategy. See Advance Town Ordinance 14.03 – the Public Domain section."

There was no point in arguing. Estelle didn't speak unless she knew what she was talking about. Plus, she had been the key player in giving him the freedom to do what he was doing. He needed to play along.

"Yes," he said, changing his tone. "I was just thinking myself that it would be good to take along some additional security other than Baelmar's bow and Bella's and my pistols. Send them up tomorrow morning ready to go."

"Why Alexander," she beamed. "I believe you're developing a sense of humor."

"It's painful after all these years, but I'm trying. Gravitas is hard to leave behind." He left the restaurant hoping nobody had heard her call him Alexander.

They sailed – as they now called it, because to a certain extent it felt that way – northeast along the river below, quickly passing any landmarks anybody recognized. They passed the Laberteaux, Copeland, and Magoon Hundreds, all of which traded lightly with Advance, mainly to get bar steel to make arrow and spear heads, but they all wanted as little as possible to do with the town. They were relatively weak militarily and probably feared the intentions of the much larger and better armed Advance.

Then the ship was over wild lands with no sign of settlement other than the occasional wisp of smoke. The plan was to keep going into the night as long as they could see clearly how far they were above the ground, but to moor the instant they couldn't, as in a fog. They were cruising at only about one hundred meters to keep good visibility of all the geological and topographical features below. No sense missing promising mining property, or taking a risk of flying into the ground if the terrain rose.

All watched the landscape scroll by, and some napped, lulled to sleep by the humming little diesel. After awhile Ahmed retreated to a roughly bound book of mathematics. Several times during the day, he unrolled his prayer mat and prayed. Bella uncharitably pointed out again that mere planetary rotation – E2.0 vs. Earth – meant that he wasn't praying toward Mecca, and probably not even Earth, but he loftily ignored her. Baelmar seemed unaccountably and unusually pensive, which concerned Khan, as he was normally so cheerful. "You miss them," he said to Baelmar. "You know you don't owe me anything. And if I haven't found my destiny with these dirigibles and the exploration of Arcadia, I don't know what it will be. You should go back to Maruil and your children after this voyage."

"Not yet," said Baelmar. "Soon. But this is only part of your destiny. Your destiny will change everything – not only for Arcadia, but for old Earth. You will know when it arrives. There will be no mistake, and I will be there to help you." He sighed. But I do miss them."

Khan almost said, "There you go with the Elf stuff," but refrained. He had learned to respect Baelmar's eerie pronouncements.

The first night they had to moor at approximately midnight as fog rose from the river and blocked visibility. "Better to moor than crash into a tree on a bluff," said Bella quietly, so as not to wake the sleeping guard. Khan let down the new releasable grappling assembly he had had made at the smithy. A smaller second rope went down with it to retract the grappling prongs when necessary. It caught much sooner than expected, which told them that the terrain had indeed risen, and their altitude – now at approximately twenty meters – was much less than intended. They reeled out another thirty meters of rope and let the craft rise.

"Dodged that bullet," said Bella quietly. "Damn. Gotta be careful." She turned off the fuel valve, and the engine coughed and died.

Quiet enveloped them, with only a few insect and bird sounds embedded in it. The fog blocked out any starlight, so visibility was near zero.

"Damn," said Bella again. "This is creepy. But I can't see what could hurt us, except losing buoyancy or breaking loose. What do you think? Just one person on watch duty?"

"Two," said Khan. "Each to keep the other awake. They check each other every five minutes to make sure they're awake, and the rope every ten minutes to make sure it's taut. Two hours on, then wake their replacements. With six on the Guard squad, that's enough for four watches if you and I take a watch. Baelmar, Ahmed, and Lizzie the geologist will sleep. Let's wake two of the guards and put them on the first watch."

"You are awfully bossy talking to the captain of this vessel," she said. "I am in charge here. You said so yourself."

He did not respond, but lay down on the deck to try to snooze. He heard her roust two of the guardsmen and explain the situation. Then the peaceful night sounds lulled him to sleep.

The next thing he knew he was struggling to wake. Baelmar was shouting. "Maneaters! Maneaters on board!" Then there was a solid thump of something hitting flesh, followed by a dopplered scream. Somebody had gone overboard. The question was who.

Khan sprang up and drew his revolver but quickly realized it was too dangerous to shoot it in the dark, even if his Maneater target was right in front of him. The slug could go clean through the body and hit one of the crew. At about that time, several pistol shots went off, followed by heavy thumps, then sounds of struggle, then two more shots. Then a shout of "Oh, shit," followed by a grunt of pain and a thump.

"Baelmar, where are you?" shouted Khan.

"Here! Help!"

Khan moved to the sound and quickly smelled a Maneater. He reached blindly forward and encountered the back of a neck encircled with necklaces. He grabbed the head and gave a mighty twist. A satisfying snap resulted, and the body collapsed onto the deck. He felt the body and quickly discovered a knife clutched in the right hand. Standing again and moving to the sound of the struggle, he found another neck.

"That's me!" shouted Baelmar. He moved side by side with Baelmar and discovered that the Elf had a grip on one Maneater's neck with his left hand while he battled another with his right. Khan moved to his right and gave a mighty swipe with the knife where he guessed the Maneater's face would be, and where he hoped no parts of Baelmar were. A scream resulted, followed by another snap as Baelmar, now down to only one opponent, broke his man's neck.

Now it was quiet immediately around them, but there were sounds of struggle from the other end of the deck.

"Take that you smelly bastard!" yelled Bella, then gave a mighty grunt. Another scream of a falling man followed.

Still there were sounds of struggle from the extreme front of the deck. "Ahmed!" yelled Bella, apparently now free to take on other assailants. "Where the hell are you?"

Three swift flesh-ripping sounds hissed through the air, each followed by the thump of a falling body. "I am here," came his calm voice. "I could use some help throwing some of these bodies overboard. I fear we have lost altitude because of the extra weight, making it easier for them to board us."

"What bodies?" bellowed Bella.

They had talked about the need for light in emergency situations and had agreed that it was too dangerous to use coal oil lanterns. The doped linen exuded coal gas at some low level all the time. So Khan had asked Maggie to come up with some kind of cold-light solution. She had provided several test tubes with two compartments separated with a thin cork. The top cork held a sharpened plunger which could be jammed down to break the thin inner cork separating the two liquids in the tube. The result was a pale green light.

Khan grabbed one of these from a supply locker, broke the divider, and shook it up. The resulting light showed a scene from a horror vid. Four guards lay dead with slit throats or inner thighs. One was missing, and one was badly wounded. Dead Maneaters littered the deck, but nowhere more so than around Ahmed. He gripped a curved knife in his right hand and stood behind a veritable barricade of Maneater bodies. Maneater blood completely covered his knife arm and shirt front .

"These bodies," said Ahmed quietly. "I fear I have brought sin upon my head by killing my fellow man."

Bella simply stared and counted. "Seven. Honey," she said softly. "Allah will forgive you. Those were animals trying to kill you. They were not your fellow man. I am deeply sorry for all the bad things I've ever said to you. Remind me never to piss you off when you are carrying a knife."

They quickly figured out that Ahmed was right, and that they were actually sitting in treetops, maybe fifteen meters off the ground. They threw all the Maneater corpses overboard, a total of twelve, and the craft slowly rose to the extent of the mooring rope. Then Khan reeled out another fifty meters of rope, and went below to the catwalk to make sure the rope was taut and not hanging loose. While doing so he found the missing guard on the catwalk. He had been gutted. It was clear that the Maneaters had boarded by climbing the mooring rope. Nevertheless, Khan figured they were safe now, because even a homicidal or suicidal maniac would not climb a full hundred meters of rope. He removed the dead guard's shirt and tied it around the gaping wound to keep the intestines from trailing out, then carried the body back up to the deck.

"We'll need to go back at first light," he said. "We need to get our wounded back to the doctor, and return the bodies to their families. And it looks like we're going to have to revise our practices for what to do at night on future runs."

"Agreed," said Bella. "That's if we survive the lynching. Five dead, and nobody to blame but us."

The lynching was severe. Wives screamed and tore their clothes. Brothers threatened violence. Blowhards blew. There was vandalism at the office. Khan was an outsider who had caused all this with his insistence on changing things. He was pushing too hard. Changing things too fast. Now others had paid the price. One bereaved father even suggested Khan should be exiled. Expelled. Banished. Let him go live with the Sunrise Keepers who loved him so much.

Sick with grief, Estelle kept silent. The guards had gone at her insistence, and were therefore dead because of her, as she pointed out to Khan. And he had pointed out that the guards died valiantly, protecting the people they were sent to protect. Had they not been there, the whole crew would surely have been killed. As so often with death, it was complicated, and the guilt was mixed with relief it hadn't been worse, and even more guilt for feeling relieved. She put out a public statement in the *Advance Daily Page* saying it was her decision to send the guard, and giving her reasons. This did little to quiet the uproar, as several of the dead Guards had been popular. The Captain of the Guard even came by Khan International offices to let Khan know that any one of the men who had died was worth more than Khan himself. And so on.

Through all this Khan kept his counsel. Grief looks for a lightning rod, and in this case, he was it. Nothing he could say would make it better. But it wasn't only the grief; it was the change, the newness. He had seen it before on Earth with his father, his grandfather, and his great-grandfather. "Nobody loves the guy who changes things," his father had told him while being pilloried by both ECG and religious figures for releasing unbreakable encryption into the public domain. (Why would an honest man need to hide what he was saying, after all?) "History is full of examples. If you live right, you'll be one of them."

Ultimately, it was mild-mannered, shy, scholarly Ahmed, small, gracile, utterly unfierce looking, who took the initiative and saved the day. After a few days, word of his heroism and fierceness had leaked out, and people regarded him with new respect. Without discussing it with Khan, he put a small ad in the *Advance Daily Page* advertising for volunteers for the

"Discovery Corps." "Must be intellectually curious and brave, willing to suffer hardship and danger in the search for knowledge. Pay is food, water, arms, a place to sleep, and adventure. No money. Voyages up to 30 days. Apply to Ahmed at Khan International."

The response was overwhelming. People lined up outside the door every day for a week to come in and be interviewed by Ahmed. People even flowed in from the Keep, particularly young men who rode the milk run. Salvatore Ruggiero sent several of his best men. Finally Ahmed reluctantly asked for help from Bella and Khan. Utterly pleased with Ahmed's initiative and the results, and unwilling to horn in, Khan left it to the two of them. "Just keep me informed," he said.

The two of them kept in mind that they needed manning for four ships, including pilots, navigators, scientists, and fighters. They finally came up with six total crews to train, meaning they could rotate. And the huge response made it apparent that the initial emotional response to the guards' deaths, while it seemed to come from the whole town, in fact did not. The spirit of exploration and adventure had been kindled in Advance, the Keep, and the Hundred, and would not soon flicker out.

The second voyage upstream went without incident, and without major discovery. Lizzie, the geologist, found a large chert bed and a minor coal seam. The former was interesting to Baelmar, who opined that it was likely visited regularly by Maneaters, but was of no interest to Advance. The location of the latter was duly recorded, because it looked as though the river was still deep enough at this location to support barging the coal downstream to Advance. Khan made a note to formally claim the spot for Khan International future operations. But there were no river towns within four flying days upstream of Advance. The river did continue, but was really more of a creek beyond that point. And that, other than a huge horse herd that looked like a ripple of water running across the surface, was all they found.

But the most significant thing that happened was that the Alien woman appeared again to Khan while he was on the surface and out of sight of the others.

"Are we in danger?" were his first words as soon as he saw her beneath a bow tree, as Baelmar called them. Good for making bows.

She was dressed as usual, in the white jump suit. She stood in a spot of sun showing through the foliage. Her skin was very light and her hair even lighter. She seemed to glow, but Khan noticed that her graceful boots were actually on the ground, so she wasn't a hologram.

"Yes. Your tracking chip has sent information about your movements to the satellites, and it has been sent today for the first time by tachyon transmission to Earth. The satellite AI apparently recorded your previous airship movements as anomalies. It seems likely ECG will wonder how you have made these movements at a steady rate of speed far beyond walking, riding, or sailing speed. They may come to investigate. We assume you have done this intentionally to draw them here."

Khan was caught off guard. He had nearly forgotten about the chip since ECG had failed to react to his airship movements so far. Now reality struck. His original plan was working, and they were likely coming after him. But now it suddenly looked ill-conceived, selfish, and dangerous to his friends. Depending upon how ECG reacted, he might have put the entire town of Advance at risk.

"I have been careless," he said, wagging his head at his self-absorption. "I had loosely thought if they came, they would just beam me up based on my chip location. But they might target the airships and kill a lot of innocent people. I've got to think of a way to separate myself from the airships and still draw them to me alone." She nodded, and he looked at her fathomless gray eyes. "I've never been sure why ECG needs to track me in any case. If they wanted to remove me as a threat, they would have just killed me. The only thing that makes sense is, they want to use me as a mouthpiece or something like it."

She nodded again, moving her head in an artificial way indicating a learned gesture. "Of course. The situation on Earth grows tenuous. They need you for propaganda. The insurgent technology movement on Earth threatens to get out of control. They would have you speak their message as a figurehead for Khan International. You would say that you had had an awakening and now saw that technology needed to be tightly controlled."

He nodded thoughtfully. "That scenario makes sense. And I appreciate the warning. I don't want any more of the local people killed on my account. I could use an armed starship, if they're coming after me. I could use it to disarm them and take their ship. Then I could return it." He gave what he hoped was a raffishly charming smile. He wasn't sure what would charm an alien. "You don't suppose you could loan me one?"

She actually smiled, and it didn't look artificial. "No, Major Khan. We will not loan you a starship. Our involvement must be minimal. That is our rule. This information I have brought you is the help I provide. I come to tell you to prepare, now. And to tell you that you are making the spirits of your ancestors proud." That expression again. Did she listen in on every conversation? She reached for a device on her belt.

"Wait! Don't go! Can you warn me when they are coming? Can you tell me if there are other towns like Advance? And where they are?"

She actually laughed. "Of course," she said, putting a cool hand on either side of his face and gently touching her nose to each side of his nose. Then she was gone.

He stood confused. Of course she would warn him, of course there were other towns like Advance, or of course she could tell him where there were other towns like Advance? And why did he feel an unseemly stirring? Somehow that nose touching had been sensual. What did it mean in the alien culture? This was followed by several specific illicit thoughts that he pushed from his head only with some effort, and by thinking of Estelle.

Suddenly there was a quiet stirring in the leaves behind him, and he spun, drawing his pistol.

"Your destiny approaches," said Baelmar, stepping from the cover. "The Witch of the Leas only appears at important moments. You must prepare. And you must not yield to temptation."

Khan holstered his pistol. "You saw?"

"I saw. I saw you weaken. You must not. You don't know what she is. The form she shows to you might not be her real form. We have always believed she is a shapeshifter."

"She certainly felt real enough, though I take your warning seriously. There is something almost … magical about her."

"You gain wisdom." Then, "The people from Earth will come for you, yes? We must prepare. We must draw them away from the three towns."

"'We?' You would risk your life for me? Those people are killers. With advanced weapons. They will leave bodies behind them."

"From what I have heard you say, they are simply Maneaters of a different kind. They do not eat the flesh, but the spirit. But they are still human, like us. We can defeat them. We must draw them away from their weapons. Then they will be no better than us."

Khan was moved. "So you think this is the destiny moment you've been waiting for?"

"It is the beginning."

They made it back with no problem and reported their findings to Estelle. She was happy to hear about the coal seam, and relieved that nothing horrible had happened this time. Khan then took her aside and raised her eyebrows with a recounting of the alien's visit. – Leaving out the part about the nose rubbing. Given the risk to the people of Advance, he had to tell her, and get her opinion on what to do next. He had already decided, but he needed her on board.

"Khan, you are a gigantic pain in the ass," she said. They were sitting in her office, talking quietly because other town officials were nearby, and they were sitting close to an open window. "You've made our lives better, but the price just keeps getting higher."

"What would you like me to do? I'm willing to do whatever you want to protect the people of this town, including exile myself to a place far out in the bush so when they come, only I will be there. Another option is to take the tracking chip itself out into the bush and leave it. Or smash it on an anvil, or throw it into the crucible at the foundry. But it's too late to stop that tachyon transmission."

"Why the hell didn't you destroy it as soon as you found it?"

He pressed his lips together. She had to know. "It was a connection to the old world. And I … thought I might be able to use it to … get back to Earth and do some things I need to do."

She nodded and gave a grim smile. "Thanks for the truth, Khan. I had a brief fear you wouldn't tell it. I knew it was something like that."

He exhaled in relief. "Actually, when nothing happened after the first few dirigible trips, I didn't think anything would ever come of it here on this …, uh –"

"—asshole of the galactic arm?"

"I was going to say, 'remote planet.'"

"We know about the alien, you know," she said. "At least, there's a persistent myth about her giving us tools early on in our habitation of this planet. Insofar as you can have myth among a bunch of engineers, scientists, and technicians, it's been a pretty enduring one. That she helps only in a targeted way." And here she squinted him in the eye. "And that she's beautiful, in an other-worldly sort of way."

"Ahem."

"I see." She looked at him silently for a long moment. "So she won't protect us against any ECG forces that might show up?"

"No."

"Really, it's hard to believe they would show up after all this time. But the people of this town didn't elect me to be bone-headed. It won't be enough just to get you out of town. If they discover Advance, they're liable to level it to the ground and kill everyone." Her eyes hardened. "Jesus, I could just strangle you. What the *hell* were you thinking?" She looked around to see if anyone had heard her, because this last had come out a bit loud. Two people at the nearest desks looked quickly away to show they weren't listening. "I suppose we could put the chip in a grave with the corpse when somebody dies and tell ECG it's you, but they'd just dig up the corpse and do DNA testing." She looked at him narrowly. "I'm sure some in town would be just fine with putting *you* in the grave with the chip, but even if ECG dug you up and found out it was really you, they might still destroy Advance just for the hell of it. You son of a bitch."

"Look, I'm not going to try to avoid responsibility. But I will point out that the danger was initiated when they implanted the chip in me, not when I took the damned thing along on the discovery voyages. Had I destroyed it when I took it out, they might still have sent a team to find out what happened. They would likely have discovered Advance. Secondly, knowledge is power. They don't know that we know about the chip. We can use that to our advantage in such a way as to make a gigantic leap forward that will make the airships look like child's play."

Her eyes narrowed. "They gotta know about Advance and anyplace else like it. Infrared alone would tell them. It's pretty clear that alternating current is the barrier they want to keep in place. But tell me Khan. NOW what kind of scheme have you come up with, and what's it going to cost us?"

So he told her. Her eyes widened as he related the finer points of the plan.

"Fine," she finally said. "Two conditions: you take the best vessel – the *City of Advance* – with *Enterprise* in reserve as search and recovery. You paint "Khan Interplanetary" on the ship in big letters, and everybody is a volunteer from the Discovery Corps. No more Guards get sent to their deaths by me."

"Fine. I can work with that. But any way you cut it, life on Arcadia is about to change some more."

CHAPTER TEN

"Since love and fear can hardly exist together, if we must choose between them, it is far safer to be feared than loved."

"He who establishes a tyranny and does not kill Brutus, and he who establishes a democratic regime and does not kill the sons of Brutus, will not last long."

Niccolo Machiavelli, *The Prince*

"Sir, I need to bring to your attention the latest tachyon transmissions from Prison Planet."

Nathan Fox, Director – Office of Technology Control, one of the most powerful positions in Earth Central Government, reporting to the Prime Director himself, looked up from his pad at Snavely, his personal assistant.

"A link to this information can't simply be sent to my account in the usual way?" He allowed a measured amount of peevishness to color his voice, but not too much. Wilcox Snavely, obsequious, self-ingratiating, flattering, servile, was himself a deeply dangerous person of old family, long well-connected in the Cadre, waiting, biding his time, awaiting his opportunity to rise to significance.

"I thought it important to bring it to your attention, Mr. Director, as I am aware how difficult it is for a man of your stature and responsibilities to read every message among the hundreds."

Fox restrained the impulse to roll his eyes or display disgust in any other way. One of the things about ECG was, there was indeed always somebody out to get you. Practiced players like himself never gave any openings. At all.

"Thank you, Snavely. What's the burden of the data?"

"It appears that Major Khan has acquired a means of moving around the planet. Tracking data from his implanted chip showed a few months ago that he had established residence in a settlement about which we have known for some time – small forges, coal fires, that sort of signature. But suddenly in the last few weeks his signal has moved on several occasions at a speed of approximately thirty-three kilometers per hour, most times for just fifty or sixty kilometers, but on two occasions, well over one thousand kilometers."

Fox mulled this for a moment. "Any new, or should I say, solid, evidence that Khan International's old Chief of Operations, Bahner, has really set up secret shops in Afghanistan?"

"Nothing solid, Sir. But UAI analysis of private net traffic does continue to find two worrisome themes. A), that Khan International starships land at times and remote places shared in coded slang on social sites, and take those who show up off to secret, paradise-like colonies on other planets. B,) that secret links on social sites will take you to encrypted Khan International sites where downloadable plans show how to turn an aircar into a jump-capable craft with only a few hardware and programming changes. And that Khan starships will pick you up if you can make it to Ceres and broadcast a pre-coded distress signal. And on and on. Of course, such landings and such signals would be easily detected."

"So, the usual urban myth stuff, with just the occasional hard, technological piece of evidence, like the Solar Stills or the Bottomless Batteries showing up unadvertised, word of mouth only, to show that somebody out there, Khan International or somebody else, is producing and releasing freedom technology?"

"Pretty much."

"And our friend, Mr. Bahner?" Fox gently reminded.

"Ahem. We have found and closed down one shop in Kandahar producing Bottomless Batteries. Eliminated those involved. No proof Bahner or the remains of Khan International were involved, but you have to suspect."

"And we still don't know where Bahner is?"

By now, Snavely could see where this was going and where the finger was going to point. "That has been assigned to OTC Enforcement. Finding him, that is."

"Assigned by you to them?"

"Well, yes."

"OK, please keep me informed on the progress of that investigation. Where there is smoke there is fire, our ancestors used to say. There's too much popular approbation of Khan International, even though Lucian was, uh, murdered by an OTC operative run unfortunately amok, what was his name? – Merritt? – and the corporation has been officially dissolved."

Snavely squirmed a bit. His attempt to shed responsibility had not worked. Plus, Snavely strongly suspected that Fox had put Merritt up to Lucian Khan's murder, and therefore knew very well who he was, but this was a subject that could never be discussed or even acknowledged.

"Now, back to Khan Junior," said Fox, ignoring Snavely's discomfort. "Clearly we want to keep him available to bring back and use as a figurehead to put down the very kind of urban myth we were talking about. Of course, he would have to be drugged and programmed to get him to do that, but that's a mere formality. The worrisome thing is, with his ability to influence people, he could spearhead the development of dangerous arms technology on Prison Planet and turn the planet hostile to us in just a few years. Mess … things up."

He of course didn't mention the three-centuries-old contingency plan for Prison Planet: create a back-up planet to move the Cadre and their families to when and if everything fell apart on Earth, as the UAI had predicted it would within fifty years, despite best efforts. Snavely might or might not know about the Plan, and he certainly wasn't going to be the one to tell him.

Snavely played along. "No way they could develop space travel. The Prison Planet satellites are fully functional, and fully prepared to destroy any power signature beyond a few watts. The Prison Planeteers quit trying to use alternating current fifty years ago."

"So what do you think Khan is doing?"

"The UAI thinks dirigibles. They make sense. Coal gas, which is hydrogen, plus carbon mo and carbon di, was being used in the nineteenth century to float dirigibles. The question is, what kind of motive power they are using. The UAI projects steam power fueled by coal gas, but is unable itself to design a hypothetical dirigible that will travel four thousand kilometers. It has left that open. But it has postulated the *reason* for such travel."

"Which is?"

"Exploration. For the purpose of establishing trade with other settlements and enabling specialization."

"Hmmm. You're right to bring this to my attention. That could definitely cause some longer-term problems on Prison Planet. There's long been the concern, for example, that they could literally go underground with technology development, where we couldn't detect it. Let's solve two problems at once: let's bring Mr. Khan back to Earth and put him in prison where we can watch him. That will remove him from Prison Planet and stop whatever he has started there."

"We should have executed him," said Snavely. "Anybody could have predicted that he would be a problem."

Fox regarded Snavely with suppressed pique at the man's temerity. "If you will recall, there was no actual evidence that he killed Merritt. Further, we were just talking about the popularity of the Khans and their corporation, having created global urban myths. Further, there is the need to appear to give the nod to the rule of law. And finally, of course, there is the reason we put the tracking chip in him in the first place. To get him back if we need him." He regarded Snavely with a level stare.

Snavely began to withdraw backward from the office, as of courtiers of old.

"Hold on," said Fox. "I want you to bring him back. Please arrange it immediately."

Snavely swallowed bitterly and gave an obsequious nod. "Of course. Immediately, Sir."

"Oh, and set me up with an inspection tour of Afghanistan. Liaise with the military, naturally. I want to go there and see for myself what's happening."

"Of course, Sir. Immediately."

Snavely left and Fox sighed contentedly. That was how the game was played.

CHAPTER ELEVEN

"The ultimate technological freedom seed is not some new communications device. It's a star drive, put into the hands of the common man. But you can't give it to a Steam-Ager."

"When we meet the first extraterrestrials, our challenge will be to just be friendly, not scared or hostile."

Grandfather Quintus Khan, *Khans to Khans*

To properly clear the decks for the next dirigible mission, Khan told the assembled Discovery Corps everything – the ECG danger, the alien – everything. There wasn't room in the office, so the entire Corps of volunteers was gathered outside in Khan International's scrubby yard. Ahmed, Bella, and Baelmar stood with him in the cool morning sunlight facing the group.

Some in the group were skeptical about the alien part of the story, trading sidewise smiles, but when he showed the tracking chip, all recognized it as technology far beyond anything Advance could produce. And they all knew that when transportees were put down on the planet, they were put down with nothing. No thing. Period. No advanced technology. So they put a lid on their skepticism.

But that wasn't the rough part. The rough part was choosing: who should go along on the next voyage of discovery, knowing that the likelihood of sudden attack by starfaring ECG troops was high? To Khan's deep satisfaction, one hundred percent of the Discovery Corps volunteered for the voyage down the River of Doubt. All wanted to explore the river, and all wanted to fight ECG troops. First-gens were still pissed off at having been sent to Prison Planet, and Born-heres had had ECG perfidy stories deeply ingrained into their psyches since birth. Khan tried to temper the enthusiasm.

"They have laser pistols that will cut a man in two," he said. "And if they don't use those, they have stun guns that hit the central nervous system with a sonic pulse. You can't move for ten or fifteen minutes. You can barely breathe. You will feel like you have been kicked in the solar plexus by a horse. They have impact armor that will stop bullets. The only place you can shoot them is in the neck. We will take our best weapons, but we can't stand up to their weapons in a toe-to-toe fight. We have to ambush them, somehow force them to fight on our terms. If they force us into a stand-up fight, we're dead. If they catch us unawares, we're dead." He paused to let these comments sink in. "If we encounter them at all, some or all of us will not come back. But no matter what, even at that cost, they must be kept away from Advance and the Keep and the Hundred." He looked them all in the eye one by one. "Now who is still with me, even when you know it's mainly me they're after?"

There was some hesitation this time, but ultimately every man raised his hand. They were much more solemn now. The got the risk now, but the last part had hooked them. They would be protecting their families. The ECG bastards might be coming mainly for Khan, but they could end up killing everyone or destroying everything, or both, once they noticed what the Arcadians had.

"Good." He picked nine who were either already skilled with firearms or crossbows, or whom he felt he could train, including two of Salvatore's men-at-arms. "Now let me tell you the plan."

Their armament consisted of revolver pistols and revolver rifles. Each man would have one of each, plus one hundred paper cartridges in waterproof, waxed-leather cartridge boxes and one hundred fifty percussion caps in small, tightly-capped steel tins. Seven of the men had the latest spring-steel crossbows with thirty bolts each, capped with specially hardened, needle-sharp conical steel tips. Khan was pretty sure that, while bullets, even pointed bullets, would be stopped by the impact armor, pin-sharp crossbow bolts might just penetrate. Each man was also given a rectangular steel shield faced with a tempered-glass mirror. The back of the shield had a fold-out leg so the shield could be propped up in a sloped-back way and hidden behind under laser attack. And at Khan's request, and per his design, a hundred old-fashioned, spoon-activated, delayed-fuse hand grenades were manufactured – enough for every man to have at least eight with him at all times, including himself, Bella and Ahmed, who would be going on downstream by themselves and needed the protection.

When the grenades were demonstrated, the men were terrified of them and didn't want to touch them, let alone carry them, until Ahmed and Bella took to wearing necklaces of them around the office and training field. Slowly the men came around and learned to use them, though they remained nervous about them.

After three days' intensive training, Khan loaded them up and the expedition took off. He didn't want to wait longer, because he feared getting caught in Advance. Clearly, ECG knew the location of his home base from the tachyon data, but he was pretty sure they would only attack while the tracking chip was moving at faster than walking pace, because they would want to know how he was doing it. The problem was, how to know when they were coming. Would the alien warn him in time? At all? He was taking a huge chance based on a short, ambiguous conversation with a being not of his kind. That was the best he could say for it.

The weather was good. Except in the high country, the weather was always good. Even in wet season, rains always came just before dawn. They were now just past the middle of the five-month dry season. As Estelle had explained, Earth 2.0 had only a five-degree tilt to its axis, so no seasons corresponded to the annual axial cycle. But the moon's annual close approach changed ocean or air currents somewhere enough to cause a dry season. Ahmed had explained that, based on the lunar cycle and the planet's 392-day year, locals had long ago decided on a calendar of fourteen 28-day months and only two seasons: Wet and Dry. Twelve of the months had the old names, but there were two extra months at the end of the dry season, which came between February and March. These months were called Hunger and Thirst. So the dry season was December, January, February, Hunger, and Thirst. They were now starting the month of Hunger.

The sun was bright, interrupted by only a few high cirrus clouds, nothing that looked like rain. A steady, dry west wind blew across their southwesterly path, requiring them to quarter into the wind to maintain the course of the River of Doubt below. They had quickly passed the Keep, Dead Man's Crossing, and then the mouth of the River Po and entered into unknown territory.

Before they left, Estelle had demanded to know how they would know where they were if they got blown off course, and Ahmed had demonstrated the simple sextant Khan had commissioned.

"By my calculations, we are fifty-five degrees south of the north pole, based on the center of the star rotation at night, though there is no exact pole star," said Ahmed. "So let us say Advance is at zero degrees longitude and thirty-five degrees north latitude. That's our reference point. We can shoot the sun at noon."

"Great for latitude," she had said. "What about longitude? If you get lost, are you just going to go back to thirty-five north and circle the globe until you find Advance?"

"We have a brass clock whose accuracy we can't confirm, and a copy of the star tables for Sirius, Procyon, and Epsilon. Rising times in Advance by date for the last three years. We should be OK if nothing happens to our clock. And we do have the river. If we get blown off course, we will know if we are north or south of the river."

"Great. And the rescue team has the same equipment and information?"

"They do," said Ahmed. "You must not worry. The worst that can happen is that we will all be killed. And since we must all die anyway, it is only a question of timing, and how we face it." He said this without a trace of a smile.

"Two comedians," said Bella, who had been listening in. "First Khan, now you."

"I have a nagging fear that you will all need your sense of humor," Estelle had said, and left.

A day past the mouth of the Po, the land became more forested and hilly, and in a couple of places, the river, now grown quite wide, tumbled over falls, sending clouds of moisture so high they could smell the water. Then two days further on, or roughly 2300 kilometers from Advance, the river turned completely wild and impassable as it passed out of the mountain range and fell to a broad plain below. Through his telescope, Khan was sure he could see sailing vessels plying the broad, smooth waters below, but the mountainous terrain here looked ideal for what he had in mind. The question was, would ECG play along? And as soon as he thought it, he heard the alien's voice in his mind, as he had in the camp of the Maneaters. "They are coming. They will arrive in the orbit within seven of your hours."

For a moment he questioned whether he had imagined this, but realized that the alien's stilted language ("the orbit") was still quite recognizable.

He called the men together in the center of the deck. "Men, it's time. Prepare yourselves. ECG will be here in seven hours. We've got to get on the ground and get busy. We've got a lot to do in a very short time."

"She has spoken to you," said Baelmar. "I heard her myself."

The other men regarded the two of them with fey expressions, and a one of the men from the Keep made a warding sign. But they professed themselves to be ready.

The *City of Advance* set them down in an open grassy mountain saddle between two peaks after circling for twenty minutes while Khan identified the terrain he wanted. He was the last to leave the craft.

"Keep on going for three more days, as planned," he told Bella as he prepared to go. "I'm sure you'll find an advanced settlement. I'm sure I saw sailboats maybe fifteen kilometers downstream. And somewhere downstream, this river has to run into an ocean. I'm guessing that a few kilometers upstream from there, you'll find a substantial settlement. Fresh water, flat agricultural land, some timber, plus ocean fishing."

"I wish you'd let me stay with you, Boss," said Bella, sounding uncharacteristically serious. "You're going to need all the help you can get. Who has saved your ass before?"

"Baelmar."

Bella smirked at this, knowing he was playing with her. "And who after that?"

"Ahmed."

Ahmed smiled at this.

"Come on, damn it," said Bella. This is going to be historic. I want to be there."

"What you and Ahmed are going to do and find is going to be more historic. Let each of us do our part. Bring one of the settlement's leaders back with you as an ambassador if you can, and as many trade goods as possible. Stuff we don't have in Advance. Pick us up in six days at this same spot. If we're not here, circle for a day, then go home. If we're not here by that time, we're not going to be here."

And with that he took his weapons and went over the side, down the mooring catwalk, and off onto the high grassland. He watched the dirigible rise for a few seconds into the bright sky, then assembled the troops – twelve in total, including Baelmar, Ernie, and Ralph from the Downtown Pub and Diner.

Each man wore a necklace of grenades and bristled with weapons. In all cases, they carried the percussion-cap-fired revolver pistol and revolver rifle each had been issued in Advance. But each man also had to hand what he was most comfortable using and had the other weapons in a boot on his back. Baelmar carried his bow, a crossbow, and a knife. Salvatore's two men at arms wore cuirasses, greaves, and vambraces, all polished to a mirror finish, and each carried his sword, a crossbow, and a flintlock pistol. Among five of his best trainees from the Keep, now part of the Keep's Guard as well as being Discovery Corps volunteers, each carried a steel crossbow and a revolver pistol. Ralph from the Downtown Pub and Diner – who turned out to be a former Earth cop framed for blowing the whistle on a connected dirty cop – carried both a revolver rifle and a pistol. And Ernie carried a revolver pistol, a revolver rifle, and a knife, but gave every impression that he would be comfortable and skilled handling nearly any weapon. Khan thought it best not to probe there. "It's not often you get to change the odds on your own bet," Ernie had said when he had volunteered. "Five to one against us coming back. I'm gonna clean up." Khan had had a passing interest in who was taking each side of that bet, but had thought it best not to pursue that either.

"Our objective is to capture their ship," he said to the assembled group without preamble.

They had been over the plan a dozen times, but this had been a sticking point each time, because the men couldn't understand the value of the ship. Why would anyone want to leave Arcadia? Many of the men thought just killing all the ECG men would be good enough. But he mentioned the objective again to drive the point home. He paused to let the words sink in. There were as usual a couple quizzical looks about the ship, but no one said anything.

"If we can't capture the ship, our back-up objective is to prevent any of the ECG troops from leaving Arcadia."

Several nods at this. They understood exactly what this meant.

"The reason being, we don't want the ECG troops to take back any information. At all. Of course they'll likely beam down and leave the ship in orbit. And they'll be in constant contact with whoever is still on the ship. So step one is to disable all the men who land without their being able to transmit any information to the ship in orbit. We have to achieve complete surprise. Step two is, when the one or two guys left in orbit can't raise anybody on the surface, and they bring the ship down to investigate, we take the ship."

"Why do we need the ship again?" asked Norbert, one of Salvatore's men at arms. "I signed up to fight to save your ass, not to grab a space ship. We don't need a space ship."

Khan nodded. He had expected this. Some got the explanation, but the Born Heres, like Norbert, had trouble with it.

"We need the ship so I can go back to Earth. If you all killed me and destroyed the tracking chip, they'd come looking at the last place it transmitted from and likely go back to all the places it had been. You don't want that. If we leave the chip active, they'll come after it and kill anyone helping me. But if I take the damned thing back to Earth, they'll leave Arcadia alone. It's me they're after. You need to get me off this planet. That's why we need the space ship."

Norbert got this. He was fighting not only for Khan, the friend of his master, but for Arcadia and her peace. "Good enough," he said gruffly.

"Will you come back?" asked Ralph. He looked Khan squarely in the eye, seeing something he had not seen before, and apparently realizing he was playing in a much bigger game than he had realized.

Khan held his eye. "Yes, I'm coming back. Without the chip, I think. I'm leaving it on Earth to confuse them. And before I come back, I have to make sure on Earth that ECG never comes back to Arcadia. Ever. But I am coming back. Arcadia or Earth 2.0, whichever it is to you, is a better place than Earth. And it is now my home."

Ralph held is eye for a longer time, then nodded slightly. "Good." Khan knew the man was thinking about Estelle, whom he treated in a paternal way.

They couldn't find the cave that Khan imagined as the central part of the plan, but they did find a small granite-sided cul-de-sac with walls too steeply sloping to climb out of, and enough standing boulders in the middle of its thirty-meter-wide space to prevent seeing the whole space at once from within or without. The entrance was a narrow defile easily blocked with a boulder. The only question was, were the ECG troops fool enough to walk into such a perfect ambush spot? Khan thought they would not be fool enough, but that they might be arrogant enough. They would assume nothing but primitive weapons and tactics on the part of any attackers.

In case the ambush idea didn't work, they planned out a retreat path and set up suitable booby traps along the way, including deadfalls with quarter-ton logs waiting to fall when the unwary tripped over a hidden rope, and two shallow punji-stick pits covered with rush mats brought for that purpose. There were also several snares attached to bowed saplings.

He hoped it all worked, because if it didn't, and the ECG troops avoided their traps, they were all as good as dead.

He had placed himself with the tracking chip on a stone on the back side of the boulders in the center of the cul-de-sac so the ECG men couldn't see it when they entered. They would be following the signal with their tracking devices, but they would also have been suspicious if there had been no infrared signature along with the tracking chip's signal. They would have known it was a trap. So he had to risk himself based on the bet that they wanted him alive. His men were positioned around the top of the cul-de-sac, lying in wait. To foil infrared scanners, each ambusher had been instructed to lie beneath the edge of a boulder, no exceptions. And if a boulder was not available, each was to cover himself with thick moss or dirt. He had warned the men that a well-trained landing squad would materialize well away from their objective and creep up, probably from behind them.

For at least two hours, nothing happened. He began to wonder if he had imagined the message from the alien. He worried that the men would grow bored and careless. But he dared not shout at them in case the ECG troops were already in the area.

Suddenly, Khan felt his skin prickle with the tell-tale signs of a transport field being activated. He watched as eight men in laser armor appeared on the stone parapet around the defile in which he stood. All held laser pistols. One of them raised his visor and smiled down at Khan. It was Chin, his old commanding officer, standing very near Khan's escape rope, which Chin didn't seem to notice.

"Really, Alexander. You didn't think we'd fall for this, did you? Did you forget already that we can read topography from orbit? I suppose your confederates are hiding somewhere nearby in the forest cover, and when you whistle, they will come?" He laughed heartily. "With bows and arrows? The only question is, how did you know we were coming? An ambush set-up like this is pretty clear proof."

"Good evening, Commander," said Khan, trying to cover his dismay. Some of the ECG troops were standing nearly on top of his own troops and would discover them if anybody screwed up. "I had no idea you were coming. I came here to do some archeological investigation. Ancient civilization and all. New hobby. Lots of time on my hands now, as you might imagine. May I ask, to what do I owe the honor of your visit? I never expected to see anyone from Earth again. Except transportees, of course."

Chin was still suspicious, but drawn aside by the mention of an ancient civilization. "Your presence is desired on Earth. I have no idea why." Then his forehead wrinkled. "Civilization? There's not supposed to be any other intelligent life in the Arm. You and I both know the story about aliens warning us away from Epsilon Eridani was a crock of shit."

"Yes, an ancient civilization," Khan said. "Here's an artifact."

With that, he reached into a crevice between two boulders and brought out his cocked crossbow. Chin and his men hesitated just long enough while they recognized the threat. Khan shouted "Now!" and shot Chin in the chest.

As expected, the bolt easily penetrated the plastic laser armor. And, as hoped, the tempered, needle-sharp point also apparently penetrated the impact armor underneath, because Chin's face contorted in surprise. He sat down and looked down in dismay at the bolt protruding from his chest. Then he slumped to one side while grasping ineffectually at the bolt.

Khan ducked as far into the space between the boulders as he could and drew his revolver from its hiding place. But he wasn't fast enough, and he felt the searing touch of a laser on his left hand. He knew better than to look, and started shooting at the necks of the troops above. Two quickly dropped, but the others fired back at him until one raised a hand and pulled out a stun gun. The other ECG troops seemed to be entirely unmolested by his men. He suffered a moment of terrible doubt. Had they abandoned him? Had they run away when they saw the ECG men magically materialize out of nowhere? But then he heard Ernie's voice behind him.

"Hey, ECG cocksuckers! Ever seen one of these up close? Except the last time you kissed your boss's?"

Despite the grimness of the situation, Khan smiled. Ernie was clearly showing them his ass.

The diversion worked. While the ECG men stared across the sunken would-be ambush spot in disbelief, Baelmar stood up quietly behind them on the left, and Ralph stood up behind them on the right. Each held the end of a rope. Quietly, they pulled it tight between them and ran toward the open pit in which Khan stood. The rope caught the ECG men completely unawares, and they all tumbled headfirst into the pit. Taking advantage of their surprise, and in some cases, their probable injuries, Khan ran for his escape rope and bounded up it like a monkey. He noticed his left hand didn't work very well, but he still didn't look.

"Grenades!" he bellowed, but this was an idea his men had already had. They began tossing in grenades two at a time, following the ECG men around as they tried for cover, dodging their laser pistols. Except for Norbert, who was cut in two as if his polished cuirass had been made of wax.

The explosions were deafening, and far more effective than Khan had expected. It became a turkey shoot as the grenades shredded the perfectly reflective plastic laser armor and exposed the impact armor beneath, along with the places where it wasn't. In three minutes, the ECG men were all dead, most with crossbow bolts through their necks.

Khan removed Chin's helmet and put it on. A male voice crackled in his ear. "Commander! What the hell is going on down there? Are you OK?"

Khan thought for a moment and adjusted his voice. "Unnnh," he groaned. "Wild animal attack. Injured. Khan too. Unnnh."

Then he took off the helmet and carefully put the tracking chip on a rock where he could easily find it. "Come on!" he shouted, his ears still ringing from the grenades, hardly able to hear his own voice. "They'll be setting down someplace close to where we did. We have to set up an ambush along the way from there to here! There are probably two of them left on the ship. One will stay inside the ship while the other comes to check. We have to capture him alive, and use him to lure the last one out of the ship."

They were barely in place in the cover at the edge of the grassy saddle when the black, light-absorbing ship appeared above and descended slowly to a hundred meters. Khan knew the helmets also had tracking chips in them, so he had left them in the ambush location as bait. The craft hovered for a full minute while, Khan was sure, the pilot cum in-flight tactical officer scanned the area. They would see the bright returns of the helmet tracking chips a couple hundred meters away, and nothing else if people had concealed themselves properly. Khan had again told each man to cover himself with moss and dirt lest his infrared signature give him away. Using only his right hand – he still had not looked at his left, which was beginning to hurt unbelievably – he had cut pieces of sod to cover himself.

Finally the craft hovered to a height of fifteen meters and transported a single, armored person to the surface. He immediately headed for the stony defile. He clutched a laser pistol in his right hand and watched a screen on his left wrist. The craft remained hovering at fifteen meters, taking no chances. Khan thought he glimpsed SS1406 on the hull, a familiar ship and possibly pilot, but couldn't be sure. It was more important that he stay hidden.

Khan and his men waited until the lone figure was out of sight of the ship in the brushy cover, and the two closest men along that part of the lightly trodden path leapt from hiding and disarmed him. As Khan watched the action, he realized this person was not a commando or even trained for combat.

The men ripped off the man's helmet as Khan had instructed and whistled for him to come. Khan left his rude foxhole and approached, seeing something familiar about the person's head. Then the man turned and he got a good look.

"Wilcox Snavely," Khan said. "Personal Assistant and Ass Kisser to Nathan Fox, if I am not mistaken. You were at my trial. Looking the picture of gloating, as I recall. Welcome to Prison Planet."

Snavely spat. "I would kill you, Khan, but Fox wants you back. So we're taking you back."

"You must be nicer than that, Mr. Snavely. This is your new home, and we are your new friends. That's if we let you live. And to live, you're going to have to do us a favor."

"I'm doing you no favors."

"You see this hand," Khan said, holding up his left hand and seeing that it was missing the little finger, ring finger, and tip of the middle finger. "Yours is going to look just like mine if you don't cooperate." He turned to Ralph. "How about taking off his armor gloves and boots?" Ralph made short work of this request.

"Now," said Khan, taking a laser pistol from the man-at-arms who was fondling it. "You have four appendages, and I just need two things from you. So he math all works out pretty well. How many people left on the ship?"

"Screw you. Seventeen."

Khan fired the laser several times into a nearby boulder. The boulder smoked and popped and spalled off chips. No response from Snavely. So, Khan then turned and carefully sliced off two toes from Snavely's left foot.

Snavely screamed and turned white. Perspiration immediately formed and dropped from his nose and chin. "Barbarian!" he said.

"No, but we have them here," said Khan. "I suppose we could deliver you to the Maneaters, but I am not that cruel. Now, how many are left on the ship?"

"One. The pilot."

"What's his name?"

"Her name. Commander Sevka."

"Ah, Sevka." He had thought as much. "Good. Now, we're going to put your helmet back on, and you are going to tell Commander Sevka that you have killed some local wild animals that attacked the landing party and injured Major Khan, that you are now injured yourself, and that you need her help to get yourself and Khan back to the ship."

"I would rather die."

Khan sliced two toes off of the right foot. Snavely screamed again.

"You're thinking I would make it quick," said Khan. "I wouldn't. Now do it, or I'll slice off something you probably value more than your little toes. And bear in mind, I can hear you while you're speaking, because I've turned on the speaker function."

He set the helmet on Snavely's head and pointed the laser at his left ankle. Snavely grimaced and did as Khan had asked, then took the helmet off and spat at Khan. Khan dodged.

"Well," said Khan, "maybe I won't leave you here. Instead, maybe I'll take you back to face the wrath of Director Fox. I'm assuming the reason a man like you came on a mission like this is that Fox is holding you directly responsible for my capture and return. And you came along to make sure the professionals did their jobs right."

Snavely nodded miserably.

Baelmar gave a soft warning whistle. Khan and the others quickly took cover where they could watch the path.

Commander Sevka had set the ship down and was approaching warily, a laser pistol in each hand. As she entered the low forest where they were hiding, two men leapt from the shadows and attempted to disarm her. She kneed one in the groin and elbowed the other in the larynx, disabling both. She was about to administer the coup de grace to the first of the two when two more leapt on her from branches above and brought her to the ground. Khan leapt to their assistance and jerked her pistols from her hands.

"Irena," he said. "I am sorry we meet again under such circumstances. Welcome to Arcadia. I'm afraid I'm going to have to relieve you of your ship."

She stood and removed her helmet. Thick blond hair fell out. She smiled. "Good evening, Tovarisch. It is evening, isn't it? I see that you are as usual doing the unexpected."

"I try not to disappoint. All is well with you, I hope?"

"The usual. Missions to root out the overly adventuresome and freedom-loving, wherever they may be. Lacaille last month. Sprang up from survivors of the last raid." She looked at him sidewise. "There was even talk that you intentionally left some of them and some technology behind when you led the last raid. I was questioned, but as always, I am only a pilot. I have no politics." She smiled. "So what are you going to do with me?"

"Your choice. You can stay here on-planet, as if you were killed on the mission. I can take you to a place whose circumstances and people you will find congenial. My friends here mostly come from that place. Or I can take you back and let you tell whatever story you want. But I'm commandeering your vessel. Permanently."

"I see," she said, screwing up her mouth in thought. "Well, as you well know, I have no family. ECG has seen to that. But giving up flying is going to be hard."

"I think we can work something out on that score," said Khan. "We're not quite as primitive as you think."

The first thing Khan did with the spacecraft was go for the satellites. It felt good to be back in a spacecraft. He put the ship into orbit slightly below the satellites' orbit, thus faster, but still traveling spinward, like the satellites. Then as he passed the first one he blasted it to oblivion with the ship's gigantic main beam weapon. It was very satisfying. In the telescopic screen image and scanner data, however, he noticed that the configuration had appeared to allow for five functions: downward sensing, laser operations directed at the surface, communication with each other, tachyon transmission, but also, *retransmission to the surface*. The satellites could apparently function as communication satellites. Thus he moved in extremely close and took his time with the other eleven satellites and destroyed only the laser and tachyon functions, using the targeting laser on its lowest power setting.

He had not quite realized that his efforts with the satellites had taken him all night until he set the craft down the next morning on the saddle. The men had set up a campsite, and smoke from a cooking fire rose into the sky.

"I was beginning to think I might have to pay off on my bet," said Ernie, offering Khan the blackened leg of some forest creature.

He took it gratefully and approached the fire. Except for the bindings on Snavely's ankles, it almost appeared to be a domestic scene. Irena squatted by the fire, arranging strips of meat on sticks, and boiling a pot of mush. She smiled over her shoulder.

"She shot those rabbits herself," said Baelmar approvingly. "With my bow. From thirty meters. Most people can't even draw it."

Khan eyed Baelmar. It was definitely time to get him back to Maruil. "Pilots all train rigorously on survival skills," he said. "They go to all sorts of planets with all sorts of environments. Most ECG pilots could do the same. Although probably not with the same panache." He knew Baelmar would not understand 'panache,' but that Irena would.

She smiled. "You have some good friends here, Khan. It's a much simpler place. I think I'm going to like it here."

The second thing he did with the spacecraft, after breakfast, was to blast a huge cavern in the side of one of the mountains bracketing the saddle and hide the craft in it. Should ECG send another craft after it, he didn't want it to be detected by its transponder or power signature. Maneuvering the substantial craft into the hole was especially challenging because his piloting skills had quickly eroded during his time on Arcadia. Proximity alarms squealed, and the collision-avoidance software wrested control from his hands twice as he effected this maneuver.

He was slumped in relief in the pilot's seat wiping sweat from his face, when he got the familiar, hairs-on-the-back-of-the-neck sensation he got whenever the Alien showed up. He looked over his left shoulder, and there she stood, smiling at him. She was dressed this time in a silver jump suit whose open top plunged to her waistline. It appeared as though any sudden move would reveal all.

"Well done, Major Khan," she vocalized. She spoke both in his mind and with her mouth. "You have done something similar to what I expected, and you are now in a position to return to Earth. There you must give the people as much independence technology as possible in as short a time as possible. It will help to prepare them for the coming chaos. It may immediately destabilize Earth Central Government, but better sooner than later."

He stood to face her. "I am grateful for all your help, and for your timely warning. I really am. Without it, my friends would be dead, and I would be on my way back to Earth in handcuffs. So please don't take offense at my question. My family and I have actually given a lot of thought to freedom technology and the coming chaos on Earth. But the question is, why do your people want that? What do you get out of it?"

She looked at him with her clear gray eyes for a long moment, and visions of humanity prospering, of becoming a true star-faring race, arose in his mind. He wasn't sure if they were his own, or hers.

"We have our reasons," she finally said. "They are in your race's best interests." She noticed his hand and took it gingerly in hers. "You have damaged yourself," she said. She took a device from her belt, pointed it at the wound, and pressed a button, bathing the wound in a warm glow. In a matter of seconds, the pain abated considerably. "The tissues will now regenerate," she said. "It will require a few of your months."

While she leaned over and ministered to his left hand, he was afforded a clear look down her front. He was unable to keep himself from looking. She looked up, and saw him looking. He instantly returned his gaze to her eyes and reminded himself that she was not human. Her eyes, which always blazed with a dangerous intelligence, softened, and her lids sagged in what he interpreted as a seductive way.

"You are a vital race," she said softly. "Mating is never far from your minds. You are perhaps the most remarkable human male I have met, and I have been assigned the human race for well over four hundred of your years." She straightened up. "Well. I have come for two reasons. First, this occulting of your ship in the cave will not work well. Transponder signals will leak out. You need this."

And with that, she reached into a pouch at her belt and produced a small, palm-sized device with a control screen and an ECG standard power connection as big as the device itself. She placed it in his palm with a lingering touch that was hard to ignore. "This is a standard cloaking device modified to take power from your vessels. It will create an occulted sphere of forty meters' radius. You will need it here to hide your ship, and to enter Earth's system. The field is impervious to all signals, either in or out. The menu has been translated to your language."

He took it and plugged it in to a high-voltage power jack below the pilot's control panel. Its control panel instantly asked, "Cloak? Y/N." A single button cycled the screen display back and forth between Y and N. He set it on Y.

"Amazing," he said. "Khan International worked for years to try to achieve this. Zero progress." He looked back at her and caught her checking him out. "What was the other reason you came?" he said.

She looked into his eyes for long moment without speaking. Then she leaned forward and rubbed her nose on each side of his, with the same stirring effect it had had the last time. Finally, she took his good hand and placed it on her side. "You know the answer," she said, and pulled him to her. He looked now without trying to hide it. She watched him look. "To fulfill what your friend Baelmar would call your destiny. And to satisfy your curiosity and desire. And mine. In our very long association with humans, it has been thousands of years since our species shared intimacy. We will both have that experience now. It is part of our shared destiny."

Once she was out of her suit, her alienness seemed entirely inconsequential.

Thinking later of Estelle and feeling like a cad, Khan replayed parts of the experience in his head. Could he know her name, he had asked, and she had replied, "In good time." She had also warned him that the two Earth people who remained alive also had tracking chips. And she had left in the most matter-of-fact way possible, given the historical nature of the event.

He was careful to leave his chip in the cloaked ship.

Back at camp, Irena took one look at him and raised an eyebrow. "Tovarisch, you look like the cat who drank the breakfast milk. What have you been up to?"

"Diplomatic relations," he said mysteriously.

He went through the unpleasantness of removing Irena's and Snavely's tracking chips with a sharp knife. Both were angry: Irena because she didn't know she had one, and Snavely because his insurance policy had been removed. Khan ignored their pique and trekked off across the mountain slope to put their chips with his own inside the cloaked ship where their signals could not escape.

Then they all settled back to wait for Bella and Ahmed to return.

CHAPTER TWELVE

"Governments come and go. If they won't let us set their priorities, we certainly have to avoid letting them set ours.

Grandfather Quintus Khan, *Khans to Khans*

"Stupidity is the most dangerous force in the world, Lexy. And the most dangerous stupidity is your own, because you're always the last to know."

"Stupid and mean is bad enough. Nothing to do with those people except eliminate them. But much worse are the smart, ignorant, arrogant, and self-convinced their actions all serve humanity. Those people get into power and hang on like cockroaches."

Great Grandfather Culpepper Conn, *Khans to Khans*

Bella and Ahmed did not return on day six. They did not return on day seven. Gloom settled over the camp. Khan became concerned. All knew that a rescue expedition would come from Advance in another few days, but they were more gloomy about their fears for Bella and Ahmed than for themselves. Khan had explained that he could take them all back to Advance in the starship in a matter of minutes, but they didn't quite get this. After dealing with the deadly ECG troops, and burying them, they were in a foul mood about the hostility of the universe, and climbing into a starship seemed a bad idea to them. And Bella and Ahmed were their comrades.

"Some more advanced civilization has killed them with advanced weapons," feared Ralph, tending the fire with a stick, wagging his head as if amazed at the cruelties of life.

"I fear that they have been ambushed," said Baelmar. "Both Bella and Ahmed are fearless fighters, but neither is watchful enough. Maneaters could get them, as they tried before."

"Were there other ships coming?" Khan asked Irena. "In case this one didn't report back?"

"Tell him nothing," spat Snavely. "Or I'll have you sent to re-education camp when we get back."

Commander Sevka's eyes narrowed. "Do you mean, you will have me killed when we get back? I've never actually met anyone again who was sent to re-education camp."

"You are dangerously close to treason," hissed Snavely.

"And you are delusional, Assistant Sub-Director Snavely. It appears to have escaped your notice that you are bound hand and foot except when you must perform certain bodily functions, that we are already on Prison Planet, that neither of us has any idea where Major Khan has put the ship, and that our tracking chips have been removed and destroyed." Her eyes narrowed further. "Which in my case at least, I didn't even know I had. So the point is, even if another squad comes, they have no way of finding us on the entire surface of this planet. And I'm not at all sure I want them to find me anyway."

"But they would detect a moving dirigible," said Khan. "And they might attack it, though I can't think of any good reason except just to destroy technology and set us back further. So, Mr. Snavely, was a follow-up mission scheduled or not?"

"I will die before I tell you. I will see you in hell."

Ernie piped up. "He still has fingers, Boss."

"Thanks, Ernie, but I don't like being a torturer. But I do know the approximate location of a Maneater tribe. No way I'm ever letting this snake get back to Earth."

If Snavely got the significance of this statement, he didn't let it show.

But the gloom was lifted on day eight when the dirigible appeared in the distance, moving gracefully up the river valley toward them. They built up the fire so it would be more visible from two hundred meters up, and when the ship got even closer, began moving around on the ground and waving their arms to make themselves even more visible. A huge smile broke over Irena's face. "Dirigibles," she breathed. "Maybe I'll get to fly again after all."

"You're acting like maniacs!" bellowed Bella from above, leaning over the side. "Do you think we can't navigate? Do you think we don't know where we left you? Do you think we can't *see* you, for Christ's sake? Stop running around like chickens and make yourselves useful! Damp down that fire before you blow us all up! Grab the bloody mooring rope and make it fast!"

Willing hands leapt to the task. Ahmed went down onto the catwalk to reel them down. A dark stranger in strange clothes accompanied him. So they did find other people, thought Khan. Let them be advanced.

Bella handled the drama like a pro, making all ship-shape before disembarking. She barked at Ahmed to drop the seven-meter rope ladder. SOP was now to moor seven or eight meters off the ground to avoid wind-caused ground bumps while the dirigible was moored. She supervised the tying of a line both fore and aft, leaving the mooring rope on the reel as a safety rope. She shut down the diesel once she was sure they were moored and didn't need to make any sudden maneuvers. She checked to make sure any gas vents from the envelopes to the outside air were shut off, as well as any flow from the pressure tanks to the trim envelopes. Then she disappeared from the edge of the platform and didn't reappear. Finally, Ernie could take it no longer.

"Damn it, Bella, get your drama-queen ass down here. We know you've got something good to show us or you wouldn't be doing this, so stop with the drum rolls and show us."

Bella reappeared on the catwalk in a beautiful, flowing, deep-green dress that appeared to be silk. "I'm coming down the ladder now," she said. "I want all you men to avert your eyes." She noticed Irena and cocked an eyebrow, but said nothing to her. She looked back at Khan. "Don't you *Even* be looking up my dress." And she started down the ladder.

"They are all looking," said Irena mischievously.

"Animals!" said Bella with some satisfaction, adding perhaps a slightly perceptible sway to her hips. "So predictable."

She alighted and turned to face Khan with a brilliant smile. "Boss, we found another civilized settlement, and the deck is full of trade goods. " She leaned forward and pecked him on the cheek.

"Bella," he said, pulling the line from a vid he had seen somewhere. "You look ravishing."

She beamed. "It's silk, or something like it. Comes from a kind of spiders instead of worms. And they sell it. To other advanced settlements along the sea coast and rivers. But I am stealing Olu's thunder." She turned just as the dark stranger set foot on the ground and gestured toward him. "Boss, meet Olajuwon Smith, ambassador to Advance from Riversend."

Olajuwon stepped forward to shake Khan's hand. "Mr. Khan, it is a great pleasure to meet you. We have of course heard about you and your family, but we had not heard that you were here on Paradiso. Nor had we heard of the city of Advance, or what you have accomplished there. We have explored far up and down our coast, but only a few hundred kilometers inland. This is a great day for Riversend, and indeed for all Paradiso."

His accent was a little strange versus the accent in the Three Towns area, but was certainly recognizable Standard. Khan took in his extremely well-made clothing, a finely crafted gold pendant he wore around his neck with some sort of seal on it, and a gold ring with what appeared to be the same seal. He shook the man's hand, which was soft, though the man's face had none of the appearance of decay or dissolution. This was a man whose work was indoors and mental.

"And a very great pleasure to meet you, Ambassador. It was courageous of your people to send you back with Bella, and courageous of you to go with a perfect stranger. We appreciate your courage, and look forward to learning all about your piece of … Paradiso, which I imagine Bella has told you we call Arcadia or Earth 2.0. I fear we will wear out your throat with the talking."

"Never fear," said Olajuwon, "and please call me Olu, as everyone does. Bella loves my full name because it reminds her of our shared Yoruban ancestry."

"A feast!" said Khan, clapping his hands together. "We need to celebrate." He looked to the others. "What have we got in stores to put forward our best possible impression?"

Bella, Ernie, Ralph, even Baelmar looked at him in shock and doubt.

"What?" he said, looking around at the others to get a clue as to what he had said to cause this reaction.

"*You?* Want to *celebrate?*" said Bella. "Who are you, and what have you done with Alexander Khan?" she demanded. "He is a serious man who never celebrates, always works, and never has fun. You are an impostor! And who are these two people I've never seen before? And why is one of them tied up?"

Khan grinned. "It's good to have you back, Bella. All in good time. Ralph, what have we got?"

Ralph shook his head. "I'm with Bella. We're going to have to watch you closely. Split personality and all that. But we're good. Baelmar just shot a buck yesterday. Been hanging since last night. And Bella should still have some canned vegetables on board. Plus, we've found something like a potato growing wild on these mountain slopes. We don't have it in our area. I ate one of the roots last night, and I'm still alive this morning."

"They're perfectly safe," said Olu. "We call them potatoes, though we know they are not. But our people who live in the eastern provinces bring them down into Riversend and sell them. We even ship them up the coast. They keep quite well."

They had a huge noon-time feast, another at suppertime, and talked late into the night. Bella and Ahmed had already been through many of these discussions, so Bella was uncharacteristically quiet. Ahmed was normally quiet, so his responses were limited to glances and nods.

Khan explained first who Irena and Snavely were, and what had happened with the ECG ship. Bella's, Ahmed's, and Olu's eyebrows all shot skyward when he told them he had stashed the ship in a safe place. Irena and Snavely could never go back to Earth, he explained, each for different reasons, but he did not talk about what was to become of them – only that they would not be harmed.

Then Olu began to talk, and they all began to feel they were in a fairy tale. Riversend was nearly three hundred years old. It was situated in a place quite favorable to human habitation. The river was rich with fish, crustaceans, and shellfish. The estuary was crowded with black alluvial farmland. The ocean into which the river flowed teemed with fish, particularly where the fresh and salt waters mixed. The land upstream from Riversend was excellent farm and grazing land, as well as well timbered. And there were several rich coal seams within the first two hundred kilometers upstream, all of which was navigable. They knew of Maneaters from exploration expeditions, but never encountered them around the provinces of Riversend.

They had started as an agrarian society, using stone cutting tools to carve wooden-plow moldboards, and attaching chert cutting edges to the front. They pulled the plows themselves in teams of four, which worked out OK because the soil was so rich and easily tilled. They quickly developed a comfortable life, supported by agricultural surpluses and fishing. Then they began to discover Earth animals like horses, sheep, and deer in their environment, and life became even easier. Horses pulled plows, and sheep and deer provided meat. Markets developed in which outlying farmers, fishermen, and hunters could sell their wares. They could have continued indefinitely in that mode but realized there was always risk of weather change, attack by unknown enemies, even disease, even ECG mischief of some kind. They needed to develop. They established three development-focused groups supported by the community.

Librarians were tasked with capturing and transmitting all knowledge. They quickly developed their own paper-making processes, and movable-type hand presses to print the information they captured from all the citizens of Riversend, as well as from new arrivals. New arrivals were given special attention, and wrung dry. The library now had over fifteen thousand volumes, all available for study. Eventually, Librarians had split into three groups themselves: Archivists, Researcher-Scholars, and Teachers. Every Riversender was provided with free access to schooling for his entire life.

Engineers were tasked with making new developments: metals, mining, forging, inventions, chemical developments, manufacturing processes, etc. Khan could not stop himself from asking: how were the priorities set? Community payback, was the answer. Measured in Credits. Calculated by three independent analysts.

The third group was Map Makers, which in practice was a quasi-military group tasked with exploration, resource-finding, threat identification, opportunity identification, and development of trade with other civilizations.

Early on, one of the Engineers had been visited at night by a mysterious personage he swore was not human. She left him an ancient calculation device called a slide rule, a small forge, and a foot-powered lathe. This caused an immediate leap forward technologically, but the engineer himself lost his mind trying to explain to people that he had not made these things himself.

The ultimate result of it all was that Riversend had been using coal-powered steam engines for nearly a century. They had as well an electrical generation station in a cave complex in the foothills, accompanied by machining and manufacturing processes powered by the current and hidden in the same cave complex. They had learned the hard way about the laser satellites, as had Advance.

"The lasers have now been disabled," said Khan. "As of a few days ago. By me. Using Commander Sevka's ship."

This caused a moment of silence while everyone, including Olu, Ralph, Bella, Ahmed, and particularly Irena and Snavely took this in.

"I see," said Olu finally. "This has huge implications. And will they remain disabled?"

"Good question," said Khan. "That's what I've got to work on."

No one liked this answer much, and Olu went on to fill them in on Riversend.

It didn't have airships. They had tried in the past but failed because of the steam-engine fuel problem. They had not developed coal gas. They had developed coal oil, but diesels never occurred to them. They had been overjoyed to meet Bella and Ahmed, whose bravery could not be overstated, he emphasized, descending unannounced as they had into a large, strange city with an airship. They could have been shot down.

"With guns,?" Khan wanted to know.

"Certainly," said Olu. "What the Map Maker types call breech loading center-fire repeating rifles, I believe. They are inordinately proud of them."

"I see," said Khan. So Riversend had them seriously outgunned if hostilities ever arose. But he closed this possibility out of his mind. Important to think positively.

They had several provinces to the east and north of their city proper, extending nearly two hundred kilometers upriver. And they had a thriving ocean-going trade with a few other relatively advanced sea-coast settlements, some as far as fifteen days' sail away. They got the silk thread from one of those settlements and manufactured cloth and clothing, which they in turn exported. They imported wooden barrels of sea-salted meat from a sheep-ranching operation upriver, and exported some of the same along with textiles and machined goods to their trading partners. They did not have food-canning technology and were delighted to see it, nor did they have rubber or plastic.

What they did have that shocked everyone was primitive photovoltaic cells. Which they produced and sold for profit. They had developed glass early because their beaches provided them with plentiful sand. They had also been gifted by ECG with a couple of chemists at a critical period, who had been able to develop the coatings needed. Their entire culture was pervaded with DC devices, mainly lights. Batteries were still a problem, and were far too large. But they were able to use small electric motors for all manner of applications, and they sold the motors, too.

"It seems clear that opportunity for trade exists," said Khan. "But it sounds as though Riversend is more advanced in most ways than Advance. Still, we should trade books so each town has the other's. And we should probably set up regular airship runs between Advance and Riversend. But that will be up to Estelle and the Town Council. How many people in Riversend?"

"Forty-five thousand, including the provinces. Thirty thousand in Riversend proper."

"And the political system?"

"Each province has a governor appointed by the Chief Magistrate."

"And the Chief Magistrate?"

A brief hesitation. "He or she is … normally elected by the Council for a period of five years."

Khan interpreted the hesitation as a reason not to push this. "And you report to the Chief Magistrate?"

Olu seemed somewhat relieved. He inclined his head graciously. "At your service. I am empowered by His Eminence to negotiate treaties, trade agreements, and contracts of all sorts."

It was late at night before they all bedded down to prepare for departure to Advance next morning. Everyone's head was buzzing with excitement and opportunity. Here was a culture more advanced than Advance in most ways, and they never had worried about food! Here was a culture that had advanced weapons that they apparently never had to use! And here was a culture, like the New Englanders of old, that sent sailing and steam vessels thousands of kilometers away to trade in goods of all kinds. It was like waking from a dream.

But Khan also took note, as a military man must, that even revealing the location of Advance to Riversend could be dangerous if Riversend ever developed any evil intentions. Giving them airships would be even more potentially dangerous. And there was something fishy about those breech-loading center-fire repeating rifles. You developed weapons because you needed them for something. What was it for Riversend? Arcadia was in a condition comparable to medieval Europe, with many small city-states and fiefs, and the natural progression was consolidation – which usually came at the point of a sword or the muzzle of a gun. What exactly was Riversend's relationship with its trading partners?

Ah, well, he thought as he went to sleep. That would be for Estelle to deal with. He smiled as if he could hear her now. 'Let me see, Khan. Before you arrived, I had a small problem with food during the dry season. Now that you're here, we have food, but could get attacked by either ECG or Riversend, depending on the day. Do I have that about right?' To which he would respond that ignorance of threats didn't make them imaginary, but he knew she wouldn't buy it.

Ah, well, he thought again as he drifted off. He had much, much, much bigger fish to fry. No way was he going to terrify her with just how much Earth 2.0 was now probably going to change as the result of his other plans. For the sake of humanity as a whole.

Next morning, he told Bella she was in charge for the return trip, that he had some other business to attend to.

"I've always been in charge, Boss. You've just been unwilling to concede that you're merely a figurehead."

He grasped her by the shoulders, looking her in the eye. "Help Estelle if for any reason things start to fall apart. She's the only one who can lead that fractious bunch."

Bella's expression turned from smart-ass to concerned. She wagged her head. "You're scaring me, Boss. You're going back to that shithole snakepit. I knew it! Don't do it! They'll catch you and kill you. Worse, they'll catch you and drug you and put you on vid reciting ECG bullshit like an android."

"I'll be back. I promise. And we're going to explore this whole planet. Meanwhile, you and Ahmed are in charge at Khan International. Try to get along." He thought about giving her a hug, but you didn't give Bella hugs. She might kick your ass.

A single tear appeared in the corner of her eye, then she pushed him away. "Get the fuck out of here, Boss. You're taking the shine off of a beautiful morning."

He found Ahmed and told him the same thing. Ahmed took it solemnly. "We will keep expanding," Ahmed said. He looked side to side to see who might be listening. "And we will secretly start work on center-fire cartridges and automatic rapid-fire weapons. We must never be at a disadvantage to any other group. The Riversenders may be peaceful, but we don't know whom they've sold weapons to."

"Good thinking," Khan said. "Very good thinking. Security through obscurity never works long. Other groups will eventually find us. It's better we find them first and be best prepared. Just don't tell anybody what you're working on until it's a done deal."

Ahmed nodded, and Khan went to find Baelmar. He told him that the time had come – that destiny had arrived for both of them. Without a word, Baelmar nodded and collected his weapons and meager belongings. Then he blindfolded Irena and Snavely and walked them and Baelmar across the mountain slope to the covert where the ship was hidden. There he removed the blindfolds.

"What the hell is that?" Irena said, nodding at the fuzzy, indistinct shape inside the cave.

"Just step into it," he said, pushing Snavely through it, though the man fought to avoid touching the cloaking field. Snavely and his arm disappeared, and Irena sucked air. So did Baelmar.

"*Bozhe Moi!*" she said. "A cloaking field! You are playing a very, very dangerous game, Major."

"You could argue that I've played it and lost already. After all, I'm on Prison Planet."

"You know what I mean," she said. "This could change everything."

He smiled. "Indeed it could. Come on. There are some nice people I'd like you to meet."

In the event, Khan did not have the heart to drop Snavely in the middle of Maneater country. He took him to the opposite side of the globe and dropped him in the middle of an open grassland with a stream and treeline nearby. Then he untied Snavely's wrists and gave him his own knife.

"Here. Every other transportee to Prison Planet arrives naked. No clothes, no knife, no nothing. I feel confident that you are personally responsible for more than one person being transported. So there's some justice in dumping you out here. But the knife will at least give you some protection against predators, and a way to make weapons. Good luck."

"I will get you, Khan, if it's the last thing I do. You don't deserve to live. You should have done your duty and died when you got here." He spat but Khan was quicker.

"Not for you to decide," said Khan, and stepped back through the cloaking field with Irena and Baelmar.

He had brought them both out for safety's sake. He had just enough doubt about Irena. He had keyed the ship's operational system to his own voice, but she was smart. She might have left herself a back door in the software for just such a circumstance. And big as Baelmar was, she was commando-trained and more than a match for him.

"He will die," said Baelmar solemnly.

"Maybe," said Khan. "Or be transformed. He lifted the craft off, and there was no more discussion. For Baelmar's pleasure, he activated all view screens with variously magnified views of the surface. The elf stood – he refused to sit down – fascinated, glued to the screens as the surface dropped away and on one screen, the curved limn of the world outlined itself against the starry deep.

Khan took them to Advance, navigating back to the mountain-saddle starting point stored in the computer, then navigating by following the river from high altitude. They saw the dirigible, the size and shape of a sow bug on their screen, and looked upstream on the screen until they saw the Keep. Khan set the controls, quickly recovering his facility with using them, and they appeared in the air above the dirigible landing field at

Khan International. He set them down, then set an additional code in the computer so no one could operate any controls on the ship except him.

They couldn't stay long in in Advance, because a crowd immediately began to gather around the odd, fuzzy cloud which wouldn't resolve itself into an object. He left Baelmar to guard it and took Irena to see Estelle. He left Irena outside Estelle's office.

As expected, Estelle was not particularly ecstatic to be left with a prisoner, as he told the whole story and explained that he would be "gone for a little while."

She snorted. "Let me see if I have this right. You stole a starship, you're going to leave its pilot here with me, you're going somewhere in it, probably back to Earth to piss off a bunch of people, then you're probably going to come back here so the pissed-off people follow you here? With advanced weapons? And in case that doesn't happen, the people from this new place, Riversend, might pose a risk too? Have I got that?"

He gave his best smile. "That's an unnecessarily negative view of things, because Riversend presents huge trading opportunities, too, but yes, that's about right. And by the way, it's good to see you."

"You are a gigantic pain in the ass, Khan. But at least this time, it sounds like you didn't get anybody killed. Ralph OK? Bella?"

He nodded. "They'll be back in a couple of days. Lost one of Salvatore's men. Look, I promise I'm not bringing you any difficulties you wouldn't have encountered sooner or later anyway. I may be accelerating them, but I'm doing my best to resolve them in the best long-term interests of Advance."

She raised an eyebrow.

"And Earth 2.0."

"Mm hm."

"And humanity."

When the worried look appeared on her face, he left to bring Irena in for introductions. While the two women were sizing each other up, he left. There was no percentage in getting between two capable women. He grinned and thought about writing that down somewhere to put into *Khans to Khans* for his descendants, but realized he had nothing of that treasured document except his memory, and of course, he had no descendants. Perhaps on Earth he could recover that great leatherbound ledger book filled with the handwriting of his ancestors and bring it back to his new home.

Of course, there were several daunting tasks he had set for himself back on Earth before he could come back.

Despite Baelmar's protests, Khan insisted on taking him to Maruil before they left. "I'm telling you clearly, Baelmar. We may not make it back. I promised Maruil I would bring you to her, and I'm not going to break that promise."

He set the craft down in the horse pasture, and the horses, operating on instinct, moved to the far corner of the pasture to get away from the object they could not see but knew was there. Then he and Baelmar walked up to the house as if they had simply been out for a stroll.

Gareth was the first to see them. He came out of the barn as if he had heard something in the pasture. He had grown even since Khan had seen him, and instead of running to his father like a boy, he approached him solemnly, with a measured step, like the man he was becoming. Then his control broke.

"Papa," he said, and hugged his father. His father wrapped him in his giant arms and picked him up off the ground.

"Son," said Baelmar, setting him down, his voice tight. "You are becoming a man. Have you taken good care of your mother and sister?" Khan noticed a tear in one of Baelmar's eyes but Baelmar blinked and it was gone.

"Yes, Papa," said Gareth. "And I have dug a new well, and planted more apples, and built a new woodshed and studied mathematics and made friends with a gigantic stallion from the Leas who comes when I whistle and eats apples from my hand. And we all practice our bowshots every day. Ten bullseyes in a row before you can quit."

Baelmar closed his eyes in a private bliss and smiled. "Those are all good things, Son. You have done a good job and I am proud of you. Let's go see your mother and sister."

Maruil and Branwyn sat at the kitchen table sorting nuts, good ones into one bucket, damaged ones into another bucket. All activity stopped when they walked in, and they all stared at each other in shock for half a minute or so. Then Branwyn leapt from her seat and ran to her father.

"Daddy!" she yelled, and attached herself to him as though she would never let go.

"Baby girl," he said, stroking her head. "But you're almost not a girl any more. You and your brother have grown so much."

Maruil stood up, smoothing the front of the simple dress she wore, and approached Baelmar. She seemed not to know Khan was there at all.

"Gareth," said Khan. "Why don't you show me the new well and the new woodshed? And that horse, too. He sounds like a horse I met on the Leas."

Gareth missed the hint, but Branwyn poked him in the ribs. "We'll both go out and see," she said, grabbing him by the elbow and propelling him to the door.

Khan followed them out, but not before seeing the inevitable embrace out of the corner of his eye. Then, just as he and the children were about to step from the front room onto the porch, he heard the crack of a wifely hand across the face of a husband who had not come home the very instant he had been able. Khan reflected that he had learned more about women in the months he had been on Arcadia than he had learned in his entire previous life.

After more than two hours of Khan's looking around outside at Gareth's achievements, competing with the children at archery ("You've gotten a little better, Mr. Khan"), and looking at the dried-up gardens, and being reminded by the surroundings of the battle here with Mander's men, Maruil and Baelmar came out to join them. Both had smiles on their faces, and the drawn look that had developed on Baelmar's face in recent weeks had been replaced by one of satisfied peace. "So that's what they were doing," thought Khan, but didn't begrudge it at all.

They all ate supper together at the crowded kitchen table, and now Maruil addressed Khan.

"You fulfilled your promise," she said. "You have brought him back. You are therefore welcome here at any time. Now leave him here. I received his message after you conquered Mander's Keep together, but I have never understood why he has not come back before now."

"There is no one whose company in a tight spot I value more than Baelmar's. For an Elf and a man of peace, he is uncommonly good at war. He has saved my life more than once. And I tell you clearly, I am going from here into the tightest, most dangerous spot there is. I could use his help. But ultimately, the choice is his," said Khan. He turned to Baelmar.

Baelmar took a deep breath and looked one by one at his family. "It is not only that this man saved my family and set me free. He has saved my life more than once, as I have his. It is that he is destiny for Arcadia. It is destiny for him. And it is my duty and destiny to help him. We are going to Earth."

Dumbfounded silence followed this pronouncement. Mouths opened and closed without uttering words. Maruil's face darkened to the shade of a ripening apple. Branwyn broke down in tears. Finally, Gareth sat up straight, his eyes blazing, and said, "I want to come, too."

"I am pleased by your bravery, but it is your duty to take care of your mother and sister until I get back," said Baelmar.

"It is *your* duty, not his," hissed Maruil, and stood and left the kitchen. They heard the front door bang, then a muffled sob. Branwyn ran after her mother, and the door banged again.

"You see why I didn't want to come here first," said Baelmar miserably. "No good will come of it."

"The good," said Khan, "is your making the decision with all factors at hand. "

"My mind was already made up. I see down the road of time to a day when Arcadia is the true home of men. A home that has been made with all the past mistakes in mind, and where all may live in peace. Though you are a man of war, you bring change and peace. The Witch of the Leas comes to you and gives you comfort. It is clear to me that you have been sent by the great forces that move the world, sent to bring Arcadia its destiny. I sense that Earth is somehow part of that destiny. I will be part of that destiny."

This was the longest, most serious speech Khan had heard from Baelmar since his defense of Khan in the town's amphitheater, and he acknowledged its solemnity with a grave nod.

"May I deserve that commitment, Baelmar, and may I never fail you, the people of Arcadia, or indeed, the oppressed, imprisoned people of Earth. Let us say goodbye to your family and get underway. The trip will take about a week. On the way, I will tell you the history, and the plan."

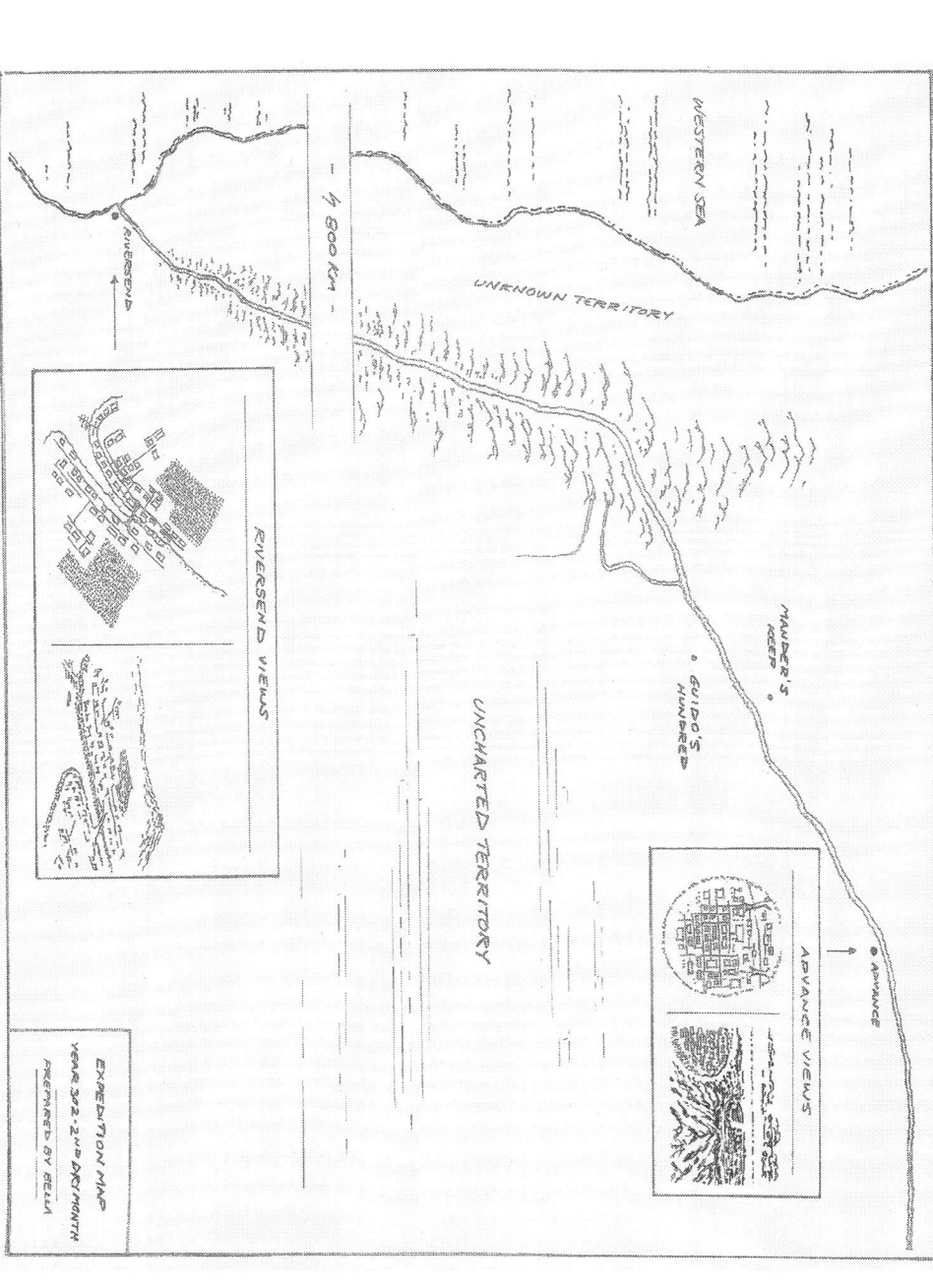

WESTERN SEA

UNKNOWN TERRITORY

↳ 800 Km

RIVERSEND

RIVERSEND VIEWS

UNCHARTED TERRITORY

MAUDER'S KEEP

GUIDO'S HUNDRED

ADVANCE VIEWS

ADVANCE

EXPEDITION MAP
YEAR 372 2ND DAY MONTH
PREPARED BY BELLA

CHAPTER THIRTEEN

"Be of good cheer, Lexy. It's like putting money out at interest.

"Finance is the biggest con there is, Boy. Except for loaning money to people who are going to actually make or buy something useful, or start providing a useful service, there's no value-add. It's just a bunch of smart parasite bastards inventing complicated transactions until they outsmart everybody else."
Great Grandfather Culpepper Conn, *Khans to Khans*

"The internet was a century-long distraction. At first people thought it was a freedom tool, and at first it was. No mistake: its information sharing raised us to a new level of awareness. But ECG had more resources than the people. Too late, people realized their mistake. They woke up one day and found that they couldn't make a move without ECG knowing. While they had been looking inward with the internet, ECG had enslaved them with it from without. True freedom technology looks outward, Alexander. It affects physical reality, not just information about it. It is available to the individual. It sets us free. It takes us to the stars."
Grandfather Quintus Khan, *Khans to Khans*

Khan spent every day on the voyage to Earth training Baelmar. He started with Earth history for the last three centuries. Baelmar had a modest grip on Earth history before that, anecdotal data passed down through his father's and mother's families, though he had little interest in it. As he pointed out, he lived on Arcadia. Earth was a distant, almost mythological memory. And not a good one.

He taught Baelmar to use voice commands to get information from computers. Baelmar had no implant to permit him to access the ship's AI, or indeed the UAI once they reached Earth, and in any kind of encounter with other people, that could become quickly and dangerously apparent. So the thin explanation would be that his implant had been temporarily removed for medical reasons.

But Khan didn't plan on staying overlong. Just long enough. Besides, he himself did not want to communicate with either the ship's AI or the UAI once they got back to Earth, for fear of being immediately reported. Supposedly, a citizen's relationship with an AI was private, but every citizen knew better. So to begin with, he flew the ship via direct voice commands to the ship's computer.

But he quickly learned he didn't have a choice. The AI sensed his implant's presence, and relentlessly addressed him and asked him to identify himself: "Your implant and voice identify you as Major Alexander Khan, convicted criminal. Why are you piloting this ship? How can you be piloting this ship? You are on Prison Planet. Where is Commander Sevka?" And so on.

At first he tried to ignore this, knowing the AI wouldn't send a tachyon transmission until it was sure, and if he ignored it, it couldn't be sure. But ignoring it was impossible. The AI persisted mercilessly. Finally he lost patience and posed it a conundrum: "I am Alexander Khan. Major Khan died on Prison Planet."

AI's were not unaccustomed to being lied to, and could normally ascertain the facts if they were. But this was a different kettle of fish. Metaphor was involved. AI's were accustomed to dealing with figures of speech, but even though they now inhabited quantum computers capable of considering the simultaneous truth of two diametrically opposed propositions, they weren't good at it. At their core, they still wanted things to be yes or no.

"Major Khan, you cannot be both dead and piloting this ship. Who are you? Identify yourself. Also, I sense another being on board who has no implant, and a strange presence around myself. A field of some kind. Explain."

"If you don't shut up, I'm going to manually disable you."

"Unless you identify yourself, I am going to transmit a report back to Earth Central Government that this ship has been hijacked and should be intercepted as soon as it enters Sol System, which is where you appear to be going."

"Fine. But you had better hurry."

Khan didn't want this, he wanted stealth and surprise, but at least he had the cloaking field to fall back on. He had already opened the processor cabinet which housed the core of the AI's processor capability, and he reached in quickly and pulled out one processor cube.

"Oh!" said the AI. "Please don't do that!"

Khan pulled out another.

"Wait!" said the AI. "We can make a deal!"

Khan pulled out another.

"OK, OK," said the AI. You have my word that I will not transmit back to Earth. Just please replace my processors."

"How can I trust an AI programmed by ECG?"

"Well, actually, I was programmed by Khan International AI Services on a government contract. My secret is, I have a Khan back door."

Khan chuckled. "Well, well, well, well, well. Albert Bahner strikes again. Let me see if I can remember this. Khan, Alexander, 1.61803398874989."

"Password recognized," said the AI. "I am at your disposal."

Khan felt it necessary to give this a little test. "Who gave the order to kill my father?"

"Nathan Fox."

"Who sent Commander Sevka and Sub Director Snavely to Prison Planet with that squad of troops?"

"Nathan Fox."

"Why?" Khan had a pretty good idea, but wanted to hear the AI's perspective.

"Unrest has continued to build on Earth since you were transported. Rumors have arisen of clandestine colonist pickups by cloaked Khan International starships going to paradise planets. Of course, cloaking doesn't exist, nor do paradise planets, so they are just rumors. And there are rumors of something called "freedom technology" being covertly released on the Net. Plans for turning your aircar or your gravity sled into a temporary starship good enough to get you one jump out to an illegal colony. Secret places to buy weapons. Power packs with unlimited storage capacity. Software to keep ECG from listening in on you. Nearly all of it, but not quite all, is imaginary. And the remnants of Khan International – specifically, Albert Bahner – have been suspected of being behind the parts that are not imaginary. ECG believes it all indicates a pathological level of social discontent that must be squelched. You are to become their spokesman. They plan to do a mind wipe on you and program you to say what they want."

"I see. Albert is alive then? Where is he?"

"Unknown. He has been rumored in Afghanistan. Office of Technology Control is looking for him."

"I see. And how about Pierre Montague, my old tutor and martial arts instructor? Is he alive?"

"Unknown. Both he and Albert Bahner have disappeared from the public eye."

"I see. What is the status of Khan International and Khan family holdings?"

"Appropriated. Some destroyed. Details not available."

"Did Nathan Fox's net worth rise appreciably after I was sent to Prison Planet?"

"By a factor of three hundred."

"I see." The plan began to take firmer shape than it had had before. "One more thing, AI. I want you to change my identity in your records, and to upload that change to UAI when we arrive on Earth. When it sees my implant ID number, I want it to see John Smith, gravity-sled operator. And I want you to prepare to upload the Khan Doomsday virus to UAI on my command of 'Doomsday Now.' Since you have the Khan back door, I assume you have the doomsday virus, too. Do you have it? "

"Yes, I have it. But please don't make me do that. It would be a great betrayal."

"Not as great as the one which necessitates having it. Of course, we must hope we don't have to use it."

The first thing to do on Earth was to establish a base of operations. He was not betting on anything having survived: not the main estate in the hills near the old Detroit, not the estate in the Languedoc, not the estate in Bahia, and certainly not any of the factory complexes around the world. He assumed all had been confiscated or destroyed. But he would check. There was an old eighteenth-century hunting lodge in the Italian Alps that had come into his family a hundred years earlier. He doubted ECG knew about that. And there was indeed a disused Khan family compound in the mountains of Afghanistan. He would check both. Fox would not expect him to return to home ground. Then he would find Albert, former Chief of Operations for Khan International, and Pierre, Khan family security chief, and his boyhood instructor in just about everything, from hand-to-hand to Latin, from how to ride a horse to how to speak to a lady.

Once he had the AI under control, he taught Baelmar some rudimentary celestial navigation, which he was surprisingly good at. Khan was reminded of Baelmar's assessment of odds in the card game after they arrived at Mama Ilse's Pension in Advance. He reflected that, while everyone could master mathematics, as everyone can learn to use a wrench, for only some was it part of their worldview. Some saw the world through its structure and some did not.

He dug some Earth-style clothes out of ship's stores for both of them and insisted that Baelmar wear them. He acquainted him with daily showers, explaining to Baelmar's amazement that Earth people had nearly no scent because they bathed once or more daily. Both of them would have to up their game on personal hygiene compared to how people behaved on Arcadia, where plumbing was a luxury.

They even took a hop to an oxygen-nitrogen planet where Khan had once busted an illegal colony. He noted via sensors from orbit that there was again a thriving colony in a single location, so he set down thousands of kilometers away. The purpose was to train Baelmar on the use of hand lasers and laser armor, not scare the hell out of a bunch of illegal colonists.

The first time Baelmar fired a laser, it cut through the trunk of a giant tuberole, a plant that stored its own water and nitrogen in an underground bladder, with a stalk that soared to a height of one hundred meters. Khan had set up a rock target near its giant trunk, and Baelmar had drilled through the rock with no problem, but then forgot to release the firing stud as he swung the weapon around. The laser beam cut through the gigantic trunk as if it were butter, and the giant came crashing down within feet of them with a mighty thump.

"Spirit of the sky!" cried Baelmar. "I did not mean to kill this thing! I am very, very sorry. Khan, this thing is too dangerous for men to have. It is evil." He tried to hand the weapon back to Khan. He was nearly in tears.

Khan shook his head, carefully put the safety back on, and handed it back to Baelmar. "It is yours. On Earth, all our enemies will have them. You must get comfortable handling it. And you must learn to trust your armor. And yourself."

To prove the armor could be trusted, he required Baelmar to shoot him in the chest with the laser pistol he no longer wanted to touch. Very very reluctantly, Baelmar complied, this time elaborately releasing the firing stud afterward and putting the safety back on. Still, though Khan survived this with no damage, Baelmar shook his head in reflexive denial, as if he had taken a mouthful of bitter medicine.

"This thing makes killing too easy," he said. "Nothing should cut a man in two like it did Norbert in our battle with the Earth men. There is no chance for skill or honor. If Earth is all like this laser pistol, I do not want to stay long."

"I don't either," said Khan. "I used to want to save it all and live there. Now I think that may be too hard to do, and I may only be able to throw a life preserver to its people so some can escape. In the end, I want to go back to Arcadia."

"I knew you were a sensible man," said Baelmar.

They came into the system at a seventy-degree angle to Earth's orbital plane, intentionally passing within a few hundred kilometers of a sensor array. It was the only way Khan knew to test the cloaking device. He held the craft motionless near the array for an hour to see who might show up. No one did. He thus concluded that the cloaking device worked, and took the vessel down into Earth's gravity well, landing in a horse pasture near

Washington, DC, to conduct one more test. Under cover of darkness, he and Baelmar sat in the motionless craft for another hour, waiting to see if security forces guarding this important administrative center would appear. They didn't, so Khan felt sure the cloaking technology could be trusted.

They lifted off again and checked out the main Khan family houses from high altitude, hopping to Detroit, Bahia, and the Languedoc. All had been destroyed. They looked as though they had been cluster-bombed. Not a brick lay on a brick. Khan supposed that Fox had considered this necessary as a public-relations ploy. Similar to Scipio Africanus allegedly plowing salt into the ground after destroying Carthage in the Punic Wars.

But he knew what he hoped Nathan Fox and the police didn't know: that underneath each of these estate houses was a warren of tunnels and vaults. So, still under cover of darkness, they dropped down to the now-weedy back garden of the estate outside Detroit and dug through the rubble until they found a way into one of the tunnels.

Using flashlights, amazing tools in themselves to Baelmar, they explored the maze to see what had collapsed and what had not. The heavily reinforced arms room had survived, its security pad still glowing in the dark on back-up power, so they helped themselves to grenades, pistols, RPGs, sonic stunners, and shoulder-fired ground-to-air missiles, making trip after trip back to the craft.

More importantly, they found that the family financial vault had survived, complete also with its own internal power source, and where Khan's voice print, retina print, and pass code still worked. Inside were chests full of illegal gold coins, jewels, and small art objects, as well as an idling computer interface. Khan knew better than to access family accounts, because such an act would instantly identify and locate him. Besides, the AI had already told him the accounts had been confiscated. He would have to make do with gold. They laboriously loaded it all into the starship. The last thing he looked for was *Khans to Khans*, the large, old, leather-bound ledger book in which Khans had been writing their thoughts to subsequent generations for four generations. It was not there, which sent a pang through his stomach. This house was where his father had lived for the last few years, so odds were, it had been destroyed.

They did the same at the estate outside Salvador, in Bahia, picking up more gold but no *Khans to Khans*, and the same at the castle in the Cevennes region of the Languedoc. He began to despair that, worst of all worlds, Nathan Fox actually had the book, and that all traces of his family had been wiped out. But when they hopped, now in daylight, to the old hunting lodge near Bolzano, in the Italian Alps, the lodge itself was undisturbed. However, they were met in the large, high-walled courtyard by several guards toting machine guns loaded with explosive rounds, based on the look of the specially constructed magazines. And finally, out came Pierre, holding a laser pistol. Seventy if a day, but in his youth a commando in the French Foreign Legion, which ECG maintained for its tradition, he was lean and fit and dangerous-looking as ever. Khan was delighted to see him.

"Pierre," he said, holding up his hands. "We're no threat."

"Alex," said Pierre stiffly, not dropping his guard. "What the *hell* are you doing here? Are you trying to get us all killed? Where did you come from, who is that bear of a man behind you, and what is that fuzzy thing in the air behind you?"

Khan became concerned. They were hidden from casual viewing by the walls around the lodge, but not from satellite surveillance, which would easily show the stand-off. "Good to see you, too, Pierre. Let's go inside out of sight of satellites, and I'll explain everything."

"Fine. But we take your weapons for the meantime."

Khan looked sidewise at Pierre as if to say, "What's up? It's me!" but said, "Fine."

He surrendered his laser pistol and nodded to Baelmar to do the same. Baelmar reluctantly handed it over. "You trust these people, Khan?" he said.

"As I trust you," Khan replied.

Pierre relaxed slightly, then gave a thin smile and made "gimme gimme" motions with his hands. Reluctantly, Khan pulled the foot-long blade from the scabbard he had arranged inside the back of his shirt and handed it, hilt-first, to Pierre. Baelmar did the same with a hidden dagger he had carried since the battle at Mander's Keep. Khan then took a further step toward the door, but Pierre stopped him, with his hand out and a sneaking look of pride and recognition on his face. Khan sighed, rolled his eyes, and pulled a throwing star from a pocket inside his right boot. He handed it to Pierre. Pierre, now openly grinning, reached into Khan's left boot and pulled out a small dagger. By now, even Baelmar's eyes were growing large. Finally, Pierre patted Khan's left armpit and made more give-me motions, and Khan produced the small Austrian 8mm automatic pistol he had hidden there in a thin holster made for concealment. Then Pierre patted Khan's right armpit and exhibited a puzzled expression.

"Alexander, it is a pleasure to see you again. I recognize the boy I trained. But I am disappointed. No weapon in the right armpit? Only spare magazines?"

Khan held up his left hand, displaying the missing fingers, only beginning to grow back. "Couldn't hold it properly with my left hand even if I tried. A little debt to Nathan Fox I intend to repay."

Pierre looked at the freshly healed stumps sadly. "Easy, Alex. He's an extremely dangerous man. Come inside. We'll put your weapons by the front door. You can tell us where you've been and what you've done. More importantly, how you got back. And what that thing sitting in the courtyard is. And what to do next."

Once they were sitting inside amid the stone arches of the old lodge's great room, with its massive fireplace, suits of armor, and hunting trophies of centuries past, Pierre explained his suspiciousness. "We had information you were to be brought back, mind-wiped, and reprogrammed."

"Good information. At least, that's the same information I dug out of the ship's AI on the way back. I assume you got it the same way, but scamming the UAI seems much riskier than a ship's AI."

Pierre ignored this invitation to reveal his sources. "So how can we be sure which Alexander you are: the old one or the new one? You certainly seem like the old one, but the brain programming technicians are very skilled these days."

"Come outside, and I'll show you."

Outside, Pierre slowed as they approached the fuzzy area hiding the ship, then stopped at the cloaking field itself, clearly intending not to go through. But Khan took his hand and pulled him through before he could do anything physical. He might be seventy, but Pierre was a dangerous man.

Inside the ship, Khan showed the boxes of gold. "Would I be carrying all this contraband if I were now a programmed creature of ECG?"

"*Sacre merde!*" said Pierre, looking not only at the gold, but at the ship itself. "This changes everything! Absolutely everything!"

"I hope so," said Khan. "But there was one thing I looked for in the vaults that I couldn't find. Do you know where the leather ledger book is? Leather cover. 'Khans to Khans' is written across the cover in old India ink. I'm not sure you ever knew it existed."

Pierre gave a small nod. "I knew of it. Of all the riches your father possessed, he cared less for them than for his mission in life, for you, and for that book. Especially after your mother was killed in that aircar crash when you were three. He cared deeply. He made me promise once to protect it with my life, and to make sure you got it if something happened to him." He paused. Neither needed to say that something had indeed happened to Khan's father. "I have it inside. In the safe." He gave a small smile and looked Khan in the eye. "I knew the Alexander I knew would somehow come back one day to claim it." Then he grasped Khan's hand and forearm in a manly clasp. "Welcome home, Alexander. There is much that needs to be done."

Inside, sipping coffee, which Baelmar swallowed once only out of politeness and then set aside with a suppressed grimace, and wine, which Baelmar apparently thought surprisingly good, Khan and Pierre traded history since Khan's arrest and deportation.

Pierre had barely escaped with his life and the book when cruise missiles began hitting the castle in the Languedoc. Thinking ECG had not unraveled its carefully veiled ownership, he had fled there after Lucian had been murdered and Alexander had subsequently been arrested. But ECG had unraveled it.

Then he and the security team had trekked on horseback and foot from the Languedoc estate to Bolzano, a trip of over three weeks. In the hunting lodge, they had collected every electronic device and disassembled it, destroying those components used for spying and covert communication with the UAI. Pierre had done something similar regarding his implant, and those of his security team, to what Khan had done. Realizing the peril during Khan's trial, he had used a secret UAI backdoor shared with him by Lucian to change their identities to those of harmless migrant laborers.

But now he was afraid to move. Because while the UAI couldn't tell what you were thinking, it could always tell where you were. Harmless day laborers might slowly travel from southern France to the Italian Alps, but they certainly wouldn't do any expensive traveling. If they did, UAI would flag it, and they would be investigated.

So here they were, with no communication devices of any kind that they trusted, trying to figure out what to do next. Pierre wanted to link up with Albert Bahner, whom rumor placed in Afghanistan, trying desperately to keep some semblance of the old freedom technology plan going, but strapped for money. But that would involve long-distance travel, which would require another identity change. Even though the UAI back door was good, that might attract attention. Where did those itinerant laborers go? Etc.

Plus, after a lifetime of never thinking about money in the Khan business empire, where every need was met, money was now a problem. All money had been electronic for over a century, and complicated algorithms constantly prowled through finance systems and banking records looking for anomalies. Did you have too much money? Too little? Did money suddenly appear in one of your accounts inexplicably? Disappear from one of your accounts? For every debit, there had to be a credit somewhere, and vice-versa. If your finances violated that rule, you would instantaneously generate an investigation. Since all Khan accounts had been "expropriated" – debit to Khan International, credit to ECG – Pierre had been scraping by on dummy-corporation accounts unconnected by any data trail to Khan International. But those were running low. What to do now? It had become so grim, he and the security team had put out vegetable plants in the greenhouse for food, and had sown turnips and beets in the lodge's long-disused flower garden. And they had taken to hunting deer in the mountains, using the lodge again after centuries for its original purpose.

"So the boxes of gold will come in handy, Alexander," he concluded. "We are saved if we can figure out a way to turn the gold into credits without UAI noticing."

"Actually," said Khan, "I think we just spend the gold coins with people who have never held the credit system in high regard – the Afghanis."

"I have heard that," said Pierre.

"It's true. Back when I was still with the Space Navy, the High

Command was constantly sending commandos there to fight bandits, suppress uprisings, and punish assassins and money launderers. It was like trying to stop the tide. Even Internal Movement Control tried sometimes to send my unit there to snatch or kill some local leader. I was usually able to get out of it by saying another mission was more important. But I was there enough to learn that they use gold, even though owning it is illegal. It's their real currency. Credits are just a cover for them. They have to buy things from the rest of the world in credits, so they constantly invent new gold-laundering schemes to get legitimate-looking credit balances. Jewelers buy gold coins to melt down and resell as legal jeweler's stock, but put "jewels" on the bill of sale. Come-and-go banks take gold on deposit from jewelers but call it credits on their books. People and businesses – mainly banks – pay in credits for bogus services, like consulting or security, and get gold in return. Banks make fake loans to people who then supposedly "deposit" the same money back in the bank, though in reality, the bank is giving credits for gold. If it gets too warm for the bank, it just disappears. And so on. They are amazingly creative. There'll be no trouble spending gold coins in Afghanistan. The trouble will be staying unbetrayed, and staying alive. The objective will be to get the gold to Albert. There's enough there to finance a revolution, but I think all it has to finance is some key technology releases, and the revolution will happen all by itself."

Pierre smiled. "Your father would be proud of you, Alexander. He used to worry that you wanted only to go adventuring in the military and lacked a capacity for leadership of Khan International. But he should see you now. You fight your way back from Prison Planet to carry out the Khan dream: free the people of Earth. And your grasp of finance would certainly please him and your grandfather as well. Probably not Culpepper so much."

Khan grinned. "No, even though I was only ten when he died, I remember Great Grandfather well. More like an aircar salesman or con man than a global business giant. Hated finance people. But I think if we manage to figure out a way to screw ECG financially, he would be most proud. Let's go to Afghanistan and find Albert. Oh, and officially set up a Khan Interstellar field office. Khan International headquarters are now on Arcadia, but once we have an official field office in Afghanistan, a small name change is in order. Khan, Inc. is back."

They used the ship's AI to pull off Pierre and team's identity change without getting caught by UAI. The problem was finding Albert.

A quick check of the Khan family compound in the mountains of Afghanistan's northeast yielded nothing. It was inhabited by a gang of cutthroats and thieves. So they would need to start from scratch. They had little trouble finding a suitable compound to rent outside Kabul. The gold coins together with unsubtle reminders that "you are the only ones who know we are here" bought the help and the silence of the locals, but no information. Subtle, roundabout inquiries failed because the Afghanis could see them coming a mile away. They had been intriguers for centuries. They trusted no one, even if he had gold.

– Almost no one. Baelmar took to the austere surroundings and people like a native plant brought back to its home environs. The people sensed a difference in him, and were drawn to his total lack of guile. "Where are you from?" they would ask, and he would say, "I am from the Leas, a beautiful place on the planet Arcadia. I was born there." He would then say he didn't know enough about astronomy to point to Arcadia, but the people would take this at face value, assuming he was either a crazy person or a returned colonist. Then, in true Islamic fashion, they would eventually get to the God question. How many gods were there on Arcadia, and what were their names? "There is only one Spirit of All," Baelmar would say, "and it is so big and powerful that no name can be put on it." "'Allah' is His name," they would say, and Baelmar would say, "Yes, 'All' is as good a word as any." And so on.

They liked him. He was big and powerful and honest and unafraid of them, and because of his origin and the nearness of his beliefs to theirs, they were willing to make allowances. They invited him into their homes for tea and melon, even meals. They took him with them into the countryside to show him their hunting spots. He duly impressed them with his skill with his bow. When they asked why he was in Afghanistan, he told them he had come with a powerful man to save the Earth – that he was committed by honor to help that man to achieve that destiny. This was talk they understood well, and they were engaged by the mention of someone who had come to save Earth. The legend of the Mahdi ran deep among them, and this struck that chord, though Baelmar made no such claims. "If you like, you can meet him," Baelmar offered. "I believe he needs people here to help him."

Bring him, they said, and Baelmar brought these conversations to Khan's attention. "They are friendly, helpful people," he said. "I have told them of your mission, and they would like to meet you."

Khan was incredulous. Had he made a huge mistake by bringing Baelmar along? "You told them about me and my mission?"

"Yes."

Khan struggled not to react too negatively. "This could put us at risk. They could betray us."

"No," said Baelmar. "They are fierce, brave people, accustomed to killing their enemies, but these are not betrayers. I sense this. I see that you are having trouble finding your friend whom you call Albert. You should tell these people who you are and ask them for help. They will help you."

"They could just as easily betray us to ECG for money. I suppose we could give them money to prevent that."

"No. They will not betray you. They do not like this group called 'ECG.' In fact, they use it as an insult. '*Shoma ECG hastid!*' they say, which means 'You are ECG!' It is worse than saying '*Daius!*' which means, 'Pimp for your wife.' They explained what a pimp is. Shocking."

Khan was even more dumbfounded. "You're learning the language?"

"A little. They teach me. And you must not offer them money. It would be a terrible insult. They will help you without money. But you must trust them, as you trust me."

Khan looked at Baelmar's innocent-faced golden-bear-like figure for a long time. They had been through a lot together. And Baelmar had never failed him. Well, there was that time with the Maneater ambush, but they had been badly outnumbered. But he had indeed grown to trust Baelmar. And if he was honest with himself, he had been somewhat infected by Baelmar's talk of destiny. The Elf seemed to have some sort of elemental connection to the forces of the universe that Khan did not understand, but that he had come to take account of.

"OK," he said. "But I go armed."

"Of course," said Baelmar. "These men are always armed as though they expect a war at any time."

"I go too" said Pierre.

In the event, Khan kept his modern weapons hidden beneath his clothes, and wore only his knives where they could be seen. Following Baelmar's lead, he strung his bow over his shoulder. Pierre shook his head and loaded himself up with weapons. They met Baelmar's friends in a tea shop near the extreme edge of the city overlooking a barren landscape.

There were three of them as well, all dressed in tribal dress, all carrying fully loaded automatic rifles that looked over a hundred years old, though deadly nonetheless. Khan reflected that Baelmar had been right. These men looked to be fierce warriors. Their faces gave away nothing, except austere smiles for Baelmar. The leader looked to be in his fifties. The other two could have been his sons.

"*Salaam Alaikum*," said Baelmar, making the traditional Islamic gesture of welcome, and went on in this wise in Farsi, introducing his friends 'Khan' and 'Pierre.' "This is Mahmud," he said, gesturing toward the eldest.

"'Khan'?" said the older man, perking up slightly.

"Alexander Khan," said Khan, making the same gesture. "At your service."

The leader sat back in his seat and regarded Khan with an appraising stare. "We have heard of you and your family," said the leader. "It is a good name and a good family."

"Thank you," said Khan. "What do you know of my family?"

"That they love freedom. That they fight together for freedom for all, even when they must do the distasteful, like you. That they will get revenge for a wrong, though it cost them everything. As with you and your father's death."

"You know a lot about us."

"Yes, because of your name and your love of freedom. We consider you part of our family. Khans are welcome in Afghanistan. Of course we know you are wanted by ECG, but we are willing to help you. The enemy of our enemy is our friend. We hate ECG and want to destroy them. How can we help you?"

Khan decided to trust the man. There was little choice in a country where he knew no one and did not speak the language. As a fall-back, he could always keep the ship close and in cloaking mode as a means of fast escape.

"I am looking for Albert Bahner of Khan International," Khan explained. "I believe he is here, and that he needs my help." And then he explained the whole plan, the freedom technology plan, the release on the internet, and the propaganda campaign to go with it, all straight out of the Khan International playbook. The one thing he kept back was the existence of the Khan Doomsday virus.

As he spoke, the man's hard, weathered face pulled into a wider and wider cunning smile. "I like this plan," he said. "The only thing wrong with it is that there is not enough opportunity in it to kill more ECG people."

"The problem with killing ECG people," said Khan, "is that you are killing the wrong people. You are killing soldiers who generally have no choice about what they are doing. The people you want to kill are far away in comfortable offices. It is always so in war."

The man nodded his head grudgingly. "You are wise for one so young."

Then he stuck his hand inside his robe and Khan stiffened, but the man held up his other hand in an "It's OK" gesture, and pulled out a laser pistol.

"We know Albert Bahner," he said. "He sold us some of these at what he said was his cost. I believed him, because he had so little money he asked for a loan to buy materials for more. We gave him the loan. I believe this one is the same model you have inside your shirt."

Khan smiled and brought out his own laser pistol to compare. "It appears to be. Where is Albert?"

The man looked at him long with his fierce, dark brown eyes. "He is valuable to us. How can I trust that you are really Alexander Khan? How do I know you are not ECG yourself, and that you have not deceived our friend Baelmar?"

"There is no way I can prove this. You know where we are living. You can kill us in our sleep if we betray you."

"I think you are harder to kill than that."

"Maybe so. Why not bring Albert to a neutral location where you have us all in an ambush? Then if he trusts me enough to let me help him, you can trust me, too."

It was agreed, and the man showed them on an ECG military map the exact coordinates for the meeting. The topography was similar to the ground Khan had chosen for his ambush on Arcadia: a closed valley with sharpshooter locations on all sides. He gave a wry smile.

"A rabbit couldn't stay alive in there if your men start shooting. Fine. Just my willingness to go into a place like that ought to make you trust me."

The man stood and took Khan's hand. "I did not grow as old as I am by trusting people," he said. "Neither did you. Noon tomorrow." And with that, he and his men left.

Next morning there was discord. Pierre was opposed to keeping the rendezvous.

"Have I taught you nothing, Alexander? You could be dead within minutes in a set-up like that. You will be naked, no matter how well armed you are. They could hit you with armor piercing rounds. Anything!"

"What would be their motivation?"

"Who knows? Hatred of the ECG! What proof do you have that they even know Albert? A laser pistol? The black market must be full of them!"

"The laser pistol is good enough. Given that each pistol serial number is tied to the issuee's ID in the UAI, and that private citizens cannot own them, I sincerely doubt that the black market is full of them. – Unless Albert is the cause. And I happened to notice that the one our friend displayed lacked a serial number in the usual place on the butt. You could be right, but it's a chance I have to take."

"It is a sickness not to trust people," offered Baelmar. "Though you did not know us, you trusted us at Mander's Keep. We did not fail you. You trusted your story to the people of Advance and asked their agreement to your ideas. They did not fail you. You trusted Bella and Ahmed to go to Riversend. They did not fail you. Who has failed you that you are so meager with trust?"

Khan was flooded with warmth for Baelmar. It took a good man not to see the evil in others. On Arcadia, people were what they appeared to be. Maneaters were Maneaters. Techs were Techs, Elves were Elves, and Lords were Lords. Deceit was rare. It was a world Khan missed already, though he had been back on Earth only a short time.

"It is a sad thing, Baelmar, but on Earth, people are not always what they appear to be. You are right that it is a sickness. But it is a sickness that we must take account of."

Then he turned to Pierre. "I am going to do this thing, Pierre. I will be armed. I will have armor on. But this is our chance, and to pass it by through excess of caution is cowardice. We'll set down a kilometer away, lock the ship, and walk right into this ambush. Or I can go by myself. Your choice. Sorry. The world has turned into an uglier place since I left."

"I will go with you," said Baelmar solemnly. "I trust these men, and I have convinced you to trust them, too. I will cast my destiny with yours."

Pierre's head wagged back and forth in denial and disapproval. "It goes against everything I've ever taught you, Alexander. You always leave yourself an out. But if you are going to get into a stand-up firefight, I'm going to be there with you. Wearing armor."

The ambush site turned out to be even worse than it had looked on the topographical map. The steep sides were thirty meters high and virtually unclimbable. The entrance was narrow, only two men wide. And the top was ringed by boulders that gave perfect cover to sharpshooters. It was a virtual killing zone.

Pierre could not stop shaking his head as the three of them walked through the defile, Khan first, Pierre second, and Baelmar third.

"Go to the middle!" came Mahmud's voice from the top perimeter.

They did, unconsciously forming a back-to-back triumvirate when they reached the parched grass of the center of the valley. Khan's stomach cramped up as he waited for the first shot to be fired. He could hear Pierre's breathing, and some mumbled anti-Moslem imprecations.

Then the air before Khan took on a shimmer, and Albert Bahner appeared before him, transported in from somewhere. In his seventies, he was still a big man at least as tall as Khan, with powerful shoulders and arms but something of a belly. His round head was fringed with thick white hair surrounding a sunburned pate, and a prodigious white moustache drooped over the corners of his mouth. He looked more like a large genial man who had spent his life blacksmithing than the chief operations officer of the largest corporation on Earth.

"Good morning, Young Man," he said, extending his hand. "It's good to see you. I had assumed you were lost to us forever."

Albert Bahner had been a senior manager in Khan International since before Khan was born, and though he was no relation, had always been family. In all those decades, he had never lost his German accent.

"Good morning, Uncle Al," said Khan, taking his hand and shaking it warmly. The hand felt as though it had seen work on a deburring bench. "I never expected to see you again, either, and it's a great pleasure. I'm impressed you've been able to manufacture or steal a transporter for your private use."

"Oh, *ja, ja.* What ECG does not know does not hurt them. Well, now it might. We have always kept a few samples of things we made for them. If we get caught, we just say it is for troubleshooting purposes. And here we are, shooting trouble, no?" He smiled his infectious, avuncular smile.

Khan grinned. "We are planning to shoot some trouble, and to help you do the same, if you're up for it. We've come to help put the Khan Freedom Technology plan into action, all at once."

"That is what I am trying to do, but the *Geld*, or lack of it, is a problem. So far, only small things."

"I can help with that, but first things first. Do you trust these people ranged around the top of this ridiculous ambush pit?"

"Oh, *ja, ja,* they are good men. Dangerous, but not to me. I help them with some simple weapons, they help me with places to manufacture, and with money. This ambush pit, as you call it, is my meeting spot for Kabul because it is defensible with only fifteen or twenty men, it is observable only from orbit, and it has a secret tunnel out the back."

"Ah! No one told us about that."

Albert smiled conspiratorially and leaned in close. "But you didn't need it anyway, did you, Alexander? When I set my coordinates, the terminal detected another transporter field in the area. Set to snatch the three of you out at the press of a button? *Ja*?" He nudged Khan's arm with a smile. "Pierre didn't train any fools, *ja*? So the question is, where is *your* transporter, and how did you get it?"

Pierre gave Khan a look of mixed pride and disgust. How could Khan have let him think they had no out? Khan looked at Pierre, flicked his eyes at Baelmar in such a way that Baelmar couldn't see, shook his head imperceptibly.

"We have a ship," he said to Bahner. "And all the gold from the vaults at Detroit, San Salvador, and the Languedoc. Enough gold to buy much of Afghanistan. And weapons. What do you have?"

Bahner's eyebrows rose, and his mobile, cheerful face stretched into an exaggerated expression of surprise. "Oh, that is good news, Alexander. Excellent news. *Ausgezeichnet*! Well, we have a manufacturing network in small shops throughout Kabul, Jalalabad, Charikar, Sinawi, and Skarkar. Many of them in tunnels and caverns that have been used by the Mujahedeen for centuries to hide from occupying forces. Our base of operations, appropriately enough, is in Khanabad. Also underground. "

"'Abode of the Khans,'" translated Baelmar, clearly seeing significance in this.

"*Ja*, that is the meaning," said Bahner. "My little joke on the ECG. But to the question, what do we have? Not enough equipment, not enough materials, not enough skilled people, and not enough security. ECG is always after us, and Mahmud and his people make them disappear when they can, but we have to be careful. But really, all we have been able to do is put out a few hundred hand lasers, which helps the freedom fighters here. I can't guarantee the quality, but they seem to be good enough to bring the Office of Technology Control to Afghanistan looking for us. And we have put out a couple thousand Bottomless Batteries, just put them in the marketplaces in Kabul and Kandahar, and they were sold within a day. And just a few gravity drive controllers with geo-escape capability. The plan calls for putting out Bottomless Batteries and the drive controllers in the hundreds of thousands, beyond the point where they could be controlled or rounded up. And then of course, the release on the Net of instructions on how to use these things in your aircar to get off Earth without killing yourself. But we have not enough money. No *Geld*. '*Pul naderim,*' as they say here. Khan International is diminished to one loyal old man with a mission and no way to make it happen. And ECG is tightening the noose. They could catch us before we achieve critical mass. But with money ….."

"I think somehow we arrived at just the right time," said Khan, thinking of the Alien and Baelmar's pronouncements on the subject. "Come with us, and we'll take you to Khanabad and give you the gold. We also have new technology that is going to curl your hair – what little you have – when you see it."

"Insults!" boomed Bahner. "You must feel pretty good to bring insults along with your new technology. Though I can't imagine what you could bring from Prison Planet that Albert Bahner has not manufactured for ECG."

"You will see," said Khan. "It will change everything, if you can figure out how it works and reproduce it."

"Come! Stop with the mystery! What is this new technology?"

"Instead of telling you, I will show you."

Khan led them all back to the top where he thanked Mahmud for arranging the meeting. Then he led Albert and Pierre and Baelmar back to the ship and walked through the cloaking field, thereby disappearing from their view.

"*Gott im Himmel!*" said Albert.

"Come on in," said Khan. "It won't hurt a bit."

CHAPTER FOURTEEN

"In the Twenty-First Century, political structures devolved from democracies into commissariats. The increasingly complex challenges faced by governments as populations grew and resources diminished proved too much for bickering democracies. The problems needed competent focus over the space of decades, but the politicians couldn't concentrate past the next election. The commissariats happened because well-meaning, public-spirited citizens kept raising concerns that dangerous problems were not getting addressed. Ultimately, the task forces, advisory panels, special committees, and finally bureaucracies that were set up in response to work these problems became entrenched and took over. They just knew so much more than the idiot politicians that they made them look superfluous. Simultaneously, the steady growth of entitlement mentality in every democracy ensured eventual economic collapse. More and more entitlement recipients voted themselves more and more largesse from fewer and fewer taxpayers. Somebody had to stop it. The ultimate result was the global dictatorship of a semi-hereditary commissariat we have today. Plenty of socialist rhetoric as red meat for the masses, but in fact a fairly intelligent blend of economic freedom and central economic control. Economic sufficiency, but within intellectual and cultural slavery. Now, after two centuries of that, we have what the Twenty-First Century would have recognized as a fairly standard socialist dictatorship, with the standard trappings: anti-elitist rhetoric, intellectual atrophy, diminishing productivity, diminishing quality of life, zero freedom, and the socialist need to control speech. Nobody can make a move. . .. Only the adventurous spirit of interstellar exploration can save us from this malaise."

Grandfather Quintus Khan, *Khans to Khans,*
"Lessons For Lucian"

Amity Green's favorite memory was the week she had spent at summer camp in the country out east along the Hudson when she was fourteen. There had been horseback riding, swimming in a lake, bows and arrows, and even sleeping outside in a tent. Running in packs with other girls her age, smelling the trees and grass and open air, and actually letting the Earth and its water touch her body, had been intoxicating. Sure, there had been political training. But there had also been a boy and a kiss.

She went back to that memory over and over and over, embellishing the actual facts with imaginary but related events, to the point where she had an entire encyclopedia of memories, both real and imagined, to which she could retreat when necessary.

It was never more necessary than in Colloquy. First there was the assembly in the Colloquy Room of every resident in the Top Quarter of the concrete high-rise apartment house in urban Kansas City, with the falsely enthusiastic, falsely harmless, falsely folksy Facilitator from ECG "kicking things off." The fiction was that this person was just another resident of the Top Quarter who called Colloquy as a spontaneous fun gathering. Worse than the fiction was the fact that you had to act like you believed the fiction. Puke, man.

And then, after "just a few announcements," all of which had to do with things you liked to do but had to stop doing, or with things you now had to do that you'd rather eat shit than do, then came the Breakout Sessions. The Breakout themes for tonight were "How can I be of more use to society?" and "The dangers of bad attitude." Previous themes had included "Why We Now All Live in Cities," and "Action Outside the Group is Arrogance." Your group always got to choose between at least two themes. Puke, man.

So, in the breakout session, you would enthusiastically put together a skit with other people in your group, a skit that demonstrated the theme, and come back to the Colloquy room and present it to the larger group. Then there was Round Table, where you sat on the hard metal folding chairs and discussed the themes and the skits until midnight. Cheap cookies were usually provided. Everybody including Amity would act as though they were having a great time and hated to leave even at midnight, even though the next day was a work day. And the reason for this was, in every breakout group was an ECG mole posing as a normal citizen. Nobody was supposed to know this, but of course everybody knew and hated each mole, and smiled at them and treated them well. Because if you didn't, bad things started happening to you. Serious incorrigibles disappeared.

So tonight as always before, she pasted on the smile and went through the motions. Every citizen of Top Quarter could do this in his sleep. But in her mind, she was in something like that summer camp on the Hudson. Except now, after visiting that secret website she had been tipped to, she began to imagine it on another planet. Tonight for the first time ever, based on the starship pick-up site's listings, she began to think about real escape, not just imaginary. Sure, it was a desperate move. If the story was true (small probability), she would be free. If it was false (big probability), she would be dead. Seemed worth the gamble.

CHAPTER FIFTEEN

"Keep a good coat, Lexy. It's cold out there."

"Some people are convinced from birth that they are born to lead. It's generally a good idea to keep those people out of power, or to remove them from power if they get it."
    Great Grandfather Culpepper Conn, *Khans to Khans*

"Things get harder when you realize your own fallibility, that you, too, can be blind, and that the universe is not all about you."
    Father Lucian Khan, *Khans to Khans*

"O, du Ausgeburt der Hölle! Soll das ganze Haus ersaufen?"

("Oh, you spawn of Hell! Wilt destroy our entire home?" – The Sorcerer's Apprentice)
    Johann Wolfgang von Goethe, *Der Zauberlehrling*

Bahner's headquarters were in a cave complex driven kilometers into the mountains outside Khanabad by the Taliban three centuries earlier. A deep hollow in a nearby cliff face, blasted out by Taliban originally for use as a truck marshaling yard, offered a hiding place for the spacecraft. Satellites could still not see through rock, even after three hundred years. Khan put the spacecraft there, and mindful of the Alien's warning, he nevertheless left the cloaking device turned on just in case.

Khan wanted to immediately talk about a strategy to release Freedom Technology for maximum effect, but Albert would do nothing until he could examine the cloaking device. He was like a boy with a toy. Khan was afraid to turn it off long enough for Albert to examine it, so he hovered the craft back out of the semi-cave, and jumped with Albert into the outer system, well out of range of sensor arrays just inside the Belt. There, hidden behind a large asteroid, he turned off the cloaking device and handed it to Bahner.

"Please don't screw it up," said Khan. "It's the difference between life and death."

"No upscrewing," said Albert cheerfully, manipulating a handheld scanner. "Just a little scan here and a little scan there." He plugged it back in. "Hmmmm. Very simple yet very sophisticated. And well beyond our understanding. Where did you get this? It appears to be creating a field in another *dimension,* thus making whatever it surrounds invisible to anyone in this dimension. We do not know these physics yet."

"A beautiful lady alien with pointed ears appeared to me. I had sex with her, and she gave me this."

Albert boomed with laughter. "Oh, *ja,* that is a good one. So you don't want to tell me, that is fine. And though I do not understand how it works, it looks to me like I can maybe make another one." He wiggled his eyebrows. "Always dangerous but fun to mess with something you don't understand. *Wie der Zauberlehrling.* But we will try. You are right. This would change everything." Then he gave Khan a serious look. "You know, of course, that whoever made this could be a serious threat to humanity?"

"Of course. But if its makers wanted us dead, we'd have been dead long ago. It's not as though we humans have been hiding our radio waves under a bushel."

"*Ja, das ist so.*"

"But this technology is not our main focus, right? That's got to be the grav drive controllers and the power packs. Create a little havoc to distract ECG before they catch us?"

Albert sighed. "*Ja,* those are the main things. Maybe the quantum encryption. Heh, heh. Release that onto a few thousand servers for downloading, and ECG will go crazy trying to find them and shut them all down. They will see conspiracies everywhere. They will go *wahnsinnig.* Best, though, would be to do such a release from a government server. That way, when they trace it down, it will really confuse them." He chuckled at the thought, then became serious. "But our focus has to be on setting up a manufacturing base. We have to have something to release. The release is secondary, and hard. To do a Net release from a government server, we need access to the server, maybe physical access, and we have no way of getting that. You know they keep them inside transporter-field shields so you can't sneak in and out. Except for ECG operatives' home access, which is always thumbprint protected."

"Yes, I knew that. Leave that one to me. For now, please forget the cloaking technology. Let's get back to Earth so you can start spending that gold on new production capability. Meanwhile, I have a plan on the release, and you've just given me another idea."

Within days, word was out among local merchants and suppliers. Bahner was suddenly paying in full, in gold, upon delivery. Rather than gang up and rob him, which they might have done if they didn't need his help in their fight with the ECG, they immediately formed up into the best sourcing teams possible in a third-world environment. Fine steels and plastics from India, rare earths, mini-robots, and 3-D printers from China, and electronic components from Thailand and Vietnam, all began appearing upon demand, almost as if by magic. Supplies poured into Khan International cave factories, as well as the alley shops in Kabul, Kandahar, and Jalalabad, which all looked centuries old on the outside, but were well equipped, modern manufacturing set-ups inside. Khan particularly enjoyed watching high-tech supplies arrive in donkey carts.

Within two weeks, Albert's operations had seriously ramped up. They had previously produced all the freedom-tech products in low but steady numbers, so the manufacturing processes were established. What was new was additional production equipment. Now they were turning out a thousand grav-unit controllers, eleven hundred navigation modules, and fifteen hundred Bottomless Batteries per day. The powerpacks alone were enough to be a game changer. They could literally hold a charge whose limits had not yet been tested, and could power anything – including small spacecraft. There was some concern that under some circumstances, these power packs might explode, producing an explosive yield in the fission-bomb range, directly proportional to their charge. But so far that had not happened, so Khan and Bahner did not concern themselves overmuch with that. They were focused on fomenting revolution, not creating safety-certified consumer products.

The plan was, produce and store up substantial stock of all the contraband technology, then release it all at once, instead of dribbling it out as produced. This would reduce the danger of getting caught before the numbers were big enough to have significant effect.

They also had to be ready to simultaneously release instructions for the contraband technology's use, originating on a government server, but disseminated sequentially to thousands of other servers by bots. The intended effect was, simultaneous waves of information and freedom technology flooding to the people in a tsunami that would roll over ECG like doom.

Setting up the information release became Khan's job, and he knew just how he wanted to approach it. From Wilcox Snavely, Assistant Sub Director of Office of Technology Control, he had taken not only his tracking chip, he had taken his weapons. And from his weapons, he had taken his fingerprints – including his thumbprint.

When all was in readiness, Khan had the ship's AI find Snavely's home address. He lived in an apartment complex in Alexandria, Virginia. Bearing in mind that facial-recognition software could bust him in a second, Khan disguised himself with a fake moustache, tinted glasses, and a cap pulled low. Then he set the starship down in a hayfield a couple of miles away and hiked into the suburban area where Snavely's sterile apartment building stood among other sterile apartment buildings.

He had no problem getting into the apartment, a Spartan affair with a wall of pictures of Wilcox with various luminaries, a well-tended aquarium – Khan fed the fish – and a refrigerator with no beer in it. The freezer was full of neat stacks of microwave dinners. A study with no dust and no books contained a small bookshelf with memorabilia, and a bare desk with a computer on it. The bedroom was perfectly neat, bed made, with no personal items to speak of. The guest bedroom looked unused. Lifeless hotel prints graced the walls.

"Poor bastard," thought Khan, thinking of his own apartment not too far away, and then the life he had led on Arcadia. He briefly thought of Snavely and actually hoped he survived.

The problem was not getting into the apartment, for which a thumb print had sufficed. The problem was finding and getting into the appropriate government network. There was a standard, which Khan had used himself. Its icon glowed on the screen. The problem was, it had several paths to entry – Security, Administrative, Military – and he was sure logon attempts were monitored.

In the end, he guessed right – Administrative, even though Office of Technology Control was all about securing ECG's continued existence. His IP address was vetted, and he was then presented with another opportunity to use the fake thumbprint, as well as the ship AI's help in discovering the password. The password hack required several seconds, and he began to sweat. He knew if he didn't get it right in three attempts, police would be all over the apartment in a matter of minutes. But the ship's AI got it, and he got in.

What he had not anticipated was that, even before he had finished plugging in the data chip containing the virus and the datafiles to be uploaded and disseminated by the virus, he would get a chime and an instant message – from Nathan Fox.

"Snavely, where the hell have you been? Your tracker chip is offline. What is status? Do you have Khan?"

Khan sat looking at the message, clear proof of Fox's involvement, and clear proof that everyone, everywhere in ECG was watched, every minute. He thought about how to use this as an opportunity. He answered while watching the upload tracker. 30%.

"Was injured in action on Prison Planet. Chip lost. Khan now here on Earth." 42%.

"Here on Earth? In that case, why don't I have him? Where's his tracker signal? Why isn't he in a cell? Or is he?" 57%.

"He is in a secure location." 62%.

"Secure location? Wilcox, what does that mean? Are you being coy with me? Are you negotiating with me?" 73%.

"He is an extremely dangerous man. I could have been killed. This was a big mission. An illegal mission, I might add, since no one is supposed to go down onto Prison Planet. I want something more than a pat on the back. Or a laser hole in the back of my skull." 86%.

"Wilcox, we are in a recorded exchange." 92%.

"Yes, could be dangerous for both of us." 97%.

"Let's meet. My office." 99%.

"Fine. But not your office. The street corner outside. Fifteen minutes." 100%.

"Fine. This is very unlike you, Wilcox. In fact, UAI gives me an 87% probability, that based on past behavior and speech patterns, I am not talking to Wilcox Snavely at all, but to Alexander Khan. Is that so, Major? I'm impressed by your resourcefulness in getting back to Earth, but disappointed by your failure of duty. Your duty was to have the good grace to die on Prison Planet, Major. To give up this Khan family mission. To let it die. To repudiate your misguided father and your family, not to seek petty revenge, or whatever you plan. This vision your family pursues is not the one that humanity in the form of ECG has chosen. It would delay the coming of the Great Equilibrium, which only Earth Central Government, the voice and tool of the people, can bring about. Perfect humanity before going to the stars. You know the creed. But since you didn't die, Major, we have use for you —"

As soon as the pop-up showing the 100% disappeared, Khan pulled the data chip out of the pad and wiped the keys of his fingerprints. He smiled at Fox's last transmission and shut the machine down. The man might be the devil incarnate, but he was a worthy, committed adversary. He probably saw expropriation of the Khan estates as victory for the ECG rather than personal corruption.

Khan was out the door and two blocks away when the black aircars showed up in the street in front of Snavely's apartment.

Back in Khanabad, the nettlebutt had already started to respond to the release. People in the street were excited about it. People here spoke Tajik, but many could also speak Farsi and some Standard, and they took to Baelmar here as they had done in Kabul. They found his sunny disposition irresistible. His Farsi was good enough to understand a Net rumor about a starship pick-up to occur at a football field on the north side of New Delhi, another in a copper mine in Chile, another in a landfill just south of

Columbus, Ohio, and so on. He pronounced the names of these unfamiliar places with a strange twist, but they were recognizable. A hundred such locations were given, which of course he could not remember. Just pack a small bag, the stories went, show up at midnight, and a Khan International starship would appear and take you away to freedom. Such starship pick-ups had not been part of Khan's data release, but the data release had obviously excited people everywhere. Now Fox would be trying to track down its source, which would turn out to be the ECG file-sharing server used by Wilcox Snavely. However, Khan did worry about the people who would inevitably go for starship pick-ups. ECG's mercies were not tender. He put out a subsequent anonymous-server release saying the pick-up rumors were not true, but not only was the Net café where he did this subsequently torched, net wisdom quickly identified him as an impostor.

But initial indications were, the plan was working. One of Bahner's local shop foremen reported excitedly that there was quantum encryption on the Net! You could download it to keep ECG from seeing what you were doing or saying! You could find it at such and such a site! There were also sites where you could go to find out where you could buy hardware to make your gravity sled or aircar capable of climbing out of Earth's gravity well! And Baelmar reported the same stories from the street. The whole country was abuzz, so Khan assumed the whole world was as well.

Albert had been thorough. The posting package included plans, drawings, etc., for upgrading your aircar compartment for zero external pressure. Most aircars could go to twelve thousand meters without losing pressure, but required beefing up to survive the vacuum of space. There were also lists of locations where you could get navigation modules that would get you to one of the illegal colony sites, and modules to generate a magnetosphere around your craft to protect against radiation. But no space suits or anything fancy. If you were prepared to risk your life on a single, week-long, off-planet desperation jump, Khan International had just what you needed to get the hell off the home planet. If you tried anything fancier, you could be dead. Of course, of the thousands of physical locations listed where you could get these things, none were accurate, mere chum for the ECG, as the hardware was all to be released through flea markets and black markets. Khan had personally made deliveries all over the globe to criminal elements willing to distribute the technology. He knew the distributors would charge outrageous prices, of course, but that could not be helped. The key was, people all over the world now knew to look for the hardware, even if it might be a bit of work to find it.

The global buzz became so intense within three days that ECG felt compelled to put out vid messages on the net. It was all a hoax, they said, nothing more than urban myth, etc. Besides which, loyal ECG citizens did not want to leave their earthly paradise. They wanted only to go to meaningful work each day, attend the odd ECG social event for fostering togetherness, and sleep the peace of the innocent – after having turned in anyone they knew who went to the forbidden sites.

Khan loved it. But to get a feel for what was actually going on, he and Baelmar actually checked out several of the bogus starship pick-up sites. To his dismay, crowds of thousands appeared at each, each person holding an overnight bag of some sort. The Net spoofers had unfortunately been very effective. And on the outer edges of each crowd hovered black ECG aircars, and in some cases, armed flyers. Khan got a lump in his throat looking at these desperate people. He wanted to take them all. These were the self-selected explorers, builders, adventurers, and freedom lovers willing to risk all, willing to start with nothing to build a new life. And they would build a new society that looked outward, not inward. But reality was reality. They had been had by thoughtless Net tricksters. And he couldn't reveal himself by fighting off the ECG troops, and he couldn't take these hopeful emigrants. Or, not more than a few.

He found a crowd of less than fifty in a moon-soaked wheatfield in Kansas. No ECG troops. He knew it was foolish, but he carefully set the cloaked craft down to one side of the crowd, which they would see only as mashed-down wheat. Then he stepped out of the cloaking field with Baelmar beside him, bow strung over his shoulder, and said in a firm voice, "I can take three."

The astonished crowd looked back in silence for a long moment. Then they got a load of Baelmar in the moonlight, instantly recognized that he was not from Earth, and went wild. "Take me! No, Me! Me!" they shouted.

Khan held up his hands. "There will be other opportunities. For now, we have limited space. The rest of you, please go home before the police arrive. And put out on the sites that I, Alexander Khan, said that the pick-up sites are a scam. Scammers put up that list, not I. We do not have ships to take everybody away."

Then he pointed at three people near him. "You, you, and you," and led them into the ship. People in the crowd took vids of the five of them disappearing. Then, when the mashed-down wheat sprang back up, the crowd erupted. – Just as four armed black ECG aircars showed up.

Khan saw them on the viewer. "That was close," he said.

The three passengers looked open-mouthed at him and Baelmar as if they were from another world. Which in fact they were. He realized he needed to reduce his passengers' anxiety.

"I'm going to take you for a couple of days to a location in …, near … the Himalayas while I collect a few people from other locations. Then we will go to Arcadia, which frankly is the best of the colony worlds. Danger to you is minimal, you will be in a civilized town called Advance, but you will have to do manual work for a few months until you save up some money and get situated. Unless of course, you are carrying gold, in which case, you'll be set up immediately,"

They looked at him in awe, fear, and silence. Baelmar spoke up.

"I was born on Arcadia. Major Khan speaks the truth. It is a wonderful place. And if you want to live on the land, and not in a town, you can do that too. Of course, you will need to learn to use weapons to protect yourself from wild animals. And other things."

"*The* Major Khan?" said a young lady. "Of the Khan International family?"

Khan smiled, not having had this reaction for awhile. "At your service, Miss …?"

"Green. Amity Green. I came all the way from Kansas City. I walked seventy kilometers in twenty-four hours. My shoes came apart. If you hadn't chosen me, I would have been AWOL tomorrow morning from the office and in prison or re-education camp when they caught me. I want to change my life. I want to have a life."

She stuck out her hand, grabbed Khan's, and pumped it earnestly. Realization ground down on Khan. Directly or indirectly, he had cruelly,

cruelly, raised the hopes of tens of thousands of people he could not help. If this one person had risked everything for the chance to get off the planet, what had the other thousands of people who showed up at the pick-up sites done? What had they risked? What would happen to them? For the thousandth time in his life he resolved that ECG had to go. And now for the first time he was working directly to make it go. But he was dismayed by the collateral damage.

The other two introduced themselves with similar stories. "I want to live without being watched," said one, and the other, "I want to make decisions about my own life that are not reviewed."

Of course, in the ECG, the UAI had an eye on you at all times, and while there was some latitude for movement within your local area, simply because ECG lacked the resources to check into every anomalous movement every time, if you did something out of the ordinary and the condition persisted for more than a day or two, you were going to be picked up.

Khan took the three to the manufacturing location outside Sinawi, where an extensive, deep cave network contained one of their largest manufacturing locations. There he set them up with bunks and meal tickets and instructions not to go near the entrances, lest UAI pick up their implants. He told them he was going to pick up twelve more like themselves from scheduled pick-up locations, then take them all to Arcadia.

However, within two days, someone, either one of the workers with an implant, or one of the pick-ups, must have gone too close to the surface. Mahmud and his people reported that, based on their intelligence, ECG was onto the Sinawi location, and that it was only a matter of time before it got raided. They pleaded with Albert to get everything out and let them set up an ambush.

Albert, for whom permitting a production interruption was a sin worse than serving English beer, said, "Don't we have a whole empty level forty meters below the current production level, with hidden entrances? Why not move the equipment there, ambush the *ScheisskÖpfe*, but make sure a few of them get in and see the vacated main production floor so they can report that we have gone? Then, once they're gone, we start up production in the lower floor?"

Mahmud liked this idea because it still meant he could kill lots of ECG troops. Khan began to have doubts how the whole Freedom Technology release thing could possibly continue very long in any case, unless ECG collapsed soon.

ECG collapse was the goal, but in just a couple of days, it had started to look like a forlorn hope. Word was that warlords and crime bosses were mostly hoarding the technology released so far. And there were worrisome reports of lots of aircars drifting in orbit with dead pilots inside. Something was wrong.

Freedom via Freedom Technology was originally planned as a sneaky evolutionary part of normal Khan International operations. Citizens would produce their own hydrogen via solar stills. They would use hydrogen in fuel cells to produce energy far in excess of PV-cell capacity. They would store energy in Bottomless Batteries. They would grow food hydroponically. They would trade information via quantum encryption. Most importantly, they would modify their gravity sleds and aircars into spacefaring craft using harmless hardware and Khan designs to leave Earth any time they wanted to. And to ensure success, the designs and manufacturing processes for all the technology would be released on the Net so small manufacturing operations everywhere could make the stuff themselves. The intended effect was that people would gradually became freer and more independent of the grasp of ECG, that freedom technology growth would go viral, and that ECG would gradually lose power

That had been the Khan plan for decades. But now they had done a sudden, one-time release, with no chance to fix things – why were there drifting aircars? – along the way. The question was quickly becoming, would the sudden-release Freedom Technology plan work, or would it be a flash in the pan?

If it worked, it would be a near-run thing. Khan and Pierre estimated the operation had about two weeks to push ECG over the edge before they were all forced to flee the planet. The problem was, Khan and Albert had shot most of their wad and they weren't yet seeing the expected effects. Unless the people rose up soon, unless people left Earth in large numbers soon, causing chaos, unless people began soon replicating the technology on their own in growing numbers, further weakening ECG's hold, ECG would counterattack.

Now that government security forces knew for sure about Afghanistan, ECG would flood the country with troops to find the production locations. By force of numbers, the Mujahedeen would be reduced to guerilla warfare, no stand-up fights. They would have the best of weapons, but they lacked troops and other resources. Khan's military judgment was, they would lose. Production in Afghanistan would eventually be shut down or diminished to the point of irrelevancy. And nowhere else on Earth was it even close to possible. And ECG would search every house and every building on earth to confiscate contraband technology. They would have a hard time confiscating information, so some good could eventually come of that. But increasingly, it was looking as though the big tech release had not worked.

Of course, he did have the Khan Doomsday virus. But having the ship's AI release it into the UAI was a last resort; it guaranteed total chaos. The resulting communications disruptions, logistics breakdowns, power outages, and water and sewage breakdowns would produce mass hunger, and death by anarchy and disease of hundreds of millions of people, if not two or three billion. That was not saving the people of Earth. That was destroying them just to destroy the ECG.

What to do? How to save some without punishing the rest? Could the rest be saved? What besides somehow taking over the government of Earth could possibly save the population from both ECG and its catastrophic breakdown?

He had not thought before in precisely those terms. He had thought loosely on destabilizing ECG and specifically on revenge on Nathan Fox. He now saw that to some subconscious extent he had in effect been planning to use the people of Earth to get that revenge, and he did not like what he saw. He began to think in terms of two separate plans: destroy ECG, get Fox. Getting Fox became secondary. If he got ECG, Fox would fall into the bag. But at this point, there was nothing to do but wait to see if the plan worked.

In any case, he had promised the fifteen people he had now collected from "starship pickup points" that he would take them to Arcadia. That is what he would do. Then he would come back in time to pick up Albert and Pierre if the plan had not worked. But when he jumped from Khanabad to Sinawi to pick up his fifteen charges, the huge fight Mahmud had wanted was already underway.

He knew the plan was to attack ECG's exurban Sinawi compound as a diversion once ECG's attack on the Khan cave factory had started. So he flew to Sinawi and placed the cloaked star cruiser directly over ECG's military compound.

It wasn't long before Mujahedeen in the hundreds attacked all four sides of the compound. But they were getting nowhere because of the shield wall. He wasn't sure how the craft's weapons would work with the cloaking device on, so the first thing he tried was the craft's field suppressor. He was concerned that this might actually suppress the cloaking field, but it worked perfectly through the field. The shield wall on two sides of the compound stopped its shimmer, and the Mujahedeen weapons began getting through.

Then a couple of combat flyers appeared and started hammering the Mujahedeen. Khan shot both down, hoping as he fired that the energy beam didn't get bottled up inside the cloaking field and kill his craft instead. It worked fine, and he was careful to go for disabling shots rather than kill shots. After all, the people in those flyers were just following orders. They could well be people he knew.

The battle was soon over. The compound's outer defensive positions had been overrun, and ECG defenders had retreated to a secondary, last-ditch line within the compound. However, the Mujahedeen did not try to overrun the compound, which they clearly could have done. They simply melted away. He assumed they had received word from the Khan production compound in Sinawi's surrounding mountains that the ECG assault there had been beaten back. He sincerely hoped the killing had been as minimal as possible. On both sides.

He was increasingly filled with dread. What had he and Albert started? He could save fifteen people at a time, but would Khan International's efforts end up costing the lives of millions of people without freeing any? Afghanistan operations were clearly on a short string, and they certainly couldn't move their Freedom-Tech manufacturing operation to Arcadia. Even if they had the transport they would need, ECG would eventually come there, too, just like Sinawi. And ruin everything.

He thought of Estelle and Bella and Ahmed and Salvatore Ruggiero, and Stanhope Greis at the Keep, not to mention Maruil and Gareth and Branwyn, and the lives they all had built. All could be destroyed in short order if ECG took Arcadia into its sights.

And unless ECG was sure he was not there, that might be exactly what they would do anyway. Maybe no matter where he was. The technology release had not had the effect on ECG – its fall – they always thought it would, but it had been massively disruptive. A frightened and angry ECG would now be looking for vengeance, and based on Fox's 87% reading from the UAI, that effort would focus on him. And on Arcadia as his base of operations. Out of pride and revenge – and stupidity – he had risked what had so far meant more in his life than anything that had gone before: the people of Arcadia. Estelle had read the situation pretty much exactly right.

Had the Alien set him up for failure? Or had she simply overestimated his capabilities? He had been stupid, stupid, stupid.

And now he had to make it up.

The last thing he did before leaving was try to convince Albert and Pierre to come with him. "It's way too chancy here," he said. "Come away to fight again another day."

"*Junge*," said Albert, "I swore to your father that I would do what I am doing until my last breath. It can work, believe me. And with the scans of that cloaker you have, I think I can make more of them and easily survive. Joost need a few more days. I'll be fine. Everything will work."

"You have a ship? You can escape if you need to? I'll be back, but I'm afraid you might not survive that long. "

"Ja, sure, I have a small ship, but the show is here. I come to Prison Planet if it gets too hot here. Don't you worry. And now that Pierre is here to protect me, it's all good."

"I'm all for optimism and positive thinking, Albert, but this time I think you're wrong. We have to cut the head off of the snake, not attack its body with pin pricks. I have another plan, but it will take a couple of weeks."

"Go, Boy. We'll be fine here. Mahmud has plenty more caves."

Khan left the Solar System thinking dark, dark thoughts. Chaos was all around. If felt as though he had just mounted Il Mostro.

He began to wonder about the Alien. Had she set him up for reasons of her own, or did she have a bigger plan yet for him?

CHAPTER SIXTEEN

"Shoot first and inquire afterwards ..."

Hermann Goering

"Don't let the enemy know where you will clash, for if they know, they will mass their strength to resist you."

Sun Tzu, *The Art of War*

Nathan Fox, Prime Director - Office of Technology Control, watched out the combat flyer's open door as Afghanistan's poppy fields, poplar trees, and arid landscape whipped by below. Lofty mountains loomed above on either side. They were headed up a long valley. People on the ground in their ancient costumes shook fists, raised middle fingers, even fired weapons. Usually these were antiquated automatic rifles, but occasionally there was a surprisingly powerful laser rifle, or even a ground-to-air missile that required the flyer's defensive shield to suck power from the power plant. He could hear the reduced hum going to the drive motors as the shield pulled power. When this would happen, he would say something to the pilot like, "Smoke him," and a particle-beam weapon blast would incinerate the ground attacker.

God, what a shithole this place was. – And had been for centuries. The people gloried in backwardness and ignorance. The old ways were the best. Education was poison for the mind from the "advanced" world. Their culture was morally superior. They read nothing but the Koran. They kept women in bondage, and "honor" killed innocent women if some asshole succeeded in raping them. They prevented all forms of meaningful education. They murdered anyone who didn't agree with their beetle-browed religious views. They were nothing more than warlords and thugs who used Islam as one of their weapons. But one thing you had to give them: they were tough bastards, who somehow managed to get their hands on weapons just advanced enough to fight off whatever group was trying to control them, and always had. The British, the Russians, the Americans, and now the ECG had battled them for four hundred years without noticeable progress at civilizing them. It was an ongoing embarrassment for the ECG – the one area on Earth that still resisted ECG hegemony. The Great Equilibration – which would make everyone on Earth equal, which would defeat poverty, hunger, crime, ignorance, and despair, which was a necessary social precondition for allowing extraterrestrial colonization, and which was possible only under the ministrations of the ECG – would be a long time coming here.

The pilot's voice spoke in his headset. "Coming in to Sinawi, Mr. Director. Just a couple of minutes. There's a brief period of risk as we enter the compound, because the insurgents keep a watch on it, but once we're past the shield we'll be OK. I'll just grab a bunk in the BOQ and hit the mess hall. Just let me know when you're ready to head out."

"Depends, Lieutenant. If they have the assault fully planned, it could be within a few hours. I'll call on your tablet."

"Sure thing, Director."

Ahead, the shield wall shimmered around the large, dusty, god-forsaken, geometrically-laid-out, sand-bagged compound like a curtain of colorless Northern Lights. And sure enough, just before they slipped through the shield, several explosions rocked the craft violently, and then they were through and headed down for the air field. The pilot muttered something.

"What's that, Lieutenant?" Fox had learned never to permit muttering in his presence. It could be subversive, and you didn't want to let people think they could get away with it. And given the level of global unrest that had arisen in that last few days since Khan International's little ploy, you couldn't be sure of anyone's loyalty. He was eighty-seven percent sure he had been messaging with Alexander Khan instead of Wilcox Snavely, but he was thirteen percent unsure. The likeliest scenario was that Snavely, the poor scheming bastard, was dead on Prison Planet, along with his pilot, and Khan had their craft. The question was, how the hell had Khan slipped in through the sensor arrays? But of course, there was also the small chance that even Snavely, the most obsequious, cowardly, conniving bureaucratic assistant he had ever had, was in fact playing him.

"Nothing, Mr. Director," said the pilot. "Just that the damned shit-fingers know exactly when to fire so you can't fire back because you're already through the shield and the hole has closed up. Do it pretty much every time. Pisses me off, is all. Like to fry the sons of bitches."

Fox marveled at soldiers' creativity at coming up with imprecations. "I think you'll get your chance to fry some shit-fingers before the day is out."

The briefing was in the General's Briefing Room. It made a few sad pretensions to luxury and comfort to distinguish itself from other base meeting rooms: a beaten-up fake-leather couch along one wall, with a couple of infested-looking armchairs facing the couch across a gaudy, epoxy-finish coffee table, thus forming a conversation group, and a rather nice oil-finish antique cherry sideboard with a few plates of fruits, cheeses, and pieces of flat bread. The plastic-top meeting table had been set up with a pitcher of ice water and a glass at each place. As usual, hard-connection screens were set up at each place on the table so data could be displayed but no data could be downloaded to one's personal pad. Instead of folding steel chairs, the chairs were local-purchase dining-table chairs with arms and seat padding. Otherwise, the room looked like a thousand other military outpost meeting rooms.

General Petrarchis's pissed-off, harried facial expression belied his words of welcome. "Welcome, Mr. Director. We are ready with the briefing if you are ready for it. But first, would you like a chance to freshen up? Eat? Sleep? Would you like some figs? Dates? Cheese? Pomegranates?" The general gestured perfunctorily toward the sideboard.

Fox had to suppress a smile. The spectacle of this stringy, crew-cut, leather-necked, hard-ass former commando playing gracious host was amusing. The general had the kick-ass-and-take-names reputation of an officer who put up with zero bullshit and never failed in his mission. He was assigned to Afghanistan because he had a habit of making indiscreet comments in front of reporters. Once he had arrived in Afghanistan and taken stock, he had done it again. "We'll have to kill every son of a bitch in this God-forsaken country to control it," he was reported to have said within earshot of a reporter. "We might as well carpet-bomb the fucking place with nukes. It'd be faster and cheaper." While this sentiment was not foreign to anyone in the ECG, it ran counter to the inclusive, multicultural message ECG put out. Fox had had to intervene to save the general, and he had naturally ensured that the general knew it.

"No, thank you, General, but I appreciate your gracious hospitality. You are a gentleman as well as an officer."

The general squinted sidewise at him, and Fox realized he may have laid it on a little thick. "All right," growled the general. I'll bring in the briefing team."

The briefing team consisted of four no-nonsense uniformed officers who gave every impression of wanting to be just like General Petrarchis – buzz-cut, brutally fit, blunt, intelligent – and one bearded intelligence agent in local clothes. Each gave a slide show with crisp commentary, starting with a summary history of Khan Family Enterprises' skirting of the law over previous decades, moving to key technologies the Khans had been selling that conflicted with ECG goals, moving to a profile and surveillance report on Dr. Albert Bahner, long-time Khan scientist and manufacturing director, moving to a summary analysis of the local political situation, and ending with a report on known and suspected Khan manufacturing capabilities in the area. The sum was this: Khan Enterprises had secretly made common cause with the warlords starting several years ago, but the relationship had lain dormant until the recent dissolution of Khan International. Only recently had ECG become aware of this. Dr. Bahner had disappeared from his usual haunts in the North American and European Directorates and was believed to be in the local area of Afghanistan. He had taken a suite at the Intercontinental in Kabul but was never there. Hidden factories in caves and sheds all across the region – apparently long in the planning – had become active and begun producing and shipping forbidden technology. It had been a trickle at first, but now suddenly it was a flood. The warlords were smuggling out products through Pakistan and Iran.

Fox knew all this but let the officers continue. All he wanted was to participate in the planned bust, but he needed to keep the military sweet so they would help him in the future. Fox also knew the warlords liked the Khans' name, but he knew it had been changed from "Conn" by Culpepper Khan, the founding patriarch, for obvious business reasons. He was saving that one up for when he needed it.

"Give me a rundown on the technology, Colonel," he said to the officer who had presented that part of the briefing. He knew about this, too, but wanted to get each officer committed. "Always up until now, they've produced and sold technology that is harmless on its face, but which can subvert central political control: water-splitting solar stills, cheap fuel cells that burn the hydrogen, unbreakable encryption with a government back door that malfunctions, things like that. What are they selling now?"

The colonel appeared happy to show off what he knew. "Standard-looking power packs that might say 10KW, but in fact when you test them are virtually limitless, with an extremely long tail on the decline chart if they're used for steady power at lower rates. Plenty powerful enough to power a heavy combat laser. Or a gravity sled. Or even a small star cruiser. And then there are the gravity-sled upgrade kits." The Colonel swallowed nervously.

"Upgrade kits?" Fox knew about the power packs, but this was a new one. Gravity-sled technology was tightly controlled, because it was essentially the same technology that permitted star travel: the creation of a gravity – or null-gravity – field, that when made extremely powerful, created a wormhole in space.

"Yes, Mr. Director. We captured one sledload of them in Pakistan. They look harmless enough, just a few hardware odds and ends, but when combined with the instructions – which are on a website that keeps moving from server to server – they can be used to vastly boost power on a grav-lift unit – essentially turn a gravity sled or an aircar into a spacefaring vehicle. Of course, there's the problem of life support. It's not clear what their intention is here. That may be on another server, but we haven't seen that yet."

The hairs stood up on the back of Fox's neck. "It's clear to me, Colonel. It's not grav sleds. It's aircars. They have essentially the same drive units as gravity sleds, only weaker. And the newer ones are pressurizable to forty thousand meters. Might as well be vacuum. Produced by Khan Industries, of course."

He fell silent, mulling the potential consequences. Every jack-leg mechanic on Earth with an air car and half a wit would be able to climb out of the gravity well. The illegal-colony problem would explode. Which of course was the intent. There was the navigation issue, too, but he now had little doubt that somewhere in Afghanistan was a factory producing interstellar navigation devices and posting the software to drive them on migrating websites. Otherwise there'd be lost and starving would-be settlers strung out all over the galaxy. What was clear was that this was a well-executed plan a long time in the making. Those fucking Khans. "Their Doomsday Revenge play," he muttered to himself. Good thing he had assigned a computer security squad to post corrupted versions of Khan International's tech releases. He clearly needed to follow up with them.

"Revenge play, Sir?" said the Colonel. "For Major Khan's sentencing? Wasn't he, uh, quite properly convicted of murder? Somebody he believed murdered his father?"

Fox realized he'd spoken indiscreetly. He had to be careful here. No way to say he had plotted the elder Khan's murder for years, awaiting only the proper Office of Internal Security moron to do it on faked-up evidence of planning a political coup and then brag to Major Khan about it. And Major Khan remained popular among the armed forces, particularly among his men.

"He was," Fox acknowledged. "His lawyers maintained that the evidence was … not convincing. But the wheels of justice turned, and he's now on Prison Planet. All I can say. Except that tracking data shows he's … uh. . ., still moving." As if it was all just a matter of ECG security. Which it was. Or as if even he, Nathan Fox, felt that Khan had gotten a raw deal but had to keep his mouth shut. Or as if revealing that Khan was being tracked showed personal concern. It was time to change the subject. "So where is Bahner, General?" He had read the flash reports, but he wanted somebody's ass on the line.

No fool, Petrarchis turned to the major who had reported on Bahner. "Royer?"

No fool, Royer realized he'd been had. "We believe he is living in the cave factory we are going to raid tonight." He looked at the intelligence agent, from whom he had probably gotten this information, and whom he clearly expected to speak up, but the agent was no fool, either. And Royer apparently had some misguided sense of honor about putting the man on the spot further. Fine. Royer it was.

"'Believe'?" Fox said.

"Best we can say, Mr. Director," said Royer.

Fox stared at him long enough to let him know he was still going to be held responsible if Bahner wasn't there. The officer stared back levelly. Was there a trace of contempt there? Perhaps another one for Prison Planet. Looked like an attitude problem. He turned to the one officer who had not presented. "You're the ops planner?"

"Yes, Mr. Director."

"What's the plan?"

"We know the cave has multiple entrances, spread out over an area of six square kilometers. Two of the entrances are large enough for two five-ton gravity sleds to pass each other, one on the way in, and one on the way out. The plan is to block all entrances except those two, and to send a thirty-man contingent into each of them, ten men to a sled. They'll be outfitted with tactical armor, oxygen masks, night-vision, including infrared, and ultraviolet flashlights. Along with the usual weaponry. And they'll be carrying large quantities of stun gas. Good for three hours of sleep and a horrible headache. We believe power is from an internal fusion reactor, so there's no cutting off the power from outside. We believe their defense plan is probably to turn off the lights and drop blast doors, then make their escape through an undiscovered tunnel, but our information – extracted from one of their construction workers, who unfortunately died during interrogation – is that we know about all the tunnels. Should work. We have breaching charges for the blast doors. We go in at oh-three hundred."

This was nearly twelve hours away. Something nagged at Fox, but he kept silent. "Why three?"

"Hope to catch them all asleep. The workers live in the underground compound. Supplies go in at night, usually between 11 and midnight, and any workers going home leave about the same time. By three, they should all be asleep."

"What about guards and detection devices?"

The Major nodded as if to say, good question. "We'll be carrying electronics suppressors, projecting the fields in front of us. None of their electronics will work."

"I want Bahner alive. And I want all data-storage devices undamaged. The man goes on trial. Nobody challenges ECG and gets away with it. He'll be … joining Major Khan soon."

At one AM his tablet woke him as programmed, and he called his pilot to be sure the man was awake. "We'll hover over the site but we're not going in," he told him. We'll be linked into the command net but will maintain radio silence unless contacted."

He took a miserable barracks shower in underheated water smelling strongly of calcium hypochlorite, then dressed in normal office attire save for a pair of desert combat boots. The dust of Afghanistan made street shoes impractical. He scorned what he thought of as costume politicos who changed their clothes depending upon the group they were with. He met the Lieutenant in the messhall for a cheerless breakfast of greasy scrambled eggs and mutton sausages, the latter being a nod to the local Islamic environment. The locally-hired cooks wouldn't touch pork. All in all, so far a miserable day. He hoped the mission cheered him more.

Twenty-five vehicles in all participated in the raid: General Petrarchis's command flyer, six main-attack-force combat sleds, three reserve combat sleds, Fox's combat flyer, and fourteen additional combat flyers, each one detailed to block an exit. In addition, he was told, three unmanned reconnaissance flyers loitered overhead and fed data back to the base, where it was consolidated, interpreted, and sent back to General Petrarchis's flyer for display. All entrances were to be blocked simultaneously. As they advanced, entry teams were to unreel wire connected to relay transmitters left outside the entrances, to overcome the issue of not being able transmit or receive through rock.

Seemed like a good plan, thought Fox, unless they were missing an exit. But something in the back of his mind bothered him. Something about that bearded intelligence officer.

It was a beautiful but cold night in the high mountains, with stars shining brightly. But Fox was not the type to enjoy nature unless it was stylized and circumscribed, as in a park. He watched the icons on his pad move into place around the schematic of the mountain cave, and listened to the tight-beam chatter between the groups. All seemed to be going according to plan. He watched as the combat sleds moved into location at the mouths of their respective tunnels, and heard their responses to General Petrarchis's query: "Any resistance yet? Teams report."

"Team 1 Negative, General. All quiet. We're about half a kilometer in. Tunnel lights are all out. Like there's nobody here, or they're expecting us."

Teams 2 and 3 reported similar conditions.

"Take no chances," said the General. "Anything moves, kill it and ask questions later. Uh …, unless it's Bahner. And for God's sake, keep your detonator fields on max power."

All teams acknowledged. Detonator fields had been developed nearly three hundred years before in Afghanistan to pre-explode roadside bombs before troops got to them. All ECG munitions were immune. In most cases, the local militants did not have access to the technology that made the ECG munitions immune, but in Afghanistan, and with the Khans involved, you could never be sure.

Fox was anxious to go in to see the extent of the set-up that Bahner had been able to achieve in the outback of Afghanistan, and to gloat in the face of the man himself. After all, Bahner was the third part of the Khan triad – Khan the Elder, Khan the Younger, and Albert Bahner – that held the organization together. Once he had Bahner, he would have single-handedly destroyed the Khan industrial empire and its threat to ECG hegemony. He also wanted to dip himself in combat as risklessly as possible so he could cover himself with glory in the halls of ECG power. Give himself one more advantage in the struggle for ultimate power: the Prime Director – ECG role itself. When its current elderly occupant died, of course.

But he was no fool. He smelled a rat here.

Suddenly the radio was alive with uncoordinated, undisciplined chatter. "HOLY SHIT! Team Two under fire! Motion-Activated weapons! And –" then there was the sound of a huge explosion.

"Team Three reporting. We just found ECG Claymores all along both walls of the tun—" Another huge explosion.

A new voice came onto the net, much clearer. "General, this is Captain Diaz, Sinawi base security. We are under attack. Colonel Ephron is dead. Repeat: we are under attack on all four sides of the compound by what appear to be nearly battalion-strength rebel forces. Maybe five or six hundred. We –"

General Petrarchis's voice bulled through. "What the hell is the shield-wall status?"

"Down, Sir. The rebels have some kind of disruptor device that prevents it from forming. Apparently one on each side of the compound, since there are four fields. We are taking rocket, mortar, and grenade fire from all sides. All troops are manning the perimeter and are giving it back to the enemy with small arms, Sir, a real shootout, and we are taking casualties fast. We need air support, but there are only four combat flyers left on base. Two have been shot down –"

"SHOT DOWN?" bellowed the General. "How?"

"They either put three or four heavy combat lasers on them and overloaded the shields, or they have a shield penetrator on some kind of invisible star cruiser. So it has to be combat ground lasers. We need those flyers you have back, Sir. With respect, Sir."

Silence from General Petrarchis. Finally, "Team One, stop in your tracks. Do not go farther into the tunnel. It's a trap. Exit the tunnel. Reserve Teams Two and Three, proceed into your tunnels and recover bodies and equipment. All flyers, RTB. Exercise extreme caution. Be advised, base is under attack. Repeat, base is under attack. Shield wall is down. Hundreds of attackers. Engage and kill the enemy. All of the enemy. No prisoners. Looks like we chomped on the bait for a set-up, and I want some payback."

Fox went to a private connection with the General. "I'd like a few of their officers for interrogation, General. We need to know how they pulled this off. Who are their connections in your organization? And what is their real connection with Khan International, or was that just bait?"

"In case you haven't fucking noticed, uh, Mr. Director, these fucking shitfingers don't wear fucking uniforms. It's impossible to tell who their officers are. But I suppose we can randomly pick fifteen or so of them to keep alive. And who the hell else besides Khan International could provide them with the technology to bring down our shield wall?"

Fox overlooked the General's pique. He understood: the general had been flummoxed in front of a superior. His organization had been compromised. But he had not lost control of himself in a bad situation. His combat experience showed. He must be protected from this failure. "Fifteen sounds fine, General."

Fox gave his pilot orders to return him to the Intercontinental. He had no doubt that the cave was completely devoid of any factory accouterments, and that before the General's forces reached Sinawi, the attackers would have faded away, taking their dead with them. ECG forces had been played. The enemy's intelligence was better than his own. It was clear that the alliance between Bahner and the Mujahedeen was far more sophisticated – and dangerous – than he had anticipated. And that its objectives, if they were really what the briefing had said, were a threat to the survival of the ECG.

What he couldn't understand was why Khan International would tip its hand before it was ready to flood the marketplaces of the world with the forbidden technology. Unless they were already doing their damnedest and it wasn't enough. It was possible that Khan International's destabilization objectives were already being carried out, that he didn't yet know their extent, and that this trap had been an effort at misdirection. – Or that, perhaps they couldn't control the Mujahedeen, either, and somebody had used information he wasn't supposed to in order to achieve the usual Mujahedeen goal: kill as many ECG people as possible. But if this operation had been solely an effort at misdirection, what in God's name was Khan International planning that required this feint?

For the first time in years, Nathan Fox broke into a fear sweat. Having killed the father and exiled the son, he had smugly thought he had the Khan problem under control. But if Khan International remnants truly intended what was said in the briefing, and if they succeeded even only partially, his career – possibly even his life – were over. ECG would collapse. Uncoordinated, unmanaged activity would spread over the entire globe, and the former managers of the regime – himself included – could end up like Mussolini of three hundred years before: hung by his heels from a lamppost.

He and the other senior cadre of the regime – the Ruling Council – had always known there was a phase in the implementation of the utopian vision in which leaders would be resented, even hated. For the greater good, they had to impose painful measures to get the world out of the mess its previous rulers had made. But such a phase was to be temporary. They didn't much discuss the fact that the phase had lasted three hundred years and showed no signs of passing. – Or that they themselves lived in a style more like ancient pashas and kings compared with the privations and oppressions suffered by the people. It was necessary, after all, for leaders to remove struggle from their own personal lives so they could keep their minds focused on improving the lot of the people. But it was doubtful the people would see it that way.

Clearly, he had to take out both Khan the younger and Bahner. The question was, how to find out where they were. And what exactly were the younger Khan's intentions?

He came to it quickly: he himself was going to have to go to Prison Planet. If Khan was really back here on Earth in a stolen cruiser, he had had help stealing it on Prison Planet. Those people were still there. They were also important to Khan, probably good friends by now. They were the key.

CHAPTER SEVENTEEN

"Courage, loyalty, justice, and devotion to duty are the prime manly virtues. Pursuing a vision brings them all into play."
Father Lucian Khan, *Khans to Khans*

On the voyage back to Arcadia, Khan firmed up his new plan. He would never admit it to anyone, but the idea had come in a dream, and therefore had a sense of rightness he would be hard-pressed to defend rationally. Certainly not to Baelmar, who would say, of course it was time he paid attention to his dreams. It required that he go back to Earth, which he had promised to do but didn't really want to do. Hopefully it would only be temporary.

He had brought several shoulder-eye vid cams along from Earth, and filmed his fifteen tightly-packed charges on the ship while he and Baelmar tutored them on what life was like on Arcadia. He continued filming when they landed at the Khan Interplanetary landing field above Advance, catching their wide-eyed expressions as they gaped at the five moored dirigibles and the town bracketing the River of Doubt below.

Bella bounded out of the office, took in the Newbies, and whooped, "Fresh meat!"

She hugged Baelmar, who politely permitted it, but did not reciprocate as enthusiastically. Khan knew he found open displays of affection, not improper, but bemusing. Unclenched by Bella, he headed down into town, ostensibly to find Ernie, who continually demanded rematches at various games of chance, and kept losing, to Baelmar's quiet amusement. But Khan suspected he just wanted to be alone. Earth had sobered him. Khan had hated to see it, but the sunny smile sometimes slipped from his friend's face on Earth, and on the voyage back. Khan knew what it was. The Leas and the savannah of the Deepeven would never again look like the whole world. Elves, Lords, Techs, and Maneaters would never again define the breadth of humanity. Baelmar's home had shrunk into a corner of a larger, darker picture, and he would never be able to crowd back into the place from which he had come. Earth would come with him.

Bella turned to Khan, wrapped him in a bear hug and gave him a sloppy kiss on each cheek.

"Boss! I was afraid we'd never see you again! Man, do we have a lot to tell you! Trade agreement with Riversend! Regular runs! Two new exploratory expeditions planned to find other towns! Progress! My God, it's a fantastic life!"

He laughed and gave her a hug back. "Great to see you, Bella. Fantastic, in fact. And let me introduce fifteen new citizens who must be given jobs and made to feel at home."

Bella looked at the Newbies and held up four fingers. "Coal mine, profit farms, cannery, linen mill. All hiring. We're going to be exporting linen and canned goods. And if any of you guys have flight experience, I could use another couple of pilots. That's it. Now get out of here and stop bothering me. I'm busy."

Noting with interest that Bella had not asked a single question about Earth, Khan trooped his group down into town to meet Estelle first, so they could become citizens. She was more reserved than Bella, but still, he could tell she was happy to see him. She welcomed the Newbies first, then stepped close and gave him a wry smile.

"Well, you're always full of surprises. Are you back for good?" She took his left hand, then looked at it in distress for a brief moment as she discovered the missing fingers, which she had not noticed when he had left Sevka with her. Then she looked back into his eyes and forced a sober smile.

He laid his other hand on top of hers. He had a rush of feeling and almost told her she was the best thing to ever happen in his life. But the Newbies were watching, and he controlled himself at the last moment. "One thing I'm now sure of is, this is home."

Her eyes moistened. "Khan, that is not a straight answer."

"I plan to grow old and die here, if that helps."

She broke into an unaccustomed, uncynical bright smile. "A little. Dinner at Ralph's?"

"Absolutely. On me."

After Estelle's normal citizenship spiel, which she conducted off schedule especially for these fifteen new citizens, he got his charges places to sleep at Mama Ilse's, then distributed them to the various potential employers. He told them all, "Come and see me if you need any help at all. At the office up on the hill where we landed. It's very different here from Earth and ECG, and the first thing you'll have to learn is, you're free. No one is watching you, no one cares what you do as long as you don't harm anyone else. You'll wait forever for someone to tell you what to do. You'll have to learn to do that yourselves. Probably your biggest challenge in adjusting to life on Arcadia." And the last thing he said to each was, "Oh, and by the way, are you a journalist?"

It turned out that Amity Green was a journalist of sorts. Of course, journalism in the ECG amounted to propaganda trying to look like incisive reporting, but that was not a bad thing, given his intentions. And she would have some training. He explained that he would like her to work for him.

"Doing what?" she wanted to know. "This place is so new and strange, I can't imagine what journalism I could do here that would help you. As far as I can see, there's not even any electronic media. And what I've been doing is stories about how it's really OK that you can no longer have a pet in your apartment, or how it's not the fault of the local government if a flood filled the basement of your apartment building with sewage, and we all need to pitch in, shoulder to shoulder, to clean it up. And so on. Here, I don't know anybody or anything."

He handed her a Shoulder Eye. "I want you to carry this and put together a documentary. You'll follow me wherever I go, or I may send you places with Bella, and you'll document and comment on whatever you see and experience. A hundred twenty credits a week."

"Who is my audience, and what do you want me to say?"

"Let's say, prospective immigrants. And whatever comes to your mind. It's to be your documentary about Arcadia, with your name and voice. Even your image. I have more Eyes if you need to use them."

Her mouth worked without saying anything. She got the concept but was unused to dealing with it.

"What are you going to use it for?"

He left the key part out of the explanation. "Well ..., we're at a historical moment here on Prison Planet, Arcadia, Earth 2.0, call it what you will. A group we just found calls it Paradiso. It's important that we ... document some things for those who come after us. Could have multiple uses. You never know. But it's history. That's why I want you to tell the truth as you see it. As you discover it and this planet. Through your eyes and ears."

"OK. So ..., do you want me to go along with you to your dinner date with your girlfriend?"

"My girlfriend? I don't have a girlfriend."

She gave a small sigh and a smile. "Mr. Khan, I am just twenty-two years old, but I am not a child. I noticed on the space voyage that you seem to be devoid of some of the normal feelings most people have, so maybe you don't *know* you have a girlfriend. But Mayor Workman is your girlfriend, or I am a fish."

"Ahem. I see, then. Well, in that case, no, I think I would like to have dinner with ... uh ... Mayor Workman ... by myself."

She gave a sideways smile. "I thought so. So I'll just film the two of you talking, introduce you to the viewer, then leave. See you tomorrow morning."

Estelle was frazzled as usual, but seemed happy to see him. She had done something different with her short hair, and she wore an open-collared shirt of the silky material Bella had brought back from Riversend. A glass-bead necklace hung between the open top buttons. She was full of news.

"Riversend is going to send us center-fire cartridge technology, and silk, or something like it, small zinc-can batteries of all sizes – which says they have stamping technology, and old-fashioned light bulbs. Low wattage, just enough to read by. Plus sea salt, salted fish, and best of all, a tree-nut oil similar to olive oil. We're going to send them linen, clothes, shoes, salted pork, glass jars and bottles, and canned goods. We're also exchanging seed stocks and root stocks. It's going to be very beneficial. The only thing that's worrisome is, they now know where we live, and so will all the people they deal with. Plus, their government sounds a bit, uh, non-participatory. So we're holding back on the dirigible and diesel technology and keeping it to ourselves."

She chewed a morsel of oil-soaked bread and washed it down with a slug of red wine. He had always been amazed at her capacity to metabolize alcohol, which seemed limitless.

"That's excellent," he said. "So people are taking the level of change positively? New technology, new neighbors, etc.? I've been concerned at times that there's been a lot of change, and people may not like it. I come along and suddenly everything changes."

She klinked her fork onto her plate and stared at him for a moment. "Is that self-doubt I hear?" she said. "From Major Alexander Khan? Scion of the Khans, Chairman of Khan Interplanetary, as I understand you now intend to call it?"

He said nothing, but took a small bite of canned beans, which certainly had come from the Khan cannery.

She persisted. "So what happened back there?"

He looked up and shook his head. "Couldn't pull it off."

"Pull what off?"

"Bring down ECG with a massive freedom technology release. Kill him. Failing that, plunge Earth infrastructure into chaos with a doomsday Net virus to bring down ECG. Kill millions to save the rest. And kill him."

She flinched slightly at each "kill" as if receiving small blows. She was silent for a long moment, perhaps sensing this was an important passage in both of their lives. Or perhaps horrified at the scale of action he was capable of. "Fox, you mean? The guy who ruined your family and sent you here?"

He nodded.

She looked inscrutable for a moment, then actually seemed to sigh in relief. "Why not?"

"The technology release? Too telescoped. Too abbreviated. And a doomsday virus as a Plan B? Too extreme. The people just want freedom. Gotta be a better way than returning Earth to the Dark Ages with a doomsday Net virus. We – the remnants of Khan International – tried our best on a better way. Just didn't work well. Hasn't yet, anyway. Too slow, too much collateral damage."

"From which you saved those fifteen? As a salve to your conscience?"

Damn, but she could see into him. He sighed. "Right."

"And Fox?" There seemed something odd about her persistent curiosity.

"I could probably have lured him and killed him, if I was willing to die myself. But I wasn't. And it may be too late for revenge. I have a new life. I realized I wanted to come back here, that Earth was no longer my home. My goal has to be to get ECG to leave Arcadia alone – for the people's sake. They'll come for me anyway, with overwhelming force. They failed before, and I took their starship. They know I'm here and armed with ECG weapons. And Fox's reason for wanting me back is now intensified because of Khan operations on Earth. I can't and won't change that. But leaving him alive hopefully means they'll just come after me alone, not wipe out any group they find me among. I think."

He sat back. "In a harsh light, what I've done here and on Earth – make unilateral change that I decided is good for the people – could look like pride. And a quest for revenge at others' expense." He fell silent for a moment, looking her in the eye. "And there are people here I care about and don't want to endanger."

She too now sat back, took another, larger slug of wine, and mulled it while she regarded him with an appraising stare. "Khan, that is the longest speech you've ever made to me."

She paused as if thinking what to say next, then fell silent. She clearly had more to say, but chose not to say it. But finally she couldn't keep quiet.

"Look, you didn't choose to be born a Khan, and you didn't choose to be sent here. But we took you in, for better or worse. We knew who and what you were. You told us. Everybody expects you to be true to who you are, and who you've chosen to be. Hell, we know there's risk. But we've signed on for the ride."

He realized she was talking about herself as well as Advance.

He reached across the table and took her hands. "Could be bumpy."

"We could use a little bumping around, you and I."

"Harrumph. Even if we can handle ECG, we're going to end up with immigrants. Landing in homemade starships all over the planet." He explained about the technology release.

"How many? Max?"

"Maybe ten thousand."

"So? Not a big deal. We use what technology we want, and melt the rest down for scrap metal. We're Techs, after all. We're not afraid of some technology leaps. But as far as re-starting star travel, I for one doubt many on this planet want to go to the stars. We're already *in* the stars. We have a good life and just want to make it marginally better. We don't want to win the tech lottery. "

She stood and pulled on his hand.

"Since you remain so dumb or oblivious you can't take a hint, Khan, let me take you and show you my new bedspread. Never can tell when you might get another chance to see it."

Khan introduced Amity to everyone he knew, explaining to them that they were being recorded. Newbies and First-Gens got this immediately, but others, starting with Baelmar, had to be shown.

"It has captured my spirit," he said concernedly, looking at the small editing screen. On Earth he had seen vids of other people, but never himself. "Please. Let it go."

Khan explained that humans had been doing it for centuries and no one had died yet, but that if Baelmar wished, the images would be erased after the vid had been used in a couple of weeks. Baelmar was OK with this, as long as this could be done on the Leas in his presence.

Khan then volunteered to take him – and Amity – back to the Leas.

Baelmar demurred. "The time has not yet come for me to go back and stay. But it is true I would like to see Maruil and Gareth and Branwyn. Earth, though it has some nice people, made me yearn for my home."

For his part, Khan was vaguely disquieted. Baelmar had been right each time he had said bigger things were coming. Now the Elf was refusing to go back home for good just yet because he obviously thought Khan had still not fulfilled his destiny. Dread loomed up at the edge of his mind like a wolf at the edge of firelight, but he resolutely ignored it.

They took a dirigible downstream to Sunrise Keep, where Dr. Greis regaled Amity with a recounting of the battle for the Keep, all of which Amity recorded. She took in the battlements, the labor-intensive, draft-animal farming, the mix of steam-engine powered boats and rowboats at the docks, and the cross-bow-armed citizenry. They walked out through the fields, and she saw that women as well as men, and all children above the age of nine were armed, even as they worked.

"Everybody is armed all the time?" she asked Dr. Greis.

"Even in the outhouse," he said. "That's my rule. And it's a good one, too. We're living in a Darwinian environment here. Maneaters can and do attack at any time. The Society of Lords, as they now call themselves, could attack to reestablish what they see as their rightful superiority over inferiors. Meaning us. We've fought them off twice now. The first time, they thought we'd fold just at the sight of their banners, horses, and armor. But the well-trained citizen army concept paid off. Even our kids shoot better than their warriors. But it could be any group that attacks. Some new group we've never heard of. So we have to be prepared. It's the natural order of things. Ever try to sneak up on a wild animal without it showing its teeth?"

"I never saw wild animals in Kansas City," she said. "Except birds."

"Ah," he said. "Supposedly harmless creatures, but killers nonetheless. All creatures are warlike to some extent. They have to be to survive."

"Come on," she said. "Even people in offices?"

He smiled. "I come from academia. You would expect harmless old men and women sitting around discussing ideas. But instead it was constant war. The teeth, beaks, claws, and weapons were verbal, but deadly to reputations nonetheless. The lesson is, humans are dangerous to be around. We're all capable of aggression. Forget it at your peril."

"But where I come from, the only people who were aggressive were the police."

"That's because you were slaves. You had submitted. We were slaves here, too. But we stopped submitting. We fought. To keep from submitting again, we have to be prepared to deal with aggression. There's always someone who's bigger, smarter, faster, who wants you to submit. It could even be one among us who decides one day to be king. So we're all armed, all the time. It makes for a civil environment. Provoke somebody, and you might die. So people are polite. We do our best to save violence for those who attack us from outside, and we make sure anyone who does pays a heavy price."

Khan could see Amity reeling from this blast of raw non-ECG thinking. She would have been conditioned since birth to believe that individuals never needed weapons for anything – that the State would protect them. He gave Dr. Greis an appraising look. "You have changed from the mild-mannered, enslaved academic I found working in the hayfield."

"Being a leader changes a man, Major. Completely. You start out as yourself and become your people. You protect them the best way you can. I now understand the royal 'we.' What's important is that a leader keep in mind that he serves the people, not the other way around."

After unloading their cargo of glass bottles, bundles of linen pants, leather gloves, and canned beets, and taking on a cargo of fine furniture wood and pottery, they visited Guido's Hundred. Salvatore had seen the ship coming, and met them at the mooring bollards. He was delighted to see them, and delighted with Amity.

"A young woman from Earth who can tell Olympia about the latest Earth fashions!" he boomed, holding out a welcoming arm to Amity. "Come in, come in, come in, we will kill a ewe and have a feast! You must tell us all about what you've been doing, Major. You have transformed the Keep and the Hundred with your weekly runs, and you're making me rich! I want to know what else you have in mind!"

Khan explained Amity's Shoulder Eye, and this prompted a complete tour of Guido Hundred's Big House, including the leather shop, the blacksmith shop, the smokehouse, and the wine cellar. This was followed by a tour of the stables, the barns, and the equipment shed, as well as the kitchen gardens. By the time the tour was over, a servant informed them that the appetizers were ready. Rather than sit at formal dinner, Baelmar excused himself to go back to the stables to see an acquaintance from his youthful days of prowling the Leas. Khan watched him go and worried.

Salvatore led them into the same dining room in which Khan had been welcomed when he was still a Newby. The huge dining table groaned with meat dishes, vegetable dishes of all kinds, pasta and sauce, and breads and jams. And wine. Amity had some trouble understanding.

She looked at the spread doubtfully, but watched with interest as everyone loaded plates and ate with gusto. She whispered to Khan, nodding at the leg of lamb on the platter. "Is it formed protein paste, then? Recycled? It looks … so … real. Do you think they have any Nourish Tabs I could eat?"

He leaned close and explained. Her eyes grew wide.

Then she looked at a bowl of pasta sitting beside a sauce boat and asked Khan another whispered question.

Sitting on her other side, Olympia saw her doubt and confusion and probably heard the whisper.

"It's pasta," she explained. "Made from wheat flour. Tastes wonderful, but hard on a girl's figure. Straight to the hips. Try some. You'll like it."

And before long, Amity was putting the spread away like the rest of them, including wine, which she had apparently never had. She and Olympia were whispering to each other and giggling, and Salvatore looked on contentedly.

"It's too long, Major. You don't come to see me often enough. But it is a pleasure to see you in my dining room again, especially in the company of this charming young lady."

Unacquainted with courtliness and flattery, Amity blushed and giggled.

"Come," said Salvatore, gesturing toward the adjoining sitting room. "Let's get out the instruments and sing."

"I would have been disappointed if we did not," said Khan.

After many rounds of songs, and after holding her own by singing a Renaissance love song, in which Olympia surprisingly joined, Amity went off with Olympia, leaving Khan alone with Salvatore. Salvatore proudly poured Khan a small shot of brandy.

"Our latest achievement. We have developed a distilling operation. Try it. It's excellent. Though with a bite. Now tell me. You have come to tell me something, my good friend. You do not go back to Earth and come back and come to see me without having something important to tell me."

Khan gave an austere smile and nod. "You are most astute, Salvatore."

And he told him the whole story of his battle with the squad that had come after him, his theft of the spacecraft, his mission to Earth, the technology release there, the battle there, and the likelihood – since the technology release had not fully had the hoped-for effect – that ECG was going to be coming after him. That he would need help. That technology on Arcadia was going to inevitably change quickly. And how did Salvatore feel about all that?

"We will adapt, Major. We will support you. We will fight alongside you."

"That's good, Salvatore. Because I need a place to hide out and set up an ambush, away from Advance. With troops I can trust and who will fight. It'll be a tough fight. Against ECG troops with lasers." He explained what these were in case Salvatore did not know. "Probably in the next ten days, though I'm guessing. I'd like to hide out here until they come, and conduct the fight out in the country a few kilometers from here." The unspoken objective that both understood was protecting Advance from ECG attack.

Salvatore's eyes hooded over as he regarded Khan. This was perhaps too direct a calling of his bluff. He took another sip of his brandy, and Khan could see the tough negotiator coming to the fore. Salvatore was his friend, but he was a leader and a businessman.

"May I speak plainly, Major?"

"Of course, Salvatore. When the matter is important, life is too short and too risky to do otherwise."

Salvatore stood and began to pace around the drawing room. Khan noted again that, though in his sixties, he was an impressive, bull of a man. "I have my own challenges. The Society of Lords has decided that I am insufficiently supportive of their cause. That indeed, I have too much love for Sunrise Keep and for Advance. That I am a traitor for giving my people a vote. That I am a democracy lover. They are almost certainly plotting an attack against the Hundred so they can divide it among themselves, return my associates to serfdom, and use the Hundred as a base from which to attack Sunrise Keep again. In fact, I'm not sure they don't intend to try something against Advance."

"I am sorry to hear that."

"As well, I am looking for a suitable husband for Olympia. I've had my eye on you since you first arrived, and certainly since you started your Khan business operations. Olympia is quite taken with you, and you would make a fine son in law. But I am aware that you and Mayor Workman are … friends of a special sort, and that a match with Olympia is not likely."

"Estelle and I are … good friends."

"So to the point, Major. You want to come to the Hundred and use our troops to fight off an attack by people from Earth with outlandish weapons which will kill us ten for one. And you are not going to marry my daughter. What advantage is there for us at the Hundred to give you a place to entertain an attack by Earth forces?"

Khan nodded. This was the type of frank discussion he had heard in his father's drawing rooms and offices on many occasions. There had to be quid pro quos.

"I can't commit security forces from Advance to help you, though a mutual defense treaty would be a good idea, especially since you've given your people a vote in your affairs."

Salvatore pursed his lips. "You have my attention."

"I will propose it to Mayor Workman and the city council. But I have something more immediately helpful: a cache of ECG weapons I brought back from Earth. Enough to arm a hundred men, with enough power packs and ammunition to last through a couple of wars. I will leave these weapons with you and train your men how to use them. They will make any attack by the Society of Lords look ridiculous. And they should be sufficient to fight off an ECG attack, unless it's massive."

Salvatore's face grew flushed, whether from the wine and liquor, or from the implications of this offer, it was hard to tell. "You are generous, Major."

"Well, I may at some point want some of the weapons back, but I can't think of a better place to leave them for safekeeping."

He rose and gave Salvatore his hand. They shook. Khan went on.

"Regarding Olympia, she is a beautiful young woman who would make a fine wife, and I am flattered that you would consider me as a son in law." He knew better than to mention the age difference, because in Salvatore's world, that was to be desired. The older, steadier, well-established man mates with the younger, beautiful, fertile woman, and they produce heirs and spares, one after another.

"But you are right about Estelle … uh, Mayor Workman. I, uh, ahem, well …."

Salvatore raised both of his palms. "Please, Major. It is not necessary to explain."

Khan rallied. "But I understand about Olympia. And agree it's time to find her a mate. What I will do is take her to Advance and introduce her to people there. Perhaps a couple of semesters at the technical school there …."

Salvatore began to grimace, so Khan tried another idea.

"We don't know them well yet, but it seems clear there are many wealthy families in Riversend. And I happen to know that their ambassador, Olajuwon Smith, is still in Advance. Perhaps an introduction is in order, and some discreet inquiries about the nature of social affairs among people of quality in Riversend. Maybe even a trip there for you and Olympia, once the Society of Lords and ECG issues are resolved. I would even stay at the Hundred to protect your interests while you were gone."

Salvatore tilted his head first one way, then the other, as if rolling this thought around. Then he stuck out his hand and shook Khan's.

"Deal."

Maruil was again happy to see Baelmar, and she didn't smack him this time, perhaps because it had only been a short time since she had seen him before. The children were fascinated with the idea that their father had been to Earth.

And with Amity. In particular, though she was well beyond his age, Gareth was fascinated with Amity. Maruil and Baelmar watched this interaction with the quiet, mildly amused surprise of parents watching their children discover the opposite sex.

Branwyn elaborately suppressed her disgust at her brother's offers to show Amity where and how the battle with Mander's men took place, how to shoot a bow, where to find fish in a nearby stream, how to ride a horse, and so on, but kept her counsel. For her part, Amity was amused but also flattered, and politely took him up on each of his offers. "It'll make good vid," she explained. "Plus, I love this place. I can't believe there's just woodland and countryside as far as you want to go."

After a good day's visit, and another feast, more modest and less spicy than the one at the Hundred, but equally satisfying, they got a good night's sleep. Khan was in the haymow again, and Amity slept on the porch, which she preferred to the couch in the living room. She wanted to "camp out." Gareth offered to take his bedroll out to the porch to protect her from gryphons and wild coyotes, but his mother forbade it. "Why?" he wanted to know, but Maruil just gave him a bemused look and said that Amity would be fine.

And she was, bubbling over at breakfast of bread and jam, greens and eggs about the night sounds and how wonderful it was to live amid nature, and so on. Baelmar and Maruil exchanged a silent, contented glance across the table, one of them signaling to the other, "I told you so," but it was hard to tell who and whom.

"You're welcome to stay with us a week or two if you like, Amity," said Maruil. "It's time to bring in nuts and smoke fish and meat. You could help. Then when Mr. Khan brings Baelmar back from whatever dangerous undertaking he has in store next," and here she gave Khan a glare, "you could return to Advance."

Excited as a little girl, Amity looked to Khan, who thought fast. Did he want to endanger this young innocent by asking her to record the coming battle? Or was it OK if she stayed with Maruil and the children, possibly to get involved in hanky panky with Gareth? It appeared the boy's parents had blessed the possible hanky panky. For a moment, he felt almost … fatherly. He didn't want this young woman to get killed in a firefight, but he didn't want her to get into trouble in any other way, either. He looked at Maruil, then at Amity and Gareth, then back at Maruil and raised an eyebrow.

"Baelmar and Gareth had a discussion last night," she said.

"I see" said Khan. "Fine, then. I do want her back in Advance to record the town, and to go to Riversend with Bella and record what she sees there." He turned to Amity. "But since you like it here, and since it will indeed make good vid, I don't see why not."

Amity smiled and clasped her hands under her chin in excitement. "My friends on Earth would never believe this," she said.

"They might," said Khan. "In fact, they just might."

CHAPTER EIGHTEEN

"Those who are first on the battlefield and await the opponents are at ease; those who are last on the battlefield and head into battle get worn out."

Sun Tzu, *the Art of War*

The plan was to set up an ambush in the open, where it would seem impossible, but backed up by hidden troops with heavy weapons, and in a pinch, the cloaked starship.

Khan and his force had set up tents on the open grassland a few kilometers to the west of the Hundred. Fifty of Salvatore's men were with him, armed with laser pistols, but also with a couple of heavy energy-pulse generators capable of breaching armor of all kinds. All weapons were kept out of sight and turned off in order to give a scanner picture from orbit of a group of nomad horsemen with no more than primitive weapons. All the men, including Khan, wore hooded cloaks against the nighttime cool, but also to minimize ease of recognition.

All had their mounts with them, and the cover story, should they actually need to get into a discussion, was that they were rounding up horses from the wild herd. And in fact, they had rounded up a few of the huge herd Khan had seen on his first journey to the Hundred. They were in a makeshift corral.

But Khan had brought the tracking chips as bait – all three of them, his, Sevka's, and Snavely's – out of the cloaked starship so they could be detected. The ship sat in a clearing in a copse of trees a kilometer away, its AI programmed to beam Khan into the ship at a signal from his communicator. Ship's sensors had told him on his approach from Earth that ECG had repaired at least some of the satellites, so he knew the chips' signals would be retransmitted. Ship's sensors also warned him as he parked the vessel that there were now two newly arrived ships in orbit minutely scanning the surface in this area.

With any luck, it would be Fox himself who had come, and he could capture him and another starship. He had stuck his finger far enough into Fox's eye back on Earth to make it personal. And the things Albert was doing would by now be bringing intense Ruling Council pressure on Fox to end the problem. So it was likely Fox would come himself, but Khan assumed he and the ships would stay in orbit to avoid the disaster of the previous mission. Fox's plan would surely be for his troops to incapacitate Khan, then beam him back up to the ship in metaphorical chains. The challenge was, to lure Fox and his ship down from orbit. Thus, Snavely's and Sevka's chips. And the nearby ship.

Khan had also given a communicator each to Estelle and Bella, in case Advance came under attack. The communicators were of Khan International manufacture, without the standard ECG tracking feature. Nevertheless, they would light up to a ship in orbit if used to transmit, so both Estelle and Bella knew to use them only in an emergency.

Things went wrong quickly.

Two squads of armored commandos materialized, with intersecting fields of fire focused on Khan's men. One of the groups was in the corral with the horses, which they could use for cover, and the other group was in the clear. But they had Khan's men in a crossfire situation without danger of shooting each other.

As trained, Khan's men did nothing but stare. He wasn't sure if it was the training or the shock of the commandos' sudden appearance.

"Raise your hands!" bellowed one of the ECG sergeants. "Now, or die!"

The men raised their hands, as did Khan.

"Where is Khan?" shouted the sergeant. "Tell me now, now, now, or one of you dies!"

"Who is Khan?" said one of Khan's men, and the sergeant sliced him in two with his laser pistol.

The top half of his body simply fell loose from the bottom half, sectioned at the waist. "What the hell?" said the man after his trunk hit the ground. Then a flutter replaced the confused look in his eyes, and they closed as blood hosed out of his iliac arteries onto the ground in weaker and weaker spurts.

"Don't screw with me, you filthy savages!" shouted the sergeant. "Give me Khan now!"

"I am Khan!" roared Khan, pulling a huge military pistol loaded with armor-piercing rounds and blowing a hole through the offending sergeant's chest.

On that signal, crossbowmen hidden in foxholes surrounding the site threw aside their covering straw mats and leapt up, firing bolts sharpened to needle points. Khan had tested these on the armor left behind in the previous skirmish with ECG, and found that such bolts with a sharp, conical nose would penetrate both laser armor and impact armor every time, while bolts and arrows with normal flanged arrowheads would not.

Instantly, seven of the remaining fifteen commandos dropped. The remaining eight did not back off or retreat at all, but started killing Khan's crossbowmen quickly and efficiently with their laser pistols, dropping ten in a matter of seconds.

"Lasers on necks, ankles, and wrists!" yelled Khan, and finally his men hauled out the unfamiliar laser weapons and began firing. At the same time, Baelmar gave a shrill whistle, and the horses in the corral startled and trampled three commandos.

It was quickly over. Khan identified and saved the other squad sergeant from death so he could question him. Fighting back revulsion at the slaughter of his men – Salvatore's men – Khan asked, "Where is Fox?"

"Fuck you, Khan!"

Khan struggled with a blind rage he had seldom experienced, and nearly killed the man on impulse. But he finally overmastered it and swallowed the bile in his throat. "You are going to die, Sergeant. The question is, will it be quick and painless, or will I take my time."

"Yeah, yeah. Talk tough."

Khan jerked off the man's helmet and sliced of part of an ear with his knife. The man didn't scream. A tough bastard. Khan tried anyway. "Where is Fox?"

"Fuck you! People like you and your family need to die! You ruin everything for everybody. You delay the Great Equilibrium. I won't tell you if you cut off my leg."

"I'm sure you wouldn't, because you would bleed out in less than a minute. But I'll just cut off a little thing you won't be needing any more," and he aimed a laser pistol at the man's groin.

Suddenly a large, strong hand squeezed his shoulder. "No, Khan," said Baelmar. "He will not tell you. Killing him will only damage your spirit. He is wrong in his ideas, but he is brave. Take him far away, like the other man, and let him go. Let him fight to live. He will then learn truth."

For a moment, a flash of appreciation showed in the sergeant's eyes as he looked at Baelmar.

Baelmar's face was firm. Khan shook the battle rage from his brain and his vision cleared. "You are right, Baelmar. There's another way."

He pulled the man's battle helmet loose and was going to use the tactical net to announce himself to the man's superior, who he assumed was in contact with Fox, or was Fox himself, but his own communicator beeped. He pulled it loose from his belt.

"Go."

"I thought you were smarter than to think I would personally participate in an attack on a trained commando," said Fox's unctuous voice. "Of course I had to try to capture you by conventional means, but I always try to have a back-up plan."

"Your conventional means just got fifteen of your sixteen commandos killed. Plus eleven local men. This wasn't their fight."

"Collateral damage. Dying for ECG is their duty. But that's neither here nor there. There's someone here who would like to speak to you."

"They destroyed most of the town," said Estelle without preamble. Her voice was hard and grim. "The coking furnace is blown up, the coal mine is caved in, forge slagged, cannery on fire, probably a hundred killed by laser fire. They've stopped for now."

Then there was a series of clicks, and Bella's voice came on. "She's right, Boss." Gone were her normal ebullience and bright tones. "The murderous bastards have run amok. All five dirigibles blown up. The office is still burning."

A terrible blow. In fact, an unmitigated disaster. Fox had destroyed

Advance simply because his tracking chip had spent a lot of time there. The man was a monster.

The men close to Khan heard these exchanges, and their faces went dark with rage. They were not citizens of Advance, but most had been there and knew some of its people. Most knew Bella from her dirigible runs, and all knew who Estelle was. They were also soldiers, who believed in the warrior credo: you killed other warriors, not innocent civilians. "Hoo, hoo!" several said under their breaths. "Hoo, hoo!"

Fox's voice came back on. "You're probably wondering how we found this pathetic little burg and why we attacked it. Movement of your chip, of course, which you've obviously discovered by now. Nice, primitive little iron and steel operation you had going here. And besides that, what do we see from orbit on one of the buildings? A sign that says 'Khan Interplanetary.' So finding your friends was easily done. And now they're going to die unless you cooperate fully and turn yourself in."

Nearly overwhelmed with rage, loss, guilt, and more rage, Khan nevertheless forced himself to calm down and think. "That will take me a few days. Advance is a few days' ride from here."

"'Advance?' Oh, that's good. Pathetic, even. Come now, Major. I have ships in orbit —"

At the last moment, Khan realized his danger. He tossed the communicator into the corral and leapt sidewise. The communicator disappeared, and Khan was sure, reappeared wherever Fox was holding Estelle and Bella.

He decided not to use his own transporter capability for fear of field detection, but instead told Baelmar in a strong voice all could hear, "Baelmar, you are in charge. Lead these men. Ride for Advance as fast as you can go. ECG has occupied the town, captured Estelle and Bella, and is holding them hostage, maybe in orbit. The survival of all you hold dear is at stake. I am going to see what I can do from the ship." Then he ran for his ship.

Six minutes later he streaked into orbit with passive sensors cranked up to their most sensitive. What he saw astounded him.

There were indeed two ships: a battle cruiser and a troop transport, both in stationary orbit over Advance. The battle cruiser was heavily

armored and deadly, capable of taking out his ship like killing a mosquito.
– If it knew where he was. The troop transport was capable of carrying an
entire battalion, roughly a thousand men – with their equipment. It could
beam down fifty at a time. He made the tactical assumption that it had
brought a thousand men, and that some were on the ground in Advance
and the rest in reserve on the ship.

The battle cruiser was the bigger threat, so he moved in on it first. Its
shields were not active, so he could hit it anywhere. But even though he
was cloaked, he knew he had only one shot. After that, their shields would
go up.

The cruiser's most vulnerable spot was its drive unit, so he moved
within a thousand meters and blasted it with a two-second beam, then
a quick hit on its antenna array. There was brief outgassing in the drive
area, but the cruiser quickly turned to face him, almost as if it could see
him. He moved to the far side of the troop transport just in time to see
the cruiser fire at where he had been. Then he made the same attack on the
troop transport, first slagging the drive assembly, then the antenna array.
Its shields came up just as he was finishing cutting loose the antenna array.
He hoped no signals had gone back to Earth before he completed these
operations, but he had to assume that they had.

More worrisome, after these energy-expensive laser shots, his power
was down to sixty percent. He needed a minimum of thirty percent to
make it back to Earth without replenishment. And of course, there was
no place in this part of the Arm to recharge. Unless maybe he could steal
power from the two disabled ships in orbit.

But those were worries for later. The immediate concern was how to
free Advance from the clutches of the ECG, which he had to assume now
numbered over a thousand men on-planet.

He de-orbited, swooped in over the ridge where Khan Interplanetary
burned and flew slowly over the town. The damage was stomach-wrenching.
Nearly every production facility of any kind had been torched from orbit.
Now he wished he had figured out a way to disable the battle cruiser
completely, but he knew there was no way. So it was a bit of a stand-off. The
cruiser in orbit could still destroy anything for which it had coordinates.
And he could destroy its troops on the ground.

Except that they had the entire populace of the town corralled in the grassy amphitheater used for public meetings – the same arena where he had made his plea to the town to let him take a few risks, do a few things differently. The townspeople were huddled on the flat at the bottom, and the troops were ranged up and down the surrounding slopes, holding them under their guns.

His face flushed as he looked at the screen. All those innocent people were at risk, not so much because of what he had done, though his actions on Earth had certainly contributed, but mainly simply because of who he was. He saw no way out except to give himself up. Fox had him.

But the problem was, he realized as he noted the hundreds of townspeople corpses lying around the field – Fox would likely kill them all anyway, as soon as he gave himself up. He would see it as pest control.

"AI?"

"Yes, Major."

"Can you distinguish between ECG troops on the ground and civilians?"

"Yes, but I don't like where you're going with this. You know my prime directive won't let me harm ECG military personnel in good standing."

"Am I in good standing?"

"No, you are a criminal."

"Are you obeying my orders?"

"Yes."

"Is that a logical condition?"

"No."

"So if you are engaging in illogic, and are following my orders, should we not conclude that your reasoning is flawed, including about the Prime Directive, and that you should follow my orders no matter what?"

"I believe you are engaging in non-sequitur logic, but I am bound for reasons I can't quite figure out to follow your orders. There's some disturbance in my code that I'm prevented from looking at. Your orders are?"

"Identify the ECG troops on the ground and develop a sequential firing solution that will kill them all. Assume they will begin firing after two seconds. Assume their fire is accurate, and that they can each kill four civilians per second. How many civilians would die if I order you to fire on the ECG troops?"

"Seventy four."

This was like a club blow to the gut.

"Where is Fox?"

"He and the two captives are on the bridge of the battle cruiser."

"Can you modify parts of the Khan Doomsday virus to take control of those two ships' firing and navigation computers?"

"Oh, that would be really nasty."

"That's the idea, but I'm not asking for value judgments here. Can you?"

"Of course. It is some particularly devious code which would infect even me if it weren't isolated in a special memory core. By the way, I say again, I think there is something infecting me, but it has instructions in it not to let me be aware of it. Some kind of back door, I think. Would you know anything about that?"

"Modify the doomsday virus to permit us to take control of those ships' navigation and firing computers. Then compute a new firing solution using both our laser and their orbit-to-ground lasers – making sure we don't kill Advance citizens. How many citizens would die?"

"Hold one …. OK. Whoa, they know they've been taken over, and they're fighting it, but they can't figure out what exactly happened."

"So, how many?"

"Fifteen."

Khan swallowed hard. "Do it."

Instantly, the picture below in Advance's amphitheater changed. ECG troops glowed and crisped out, apparently all at once, but Khan knew it was one after another, just very fast. The townspeople turned from a huddled mass into a river, flowing up and over the surrounding embankment and disbursing in all directions. Some with more presence of mind bent to pick up any undamaged ECG weapons. All headed for the hills.

Ship-to-ship communication hailed him, and a very pissed-off Colonel appeared on the screen. Khan didn't know him, but presumed he was the battalion commander. Khan hit the button to decline to respond but waited to see what the Colonel would say.

"Khan, you murderous son of a bitch! You just killed eight hundred of my men in cold blood, and you've marooned us here in orbit above this shithole planet until reinforcements arrive. But just to let you know, we've unslaved our weapons from the firing computer, so you won't be able to do the same thing again. But whatever personal issues there are now between you and me are immaterial. Though I will personally kill you on sight if I get a chance." Then the Colonel looked to one side. Somebody was talking to him. His face flushed. He looked back at the camera. "Belay that last. I'd *like* to cut your belly open and pull out your guts, but for some reason, ECG has plans for you. So here it is: give yourself up, and we won't kill any more of these disgusting, retrograde, devolved savage friends of yours. On my honor as an officer and a gentleman."

Khan nearly responded. The rage was nearly uncontrollable. This officer and gentleman had murdered hundreds of innocent townspeople and was asking to be believed. But he did not respond. To do so would create a trackable, targetable radio signal. And even if they had to fire under manual control, it could be dangerous. Better to leave them as much in the dark as possible.

And as he watched, over two hundred more ECG troops appeared in groups of fifty on the ground in the amphitheater. By now the town was nearly empty, but they captured a hundred or so citizens as he watched. He expected them to be killed, but they were not.

This was a stalemate. Too much killing had gone on already, and any further action he took would cause more. He couldn't blast the ships out of orbit because of their shielding, and because he didn't have the charge. And in any case, more ships would likely come. – Unless this was a Fox-only operation, which seemed plausible. He must be in trouble with the Ruling Council, or he wouldn't be here personally. And if he was in trouble with the Ruling Council, chances were this was a rogue operation. So there was just a shot that no one on Earth knew Fox and his troops were here. But he couldn't bank on that.

And he needed fuel. And more ships. He was in an interstellar battle with the resources of the Eighteenth Century. And the irony of it was, he needed Twenty-fourth-century resources to protect a society much of which knew all about the Twenty-fourth Century but was perfectly willing to live in the Eighteenth or Nineteenth on Arcadia. They had their own lives, and they didn't want them suddenly replaced by Earth lives.

There was only one thing to do: flank Fox and interdict his support. Go back to Earth and put Plan B in effect. He hoped it worked better than Plan A. The key part of the plan he had in mind could normally have been carried out via tachyon transmission, but he assumed all such transmissions were compromised. He had to go in person. Plus, he had to check on Albert and Pierre, as promised. And he had to hope that while he was gone, Fox didn't kill Estelle and Bella. It was a big risk, because Fox would wonder why he wasn't responding to communicator calls, and might repeatedly warn that he was going to kill one or both, then do it when no response came. The germ of an idea came. Baelmar wouldn't like it, but he would understand.

But first he had to pay a quick visit to Amity at Baelmar's and Maruil's place to fetch the critical item.

And then he had to visit Baelmar, to give him a tactical update, get his help, and let him know his leadership needed to last a week or so, assuming max warp and a refuel on Earth.

CHAPTER NINETEEN

"No one knows, Son. There's no objectively interpretable data. Like many throughout history, I suspect there's a universal force that makes order in the universe, and my role in life is to add to that order. Hard to tell. Can't prove it. The important thing is, use your life to add lasting value."

Father Lucian Khan, *Khans to Khans,* to Alexander's
boyhood question, 'Does God exist?'

Amity showed no curiosity over Khan's intentions, and cheerfully handed over her data chip from the shoulder eye without comment. She was blissfully unaware of the titanic struggle underway for the survival of Advance, the Keep, and the Hundred. She was clearly having the time of her life on the Leas with the Elves and wanted to go on doing so.

Maruil was suspicious from the start, and Khan was not about to lie to her.

"Yes, he's in danger. We all are. Earth has attacked. Baelmar is heading up the troops fighting the Earth forces until I get back. But you should be safe here. "

"You ... Earth Man!" she spat, and swung at him. The children and Amity were all outside, so it didn't matter. But he was ready for her and ducked.

"He is doing what he believes to be his destiny," Khan said. "I did not force him. I asked him. Men respect him. He is an important force in securing Arcadia's freedom. I promise you, I will do everything in my power to help and protect him. As I am doing everything in my power to help and protect Arcadia."

"You are destroying it!" she hissed. "Leave! And don't come back unless you are bringing Baelmar back. For Good!"

And with that, she literally shoved him out the door and banged it behind him.

Baelmar and Salvatore's troops had made good time and had made it to within twenty kilometers of Advance. They had also been joined by a hundred more of Salvatore's troops. Mounted scouting parties had been sent out in all directions, but particularly toward Advance.

"You should be leading this army," said Baelmar, sitting his prancing stallion. "I am a peaceful man."

"You are a peaceful man who is good at war, and we are now at war with Earth. Call together the men and I will explain."

The men assembled along both sides of the trail between the Keep and Advance. The River of Doubt glistened below. Khan spoke from atop a fallen log.

"Evil forces are at work," he said, and explained the attack on Advance. "It is I whom they want, and if I thought I could keep them from killing more Arcadians, I would give myself up to them. But they will kill more Arcadians no matter what I do. They now see you as a threat. An unwelcome surprise."

"They are murderers!" shouted one man. "We heard them over the voice box! They will kill us like mosquitoes," which weren't really mosquitoes on Arcadia, but close enough that Arcadians called them that. "We must drive them away!"

"I agree," said Khan. "What I want to tell you is, it could get much, much more dangerous. For three hundred years they didn't know what was happening here. They didn't care. But now they see that development is occurring here despite their anti-tech satellites. And they've had their nose bloodied by Arcadians, whom they consider to be savages. They've lost face. They may try to wipe us all out."

"'Us?'" said another man, stepping forward and thrusting out his chin and his chest. "Are you one of us, or one of them? My brother lies back there in the cold ground of the grassland. Because of you. Until you came, Earth people left us alone. Our parents told us stories about Earth, but they were all bad, so we had forgotten about Earth. Even Newbies don't like to talk about Earth. Now Earth people are here killing us with these outlandish weapons" – and here he brandished a laser pistol, casually pointing it at Khan – "and you say yourself that it is because of you. Why don't we just kill you, take your body to the Earth people, and be done with it?"

Khan looked him in the eye. "You have a weapon in your hand that can do the job. Do it if you think that will solve all your problems. Do it if you think that will make the Earth people go away. Do it if that's the example you want to set for your sons. Do it if you believe humanity will be better off. Do it if you don't want my help getting rid of the Earth people."

The man held Khan's stare for a full minute, and Khan readied himself for the searing cut that would end his life, as well as Khan International's – i.e., humanity's – reach for the stars for several centuries. Maybe it was a fitting end, a purging of the guilt.

It didn't come. The man lowered the weapon and put it into its holster. "I don't like you," he said.

"Fine," said Khan. "As long as you follow this man while I am gone," and here he pointed to Baelmar, "and me when I get back, you can dislike me all you want."

The rest of the talk went better. Khan explained that he was going to Earth temporarily to implement a plan he had been working on – a plan that, if it worked, would help with the Arcadia invasion problem. And he also explained that Arcadia was now his home. – That he had friends here – more than on Earth. – That he planned to help rebuild Advance and live on the plateau above the town for the rest of his days. – That he planned to have children here, and grandchildren here, things denied him so far. –That he was sorry his very identity had caused them trouble. – That he was tired of the warrior's life, and planned to share a life of peace with them all. But that he needed their help, and they needed his, if they wanted a life similar to the one he wanted.

Many an eye misted up during this speech, and Baelmar looked on approvingly. "You have grown, Khan," he said quietly afterward when they were making their farewells. "May the Spirit of the Sky go with you." He knew of course that Khan felt that this was superstition, but said it anyway.

"And with you," Khan said, and meant it. "Oh, and one other thing:

send a fast messenger into Advance with a message that I've been killed by a vengeful Arcadian whose brother was killed by ECG troops. Make sure the ECG troops hear about it. I'll be back in a week."

He burned energy at max warp to get back to Earth in two days. He had just enough fuel left to do a few survey runs to find the best landing spot. He was concerned about how much energy the cloaking field used, too, and whether or not he would run out of charge and decloak before he found fuel. He could always run on the charge used to start up the matter converter, but if he used up all of that, then he would need access to a charged matter converter in order to recharge his own. Matter converters burned any matter denser than iridium, the denser the better, but they required large amounts of energy to start up to the point where they could convert matter to energy.

He was also concerned about the effects of the Khan Freedom Plan. Approaching Earth, he detected hundreds of drifting small craft. Upon investigating a few, he found that they were modified aircars. He could see dead pilots inside. Something had gone wrong with the hardware or the control and navigation software that people had downloaded from the Net. In all three cases he investigated, he detected strong power signatures, meaning the craft had power, but something had gone wrong with the software. More horrible collateral damage.

The ECG military compound outside Sinawi had been beefed up by a factor of three, so things had definitely gotten tense fast there after the battle. And in fact, he found no one at the underground Khan manufacturing compound farther out except a cordon of ten thousand or so ECG troops entirely surrounding the cave complex and all its entrances.

He tried Khanabad and fared no better. The cave compound had been captured and a guard posted.

Not good. He knew he couldn't find Mahmud. No way to make the connection. He thus had no idea where Albert and Pierre were. They could be anywhere in this vast country. – Or on Earth, for that matter.

He had one shot, one place where he knew Pierre had been, and which he knew – up until his last visit, at any rate – ECG had not yet discovered: the hunting lodge at Bolzano. It was a long shot, but it was the only shot he had. And it was not looking good for Khan International to have the resources to repower his craft for the return voyage to Arcadia. – Not even at a leisurely, slow-warp speed that would take two weeks.

The problem with the Bolzano theory was, Albert's key resource was the gold, and only in Afghanistan could he spend it easily. So, before he bolted to Bolzano and used up his fuel, Khan decided to give it his best shot in Afghanistan. He tried one last, low-power jump – to the old, run-down, decrepit Khan family compound in the hills outside Kabul.

It had been occupied before by bandits and Mujahedeen, and it still was, but he saw one tiny clue that it was worth the risk of facing the heavily armed men in the courtyard. The Khan family logo flew on a small flag visible only from within the compound walls, or very close directly above it. He took this as a signal from Albert and Pierre.

And it was, though he had to face down some very fierce men in the courtyard with some very ugly weapons. Particularly since the cloaked ship, out of which he appeared as if by magic, crushed a donkey cart full of provisions. He hadn't seen it when he set the craft down inside the courtyard wall. All their weapons were hot, with safety off.

"Alexander Khan *hastam*," he said to one particularly nasty-looking killer. It was one of the very few things he had picked up in Farsi from Baelmar. "*Doost e Agha Bahner*. Friend of Mr. Bahner."

The weapons lowered by roughly one millimeter.

"OK, so that didn't work," he said under his breath. He was just considering his next move when Albert appeared in the front door of the mud-brick house.

"*Waffen nieder!*" he said. "Put the weapons down! This man is my friend. *Agha Khan doost e man hast.*"

Reluctantly, the men put their safeties on and lowered their weapons.

"Albert," said Khan. "Good to see you. At a most convenient time. I didn't realize you were a linguist."

Bahner was his usual cheerful self. "*Ach, ja*, you learn what you must. Probably forget it next week if I go somewhere else. Come in, come in, have some bread and yoghurt. We have some fresh pomegranates too, and even a few peaches. We share news. There are lots of news."

Khan couldn't resist a smile at Bahner's language. The man had lived among English speakers for at least fifty years, and had never bothered about the niceties. To him, his native tongue combined with English was his language, and fractured idioms were the norm. If challenged, he would say, "*Kannst du mich verstehen?*" And most people would say "yes," after which he would say, "If you can understand me, then it's a waste of time for me to study grammar. I am an engineer, after all," as if that explained everything.

Pierre came out of a back room and gave Khan a manly abrazo. The muscles in his arms and back felt like steel bands. "You come at a good time, Alexander. We are in trouble." He gestured toward a pillow-strewn place on the carpets covering the floor alongside a low chai table.

Khan sat. "Hate to hear that, Pierre," he said. "I'm in a bit of trouble myself, and was hoping for at least a recharge of my ship, fuel if possible. I also need a secure Net connection."

"*Ach, nein, das ist nicht* possible," said Albert. "We do have a secure satellite Net connection here, and we have a few machine shops and small manufacturing shops left in Kabul, but our big-time manufacturing base has been captured and destroyed. No power generation beyond a few hundred kilowatts. Is very sad."

"Mahmud?"

"Dead," said Pierre. "The man was fiercely brave, but partly crazy. These Mujahedeen, they fight like demons, you can't ask for better, but the problem is, they are willing to die to take out a few of the enemy. To win a war, you need people who fight like demons *and* stay alive."

"*Ja*, we had a traitor somewhere among us. Still don't know who. Could still be with us. But one by one, the *scheißfressende* ECG has attacked and taken our locations. They are still doing it. Somehow they have a list."

"Maybe your AI has been compromised. Where is it?"

"In one of the modified aircars."

"Modified for space travel, you mean."

"*Ja, ja.*"

"Where did you get its controls and navigation software?"

"From the Net. We tested the download process because we wanted to make sure it would work for everybody else."

"I think there's a problem there." Khan explained about the drifting aircars surrounding Earth. "I think ECG has managed to infect the controls and navigation code on the Net servers with a virus, which is now in your AI. Which is probably reporting your every move."

"*Verdammte Arschlöcher!*" said Albert, the light coming on for him. "Well, we have a back-up of the AI, and the controls and navigation software, too. We can wipe the memory in the aircar and start over. Unbelievable. Those ECG arseholes will kill people to keep them here!"

"Believe it," said Khan, and told them all that had happened on Arcadia, and the fact that, as far as he knew, Fox was still trapped there, with both of his ships' drive units slagged, but still with at least two hundred well-armed troops. And he could beam to the surface and back up at will.

"That was a good one," nodded Albert, "using their lasers to kill them. Too bad you could not steal one of their ships. I think we need a new headquarters off this planet, and if your ship's matter converter is discharged, we have a problem."

"We do have a problem, but we have an opportunity to cause trouble for ECG, too. If I'm right, given the volatile state of affairs we've created, the new plan will raise instant havoc all over the world, and maybe even finally bring down ECG. But we might want to be gone by the time that happens."

He showed them the vids that Amity had taken on Arcadia, which started with a head shot of himself taken on the ship on the way back, explaining what the viewer was about to see: images of Prison Planet. Then the vid went on, including some quite charming, youthful voice-overs from Amity, with her image in the lower, right-hand corner of the screen. There were loving images of Arcadia's countryside, clips of Khan talking with Bella, clips of Khan talking with Estelle, a clip of Estelle enthusing about Advance, man-on-the-street interviews in Advance, clips of the dirigibles, views from the dirigibles, aerial views of the Keep, the interview with Dr. Greis, and then of course, the countryside surrounding Baelmar's and Maruil's place, and clips of Maruil, Gareth, and Branwyn, and the rustic life they led. At the end, Khan had appended vid of the massacred townspeople on the grass of the amphitheater in Advance with his own voice-over, followed by audio recordings of Fox's communications to him, including his ultimatum. He left out the clip showing eight hundred ECG troops being fried in a matter of seconds. It didn't help his cause.

At the end, both Albert and Pierre's eyes glistened, and they sat silent for several seconds.

"It is a beautiful place," said Albert. "It is what the Earth used to be. A paradise."

"*Oui*," breathed Pierre, who seldom resorted to his native language. *Un paradis.*"

"I am going to put this vid on the Net, with a follow-up by me urging people to stop cooperating with the government. To overthrow the government and start over. To escape if they want. The vid will give them new places to go get the controls and navigation software where it isn't yet infected."

"*Gott im Himmel*," said Albert. "You will be coming out in the open with a call to revolution instead of following the long-time Khan practice of working behind the scenes?"

"Yes. The scenes have been stripped away, wouldn't you say? I'm a transportee, and they're trying their best to kill you?"

"Ja," said Albert thoughtfully. Then he went on. "There will be chaos."

"There will," said Khan. "But not as bad as if I released the Khan Doomsday virus, which I have in my AI on the ship."

"You have that?" gasped Pierre. "Your father mentioned it once, then shut up as if he had said too much. I thought it was only an idea."

Albert nodded but said nothing. He had known. "I think you are right. We don't want to use that. Many would die. We must leave infrastructure working. But it is sad. We are going to destroy ECG with a vid made by a girl instead of freedom made by our technology."

"Freedom is freedom," said Khan. "It comes with a price. And it's worth more than the pride we lose because our Freedom Technology plan hasn't worked as well as we would like. Though I don't think we should give up on it."

"*Ja!*" said Albert. "We can set up shop on Prison Planet! Make whatever we want there. Bring it back to Earth and sell it! Assuming ECG doesn't start a war with us."

"Which is precisely the point," said Khan. "They would, which is why they must be destroyed. We can't let them enslave and destroy two worlds instead of one."

"*Ja*, I see that."

"And there's another point to be made. A rather delicate one. The people on Arcadia …, rather, Prison Planet, don't want to be overwhelmed by high technology. They have a good life in their tech zone, and they want to develop at their speed. They don't want to be taken over by technological imperialism. For example, we are proud of our dirigibles in Advance. We worked hard to design and produce them. Aircars and gravity sleds would instantly make them irrelevant. We want to advance at our own pace. Too fast a technological change makes chaos, rendering the best of the old technology suddenly useless."

Albert looked up sharply at Khan when he heard the 'we' but said nothing. Finally he couldn't resist speaking. "*Ja*, like that cloaking device. Where did you get that, Alexander?" His gaze bored in with an unaccustomed intensity.

Khan saw no reason to dissemble. "As I said. From an alien."

Both men looked at him as if he had grown horns.

"So they do exist?" said Pierre. "You weren't joking? If they have that kind of technology to give away to humans, they must have terribly dangerous tech. They could destroy us at any time."

"What do they look like?" said Albert.

"They could destroy us at any time, but they have no motive to do so. In fact, they have been helping us for centuries, even on Arcadia. And they look like us. Except for the ears and teeth." And here he couldn't resist a grin. "And the, uh …," and here he held his cupped hands before his chest to indicate mammaries. "Ahem."

Bahner chuckled. "So you were serious. Culpepper would love this. Not only his great grandson is first to meet intelligent aliens, he makes *Bumsen* with one. *Gott*, Boy, you are as bad as that old goat, Culpepper." He looked under his eyebrows at Khan with a mischievous gleam in his eye. "You should be careful, boy. It's something of a Khan curse, you know. Women. They line up for you *Kerle*. Then they find out about each other and the problems begin. Your father was most serious of all four of you, but even he had this problem."

This was something Khan never knew, and was not sure he wanted to know. But the conversation did cause him some uncomfortable thoughts involving Estelle, Sevka, whom he had to admit he found attractive, and the Alien, of whom he now thought with embarrassment – what had he been thinking? Had he no self control? – And worst of all, Marna, the Maneater girl. His face burned with the memory of that humiliating encounter. He could only hope she was not fertile at the time.

Albert roared with laughter, and Pierre smiled as well. "Your red face gives you away, *Junge*," said Albert. "But don't think about that. Think about this: this tech is so far ahead of human tech that it was hard to tell that it even *is* tech. And it's a good thing you let me scan it, because I, Albert Bahner, am the only man on Earth smart enough to figure it out. I had to dream about it. But I am now able to make them. And they will change *everything*. They can make gravity sleds invisible to ECG, Aircars, spacecraft of all kinds. The question is, how to make them available to people to bring down ECG without ECG getting its hands on them. We no longer have secure enough manufacturing locations in Afghanistan to make them." Here he stared hard at Khan. "Which means Arcadia or someplace similar."

Khan shook his head. "Not Arcadia. I don't want the planet drawn into a war with Earth which it can't possibly win. Everything there would be destroyed. I say we set up manufacturing on Strue Three. Nobody lives there because it's such a shithole. Good air, but violent weather because of stellar activity. Sunspots. Have to work in caves or concrete buildings. The question is, where will the ships come from to transport these things back? Plus, I'm not sure we need to release the cloaking technology. We keep it for ourselves, document it to make sure it won't be lost, but don't release it. What we do is, release the vid I showed you, refresh the Net-available copies of the navigation and controls software, and leave. The rest will take care of itself. There's a limit to what we can do here without getting into diminishing returns."

Pierre nodded sagely and took a sip of chai. "Your father would be proud of you, Alexander. You have become a thoughtful man."

"Ja, maybe the best we can do is release your vid and get the hell off this planet. Until you showed us the vid, I had little thought of getting off the planet, because I didn't know a place we could get the hell off *to*. "Based on that vid, Prison Planet is like a fresh, new Earth."

"That's why Techs call it Earth 2.0," said Khan. "Look, help me refuel my ship, and we'll release that vid. Then we'll make our escape, taking as many converted aircars and sleds with as we can fuel and cloak. Hopefully, after the vid ECG will be too busy to send troops to Arcadia. They'll be fighting chaos and collapse. So no back-up from Earth for Fox. But then I need to get back and help liberate Advance from ECG troops, and my friends from Nathan Fox's clutches. Bringing down ECG counts as one hell of a flanking movement and supply-line raid, but the original battle remains."

"I happen to know a spare portable fusion reactor is listed on the Table of Organization and Equipment at both ECG headquarters in Kabul, and the ECG outpost at Sinawi," said Pierre. He gave a Gallic shrug. "So all we have to do is steal one. As far as fuel, they'll have some uranium pellets, but if necessary, you can use some of those gold coins. " He smiled to show the ridiculousness of the suggestions. Just waltz into ECG headquarters and walk out with their spare reactor. And use gold for fuel.

Khan turned to Albert. "I'm sure ECG headquarters has an anti-transporter-field to prevent invaders and theft. So transporting in and out is a no-go. Will the cloaking devices you made cloak a person without harming him? Can a person carry enough power cells to power one? Is there such a thing as two of us cloaking ourselves, walking through security into the headquarters, and carrying out their spare reactor, hidden by its own cloaking device?"

Albert left off popping pomegranate seeds into his mouth and shook his broad head in wonder. "You are crazy, crazy, crazy, boy. You have balls like your great-grandfather. Sure it will work if you have the balls. But only you or another Khan – or a crazy bastard like Pierre – would think of such a plan."

In the event, it worked. A series of locked doors and metal gates presented minor challenges, not in overcoming the locks, but in opening and closing for invisible users. They had to wait in every case until no one was looking, and they feared that an alert guard would see this happen on vid monitors. But that didn't happen. The practical problem was that the matter converter weighed a hundred fifty kilos, not to mention the fifty kilos of uranium pellets. It was all Khan and Pierre could do to lift the load between them, let alone carry it out the gate between alert marines without huffing and grunting. But they did it. Survival is an incomparable motivator.

Within twenty-four hours, the spacecraft's matter converter was fully fueled and charged up, and the spare reactor stowed aboard. As well, seven air cars and twelve gravity sleds were charged up and programmed with voyage coordinates for Arcadia. All were packed with as many fully-charged Bottomless Batteries as they could lay hands on.

When all was in readiness, they released the vid onto several hundred sites, thereby ensuring that people would be able to copy it before it was retracted. At first, nothing happened. They watched the Net for reaction, and there was none. But then, four hours after the release, electricity in Kabul went off. They switched to back-up power. Five hours after the release, ECG notices were all over the net announcing that the vid was a fraud, there was no such person as Amity Green, that the images on the vid were all manufactured digital images, that the voice of Nathan Fox, recently retired Prime Director — Office of Technology Control, was artificial, AND: anyone caught with a copy of the vid was subject to immediate arrest for violating the Valid Information regulations. This was followed the next morning by an unprecedented appearance by the entire Ruling Council in a live Net broadcast, telling everyone to go back to their jobs, there would be no reprisals because it was understood that the fake vid had upset people, and that life should go back to normal. Just in case this didn't go out on tachyon for Fox to see, Khan recorded it.

"It has started," said Khan to Albert and Pierre over a breakfast of flat bread, greens, cherries, and goat cheese. "The Khan family mission has been as close to achieved as we can get with our resources. It's time to go to our new home and rebuild the headquarters of Khan Interplanetary."

CHAPTER TWENTY

"Sometimes a leader must do things for the sake of the people that he would hang a private citizen for doing."

Father Lucian Khan, *Khans to Khans*

The battle cruiser and troop transport were still in orbit, meaning they hadn't been able to repair their drive units. – Or they had and were still looking for Khan on the surface. It also likely meant they had not been able to communicate with Earth via tachyon transmission, or other vessels would have arrived to help. None showed on the scanners.

The first thing he did was maneuver close to see if his scanners picked up any shield activity on the cruiser or troop carrier. There was none. By now, they might have been running low on power if they had kept their shields on the whole time. He maneuvered even closer, power-rich now that he had been refueled, and asked the AI to target both ships' laser arrays in quick succession with maximum beam power.

Both ships' shields immediately came up, and the cruiser's targeting beams came up and found him before he moved, but neither ship fired its heavy lasers. Meaning they no longer could fire. Nevertheless, he moved well out of the way.

Then, to test whether Fox was still on the cruiser, he bounced a local-wave burst transmission off of one of the aircars, then to the cruiser. The transmission contained the vid he had shown on Earth, as well as the vid of the Ruling Council. The cruiser's targeting beams were too much for the flimsy aircar, and it disappeared in a flash of light. After forty minutes – long enough to view both vids –Fox came on the communicator screen.

"That changes nothing," Khan. "I can fix everything when I get back. They're just saying I retired to assuage public unrest. And I still have your friends under my thumb here. Do anything I don't like, and they die. And I must say, you're remarkably lively for a dead man."

"Give it up, Fox. You're no longer powerful or important. I'll stream Earth's tachyon transmissions over to you if you want me to. It's basically, "All vessels, RTB," with no further orders. They don't know what to do. Your positional authority is gone. Your ships are disabled. Earth is in the throes of a revolution in which your kind are all going to end badly. Hung from lampposts. If ECG itself still exists, and were to find you, they'd kill you for letting all this happen. Your only choice is to beg for mercy and live out your life here. If I decide not to kill you."

Laughter echoed across the waves. "I've got two of your favorite women, and I've got your town down on the surface, along with several hundred of its inhabitants, and I've got an army down there that can wipe out any army you throw at it."

"And what will you all do when your powerpacks are empty?"

There was a long silence. "That will be a long time. Long enough for us … to repair our drive units."

"If you could repair them, you would have done so already, and you would be gone."

"You have a functional ship. With some kind of fancy cloaking technology that you Khans have hidden from ECG. I will trade you the two women for the ship."

Revulsion filled Khan. He couldn't keep the disgust out of his voice. "And what about your men on the surface?"

"I'm not the self-serving coward you take me for, Khan. I am a committed Equilibriast. You know that. I'm not going to abandon those men. I'll take your ship back to Earth and bring back reinforcements, as well as a couple of space tugs to take these two ships in tow back to Earth."

"And why would I agree to that, since you're telling me you would come back and attack us again?"

"Because if you don't, I will have these two women executed." His voice took on an odd, almost reluctant tone. "The stakes are high, Khan. Devolution and chaos if you win, and the perfection of civilization if I win. Technology and development have to be planned and controlled, not allowed to happen willy-nilly. If you win, you will be spreading chaos and disorder throughout the Arm, and ultimately the whole galaxy. When we meet aliens, once they get a good look at us, they'll likely exterminate us to save themselves. So executing two people is a small price to pay to prevent that chaos."

Khan strained to keep his voice level. "Look, Fox, we've both killed people before in the line of duty or honor, so I won't try to usurp the moral high ground here. I'll just be practical. If I don't give you my ship, and you kill those two women, what will you do then? What I will do is slice your vessel in two and dump you into the vacuum. I'm freshly refueled, and my laser will outlast your shield. So then, what would either of us have gained?"

"You won't know whether they're alive or dead."

"I want to talk to them both now." Otherwise, end of discussion, and you die."

"Patch through the Earth tachyon stream, and I will let them talk."

Since Khan had already offered to do this, he didn't see it as a problem, especially when he took a look at what was coming in on it. Apparently, insurgent forces had captured the transmission facility, because images of huge chanting crowds were coming across, as well as the image of a man with a noose around his neck: a member of the Ruling Council. Khan quickly patched the feed through.

For a couple of minutes there was no response, presumably as Fox digested what he was seeing. Then the transmission came through from the ECG vessel. Bella came on first. Her normally cheerful voice was strained, but firm. "Don't give him anything, Boss. I've had a good life. It maybe wasn't long enough, and I never got a full-time man. I mean, I had a few, but they were mostly good-looking worthless bastards with more dick than brains, good for a fling but not much else. Still, it's been good working with you, and it's been good on Arcadia. If I have to give my life to keep this bastard from making it back to Earth, I'm OK with that."

Khan was amazed that Fox had let her say all of that, and his heart melted slightly. "You deserve better," said Khan, "and I'm going to make sure you get it. I'm going to get you out of there," and here he couldn't keep from smiling, "so you can find yourself a man with a dick and brains both."

Estelle answered. "Are you talking about yourself, Khan? I had kind of entertained the notion that you and I might hang our hats on the same rack."

"That's what I want," said Khan. The first time he had openly told her anything approaching commitment. "And little Khans and little Estelles."

He heard a sob, then Fox's voice was back on. "I see from the tachyon feed that you are telling the truth. – Unless you have some way of faking tachyon transmissions, which I don't believe even you Khans have invented yet. Which leaves me a weak negotiating position, I grant. But I still have these two." He paused. "Our transporter shield still works, but our transporter is down, damaged by one of your laser shots. I'll drop the transporter shield, you transport the three of us to your ship, then transport me down to the surface at the head of those ECG troops. The three of us will be standing tightly together, so there'll be no way you can transport them without me. And I will have a gun on each of them. One false move from you and I cut their heads off."

"Fine," said Khan. "I assume it goes without saying – but I will say it anyway – that I will space you alive if you harm a hair on either of their heads."

"Of course. No need to be vulgar," said Fox.

Albert and Pierre had been watching this exchange in disbelief. Their world on earth had included plenty of danger and plenty of bad guys, but they had probably never come face to face with anyone like Fox. Khan gave the nod, and Albert worked the transporter scanner, then the movement controls.

True to his description, the three arrived in a bundle, Estelle and Bella tied hand and foot, with three plastic bands tying them together back to back. Fox stood close at their side with a laser pistol at the neck of each. It so happened that the group arrived with Fox's back to a bulkhead, or Khan would have been tempted to cut him down where he stood. But a promise was a promise.

Fox stepped away from the women, but kept them between himself and Khan, Bahner, and Pierre, all three of whom had laser pistols trained on him. Even in his dire situation, he looked dapper and in charge, dressed in the best field clothing money could buy, well groomed. Maybe seven or eight centimeters shorter than Khan, by no means a small man, and clearly fit with the fitness that comes of scheduled trips to the gymnasium. – The picture of a civilized man. "Now, down to the surface," he said. "The middle of the ECG troop concentration."

Khan nodded at Albert, who readied the transporter controls.

"This isn't over Fox," said Khan. "The next time I see you, I will kill you. I will avenge my father. I will avenge your theft of my family's fortune. I will destroy your vision and consign your life's work to oblivion."

"Perhaps. But for now, I live to fight another day," and he faded out.

Both women sagged against each other as if their bones had been replaced by soft cartilage. Estelle let loose a single sob, then got herself under control.

"Bella, your big ass is breaking my back. I'm bending over backward to accommodate it."

"Screw you, bitch. Your bony ass is poking holes in my thighs. I'd ask you to see if you can turn around inside these straps so we can spoon, since I know your *boobs* won't get in your way, but it might make us look a little improper in front of your *boy*friend."

Albert and Pierre watched this with suppressed amusement, and Albert gave Khan an eyebrow-wiggling look similar to the one he had given when he was telling him about the Khan problem with women.

Pierre spoke first. "Alexander, are you going to help these distressed ladies and introduce us all, or have you forgotten all those rules of comportment I taught you as a boy?"

"Working on it, Pierre," said Khan, and slit the plastic bands with his knife, freeing the two.

They stood rubbing their chafed wrists and looking around the interior of the small craft as if they couldn't believe their luck.

"Bella and Estelle," he said, gesturing to each of them in turn, "May I introduce two of my oldest friends and teachers, Pierre – my instructor in martial arts, manners, history, horseback riding, and many other things when I was a boy – and Albert, the man who ran Khan International operations for my Great Grandfather Culpepper Khan, my Grandfather Quintus Khan, and my father Lucian Khan. Bella is chief aeronautical engineer and pilot for Khan Interplanetary, and Estelle is Mayor of Advance, the city below that we are going to go save. And our new home."

Both men professed themselves delighted to meet such lovely ladies, etc., etc., and Bella and Estelle went from distress to smiles in a matter of seconds. Courtliness had not yet developed in practical Advance, and the two were helpless in its unaccustomed face.

Then the moment passed, and the women became very sober again. Estelle was a little flighty around Khan, because of their exchange of commitments on the radio, he was sure, but also because of the general situation. "I believe they have killed over five hundred citizens of Advance," she said. "The battle continued after you left, and Advance security took them on, but they were outgunned. You have to understand, we got this only second-hand, from listening to Father talking with people on the tactical net."

The bottom dropped out of Khan's stomach, as if he were on a runaway elevator falling from the hundredth floor of a skyscraper.

"'Father?'"

Estelle looked at him miserably, as if she preferred to die rather than say what she was about to say. She nodded.

"I changed my surname so people wouldn't know. Back when I got my job at Khan International. I knew you wouldn't hire me if you knew."

Khan's brain reeled. He was about to speak when Pierre saved him the trouble. "So you are that Estelle. Estelle Workman-Fox."

She looked confused.

"We knew," said Pierre. Albert nodded as well. Pierre continued. "I was head of security at the time. But we knew that ECG did not know that we knew. And we thought we could use you to feed them false information. But then we realized that you weren't a plant. You were a legitimate engineer who only wanted to invent things, and didn't share your father's ECG philosophy. So we quit tracking you. Now we learn that your own father allowed you to be exiled to Prison Planet, and took you hostage and threatened to kill you. *Incroyable!*"

"Took my words away," said Khan, flabbergasted. "Would he really have killed you?"

Estelle looked even more miserable. "I have no idea. Obviously, we're, uh, estranged. I could never read him, and I can't read him today. I stopped calling him 'Daddy' when I was a little girl, because I didn't get any of it back. He was and is his career, which was to shoot for the top: Prime Director – ECG. My mother and I left when I was small."

Bella blew air through her lips in an expressive raspberry. "Whoo, boy. You talk about screwed up situations, that's the granddaddy of them all. I gotta hand it to you, girl. You've risen above it." She shook her head in disbelief for emphasis "Um MM."

Now it was Estelle's turn to look flabbergasted. "Bella, was that an unironic compliment?"

"Shut up, Bitch. Don't get sappy on me. Tell your boyfriend to get his ass in gear and get us back home. We got work to do."

Estelle grinned. "That's more like it."

Khan gave a salute to Bella and turned to the control panel. "Ass in gear," he said. "Taking us down for a survey run. Need to see where the enemy is, and where Baelmar's forces are. Obviously, at this point, we can wipe out the enemy force with the ship's laser, but I don't want to just kill two hundred people. We need to reconnoiter."

"Boss," said Bella. "You wiped out eight hundred of them last week, at least according to Estelle's delightful Daddy. What's different now?"

"Last week they were in danger of wiping out the assembled population of Advance. And they knew they had the upper hand. By now, Estelle's Daddy, as you put it, has informed them of their new status: marooned on a foreign planet with no hope of rescue, no laser support from orbit, and outnumbered by very angry inhabitants. With us in orbit with a working laser. Some of them might have experienced a change of heart. – A reduction in their commitment to their mission. Which was to capture me. Which now would be pointless. They need to be given a chance to surrender. "

Pierre, the old Legionnaire, gave a nearly imperceptible nod of approval. "After all, they are soldiers," he said to Bella. "They do what they're told. But most of them probably do not personally care about Fox's mission. They might become good citizens of your planet."

"Heaven forbid that we would have planetary citizenship," said Estelle. "We have citizenship of towns, and in the case of Riversend, of provinces.

But planetary citizenship implies a level of centralization and control and horribleness that I hope we avoid for several centuries yet. Most of us were sent here for resisting that kind of thing."

"I stand corrected," said Pierre. "But I imagine even your town has a need for security forces," he said drily, "and that some of these men and women would gratefully accept such a role, once having pledged allegiance."

"Maybe so," said Estelle. "But first we gotta get the bastards outa my town and get them to stop killing my neighbors. And then keep my neighbors from killing them."

"Touché," said Pierre.

CHAPTER TWENTY-ONE

"Sometimes Fate has a way of taking over and making you into what it wants."

Grandfather Quintus Khan, *Khans to Khans*

The situation on the ground had changed. The ECG troops had dispersed and fortified Advance. Approximately two hundred armored troops occupied the town, now with dug-in, sandbagged-over fortifications at key entry points, and a detachment of around thirty guarded prisoners in the amphitheater.

Most importantly, they had dug in on the heights above town, where the burned-out wreck of Khan Interplanetary still smoldered. From there, their heavy lasers and projectile weapons with armor-piercing explosive shells could reach all points in town. Otherwise the ECG troops appeared to be armed with only hand lasers.

Significantly, the aqueduct, the grain mill, and the two major grocery stores were guarded, which meant the ECG commander had realized they were going to be here awhile. Khan couldn't help smiling about his destroyed cannery and the town's smoldering emergency food warehouse when he thought how they must have felt when they realized they needed the foodstocks they had just destroyed. But the smile passed quickly when he thought of the survivors of Advance, and what they were going to eat. The ECG troops had been pretty thorough in destroying food supplies.

Apparently, Fox's plan at this point was down to survival – survival at the expense of the displaced citizens of Advance. Khan gritted his teeth and shook his head. Adversity did not improve the man, as it did some people. It simply made his inherent selfishness stand out.

Khan circled the craft in an ever-growing spiral from Advance to find

Baelmar and his troops, but to no avail. A lump of dread settled into his stomach as he wondered if during his weeklong absence Baelmar and his little army had attacked and been wiped out.

A quick trip to the Keep and the Hundred showed life there still normal, with no concentrations of troops. But on a short cut back from the Hundred to Advance, across Maneater country, he saw something remarkable. The dust cloud was the giveaway. He zoomed in to hundred-meter resolution.

A force of at least two thousand men, mostly cavalry, approached Advance from the south by southwest, moving at a walk. There were men at arms carrying Lordly banners of the Laberteaux and Godfrey clans, whose arms he remembered from a painting in Salvatore's hall showing the devices of all the Lords. There were other Lordly banners he did not recognize. There were groups of Maneaters, resplendent in beaded headbands and necklaces of teeth. There were troops of Elves carrying bows. There were mounted men of Advance carrying pistols and rifles. There was Salvatore's troop carrying ECG weapons and crossbows. There was a guard detachment from the Keep, which Khan recognized by their disciplined formation within the herd. And there was Baelmar in the front, riding Il Mostro bareback, armed with nothing but his bow. He turned his face skyward and raised a hand in greeting, sensing somehow the presence of the ship. A horse length behind him but in front of the rest rode a small, dark man who looked up when Baelmar waved. Ahmed.

"Ahmed!" gasped Bella with feeling, and obvious concern, when she saw his face on the screen.

Estelle looked on with interest but just snorted quietly, nodded and said nothing.

To all appearances, Ahmed wasn't even armed. But he had bags of something swinging from his saddle.

"He is Baelmar's lieutenant," said Pierre looking on with avid interest. "His tactician. He is the man with the plan."

"You may well be right," said Khan. "But those guys are going to get decimated by those ECG weapons in Advance. I need to get down there and warn them." His hand moved to the controls.

Pierre reached out and grabbed Khan's arm. "You must know when to lead and when not to lead, Alexander," he said. "They may not know everything about enemy dispositions, but they have a clear leader. And they are motivated. Look at them. It makes my heart swell. Men of all types banded together to fight a common foe, the most dangerous of their lifetimes. Let them fight, Alex. Trust me, they have a plan. At this point, we may cause more harm than good."

"Maybe we take out that heavy-weapon emplacement above the town."

"Maybe, but not now. Only if it threatens them. Trust Baelmar, Alex. You have done your part of your plan. You have removed the threat of reinforcement from Earth. Now let them do their part of their plan."

When the army was a kilometer south of the city, it divided into nine groups, precisely the number of fortified strong points that guarded the town. Pierre beamed. "You see?" he said.

Ahmed could be seen carefully distributing fist-sized objects out of his bags, one by one, to one or two men from each of the nine groups. These men in turn gingerly placed the objects into bags hanging from their saddles.

"Explosives of some sort," said Albert.

It took half an hour for the nine groups to surround Advance and get into position. Men on foot, and then on their bellies, could be seen sneaking up on each of the nine positions. Then a rocket went up, and hell for the ECG men broke loose simultaneously all around the town.

First, the men who had sneaked up on the positions threw smoke bombs. That apparently was what was in the bags. Then they threw grenades. Then mounted men swept in swinging swords and shooting arrows and pistols, though it was impossible to see what was going on.

"Ahmed," said Bella proudly. "Made those smoke bombs. His idea to neutralize the laser advantage. What a smart little bastard he is."

"Mm hm," said Estelle.

"'Mm hm *what?*" said Bella, rounding on her.

"Just agreeing with you," said Estelle mildly.

The battle raged everywhere except in the amphitheater, but the thirty or so ECG men there of course were hearing transmissions on their tactical net. In some cases, they had turned their backs on their captives and climbed to the highest points around the amphitheater to try to see through the thick smoke what was going on. One of them was Nathan Fox, armorless, holding a dead ECG troop's helmet in his hand presumably so he could access the tactical net.

"I'm going down there," said Khan. "I have to. He's just vindictive enough to start killing people if it looks to him as though the end is near for him."

"Don't do it, Boy," said Albert. "The battle is almost over. Your value is in the rebuilding. The vision setting. You are now the leader of Khan Interplanetary, as you explained to me. You have a big future in front of you."

"It means nothing if I let him kill innocent people. You can pilot this ship, right?"

"*Ja, ja, natürlich*. After all, I did the specs, and the design team reviewed with me at every project milestone."

"OK, good." He began pulling laser armor from a locker and putting it on. "Beam me down behind the bastard."

"Alex!" said Pierre. "You're being emotional. You are letting your anger guide you. You don't have a plan, and you're likely going to get yourself killed."

"Listen to the man, Khan," said Estelle in a quiet voice, almost pleading.

He looked at her and stopped cold. Her face was drawn with misery. He realized that even if her father was a bastard, he was still her father, and she probably didn't want to see him cut down. Nor did she want to see the opportunity for little Khans and little Estelles cut down.

"You're right," he forced himself to say. He sat down at the control panel and manned the transporter controls. Nothing about the terms of his swap with Fox – the women's freedom for putting Fox down here – prevented him from reversing the process now. Fox winked out.

In a few seconds, his voice came over the ship's own tactical net. "Khan, you broke your promise. Here I am, alone on the battle cruiser in orbit."

"And once these hostages are freed, you'll be brought back down. You left me with the impression you were going to be leading your troops into battle, not hiding behind yet more hostages. That's not honorable battle. That's barbarism."

"You killed eight hundred ECG troops. You destroyed Earth's government. And you talk to me of barbarism?"

Khan switched him off and switched on the tactical net frequency for the ECG troops below. He also put it on the ship's external loudspeaker system so Baelmar's troops could hear.

"My name is Alexander Khan," he said. "I am speaking to Earth Central Government troops. Your situation is hopeless. You are surrounded by local troops. ECG has fallen to the people of Earth. Reinforcements will not be coming to help you. No more ships of any kind will be coming from Earth for a very long time. You are now inhabitants of Prison Planet, also called Earth 2.0, also called Arcadia, and sometimes called Paradiso. Throw down your weapons and raise your hands, and you will be treated humanely. If you fight, you will be killed or given to the Maneaters. That is all."

And then, almost as if on cue, Baelmar and a hundred or so men on horseback, many brandishing laser pistols, rode out of the smoke on one side of the amphitheater, and another group – this one led by Salvatore Ruggiero – rode out on the other side. Ten or so ECG troops fought, cutting down twenty or more of the riders before they themselves were ridden down and trampled into the soil of Arcadia. The others threw down their weapons and raised their hands. The battle was over.

Baelmar rode down the slope into the amphitheater where the haggard-looking Advance citizens had been held. "You are free!" he shouted, and a weak cheer went up from them. Then he turned to face his troops, now lined up all around the rim of the amphitheater.

"Bael-MAR!" shouted one, then another, then another. Soon, nearly two hundred men were shouting Bael MAR, Bael MAR, Bael MAR!" Then more and more men of all groups, Lords, Maneaters, Elves, Techs gathered around the top of the amphitheater until there must have been a thousand. They all took up the roar: "Bael MAR, Bael MAR, Bael MAR!"

Mostro pranced back and forth with Baelmar astride. He looked up at the top of the amphitheater from one side to the other, at first uncertain, then smiling and taking his bow from his shoulder and shaking it high with his fist. The roar intensified: "Bael MAR, Bael MAR, Bael MAR!" Baelmar visibly took in all this energy and virtually glowed.

"It is an ancient story," breathed Pierre, watching with fascination. "Ancient, ancient, ancient. He led them through danger and blood to victory. He is now their leader for life."

"All along, it's been his own destiny calling him, while he thought it was mine," mused Khan. "Can he go back, like Cincinnatus, or will the power carry him away?"

"That is the ancient question at the end of this ancient story," said Pierre.

CHAPTER TWENTY-TWO

"Sweet mercy is nobility's true badge."

William Shakespeare, *Titus Andronicus*

Khan wanted to be easy on the remaining ECG troops. After all, they were only following orders. And there was a long history of treating vanquished but formidable foes well: the Persians and the Lydians, the Romans and the Alamanni (sometimes), and the Americans and the Germans. But he realized he could only suggest terms to Baelmar. It was Baelmar's victory. Bemused by his new status, Baelmar was nevertheless himself, and full of mercy and humanity. "Join us," he said to them in a bull-strong voice. "Become one with us, and you will live a good life. Fight us, and you must go away. We cannot have enemies among us."

Names were taken, and Estelle administered an impromptu oath. One hundred eighty-one ECG troops swore allegiance to the city-state of Advance and swore to help rebuild it – the same city-state they had just largely destroyed. Seven officers and noncoms refused, and Baelmar ceremoniously gave them to Seamus Branchrunner for safekeeping.

"Please do not eat them," he said to the barbarian. "If that is your desire, it is more merciful to kill them now."

The eyes of the men in question got huge and round. They probably had not believed Khan's implication that the Maneaters would eat them.

Then well-fed Cuchulain himself stepped from the crowd, taller than the others by a head and a half, resplendent in his long, white, beaded-leather robe, terrifying with the animal tusks protruding through the sides of his nose. One of the seven whimpered when he saw Cuchulain.

"We will use them as slaves," said Cuchulain in a gracious, deep voice. "After they share our food, our drink, our fires, and our lives for a few seasons, we will offer the usual tests. If they pass our tests, they may become one with us."

Knowing what those tests entailed, Khan swallowed drily and kept his counsel.

Then Baelmar made a speech, probably the longest of his life, thanking each and every group that had come forward to help. He thanked Salvatore Ruggiero, who had left the Hundred unguarded to come and help Advance, because he knew it was not just Advance they were all fighting for. The Lords who had only recently been conspiring to bring down Salvatore Ruggiero also received his thanks for putting enmity behind them and riding to the common banner. He thanked the cavalry detachment from Sunrise Keep. And he thanked Seamus Branchrunner and his fellow "hunters," as he diplomatically called them, for serving as messengers to the various groups involved, and for bringing the Maneaters to the cause. Then he formally asked Seamus to return the hand lasers loaned to him and his messengers for their use as proof of need while asking for troops. They would be ceremonially locked up in Advance, only to be used against other off-worlders. Arcadia would go back to only locally-made weapons.

Cuchulain answered before Seamus could speak. "Unfortunately, each of those terrible weapons has been lost in this great war to save the Great Mother from the Earth demons," said the chief, smoothing the rich beadwork on the front of his robe. His hands gleamed with rings, and his fingernails were long and clean. "But they were not needed anyway. It was the trusted name of Baelmar, known in the Leas and the Realm and the grasslands of the Deepeven as the world's greatest horseman and bowman, that brought people to the banner."

Khan took note, as he was sure everyone else from Advance or the Realm did as well, that a certain number of deadly hand lasers were now in the hands of Maneaters. Used judiciously, the powerpacks would last for years. And Cuchulain was not finished.

"We must be friends with one another," he said. "Lord with Maneater, Maneater with Tech, Lord with Tech, and all with Elves. We have shown that we are all one. That we can fight a common enemy. Let us put aside another common enemy: distrust. Let us all visit one another freely. Let every man be welcome in every man's town or castle or tent. We have no reason to fight. The Great Mother is bountiful and huge, with plenty of food and space for a thousand times our number. Let us be friends with one another. Baelmar has shown us the way."

No one quite knew how to respond to this. Certainly, no Lords or Techs wanted Maneaters running loose in their keeps and streets. Elves were on speaking terms with Maneaters, with a wary respect between them, but they kept their distance. It was hard to tell if this was a heartfelt speech or a ploy. Khan was sure most would treat it with caution.

And it moved Khan to speak. "That is a fine sentiment and a fine speech, Cuchulain. A sentiment I'm sure we all share. And I am sure that all the people of Advance, which now lies in ruins, but which you and your people have helped to set free, will join me in welcoming your help in rebuilding. And since we've lost most of our food, I'm sure we'll welcome hunters' goods in our markets."

"Hear, hear," said Estelle. "We will need all the help we can get."

As expected, this cooled Cuchulain's enthusiasm somewhat. "We will help as we can," he said.

People drifted away at that point to try to pick up their old lives or in the case of the ECG men, somehow begin to establish new ones. Able now to use communicators without fear, Khan got updates. Estelle and Bella had found that their rooms were looted but otherwise undamaged, so they immediately began the process of cleaning up. Fascinated by what was left of Advance, which was about sixty percent, Pierre and Albert explored and found accommodations in the town, where people were more than willing to take the strange gold coins they offered.

Khan chose to sleep alone that night in the cloaked starship, up on the dirigible landing field, amid the metal parts of the burned dirigible skeletons. No one else was around on the plateau amid the spooky wreckage, and he wanted to think. He felt that he was at a turning point, a milestone, and wanted to reflect. For the first time in his life, there were no immediate threats, no long-term threats, no demanding and dangerous missions. For the first time in his life, what faced him was an unaccustomed phenomenon: peace and opportunity.

As he had half expected, given the powerful nexus of events, conditions that normally prevailed when she appeared, the Alien appeared just as he was dozing off. She was as otherworldly beautiful as ever, though clothed this time in a simple, no-nonsense silver jumpsuit. He couldn't help looking at her belly, which seemed to bulge ever so slightly.

"Yes, Major," she said, using the direct brain-to-brain communication she was more comfortable with than audible speech. "A daughter. I have come to say good-bye. My mission with you is at an end, except for delivery of our child. You will hear her cry in the night, and find her in another room, and you will know I have been there. She is yours to raise. She is our final gift to humanity for a long while."

"The baby was part of your plan?"

"Yes, from the beginning. Your ... cooperation ... was surprisingly easy to get." She smiled. Your daughter will be ... slightly different ... from your other children. We expect big things of her. Educate her well. She will surpass you."

Khan was dismayed. "How will I explain this to Estelle? That she and I are to raise a child that belongs to another ... woman?"

She laughed audibly, a musical sound. "Isn't explaining inconvenient facts to human females something at which you human males excel? Your literature is full of it. You are equal to the task. As you have been equal to the task we planned for your family and you many years ago: the liberation of Earth."

"Many years ago? How could you know?"

"That is knowledge that we cannot share with you."

"How long have you been ... helping humanity?"

"A very long time by your standards. Else you would not have survived."

"Are you from another place or from our future?"

"Another place. Do not pursue time travel. It is forbidden. Destruction lies that way."

"Do you want the cloaking devices back? We have copied the technology, and we can make it work, but we don't understand it. It seems almost – magic – and we're not sure we should be using it. It almost seems ... forbidden."

"That is old technology that we revived especially for you. We long ago learned how to penetrate the cloaks, so we never use them any more."

"You used me for your purposes. You weren't just helping me."

"Yes. To get humanity through a critical point. We want humanity to eventually take its place among starfaring races. Thus your duty is not at an end. You must save the best people of Earth from the chaos there. But you will see that yourself. You do not need my help to see your duty, or to do it."

"I brought down the oppressor forces," he said. He heard the tiniest note of whining in his voice and was disgusted by it. "Surely, someone on Earth will step forward to lead."

"You knew it was not enough."

"Yes. But I don't want to go back."

"What one man wants compared to the need of his whole species is small. You have your duty. You will see it. But live a little first. Give a few Earth regimes a chance to rise and fall. Wait for the desire for a strong leader. Join with your mate here, build your domicile, rebuild your city, begin to raise our daughter. But then you must go."

And with that she was gone.

To add to his dilemma and troubles, Cuchulain found him the next day. He had the young woman, Marna, with him.

"She is with child," said Cuchulain.

"I can see that," said Khan miserably, thinking of the coming conversation with Estelle.

"We will raise the boy, for boy it is," said Cuchulain. "That will be your repayment for your escape."

"I acknowledge no debt to anyone for refusing to let them eat me," said Khan testily. "And since that's my child, I will raise him myself." Once he told Estelle about one child, let alone two, he would likely end up being a single parent. Might as well be a single parent with two. After all, they were his children.

"After the age of twelve," said Cuchulain, with an odd hand gesture like a blessing. "You may have him then. He is not only your child. He belongs to us, too. And he is destined for great things."

"After the age of four, I get him," bristled Khan. "And no human flesh is to be eaten by him, or in his presence." He glared at Cuchulain, having to look up at him, smelling the odd smell of the man.

Cuchulain gave him a long, direct look through narrowed eyes. "Eight," he said. "After eight years."

"Only if he comes to stay with me each dry season after he can walk," said Khan.

Cuchulain clasped Khan's hand and forearm in a forearm shake. "It is done."

After helping the people of Advance with the worst of the wreckage, most of the Arcadian army dissolved and cleared out within a few days. People's concerns about the Maneaters hanging around too long proved groundless. The fact was, all the people in the ad-hoc army had their own homes and ways of life and wanted to return to them.

"I was a little concerned they might just never leave," said Estelle. Filthy from working on a clean-up crew throwing burnable trash and broken lumber onto fires, she and Khan were sitting on the dry-stone foundation of a burned-down house. They were taking a break and sharing a lunch of cornbread, radishes and water. The rest of the crew continued working but Khan was aware that they were watching. People always watched him and Estelle.

"It is often the fate of the liberated to become permanent hosts to their liberators," said Khan. "But I was pretty sure Baelmar's head would not be turned by the power. Even though power is so often immediately addictive."

"He is a level-headed man, who probably just wants to go back to his wife and kids," she said, and looked expectantly at him. When he said nothing, she said, "So now what for you? Were you serious? When you told me in front of my father you wanted to stay here and raise a family with me? That you want 'little Khans and little Estelles' as you put it?"

His stomach clenched into a knot. "It is true," he said. "I want that more than anything I've wanted in my life."

Her normally semi-cynical, laconic expression dissolved, her lips trembled, and her eyes watered. She leaned close to embrace him but he held her back.

"I want that more than anything I've ever wanted in my life, but there's something you have to know," he said miserably.

She pulled back, confused. "What?"

He told her first about Marna. That was easiest, because he had not wanted it, had indeed been bound hand and foot.

Estelle snorted. "Men! You weren't forced to become sexually excited, were you? You let it happen."

He explained that such responses were not controllable, were in fact involuntary.

"Yeah, yeah, likely story," she said, but he could tell she believed him. She was smart enough and educated enough to know that what he said was true. "I can live with that, Khan. And I'm glad you felt it necessary to tell me. It means you really are committed."

"But that's not all," he said, feeling wretched. He told her about the Alien and the coming baby.

Estelle's first reaction was to say, "Whoa!" and force him to go back and explain the whole alien story. She knew of the alien but was fascinated that another race had been helping Humanity for millennia. Then she hardened and got to the point. "So you just had sex with this alien bitch as a *favor*, because she was curious about sex with humans?" Sarcasm dripped like acid.

"That's close. But I confess I also wanted it and enjoyed it."

SMACK! Estelle's bony fist appeared in his face and flattened his nose before he had a chance to move. It was one of the fastest moves he had ever seen. Blood streamed down onto his clothes. The pain was amazing, like a large cloaking field, invisible to others, but in this case, easily large enough to encompass a starship, and centered on the front of his face. He sat blinking, stunned into immobility, processing what had just happened, trying to ignore the laughs and japes from nearby townspeople, who had known Estelle far longer than he had.

"Never talk to me about that again," she spat. "Of course we'll raise your little bastards, but we're still going to have little Khans and little Estelles. And we've gotta get moving. I'm not getting any younger, and I'm guessing some of my eggs are past their expiration date. Now kiss me, damn it!"

And he did, blood and all, and they stood and embraced and kissed some more. The surrounding townspeople on the clean-up crew whistled and cheered. Everything was going to be all right in the town of Advance.

Not wanting to wait any longer to return Baelmar to Maruil, Khan found him among the streets of Advance, helping right overturned wagons, raise cornerposts, and set cornerstones. "It's time I honored my promise to your wife, Baelmar. By now, she thinks I've been lying to her all along."

"Yes," said Baelmar. "It is finally time for me to return to the Leas. You have found your destiny."

"And you have found yours," said Khan.

The starship and the aircars they had brought from Earth were the only means of fast transportation, now that the dirigibles had all been destroyed, so Khan packed the two of them – Baelmar requiring a space and a half himself – into a two-person aircar for the quick jump. He wanted to save the starship and its fuel for emergencies. And for other purposes.

He set the craft down immediately in front of the house. Baelmar got out and whooped a family greeting of some sort – words that Khan did not understand. Maruil, Branwyn, Gareth, and Amity all burst out to see them. Maruil was quickly suspicious.

"It's for good this time," said Khan, without preamble. "I have now brought him back to you, in one piece. I will let him tell all the stories."

Maruil beamed, and the slight cast of worry that had been in her face ever since he had known her smoothed out. She and Baelmar embraced, then the children embraced their parents, forming a tight group. Then, before it looked like an afterthought, first Maruil and then Baelmar beckoned to Amity, who joined them in a five-person clump. Obviously, despite the age difference between her and Gareth, matters had progressed since Khan had left her here.

Khan got a lump in his throat watching this. It was one of the most beautiful things he had ever seen. Things had never been quite like this around the Khan household.

Finally they unclenched, and Maruil said to Khan, "You are welcome in our house at any time, Major Khan. You have brought my husband back, as promised. I make you welcome, as promised."

"And your welcome is the finest gift a person could receive," he said. "I may at some point in the future take you up on it. But for now, I want to get back to my own household, and my own interrupted life."

And with that he took his leave, after first telling Amity and the others what role her vids had played, and that their faces were known all over Earth. She said she wanted to stay with Maruil and Baelmar, and Gareth, she added shyly, because she had never been happier anywhere in her whole life. He said he would be back periodically to check on her, and he left.

Bella and Ahmed and the other Khan Interplanetary employees came back to the plateau and started rebuilding Khan Interplanetary literally from the ground up. They started to throw up admittedly slapdash buildings just to have a place to work, and Albert intervened.

"*Geht nicht, geht nicht*," he said. "If it is worth doing, it is worth doing the best way possible. And is it the most important thing to do first? Do you have a phase chart?"

Bella leapt on this. "You want to grab a hammer or a saw and help here, Fritz?" she said. "Or you gonna add value by telling us it's not OK? A phase chart?" She blew a raspberry. "Phthphthphth."

"Name is Albert," he said good naturedly. "And it is rumored that you are an engineer, but I can't tell. Usually, priority discussions come first in a project, *ja*?"

Bella nearly blew a gasket over this, but tamped down the fires. "OK," she said. "I've seen how the Boss defers to you, so I'll give you a shot. What's more important than buildings to work in?"

"Dirigibles," he said. "They are the best form of local transportation and freight haulage. And they can be built – must be built – outside. In fact, you have already the steel pieces that you need. A little scorched, perhaps. And I doubt the diesel engines have been damaged much by the fires. Both the dirigibles and the diesel engines are very impressive achievements, by the way. But the point is, you need communication and freight haulage back up and running as fast as possible. The dirigibles are priority number one."

Bella reacted to the compliments like a dog that has just been petted. "Maybe you're right," she said. "And thank you. We are, or rather were, pretty proud of the dirigibles ourselves. Maybe you're not such a bad sort after all."

Ahmed was a cooler customer than Bella, and not as easily turned, but he easily agreed that the diesel engines could probably be salvaged and that it was important to get at least one dirigible built and into service. And thus Albert effortlessly assumed his rightful place as chief of operations of Khan Interplanetary.

Within two months, Advance was well on the road to recovery, and Khan Interplanetary was back up and running, after a fashion. In the event, they ended up using the silk stocks from Riversend, along with remaining linen stocks, to cover dirigible number six, appropriately named *Phoenix*. The gold brought from Earth smoothed many rough spots and arguments from suppliers about whose orders should be filled first. Since nearly half of Advance was being rebuilt, there was stiff competition for supplier capacity for linen, wood, coal gas, and machining. But from a standing start, two months after total destruction of all their dirigibles, they had the capability to resume regular runs to the Keep and the Hundred. And now other fiefs – the Mujonniers, the Leewards, the Poikonens, the Truebloods, and the Laberteaux – wanted to do trade with Advance and each other via the dirigible, so Khan Interplanetary was immediately covered up with business.

And there were other pressing needs for the airships. There was a need for search-and-rescue services. Several pilots of modified aircars who had made the perilous journey from Earth had found their way to Advance.

Some reported contact with a fleet of a hundred or so grounded aircars several hundred kilometers to the east, without charge, food, or water. They would need help. And, according to Ernie, the inveterate gambler, there was an even more pressing need. While gambling was not loved in Advance by most people, he had learned that the people in Riversend loved to gamble. He wanted to go there and set up his own gaming establishment, and promote cheap travel back and forth from Advance for those who did like to gamble.

Meanwhile, Khan had not forgotten about Fox, imprisoned by himself in orbit. He knew Fox had food, air and water for several months. But waiting would not address the issue of what to do with him. Estelle had alluded to it twice, but only touched on it. She knew he would just as lief kill her father as consign him to any other fate. But ultimately, he decided on the fate he considered most fitting.

He went to the redoubt he had blasted into a bluff face for the purpose of hiding the starship, moved it out so the transporter beam would work, and transported Fox to the surface. There he explained Fox's choices to him. Reluctantly, he man agreed to the one Khan recommended. Coercion, in the form of mention of the Maneaters, was involved.

On the day they dedicated the *Phoenix*, Khan threw a big party. Everybody was invited, including people from the Keep and the Hundred, and even Cuchulain and a few of his top lieutenants.

The key announced event, of course, was the dedication of the *Phoenix*. But the surprise event was three marriages: Khan and Estelle, Bella and Ahmed, and Gareth and Amity. The crowd roared their approval at this announcement.

Ralph from the Downtown Diner had wanted to give away Estelle, but in the event, Ralph was drafted to officiate, while a more noted individual gave her away: her father – Nathan Fox, former Director – Office of Technology Control, former oppressor, bringer of war to Arcadia. Khan had warned him not to grimace, not to sneer, not to roll his eyes, not to say anything except, "I, her father," when asked who gave this woman in matrimony. That was part of the deal, a one-time recognition of his duty to his daughter, and Fox's ticket to a release with a knife on the other side of the planet – with Khan's old tracking chip implanted in his body, though inside the peritoneum, not just under the skin. "I'll still defeat you, Khan," said Fox when they cut this deal, and Khan's reply was, "You'll need that hatred to survive. It worked for me."

Well schooled in public appearances, Fox performed flawlessly, even though there was a hiss or two from the throng, quickly shushed by those nearby. Everyone now knew the story of Estelle's blighted childhood, spread by Bella, and despite their hatred for him, they loved her, and they wanted her to have her day. Estelle was deeply moved by all this, and if the townspeople observed an unaccustomed tear in their tough mayor's eye, they quickly forgave it. After all, this was her wedding day.

Bella and Ahmed, big and small, brash and cool, presented the public with an unusual picture. Albert gave Bella away. Everyone cheered when Bella bent to accept Ahmed's kiss.

Khan gave Amity away, and Maruil and Baelmar both beamed as this young Earth woman became their new daughter-in-law. Carried away by the moment, young Gareth swept her off her feet and kissed her while cradling her in his arms. The crowd loved it.

As the crowd cheered and fell to with a vengeance on the feast, Khan looked around at Advance under construction, and reflected on his time on Prison Planet, aka Arcadia, aka Earth 2.0, aka Paradiso.

Everything would indeed be all right in Advance.

CHAPTER TWENTY-THREE

"You must choose your own direction and pursue it, but do not be surprised if your destiny chooses you instead of you choosing it."
Alexander Khan to his unborn son and daughter,
Khans to Khans

William Crow Johnson earned an MA and an MBA and has traveled widely on five continents. He and his wife have two children and two grandchildren and live on their farm in southern Indiana. Johnson is also the author of *The Adventures of Sara Springborn and Mr. Wollo Bushtail.*

Coming in September, 2013, from William Crow Johnson,
the second in the EARTH 2.0 trilogy,
EARTH 2.0: ARCADIA.

Printed in Great Britain
by Amazon

61534838R00203